CW01072489

Pawns

Pawns

The Wielders of Arantha Book 1

Patrick Hodges

Acknowledgments

Book One of the *Wielders of Arantha* series is my fourth novel, and it seems the list of people I have to thank with each successive book just gets longer and longer. But that's okay, because I really like thanking people.

First, to my extraordinary family, who have supported my every literary endeavor, thank you for your endless wellspring of support. Without you, I would not be realizing my dream of being a published writer, and for that, I am eternally grateful.

To my army of beta-readers, many of whom are my colleagues at Young Adult Author Rendezvous, the best collection of YA authors *anywhere*, it's because of you that this book is as good as it is. Your feedback was beyond valuable. It was *invaluable*. I thank my stars every day that I have such an incredible resource to mine whenever I need creative input.

And I cannot forget my cohorts at the Central Phoenix Writers Group, who once a week took an excerpt from my story and told me just what the hell was wrong with it – which, in the beginning, was a *lot* – and without your myriad of opinions, skill, and verbal dexterity, *Wielders* would be a far less enticing product than it is now. I'd list you all by name, but there are too many, and the more special of you already know who you are.

Lastly, thanks to you, the reader. Though my first books dealt with the perils of childhood and middle school, my first love as a youth was always science fiction and fantasy, and being able to dip my toe in the waters of this genre is a dream come true for me. I hope that you find my efforts worthy of praise. I promise, there will be more than a few twists and turns before you're done.

Prologue

THE OLD woman lay on her bed, motionless, staring up at the ceiling of the only home she'd ever known. She was born in this room. She would die there too.

She'd laid her withered hands upon the Stone one last time the day before, feeling the surge of warm, familiar energy as it coursed through her frail body. Her mind beheld an array of familiar images: the past, present and future of her people, a history she helped shape. As the feeling of unity with Arantha began to subside, she felt suffused with a tremendous sense of inner peace. Her work finished, she would soon be welcomed into Arantha's waiting arms.

For her people, the road ahead would be difficult. Their isolated way of life, the path Arantha put them on centuries ago, would end. The chain of events she'd set in motion with her final order would see to that. And it would be up to her daughter Kelia, as her successor, to discover a new path for them. New enemies would arise, as would new allies. She saw them all, time and time again, in her mind's eye: the dark twins, the northern mage, the painted woman from the Above.

One last, lingering doubt crept through the old woman's mind. She'd prepared Kelia for her role as Protectress her entire life, and though Kelia didn't possess her mother's level of foresight, her elemental abilities were unequaled. She was a strong leader, well-respected, and wise beyond her years. But would it be enough?

It has to be, she thought with a regretful sigh. *To fail would mean oblivion for my people, and for all of Elystra.*

Her vision darkened, a curtain of blackness that stole her sight one inch at a time. Her breath became ragged, and she felt her heart beat for the final time.

As her spirit left her body, her final thought was a silent prayer:

Arantha, watch over them.

Chapter One

RICHARD'S DEAD.

Maeve blinked back tears as the *Talon* powered through Earth's atmosphere. They'd evaded the Jegg's ground-based weapons, but that was merely the first line of defense.

Once they hit open space, their problems increased exponentially. She didn't have to look at the sensors to confirm the Jegg ships were following them. The *Talon* was the first Earth ship to be airborne in five years. Even though the hull was black and silver, it may as well have been pink and yellow with a huge bull's-eye painted on it.

For eighteen months, they'd planned this mission. With the help of his contacts in the Underground, Richard not only restored a junked Space Corps cargo ship but somehow combined a Jegg quantigraphic rift drive with a Terran supralight engine. Two completely different technologies, and he miraculously got them to speak the same language. This brilliant engineer, the man she fell in love and had a son with, was the key factor in the Underground's last-ditch effort to find a way to escape the alien conquerors who had subjugated the human race.

They'd celebrated last night, the ten of them: Maeve, Richard, their fourteen-year-old son Davin, Richard's protégé

Gaspar, and the entire team that toiled in utmost secrecy to get this bucket off the ground. The mood was ebullient, as it seemed their mission would finally commence.

Mission! Maeve snorted as the ship burst through the stratosphere and out into open space. *A Hail Mary is what it is. We're hanging our last hope on the word of a shimmering alien being and praying there's a pot of gold at the end of the rainbow.*

Brushing strands of her purple, shoulder-length hair away from her face, she cast a sidelong glance at the copilot's chair. Seeing its emptiness, a tear escaped her violet eyes.

Richard's dead.

My husband is dead.

So are Manny, Kacy, Calvin, Ji-Yan, Suri, and Mahesh.

She chided herself. Now was not the time for these thoughts. They threw her adrenaline rush out of whack and disrupted the concentration she badly needed right now. There were still three lives to save, including her own. Fighting down her emotions, she called upon the piloting skills she spent fifteen years in the Space Corps sharpening.

Jegg fighters were nearly impossible to detect unless they were right in front of you, one of the reasons the Terran Defense Forces had been so helpless against them. Gaspar increased the sensors' capabilities just enough for them to know fighters were in pursuit. Judging from the number of explosions detonating near the ship, causing it to rock back and forth like a kayak on white-water rapids, there had to be at least three of them.

Regaining her focus, Maeve banked sharply to the right and fired the sublight thrusters, making a beeline for the Asteroid Belt. Once they cleared that, and the Jegg dampening field that effectively rendered supralight technology inoperable, they could engage their makeshift QRD and be out of the Terran system in the blink of an eye.

The pursuing Jegg fighters increased their speed. They were gaining.

Maeve flipped a switch on her panel. "Gaspar!" she shouted. "I don't think they're gonna let us go without a fight!"

"Oh, ya think?" came a frazzled voice from the other end of the intercom.

"Any ideas?" Maeve asked. She pushed the steering column forward a few inches, and the *Talon* increased its speed. The vibrations intensified, as if the ship was about to fly apart at the seams.

"Hold on a sec," Gaspar said, pausing briefly. "I've got four canisters of D34Z ready to jettison. Let me know when to detonate. Maybe we can take a few of 'em out."

She checked the sensors, which indicated five Jegg fighters in hot pursuit. "Stand by!"

The Belt loomed in front of them, millions of rocks that had floated in space between Mars and Jupiter for eons. A few more seconds, and they could lose themselves within it. Or die a fiery death.

Davin burst through the cockpit door, threw himself into the copilot's chair, and fastened his safety belt. "Anytime you want to get us out of here, Mom ..." Sweat and grime caked his freckled face and curly red hair, but his eyes shone with fierce determination.

She returned her gaze to the viewport, gripping her controls even tighter. "Don't start, kiddo, we're in some deep-level shite here. Where've you been?"

"Helping Gaspar load the canisters into the airlock. Let's blow this pop stand and go, okay?"

"Roger that," she said as another explosion rocked the ship. Into the intercom, she yelled, "G! Eject the first three canisters ... now!"

The sound of a metal hatch clanging open echoed through the ship, followed by a whoosh of compressed air as three large, yellow containers shot from the airlock, one after the other. She followed their trajectories on the scanner, watching as the Jegg fighters pressed in.

"Detonate on my mark!"

Seconds ticked off as the enemy ships drew ever closer.

"Mark!"

A huge explosion violently rocked the *Talon* again. A control panel behind Davin sparked and began to smoke. He unhooked himself, leaped out of the chair, grabbed a fire extinguisher, and sprayed the panel with fire-suppressing foam.

Maeve checked her scanner again. Where before there were five faint blips following them, there were now only three, and one was falling behind, obviously crippled.

She allowed herself a smile. "Three down! Well done, G!"

"Major?" came Gaspar's voice, laced with desperation. "We have a big problem!"

"What now?"

"The quantigraphic rift drive is offline! That last explosion blew the containment field!"

Oh, shite. Not good. "Can you restore it?"

"Assuming the manifold stabilizer isn't fried, yes."

Maeve gulped. "Be careful, G."

"You got it. Give me two minutes."

"No promises." Maeve executed a barrel-roll, evading the maelstrom of rocks that seemed to fill nearly every square inch of the window. The two remaining Jegg fighters were still right behind them, firing in a continuous barrage.

Just then, a crazy idea came to her. "Dav, is that fourth canister ready to go?"

Davin, back in his chair, checked the panel in front of him. "Locked and loaded."

"Perfect!" She pulled back on the controls, banking upward and narrowly missing a huge, jagged asteroid. It was impossible, but Maeve swore she felt the wind of it going by.

One of the pursuing fighters wasn't so lucky. It tried to veer off at the last second, but it was too late. The asteroid clipped its starboard thruster, and it spun out of control until it crashed in a fiery conflagration on another enormous rock.

"One more down!" yelled Davin.

The last remaining fighter bore down on them, firing salvo after salvo. The *Talon* rocked again, and sparks poured from another control panel.

Maeve activated the intercom again. "G, we gotta go! Is the containment field back up?"

"Yeah!" came Gaspar's voice. "Thirty seconds to power up the jump!"

"Okay, here's what's gonna happen," Maeve instructed, banking hard left again. "We eject the final canister, and detonate it at point-blank range just as we make the jump."

"Are you crazy?" Gaspar sounded frantic. "The hull's already been weakened! You detonate that close, it'll tear right through us!"

Maeve sighed. "The Jegg's long-range scanners will think we were destroyed. It's our only hope right now."

"Major –"

"No time, G! Prepare to eject! Twenty-second countdown till jump, *mark*! Get yourself to safety!"

"On my way," he said, and the intercom cut off.

Maeve and Davin both held their breath.

The *Talon* twirled around another flying asteroid. They'd cleared the Belt.

"Eject!"

Another clang, followed by another whoosh.

Maeve's thumb hovered over a button that read 'QRD – Engage'.

"Detonate!" she shouted.

The screen displaying the ship's rear sensor array flashed fiery orange and red.

Half a second later, Maeve pressed the button. "Mark! Hang on, Dav!"

A whir of built-up energy filled their ears as the quantigraphic rift drive powered up. The control panel on Maeve's left erupted in a shower of sparks, and she felt an intense burning sensation on her arm.

Her mouth opened in a silent scream as an energy field enveloped the *Talon*.

Chapter Two

THE MIDDAY sun hung high in the cerulean Elystran sky, and the view was magnificent. Kelia shrugged her kova-leather satchel off her shoulder and took a long, quenching sip from her water-skin. She'd worked up quite a thirst during the hour-long walk from her village to this spot. She stood upon a prominent outcropping of rock, overlooking the vast Praskian Desert that stretched out between the Ixtrayan Plateau and the distant Kaberian Mountains. Over her thirty-six years, she'd visited this spot many times, but never with such a profound sense of purpose as today.

This outcropping marked the western edge of the Ixtrayu's territory, which ran from Lake Barix in the southern range of the Kaberian Mountains through the large expanse of forest north of the Plateau the Ixtrayu called home. Not for the first time, Kelia smiled at the irony that this part of Elystra belonged to a tribe of women, and not a single one of the distant kingdoms, ruled for millennia by men, even knew of their existence.

Arantha has been good to us, she thought. *Eight centuries, she's kept us safe and hidden.*

She took a deep breath of the warm, dry air and sat down in the shade of a large huxa tree that grew a few yards from the edge of the overlook. Its trunk was thick and its bark hardened to withstand the desert climate, but it seemed to welcome her presence like an old friend. She absently moved a tress of her long, dark brown hair over her left shoulder, where it hung past her breasts. She took a moment to admire the intricate braid her aunt, Liana, had woven for her, and how beautifully it complemented her loose-fitting reddish-brown robe.

Her hand then moved to the lump of lustrous brown metal that hung from the loose leather string around her neck. The necklace had been crafted by her daughter Nyla when she was only six years old. It consisted of six wooden beads strung together, three on either side of the tiny piece of metal that hung between it. Touching its smooth surface brought forth memories of her mother, as it had been Onara's final gift to her before her death.

Even though her powers of divination paled in comparison to those of Onara, she was still able to discern much from the images that flashed through her mind during her most recent consultation. Since assuming the mantle of Protectress, she'd hoped each consultation would reveal the reason Onara had decreed a halt to the Sojourns; but every time, Arantha chose to keep that knowledge to herself. Since her mother's death, not a single Sojourn had been taken, and therefore, not a single daughter had been born to the Ixtrayu. Kelia's people pleaded with her, wanting answers she couldn't provide.

For the last thirteen years, her visions had been unremarkable—frustratingly so. That morning, however, Arantha finally showed her something new.

She saw, clear as the waters of the River Ix, an image in her mind of this exact spot. She felt the image pull at her, as if her very essence was being drawn here. She knew there was something of grave importance that Arantha wanted her to see. Liana packed a satchel with provisions for Kelia, who set off from the village within two hours of having her vision. The Council suggested she not travel unaccompanied, but Kelia insisted she go alone. What Arantha had in store for her was for her eyes and no one else's.

She opened her satchel and surveyed its contents: several pieces of riverfruit, a few strips of dried kova meat, a loaf of holm-grain bread, and two extra skins of water. Liana had even included several sachets of jingal-root tea and a small metal kettle for steeping. As an Elemental Wielder, she didn't need a fire to get water to boil; she could not only manipulate water's physical form but also its temperature. She knew she would need the tea to help her stay awake and alert, since she had no idea how long Arantha would require her to keep watch.

Kelia nestled back against the trunk of the tree. Her dark brown eyes scanned the barren wasteland that lay spread out before her, searching for anything out of the ordinary. She felt a faint tingle of excitement as she wondered what Arantha had brought her there to behold.

Chapter Three

ELZOR WATCHED the riders approach at a full gallop: five men, dressed in fine, high-quality armor. The merychs they rode were well-bred and strong, with long, flowing manes; suitable mounts for those who commanded the Agrusian army.

He cast a quick glance to his right. As always, Elzaria stood at his side. Like him, his twin sister was tall, with black hair and dark eyes that blazed with as much determination as his own. She, unlike Elzor or the six hundred soldiers that followed him, wore no armor. She wore a tight, emerald-green tunic, cinched at the waist by a thick leather belt, which hugged her slim frame. She was never shy about showing cleavage: it turned the heads of men who would invariably underestimate her.

Elzor heard the crackle of energy pass through her body as her power began to manifest, making the face beneath his short, dark beard itch, and a cold smile formed on his face. She'd come so far from the submissive, broken girl she once was.

Were he one of the many gullible fools who worshipped Arantha, he might have reasoned that finding the Stone was their destiny. Without it, he and his sister would have just been two more faceless orphans to work themselves to death in the mines of Barju.

On occasion, Elzor cursed the fates for choosing to bestow so much raw power upon his sister and not himself. Her capricious personality, coupled with her deep-seated rage, made her abilities difficult to keep secret. She spent years learning how to focus her mind, until such time as Elzor could gather enough followers to seize power for themselves.

He'd been patient, cunning and industrious. His masterplan was about to come to fruition. The power Elzaria channeled made her the most powerful weapon on Elystra.

It was now time to unleash that weapon.

As the riders drew nearer, Elzor scanned his surroundings. The road upon which they traveled, the main thoroughfare between Agrus and their former homeland of Barju, was wide and flat and accommodated most of his army, whom he'd dubbed the Elzorath. Six hundred men stood in impassive silence as the riders approached. Every man had his hand on the hilt of his sword.

This particular stretch of road curved through a thick forest of deciduous nipa trees. Most of the buildings in Agrus were made from this sturdy wood, the largest exception being the Castle Tynal. The centuries-old castle was the seat of power for Agrus's rulers, and by day's end, it would belong to him.

With a chorus of merychs' whinnies and the clip-clop of their hooves, the riders slowed to a halt. Elzor waited for them to dismount, but they did not.

He stared up at their leader, whose high-quality machinite armor bore the Agrusian emblem of two crossed swords. The commander's long, fair hair spilled down from his head, his jaw as square as his shoulders were broad. Elzor waited for the man to speak, but received only a contemptuous glower.

Another useless tactic. One would think that marching an invading army, in broad daylight, straight to his country's borders, would convince him that I'm immune to intimidation. What an arrogant braga.

"Shall I destroy them?" Elzaria whispered.

"Not yet, dear sister. Patience."

She did not object. She merely cracked her knuckles in anticipation.

Finally, the commander spoke in a deep, booming voice. "When my scouts informed me earlier this morning that an army bearing no country's standard approached our borders, I was certain it was a mistake. Now that I have laid eyes upon this gross violation of our boundaries, I can see I was correct: this godless rabble has no business calling itself an army."

Elzaria's lips curled into a snarl, the quietest of hisses escaping her lips. Elzor put a steadying hand on her arm as his eyes turned back to the Agrusian commander. "Bold words indeed," he said, "for a man whose death is but one gesture away." He raised his hand, and the front line of soldiers edged their swords several inches out of their scabbards.

The man's face hardened at the threat. "I am Nebri, High Commander of the Agrusian army. I have fought, and defeated, far more worthy foes than you, Elzor of Barju."

Elzor's face broke into a humorless grin. "I see my reputation precedes me."

Nebri gave him a dismissive smirk. "And what a reputation it is: a deserter, a coward, a captain who slaughtered his commanding officers and fled Barju like a whipped tigla."

Right behind and to his left, Elzor heard the sound of a sword being unsheathed. He turned to see a bald, bearded, barrelchested man glaring at Nebri while taking several lumbering steps forward. Elzor held his hand up, halting the man's forward progress. "Stay your hand, Langon," he said firmly.

Langon stopped at the order and stood at Elzor's side. "Yes, my liege."

The big man's words elicited a peal of mocking laughter from the commander. "'My *liege*'? Great Arantha, you are an arrogant fool, aren't you?"

Elzor's eyebrows knitted together. "Taunt me at your peril, Agrusian," he shot back.

"You *are* a fool, Elzor. No other description fits the folly of your presence here."

"And what folly might that be?"

Nebri gestured back in the direction from which he'd come. "At the end of this road, the entire Agrusian army is assembled. We are better trained, better armed, and outnumber your filthy gang of heathens five to one."

He raised his voice, addressing the Elzorath. "You men! If you turn back now, King Morix gives his word that you will not be pursued. But if you dare engage us in battle, I can assure you, no quarter will be given. You will die in ignominy, your lives cast asunder by the whim of a fool."

A few of the assembled soldiers looked at each other while others shuffled their feet in momentary indecision. But none spoke, and none made a move to depart.

"As you can see," Elzor said with a smug grin, "my men are loyal to me. No quarter would be asked for."

Nebri scoffed. "Then they are as foolish as you. What self-respecting soldier would follow a leader who would bring a *woman*," he turned his glance toward Elzaria, "into battle with him? Who is she, Elzor? Your own personal whore?"

The surge of power that resonated from within Elzaria increased as her seething, silent anger turned into white-hot hatred. A blue corona of energy appeared around her body, crackling and sparking as the power of the Stone coursed through her.

The Agrusians saw it too. They sat in slack-jawed silence for a few moments before pulling back on the reins of their whinnying merychs.

Before the riders could retreat, Elzor and Elzaria locked eyes. Elzor returned his sister's pleading look with a whispered, "Leave two of them alive."

She nodded and smiled, strutting forward. She raised her arms, holding her palms outward. Addressing Nebri, she spat, "I am Elzaria, and I am your death!"

Intense blue energy shot from her hands. It diverged and formed branches like a bolt of lightning, striking Nebri and two other riders in the chest. Frozen in place, their bodies shuddered and twitched as their blood boiled from within. The three men let out a collective unholy scream that Elzor hoped could be heard by the rest of the Agrusian army. Wisps of smoke curled upward from their leather armor as their skin charred and split.

The other two riders, unable to help their comrades, turned their merychs away and spurred them back the way they came, riding like the wind.

After one final blast of energy, Elzaria pulled her hands back and studied her palms. She watched as the blue light flared and vanished, leaving not even the slightest mark or burn upon the skin of her hands. Her work done, she stepped back and returned to her brother's side.

In unison, the three riders toppled from their mounts and crashed to the ground. The merychs, though terrified, had not been touched, and would probably have bolted if three Elzorath hadn't come forward to grab their reins.

Elzor nodded, admiring his sister's precision. He glanced up, his eyes locked on the two surviving riders, who were already a hundred yards away and would soon disappear around the bend in the road.

Langon spoke up. "The archers you had me deploy behind the tree-line are in position, my liege. Shall I give the order to fire?"

Elzor shook his head. "No, Langon. Let them go."

The big man looked incredulous, but Elzor ignored him. He stepped forward and took the reins from one soldier before placing his foot in the stirrup of Nebri's merych and hauling his body into the saddle. Elzaria and Langon climbed onto the other two.

Elzor turned to face Elzaria. "I have a task for you. Have you the stamina?"

"Of course."

"Then ride with all speed to the road that runs parallel to the Saber River. When those two fools report what happened here, Morix will send messengers to his allies in the east, calling for aid. You must intercept them before they reach the northern forest."

"Consider it done, my liege," she said.

"When you have completed your task, join us on the plains northeast of Talcris. Kill any who stand in your way."

Elzaria bowed her head, and immediately kicked her merych into action. The legion of soldiers parted as she rode through their ranks.

Elzor watched her go. Two miles away, this road intersected another that bore due west. Elzaria would then follow the tree line until she reached the Saber River. He had no doubt she would succeed in her task, and even less doubt that the Agrusian army knew what lay in store for them.

On his other side, Langon gave a deep, throaty chuckle as he shifted his massive bulk on top of his equally thick-muscled steed. "I've always wanted to ride a merych into battle."

Elzor chuckled as well. "Today is the day, my friend."

Langon raised his meaty arm, and a hush grew over the assembled army as they awaited the order. A faint smile played on his lips as he bellowed, "Elzorath, move out!"

As one, Elzor's army began their inexorable march across the Agrusian border, on the heels of their leaders who urged their merychs into a slow canter.

Elzor smiled again. His men were capable fighters, and were more than adequately prepared for battle.

Victory was theirs for the taking ... after Elzaria had her fun.

Today, two legends would be born.

Chapter Four

"**S**HITE!" Maeve waved her soldering gun at the control panel. After five hours, the *Talon* still refused to budge. As she looked out the viewport, her eyes locked onto a bluish-green orb that hung, tantalizingly close, only seven light-minutes away: Castelan VI.

We can't fail now. Not when we're so close.

She took a few deep breaths and wiped the sweat from her brow. She was about to make another attempt when she heard a voice behind her.

"Mom?"

Maeve turned around to see Davin, his curly vermillion hair matted and unkempt, poking his head through the cockpit door.

"What is it, Dav?" she asked, shoving her frustration aside for the moment.

He crossed the threshold, cradling a small bowl in his hands. "I brought you some soup. You haven't eaten in over eight hours."

She tucked a strand of hair back behind her ear, let out a sigh, and put down the soldering gun before taking the bowl from her son. "What kind of soup?"

A bemused smirk appeared on his face as she lifted the spoon to her mouth. "The label just said 'soup mix', but I'm guessing tomato. I gotta warn you, though –"

Maeve took a slurp of the watery liquid and gagged. In an effort to keep the soup in her stomach where it belonged, she threw her head back and bellowed, "Saints alive!"

"... it tastes like shite," Davin finished.

"Where'd you get this from, the reclamation tank?"

He grinned. "No, you're thinking of breakfast."

Maeve made a face, abandoned the spoon, and took another hearty gulp directly from the bowl. "Yikes, that's bad."

Davin pulled a canteen from his belt and handed it to her. "Here, you may want to wash it down with this."

She grinned. "Whiskey?"

He rolled his eyes. "Water."

"Pass. Haven't had a chance to fix the purifiers yet. The water tastes worse than this soup."

"Not any more. I fixed 'em." He shook the canteen in his hand, quirking an eyebrow.

She looked at her son with pride as she took the canteen and unscrewed the cap. "How'd you find the parts?"

"Um ..." A guilty look crossed his face, as if he'd just been caught sneaking back in to the house after curfew.

"You know what? Forget I asked. I'm sure I don't wanna know." She took a swig from the canteen, letting the surprisingly refreshing water slide down her parched throat. "Whoa. That's the cleanest water I've tasted in months. Great job, Dav."

"Thanks." He took the empty bowl from her and placed it on the copilot's chair. "How's your arm?"

Maeve looked down at the field dressing on the upper part of her left arm, which Davin had applied a few minutes after confirming they'd successfully escaped from the Terran system. They hadn't been followed, so she deduced the Jegg must believe them destroyed. With the quantigraphic rift drive non-operational, they were completely vulnerable.

"It's okay. Just a minor burn. I can feel the salve working. It actually itches more than it hurts." She scratched at the surface of the bandage. "I hope my peregrine is still intact."

Davin smirked. "I wouldn't worry. That falcon's as tough an old bird as you are."

"Hey now," she said with a scowl. "That's the pride of my flock you're talking about. It's the first tattoo I ever got, right after I joined the Space Corps. It means a lot to me. And I seriously doubt there's a tat artist on this planet who can give me a touch-up."

"Yeah, yeah," her son said as he gazed out the viewport at the nearby planet. "I ... covered Gaspar up," he said, unable to keep his voice from trembling.

Maeve cursed under her breath. Her dangerous plan to escape the Jegg was a success, and by the skin of their teeth, they'd fled to the outer reaches of the Milky Way Galaxy. The final explosion hadn't caused a hull breach, but the ship was thrown sideways so violently that Gaspar lost his balance and cracked his skull against the bulkhead. By the time they found him, there wasn't anything they could do.

Another friend gone, she thought. *Another life I couldn't save.*

Fighting to quell a rising tide of emotion, she endeavored to keep her voice as comforting as possible. "We'll bury him as soon as we land. Promise."

"Okay," he said as he continued to stare blankly out the viewport.

Maeve gazed at her son, cursing whatever higher power had forced them into this predicament. *He shouldn't be here. He should be at home, starting University and chasing girls and sneaking his first beer. Not here.*

Farking Jegg.

"Is that where we're going?" Davin said, gesturing at the planet.

Maeve took another sip of water. "Yep. Castelan VI."

He sat down in the pilot's chair, stretched his arms out, and interlocked his fingers behind his head. "Looks kinda like Earth."

"Yeah, it does."

"I mean, there's only the one really big continent, but other than that ... "

Maeve stood up and took the copilot's seat. "Castelan VI," she said, reciting a report she committed to memory months ago. "Slightly smaller than Earth, with a comparable atmosphere and gravity. Rotates on its axis once every twenty-two-point-five hours, takes three hundred and eighty-nine Earth days to make one revolution around its sun. Total population is approximately two hundred sixty-three thousand humanoids, ninety-nine percent of whom are clustered on or near the coastal regions of the northern half of the main continent. There are some undeveloped areas farther inland that can support life, but most of the central land mass is inhospitable terrain: deserts, mountains, et cetera. There are a few other small islands, but they're far from the main continent and look to be uninhabited."

He nodded. "Of all the places Banikar suggested, why'd Dad choose *this* planet to come to?"

"Several reasons. We had to choose a planet with a breathable atmosphere and far enough away from the Terran Confederation that the Jegg would ignore it. Ideally, we would have chosen a world with no humanoid life, but ... well, let's just say our options were limited. Ironically, the final two choices were this world and Denebius IV. Believe me, I was not in a hurry to go back there."

"I bet. You're sure the information is reliable?"

She gave him a grim smile. "I've asked myself that question at least a thousand times. Honestly, I have no idea. What it comes down to, unfortunately, is that we really have no choice. When a trans-dimensional being tells you that your best chance to defeat the Jegg is by finding some mysterious energy source, you shut up and listen."

He scoffed. "If the Eth are so flippin' powerful, why couldn't they just get rid of the Jegg themselves?"

She turned to face him. "You may find this hard to believe, Dav, but they wouldn't answer that question."

"Great. How exactly is this energy source going to help us beat the Jegg?"

"Fark if I know. I'm just supposed to fly the ship and see to the mission's safety. It was your father and his brain trust that were going to figure that part out."

Davin sat up straight again, covering his mouth just in time to sneeze into his hands. Maeve reached under the console, grabbed a clean rag, and threw it to him. "Blow your nose, kiddo."

He snatched the rag out of midair and blew into it. Sniffling, he leaned back in the chair again. "So, what's the plan?"

"Well," she cast a dirty glance at the offending control panel, "once we get a little closer, I'm going to initiate another planetary scan. I'm not sure our sensors are calibrated to locate this energy source, but I'm hoping we can find a healthy quantity of it in one of the unpopulated areas. With a butt-load of luck, we can carry out this mission without having to deal with the locals."

"Why are you worried about them?"

"Because they're primitives, that's why. Long-range scans indicate a technology level equivalent to thirteenth-century Earth. I believe the word scholars once used to describe it is 'medieval'. They've discovered metallurgy but have yet to invent firearms or any complex machinery. I think it's safe to say they know nothing of extraterrestrial beings, so they probably won't greet us with open arms."

"Do they look like us?"

She nodded. "For all intents and purposes, they're nearly identical to homo sapiens. There are a few minor variances in terms of body chemistry, but other than that, they're no different than Terrans of fifteen hundred years ago."

"No different?" His brow furrowed. "That's hard to believe. I mean, what are the odds that, in this great big ol' universe, two planets so far apart would produce humanoid life-forms so close to each other genetically?"

She chuckled under her breath. "You're asking the wrong lass, Dav. Metaphysics and the great cosmic dice game are way above my pay-grade. And besides, we've got much more important things to worry about right now, don't we?"

He didn't answer her. He just stared into space.

She looked at her son with affection. *How is he holding it together so well after all that's happened? He's just a kid, and he's dealing with it better than I am.*

She stood up, moved over to stand next to him and placed a hand on his shoulder. "It'll be okay."

"If you say so."

With a sigh, she moved back over to the panel, sat down, and grabbed the soldering gun again. "Come on," she said, "let's get some juice into this rust-bucket's guts, all right?"

"Sure," he said. He didn't move, though. He just continued to stare, unblinking, at the nearby planet.

Maeve set to work again. She had no desire to interrupt her son's thoughts, which she knew were as heavy as her own. *We've lost so much, and the only ones left to pull humanity's collective arse out of the fire are an ex-Space Corps pilot and her teenage son.*

Saints, don't let this be a fool's errand.

Chapter Five

KELIA STRETCHED her legs, working the cramps out as she walked in circles around the small fire she'd built from a few dead branches of the huxa tree that had been her only companion during her vigil. The nights during the dry season were still quite warm, but a burning fire at least gave her something to concentrate on while she kept watch.

Since her arrival, she'd not slept at all. She couldn't risk falling asleep and missing what Arantha had brought her there to see.

She glanced once again across the darkened desert that stretched like a giant black carpet in front of her. There was no movement, no sound but the chirping of insects; not even a breath of wind.

As Arantha's vessel, Kelia assumed the energy she received from her last consultation would be enough to sustain her for the duration of her visit to this place. After nearly three days, however, her constant measures to remain awake and alert left her both physically and mentally drained. She'd used various meditative techniques to keep her senses acute, but she found herself unable to maintain that level of concentration now; her evening meal, several hours ago, represented the last of her food.

Kelia did not think, when she first set out from her village, that Arantha would test her resolve so. Her initial excitement had been replaced by a frustration greater than she'd ever felt before. She was hungry, thirsty, and so, so tired. And she needed a bath. Badly.

As she continued to pace, she weighed her options. The last thing she wanted to do was disappoint Arantha, but her abilities—and her patience—were stretched beyond their limits. If she made it through to sunrise without collapsing, she would return to the village with nothing meaningful to show for her prolonged absence.

Her leather shoes made no noise upon the rock as she paced, idly chanting rhymes from her childhood. She considered amusing herself by using her Wielding to shape the flames within the fire to her whim, but dismissed this notion quickly. She was far too exhausted to waste energy like that.

* * *

Hours passed. Sunset was already a distant memory, and Kelia began to wonder if her sanity had fled with the daylight.

A distant roaring sound caught her attention. She whipped around, looking left and then right, wondering if she was hearing the call of some great animal. However, that was impossible, for the sound continued unabated, and it was steadily growing in volume. With a start, she realized the sound wasn't coming from the desert, but from above her.

Adrenaline gave her weakened body new vigor as she cast her glance skyward. Seconds passed, and the roar grew louder and louder. She searched the heavens, praying for the sign she so desperately sought.

Then, out of nowhere, a spot of light appeared. It was tiny and dim at first, but grew in size and intensity as it streaked across the heavens, leaving a trail of incandescence in its wake.

Kelia's heart beat frantically in her chest as the ... *object*, for she had no other word to describe it, sank lower and lower in the sky, eventually vanishing as it neared the horizon. It must have come down somewhere in the Kaberian Mountains. She continued to watch for several minutes, but the light did not reappear.

What did I just witness? Great Arantha ... have you returned to Elystra after all this time?

She felt her sudden rush of adrenaline fade, and fatigue threatened once again to overwhelm her. Fighting it down, she gathered up her satchel and walked at a brisk pace away from the outcropping, back to the village.

* * *

When Kelia strode through the doorway of her home, she wasn't surprised to find Liana still awake, even though it was the middle of the night. Countless times, she'd caught her aunt, seated in the room's most comfortable chair, wide and wooden and covered with lyrax pelts, poring over one of the scrolls Kelia forgot to roll up and put back in its proper cranny in the wall of her study. A small fire crackled in the circular fire-pit in the center of the room.

Liana stood up as Kelia entered, and a welcoming smile formed on her round, wise face. In a loud whisper, she said, "Nima! I'm so glad you've returned!"

Kelia smiled back, happy to be addressed as "niece" instead of "Protectress," which only happened in the privacy of her own home. "Not as glad as I am to be back, ama," she returned, giving her aunt the same familial greeting.

Liana strode forward and enveloped her niece in a warm hug. Almost immediately, she stepped back and scrunched up her face, which looked rather comical under her short white hair. "Though I must admit, you've smelled better."

Kelia removed her outer robe and hung it on a hardened clay protrusion near the door, a sign to the Ixtrayu assigned to laundry duty that it was ready for cleaning. "You try sitting in the same spot for three straight days and see how *you* smell," she retorted. "How's Nyla?"

"Keep your voice down," Liana whispered, using her head to gesture at one of the home's three bedrooms. "She's only just drifted off to sleep."

"Sorry." Kelia stumbled forward and sat down in one of the other chairs next to the fire-pit. Leaning forward, she held her hands over the glowing embers of what remained of the fire. Warmth spread through her body, and she was grateful to be indoors, in familiar surroundings again.

"You've been gone a long time," Liana said hesitantly. She rolled up the scroll she was reading and laid it on the ground at the foot of her chair. "We were wondering if something happened to you."

"Something did."

Liana drew in a sharp breath. "Does that mean you saw what Arantha wanted you to see?"

Kelia remained silent as she leaned back in her chair, tightly gripping the armrests while continuing to stare at the remnants of the fire.

Dozens of myths were told to the daughters of the Ixtrayu for centuries: tales of a godlike being that descended from the Above. This being's name, according to legend, was Arantha, and through her intervention, a group of female slaves rose up against their captors and built a thriving community. No man had set foot in Ixtrayu territory since the village was built.

Arantha's wishes were often vague and cryptic, but she'd never led Kelia, or any of her predecessors, astray. Still, to actually *see* the distant light appear before her was … exhilarating. And more than a little intimidating.

"Yes." Kelia whispered, her eyes still fixed on the fire. Liana drew in another sharp breath.

They sat in silence for a few tense moments. Liana idly drummed her fingers on the arms of her chair. "Are you *really* going to make me ask?" she finally said.

Kelia knew Liana would not be satisfied with a simple, vague description. "I don't know what it was. I do have a theory, but I'm not sure how the Council will react to it."

"Nima," Liana said soothingly, "Arantha led you to that spot, and fulfilled your vision. She would not have done this were it not for our benefit. Why are you so worried?"

"I don't know. Maybe I was hoping that after so many years of guesswork, Arantha would provide me with some clarity." Kelia shifted in her seat and rubbed her leaden eyelids. "It feels like ... like we're traversing a raging river so shrouded in darkness we can't see the other side. The only way we can make our way across is by blindly groping around with our feet for the next stepping stone. All it will take is one false step on my part, and our people will be swept away to their doom."

Kelia bit her lip, fidgeting in her chair. "Never in all my life have I felt so handicapped by my stilted divinatory ability. How am I supposed to explain what is beyond my power to understand?"

Liana didn't even blink. "By trusting Arantha, and those who know you and love you."

"It's that simple?"

"As far as I'm concerned, it is. So tell me ... what was it?"

Before Kelia could respond, a mighty yawn forced its way through her mouth. She felt fatigue overwhelm her again, so she stood and stretched her back before she circled the fire pit and knelt down by her aunt's chair, placing her cheek on Liana's bony arm. Liana responded by gently rubbing the top of her niece's head with her other hand.

After a few deep breaths, Kelia met the older woman's gaze again. "Something has come to Elystra, ama. Something not of our world."

Liana's brow crinkled into a frown. "You don't mean … from the Above?"

"That's exactly what I mean."

Her aunt gasped, her brown eyes widening. "Oh my."

Kelia's knees started to cramp, so she rose to her feet again. She shuffled over to a small pile of kindling in the corner of the room, grabbed a few sticks and threw them on the fire. They stubbornly refused to ignite, so Kelia closed her eyes and made a slight motion with her hand. The kindling burst into flames, returning the fire to its former glory and warming the room. Satisfied, she resumed her seat in the chair nearest the fire pit.

"What are you going to tell the Council?" Liana asked, her soft voice combining with the crackle of the fire.

"I haven't decided yet."

"But you just said … it came from the Above. If Arantha has returned –"

"It would be a great and wondrous thing," Kelia interjected. "The Ixtrayu have served her faithfully from the beginning. Her return, in whatever form she may take, would renew our faith for centuries to come."

Kelia pointed at the scroll at Liana's feet. "Ever since I learned how to read, I've been studying our tribe's history. Arantha has always shown us our path. How we tread that path, however, she has always left to us. Our ancestors followed her blindly, but we are a more enlightened people now. I cannot just assume it was her return that I saw tonight, even if it *was* she who allowed me to see it. It could very well be Arantha … or it could be something malevolent. Something that threatens the Ixtrayu, perhaps all of Elystra."

Kelia's leg began to twitch, and she had to hold it steady with her hand. "But if it *is* Arantha, I have to ask myself: why didn't my mother, whose gift of foresight was far superior to my own, see this coming? And if she did, why would she not speak of it, or at least document it?"

"Perhaps she couldn't," Liana replied. "She must have believed keeping tonight's events a secret was Arantha's will."

"That's quite a secret to take to the Great Veil with you." Kelia stared into the flames, as if hoping to glean some additional wisdom from them.

"Don't fret, dear niece." Liana gestured at the rolled-up scroll she'd been reading. "You may not have your mother's talent for divination, but your ability to control the elements puts hers to shame."

"Maybe so, but right now I'd trade *all* of that ability for a fraction of hers. I fear the Council will expect more answers than I can provide, especially Susarra. She grows more difficult every time I refuse her request to have the Sojourns resume."

Liana rose to her feet. "I wouldn't worry about her. She may honk louder than most, but she won't challenge your authority." She moved off toward a room adjacent to Kelia's bedroom. "I'm going to sleep. Try to get some yourself. You look like you need it."

"I will. Sleep soundly, ama."

"Sleep soundly," she echoed and disappeared through the thin layer of kova hide that curtained the entrance to her room.

With a slight wave of her hand, Kelia subdued the fire until, once again, it was reduced to a few smoldering embers. Yawning, she walked over to the entrance to Nyla's bedroom, peeking through the curtains. Fast asleep on the pile of lyrax pelts in the far corner lay her thirteen-year-old daughter, her dark hair spilling over her cherubic face.

Kelia allowed herself a slight smile, inwardly hoping Nyla's calm repose would remain when she woke in the morning. The odds were better that Onara would return from the Great Veil. Being rebellious and disobedient was part of adolescence, and not even the daughter of a Protectress was immune to the fickleness of youth.

She took a deep, cleansing breath and crossed the threshold into her own bedroom. Too weary to even change into her sleep-robes, Kelia collapsed onto her bed and fell into a blissfully dreamless sleep.

Chapter Six

Elzor stood on the balcony adjacent to the throne room of the Castle Tynal. Many fires still burned in the city of Talcris, providing more than enough light for him to see the results of the day's work. In the distance, he heard the sounds of several skirmishes still being fought as his soldiers disposed of the last few pockets of resistance that seemed determined to defend their lost cause to the bitter end. Not that it mattered much. His men weren't taking prisoners anyway. The best enemy was always a dead one.

It had taken Elzor many years to achieve this victory, so he allowed himself a moment of contentment. He caressed the soft material of the royal cloak draped across his shoulders, and his smile morphed into a broad grin as he beheld a few drops of blood marring its otherwise clean surface. Only hours ago, he had the satisfaction of tearing this cloak off the beaten, broken body of King Morix, the former ruler of the region. His one regret about the encounter was that Morix hadn't been conscious to witness Elzor drawing a blade across the throat of his stupid gurn of a queen. The former monarch now languished in his own dungeon, manacled to his wife's corpse.

A shuffle of footsteps from behind Elzor tore him away from the scene of his conquest. Turning back, he reentered the throne room.

The place was opulent, with many ornate pieces of artwork and tapestries adorning the walls, which bore a plethora of torches held in place by equally lavish sconces. One wall was dominated by a picture of the now-deceased Queen, which Elzor made a mental note to have removed and burned as soon as possible. His mood improved again when he saw Elzaria and Langon awaiting him.

General Langon was a brute of a man, giant in stature and as thick and tough as a century-old huxa tree. His rough, bearded face bore so many scars that Elzor had stopped imagining what he looked like before they became comrades-in-arms. He stood, stock-still, oblivious to the gash on his upper right arm where an Agrusian soldier had wounded him. Much of his thick kova-leather jerkin was stained with blood as well. Elzor was certain that came from many deceased members of Morix's army.

Elzor sat down on the elaborately-decorated wrought-metal throne and faced them. "Report," he said, his voice reverberating around the room.

"Our victory is nearly complete, my liege," said Elzaria, bowing her head as she addressed her brother. "By nightfall, the last remnants of the Agrusian army will either be dead or have fled for the northern forests."

"Excellent." Elzor straightened himself up on the throne. "Any sign of our prize?"

"No, my liege," she replied. "I've had twenty men conduct a thorough search of the castle grounds. They've turned up nothing. However, we have discovered a secret level below the dungeons. We were not aware of this before."

"I trust you've searched it as well."

"Of course. There is a massive door at the far end of a corridor. It appears to be built right into the castle's foundation. It bears no keyhole, and it has confounded my every attempt to open it using my Wielding." She scoffed. "Trust the Agrusians to hide the Stone in the one place that is impervious to my power."

"No matter." Elzor waved his hand dismissively. "Whatever's closed can always be opened. Let Morix spend a few more days with his beloved wife, and he'll tell me what I need to know."

"You've taken his realm, and murdered his queen," Langon said. "What makes you think he'll tell you anything?"

"I can be ... quite persuasive." Elzor said with a sardonic tone.

"And if he still doesn't tell you?" Elzaria asked.

"Then I'll be even *more* persuasive."

Langon nodded. "Should I see to the ... *other* matter, my liege?"

Elzor locked eyes with his general. "Do it."

"Yes, my liege." Langon bowed and strode out of the room.

Elzaria remained still. "Any further commands for me, brother?"

Elzor regarded his sister, noting for the first time how haggard she looked. Not at all surprising. She'd had a productive day.

After dispatching the King's royal messengers, she joined the Elzorath on their final march to the city. She let the power within her grow to a level she never had before, releasing a blanket of blue death that killed or incapacitated half the Agrusian army on their initial charge. The second attack met with similar casualties, after which Elzaria collapsed from the strain. The Elzorath then took the fight to the remaining soldiers, claiming an easy victory.

"No, dear sister, you go rest. The queen's bedchamber is all yours. Replenish your strength, and I'll send a servant around with the best meal our new castle has to offer."

Elzaria gave a cold, chilly smile. "You spoil me."

"Well, if I don't, who will?" Elzor strode forward, taking her hand and kissing it in an uncharacteristic display of chivalry.

Elzaria smiled but didn't respond. She retracted her hand from Elzor's grasp, unsheathed a thick-bladed knife she had strapped to the back of her belt and flung it all the way across the throne room. It struck the portrait of the Queen right between the eyes.

Elzor watched in amusement as the knife continued to vibrate, as if excited to have hit its target so perfectly. He turned around just in time to see his sister's back as she swept out of the room.

With a swoosh of his stolen cloak, he made his way back to the balcony and placed his hands on the balustrade. The sounds of fighting had all but died out, and the city of Talcris was eerily silent.

He was about to head back inside when something curious caught his gaze. Up in the sky, far in the distance, a trail of light shot like an arrow toward the horizon.

He cocked his head, keeping his keen eyesight focused on the streak until it disappeared from view. Such sightings were rare on Elystra, but not unheard of. Whatever strange phenomena occurred in the Above didn't concern him. If any entity, god or mortal, was foolish enough to stand in his way, he would sweep them aside as easily as he had Morix's army.

Elzor drew in a deep breath as he reveled in his victory. He was master of this domain.

And many more domains would soon follow.

Chapter Seven

EEP IN the heart of Mount Calabur, Mizar, High Mage of Darad, stood transfixed, his mouth opened in a paroxysm of pain.

A surge of energy, far more intense than any he'd ever experienced, pounded through him as image after image flittered across his mind's eye. The stuff of nightmares, overlapping each other in a cacophony of chaos: flashes of intense light, entire villages in flames, streets littered with the blackened, charred bodies of men, women and children. Mizar tried with all his might to block out the horrific images, but failed.

As the comfort of oblivion threatened to overwhelm him, the scene of slaughter disappeared, and another, much different image took its place. With the last of his flagging mental strength, Mizar concentrated on this latest image.

Three women stood on a darkened, unknown landscape, still as statues, while a fierce battle waged around them. Each one radiated raw power; the kind of power, he noted with stupefaction, that could only have come from Arantha. Three Wielders, each one clothed by an aura that pulsed with the energy they channeled.

Mizar tried to break through the whirling torrents in his mind, attempting to discern the faces of these three women, but as he teetered on the brink of clarity, another blast of energy coursed through his body. The image disintegrated, and blackness overtook him.

Released from Arantha's hold, Mizar's body crumpled to the ground.

* * *

"Master! Master, wake up!"

Mizar's eyes fluttered open, and he became aware that he was lying, face-down, on the stony ground. With a groan, he propped himself up on his elbows, trying to will the strength back into his limbs. It felt as if someone had stuck a white-hot poker through his brain. Even the small movement of lifting his head caused a searing flash of pain to rip through it. It was all he could do not to let unconsciousness overwhelm him again, as it had a few ... *minutes ago? Hours?*

How much time has passed? How long have I lain here, dead to the world?

He cast a sidelong glance to the entrance of the Crystal Cavern, the hollow heart of Mount Calabur, where he had unceremoniously collapsed. He remembered crying out in agony. It obviously wasn't loud enough to alert the guards who prevented anyone from entering the chamber when Mizar consulted Arantha.

Inch by painful inch, he struggled into a sitting position, brushing dust and small pebbles from his clothes and his grayish-brown beard, and retrieving his black cloth skull-cap from the ground. He had fallen where he normally stood, on the Nexus of Arantha. Thousands of crystals, none larger than one of his fingernails, dotted an almost geometrical pattern over the walls and ceiling. Over the course of the five and a half decades of his life, he'd had hundreds of visions, but none had given him the sense of foreboding—or the overwhelmingly intense pain—he had just experienced.

38

He turned the other way and saw, kneeling at his side, a gangly young man dressed in a loose beige tunic. "Master! Oh, thank Arantha!" he exclaimed, relief spreading over his face. "I feared you were dead!"

Mizar clapped his palms over his ears. "Please, Sen, not so loud."

"I'm sorry, Master," Sen said, at a much more reasonable volume. "I'm just … thankful you're alive. You were barely breathing."

Little by little, Mizar's sight returned to normal. His brown, deep-set eyes scanned the Cavern. All looked exactly as it had before his ordeal. "I'm all right, Sen. Thank you for your concern."

"Can you stand?"

Mizar nodded, and with Sen's help, he was able to climb to his feet and make his way to a long wooden bench that ran along the cave's near wall. Sitting down, he glanced up at his apprentice, who continued to stare at him with concern.

Sen was tall and rail-thin, with medium-length black hair, sea blue eyes, high cheekbones and a wide mouth. Although often awkward and clumsy, he was a good, hard-working lad, and Mizar had grown rather fond of him over the previous two years. He reminded Mizar so much of himself. They were both sixteen when they discovered they could Wield. Unfortunately, after two years of training, it became clear Sen possessed only healing abilities and nothing else. Mizar, with his powers of divination and control of the elements—air, water, fire and earth—was High Mage, only the fourth in the history of Darad, which went back almost a thousand years.

A wave of dizziness shot through Mizar, and he would have toppled over had Sen not grasped him by the shoulders and pulled him back into an upright position. "What happened, Master?" Sen asked.

Mizar placed his thumbs and forefingers against his temples, trying to calm his turbulent thoughts. Within moments, the pain receded, but the lightheadedness remained. "I–I don't know. That's never happened before." He looked at his apprentice again, his forehead wrinkling in puzzlement. "The guards just let you in?"

Sen's cheeks flushed, and he averted his eyes. "Forgive me, Master. When you didn't show up for my lesson, I assumed you had other business to attend to. I waited for you in the dining hall for midday meal, but when you didn't show up there either, I asked around, and no one had seen you since you entered the Cavern, so I figured you must still be here." He grimaced. "The guards made me wait two more hours before I could convince them something must be wrong."

"So I've been lying here unconscious for … *eight hours*?"

"I think so."

Mizar harrumphed. "I'm going to have to ask His Majesty to instruct his guards to be more accommodating in the future, just in case this happens again." He closed his eyes, massaging his temple again.

"In case *what* happens?" Sen asked, his voice tremulous. "Master, what did you see?"

Mizar couldn't form a response as he tried to make sense of what he just underwent. Thankful that his memory was still intact, he focused on the images Arantha had thrust into his mind. He looked for details that he may have missed when he lost consciousness, but was unable to discern anything new.

He then realized he hadn't yet answered his apprentice's question. "I saw … evil. A great darkness sweeping across Elystra."

Sen's jaw fell open. "We must tell the King."

Mizar grasped the boy's arm. "No, Sen. Do not breathe a word of this. Not until I've had a chance to make sense of it all."

Sen saw the seriousness on his teacher's face and lowered his head in deference. "Yes, Master."

Having regained enough strength to stand, Mizar rose to his feet. "I regret that your lessons are going to have to be postponed for the time being, Sen. I have a task for you that is of paramount importance."

Sen's eyebrows raised expectantly.

"Tomorrow, I will speak to King Aridor. I'm going to get his permission to access the Royal Archives."

"Master," Sen said, looking even more bewildered than before, "you've sent me to the Archives dozens of times. We've never needed the King's permission before. Why do we need it now?"

"You know that locked vault in the back corner that no one but the King holds the key to?"

"The Forbidden Knowledge?"

"That's right."

Sen gulped and the blood drained from his face, looking as if Mizar had just asked him to cut off his own arm. "And what information will you be requiring?"

Mizar tightened his jaw. "All of it."

Chapter Eight

DAVIN DELICATELY laid the final fist-sized chunk of shale on top of the small cairn of rocks at the head of the newly dug grave. Standing up, he brushed the dust from his pants and joined his mother, who stood a short distance away.

The pair took in their surroundings. They'd landed the *Talon* in a shallow wadi between two small peaks in the mountain range that ran for hundreds of miles down the western part of the central continent, effectively bisecting the desert that stretched as far as the eyes could see on either side.

They'd made planetfall the night before. After getting the ship moving again, Maeve decided to wait until nighttime before landing, as it would cut down on the number of locals that might witness the *Talon* as it made its way through the atmosphere. Thankfully, the landing had been textbook, and the two of them slept straight through till morning.

They'd unpacked the portable generators, the purifiers, and the excavator. Next came the food synthesizer, which would give them their first palatable meal since leaving Earth. First, though, they had a burial to attend to.

The hard-packed dirt of the riverbed that the *Talon* now rested upon proved difficult to dig through. The ground near the mountain lake a quarter-mile away was much softer, so they chose a shady spot underneath a rocky overhang about ten yards from the lake's shore for Gaspar's final resting place. After only an hour of digging in the hot dry air, sweat drenched their loose-fitting clothes.

"Would you like to say a few words?" Maeve asked, her eyes fixed on the grave. "You knew Gaspar better than I did."

Davin shifted his feet. "I'm not sure what to say." He looked sideways at his mother. "You've been to funerals before, right?"

Maeve closed her eyes, nodding. "Far too many, unfortunately."

"Do you remember any of that stuff Grandma and Grandpa taught you when you were little? You know, the God stuff?"

"Not much." She sighed. "I do remember a poem my mother taught me, though." She reached her hand over, motioning for Davin to take it, which he did. Both of them bowed their heads.

Maeve spoke in a hushed, reverent tone. "*Those we love don't go away, they walk beside us every day. Unseen, unheard, but always near, still loved, still missed, and very dear.*" She took another deep breath before continuing. "Lord, I know it's been a long time since we've, um, spoken ..." She felt her mouth going dry.

Davin squeezed her hand. They locked eyes, and a wordless conversation passed between them.

Maeve exhaled, then continued. "Gaspar was ... a fine young man. One of the finest minds you've ever produced. My son and I ..." She took a step closer to Davin, who released her hand and put his arm around her shoulder. "... would not have made it here without him. Please, God, do not let Gaspar's sacrifice, and my husband's sacrifice ..." A tear escaped Maeve's eye, slicing down her cheek. Davin pulled her against him. "Please don't let them have died in vain.

"I'm sure you've noticed, humanity's not doing so well right now. Our backs are against the wall, and ... well, whatever you can do to guide us through our darkest hour, we'd, um ... we'd really appreciate it. We also ask that you welcome the souls of Richard Cromack, Gaspar Wexler, Manuel Villegas, Calvin Stockard, Ji-Yan Lee, Kacy Weatherby, and Suri and Mahesh Patel into the kingdom of heaven." She paused, glancing over at Davin, who gave a slight smile. "Um, that's it, I guess. Amen."

"Amen," Davin echoed, releasing his hold on her. "That wasn't too bad, Mom."

Maeve wiped her face. "Saints, I'm out of practice."

"Come on." He used his head to gesture at the just-unpacked synthesizer. "We'll feel better after we eat. I always do."

She couldn't fault that logic. "Lead the way."

One final look at the grave, and they made the short walk back to the landing zone.

* * *

After sustaining themselves on nothing but emergency rations since before they left Earth, unpacking the synthesizer had been like unwrapping a Christmas present, and it chased their somber mood away. Thirty seconds after hooking it up to one of the portable generators, Davin shoved a pastrami on rye into his mouth in that way that only a teenage boy could.

Maeve chuckled as the sandwich disappeared and took a bite of her own. He'd no sooner gulped down the last bite when he pushed a button on the synthesizer's control panel. A few moments later, a side-panel slid open, revealing another sandwich. He greedily scooped it up and deposited it on his plate. It was moments like this that made Maeve glad she was the only one with the machine's pass-code, or he'd eat his weight in food on a daily basis.

"Whoa, slow down, Speedy," Maeve chided him. "You don't wanna give yourself a stomach-ache. We've got a lot of work to do today."

"GnarmIknowmomnom," he said around another huge bite, washing it down with a gulp of cold water. "Sorry. I'm just ... hungry."

"Really? I never would have guessed."

He grinned. "Any chance for a piece of cake?"

Maeve cocked an eyebrow. "I know we're on a different planet and all, Dav, but that doesn't mean it's suddenly your birthday."

"*Please,* Mom? It's only three days away!"

Maeve matched her son's puppy-dog look with a stern one of her own. "Dav, come on. We're not on vacation; we're on a mission. You know that."

"Fine," he said tersely, tearing his eyes away and cramming the rest of his sandwich into his mouth. "So where're we gonna start digging first?"

They'd set up a dining table under a large overhang of rock, which shaded them from the heat of the midday sun. A fresh-water mountain lake lay off to the left, and the *Talon*'s gun-metal gray hull sat to the right, around the base of the smaller of the two peaks that dominated the area.

Maeve pointed to the larger peak, several hundred yards away. "Right there, I think."

"You *think*?"

"Well, like I said before, I don't know anything about the nature of this energy source we're supposed to find. Geological scans have turned up nothing out of the ordinary, except ..." She grabbed the computer pad from the table in front of her and tapped it.

After a few moments, she handed the small screen to Davin. It showed a topographical depiction of the mountain range that surrounded them. At the center, a red dot expanded and contracted at regular intervals.

"For whatever reason, there are several areas on this planet that the scanners can't seem to penetrate. It could be that this energy source, whatever it is, is interfering with them."

Davin nodded. "Seems like a good place to start. Out of curiosity, why'd you pick this location?"

"Because the other sources of the interference are located near populated areas. There appear to be two other large blurs: one about three hundred miles to the east, the other on the northwestern coast. I'm hoping we can find the source at this location without alerting any of the locals."

"You sure, Mom? These excavators make a ton of noise, you know."

"I know, but that's a chance we have to take. That settlement three hundred miles away is our closest neighbor, so we should be okay. Even so, I'll go out tomorrow with some portable long-range detectors and place them around the perimeter. Don't want anyone sneaking up on us."

"Good idea," Davin said. "What about that lake? Is it safe to swim in?"

"Should be, but I'll do a molecular analysis to be sure. Don't want any weird microorganisms spoiling our little outing, do we?"

He drained the contents from his cup. "Time to get this show on the road, I guess."

Maeve collected the dirty plates, opened a lower drawer on the synthesizer and shoved them in, slamming it shut with a resounding *thunk*. She turned to her son with a determined grin. "Come on, kiddo, let's go kick this mountain's arse."

Chapter Nine

"PROTECTRESS?"

As Kelia woke, she became aware someone was tugging at her shoulder. Through narrowed eyes, she squinted at the light of the morning sun that poured into the room through the window.

With a groan, she pushed herself into a sitting position. As the top layer of lyrax pelts fell off her body, she realized with a huff that she'd forgotten to cover the window. Her eyes having adjusted to the light, she turned her head to see a pretty, doe-eyed, teenage girl with long dark hair staring at her.

"Vaxi," Kelia said, stretching her arms over her head as she willed the stiffness out of her back muscles. "What is it?"

"I apologize for waking you, Protectress. One of the Council requests an audience."

Kelia rubbed the last vestiges of sleep from her eyes, climbed to her feet and began removing the dirty clothes she'd spent the last three days wearing. "Let me guess ... your grandmother, right?" she asked with perhaps more sarcasm than Vaxi deserved.

Vaxi nodded, averting her eyes. "Yes, Protectress." Though Vaxi kept her face expressionless, Kelia could tell the girl was troubled.

Every time Kelia saw Vaxi, she marveled at how much the girl had grown over the last few years. Tall, athletic, and muscular, Vaxi was one of the swiftest and most agile of the huntresses despite her young age. Not only did she bear a striking resemblance to her mother Ilora, she also possessed Ilora's compassion and affability.

It made Kelia sad whenever she thought about Ilora. They'd been bonded for only two years when Ilora died. Kelia had just taken over as Protectress, and had given birth to Nyla the year before. Had Ilora lived, Nyla and Vaxi would likely have been raised as sisters, but Susarra insisted that between Ilora's death and Kelia's time-consuming duties, Vaxi's upbringing should be her responsibility as her only living blood relative. Living under the same roof as her domineering grandmother had clearly taken its toll on her.

Figures Susarra would send Vaxi as her own personal messenger. She knows I'm far less likely to say no to Vaxi.

Kelia grabbed a clean tunic from its hook on the wall and pulled it on over her head, straightening it out so it hung loosely around her body in all the appropriate places. "Tell Susarra I will speak with her, and the rest of the Council, after evening meal. I have a great many things to attend to before then."

"I will relay that message, Protectress."

Kelia walked to her basin, scooping a handful of water from it with a ladle and pouring it into a cup before draining its contents, quenching a thirst she'd allowed to go unchecked during her vigil. Then she took another ladleful and leaned back, letting the liquid drip onto her face. Grabbing a small cloth next to the basin, she attempted to make her filthy face and hair more presentable.

Silently vowing to make a trip to the cistern for a bath at the earliest opportunity, she turned to find the girl still standing there, her eyes cast to the ground. "Was there something else, Vaxi?"

"I was ... I was just ... " Vaxi looked up, staring vacantly out Kelia's bedroom window.

"Speak your mind, Vaxi, please," Kelia said, crossing the room to stand in front of the girl. She noticed a large purple bruise on the girl's arm, but dismissed it. Hunting was the most dangerous duty an Ixtrayu could perform, and injuries were common among the huntresses.

Vaxi cleared her throat but didn't return the eye contact. "As you may know, Protectress, I am approaching my eighteenth birthday."

"I am aware."

"I was just wondering if ... if there was any chance that Arantha ... " Vaxi's willpower dissipated along with her voice.

This was a delicate subject, one that had been a constant matter of debate between Kelia and Susarra ever since Onara's pronouncement thirteen years ago. Kelia couldn't help wondering if Vaxi was bringing this matter up of her own volition, or whether it had been Susarra's idea.

Kelia put a hand on the girl's shoulder. "Vaxi, there will come a time when you will take your Sojourn, and when you do, I know you will bear a beautiful, strong daughter that will be a fine addition to the Ixtrayu. However, I regret that I cannot tell you when that time will be."

The girl nodded resignedly. "I understand, Protectress."

"Hey," Kelia said, placing her finger under Vaxi's chin and lifting it so their eyes could meet again. "I know this won't bring you comfort right now, but I ask that you not let this trouble you. If Arantha, through her vessel Onara, decreed a halt to the Sojourns, then there must have been a reason for it."

"But," Vaxi said sheepishly, "you are Arantha's vessel now. Shouldn't you also know what that reason is?"

49

There it was. The question she'd been asked repeatedly since she became Protectress, and the one question she still couldn't answer. It always made her feel so helpless, so ignorant.

"Oh, if only it were as simple as that," she responded, struggling to keep her face implacable. "Arantha's will is not always ours to comprehend, Vaxi. We mere mortals are not always privy to her designs. The duty of the Protectress is to interpret. Onara was certain discontinuing the Sojourns was necessary, and we cannot question her judgment, no matter how much we may disagree with it."

"And ... if Arantha decides that I never Sojourn?" A tear appeared at the corner of Vaxi's eye, and it was all Kelia could do to keep her heart from rending itself in two.

Kelia brushed a strand of Vaxi's hair away, placing her hands on both sides of the girl's face. "If that is your destiny, then we must accept it."

"Yes, Protectress."

Kelia gestured to the purple bruise on Vaxi's forearm. "Go see Lyala about your injury."

"Yes, Protectress," she repeated. Then, with a nod and a respectful bow, she backed out of the room through the curtain. Kelia felt her heart grow heavy as she listened to Vaxi's footsteps fade away.

With a resigned sigh, Kelia slipped her feet into her well-worn kova-leather boots and made her way into the main room. Sensing nothing but dead silence from every other room in the house, she surmised that Liana must have taken Nyla for her daily lessons.

She strode through her doorway, blinking again in the light of the noonday sun. A whiff of roasting kova meat wafted past her nose, and she felt her stomach growl. Turning to her left, she quickly descended the stairs from her home, heading directly for the source of the smell.

* * *

Kelia was silent as she ate her midday meal across from Liana. On her plate were several strips of kova meat and two slices of riverfruit. She wondered whether a tribal leader should be seen wolfing down her food like an underfed chava, but she dismissed it. She was famished, and Liana was considerate enough to let her sate her appetite without engaging her in conversation.

Three dozen of the two hundred and seventeen Ixtrayu were trained as huntresses, and this was the time of year when herds of kova, numbering in the thousands, migrated across the Plains of Iyan on their journey down to the Southern wetlands. They were large, brutish animals, generally brown or black in color. They walked around on four thick, hooved legs, and their biggest weapons apart from their size and stamina were two curved horns that jutted from the sides of their heads. To an untrained huntress, they were quite formidable. However, they were as unintelligent as they were brutish, and though their size made them difficult to kill, it was worth the huntresses' efforts. Ten full-grown kova could feed the entire Ixtrayu tribe for a whole season. In the days since Kelia began her vigil, the hunt had been bountiful.

After cleaning her plate of everything but a few bones, Kelia straightened up and exhaled.

"Full yet?" Liana asked, smiling. "Or do I need to have Aarna carve you another slab?"

"This should suffice for now," Kelia said before covering her mouth to muffle the belch that followed. "If I'd known I was going to be gone for three days, I would have brought a lot more food."

"Well, I'm just glad you're back. Taking care of Nyla is starting to become more than I can handle."

"She's not making trouble again, is she?"

"No, not trouble, she's just … bored. Like all girls are at that age. Too old to play childish games, too young to perform their duties unsupervised. All she has are lessons and training." She cast a glance over her shoulder. "At least she has Sarja."

Following Liana's gaze, Kelia spotted Nyla at a table on the other side of the room. Her daughter wore a plain, light brown tunic, snug tan pants, and a pair of leather boots. Her hair, in contrast, was exceptionally dark, almost black, a large strand of which hung in a straight line down the right side of her face, partially obscuring one of her hazel eyes.

Kelia was glad to see Nyla eating her meal with Sarja, the young daughter of her best friend Runa. Nyla and Sarja had been best friends since they learned how to walk, and she wondered, not for the first time, if their lifelong friendship would end up blossoming into a physical relationship. Also at their table was Vaxi, who appeared to still be in a dour mood despite Kelia's reassurances.

A young brown-haired woman wearing a loose tunic and a belt with many pouches rushed into the room. Kelia recognized her as Yadra, one of her cousins. She was clearly frantic and out of breath. After a few seconds, she spotted Liana and Kelia and ran over. "Gama! Protectress!" she panted. "I need to find Lyala! Have you seen her?"

"Why? What's wrong?" Liana asked.

"It's Talya! She's been hurt!"

Yadra and Talya, Liana's two granddaughters, were gatherers for the tribe. Most of their duties entailed regular trips to Lake Barix, the source of the River Ix, around which many plants and herbs grew that were essential to the Ixtrayu for culinary and medicinal purposes. It was a two-hour journey by chava to get there.

"What happened?" Kelia demanded.

"She was attacked ... by a wounded lyrax. Her leg is cut up bad. Mother's with her right now. She needs the healer! Have you seen her? She's not at the apothecary!"

"Lyala was here not too long ago," Kelia said. "She said she was going to her herbal garden under the eastern overhang."

"I'll find her," Liana said, rising to her feet. "Yadra, you run down to the stables and have Olma ready three fresh chavas. We'll join you there." Then both Liana and Yadra turned to look at Kelia, silently asking for permission to depart.

"Go, both of you," Kelia said. "Bring her home safely."

They both nodded and ran from the room.

Kelia and the other Ixtrayu present watched them go. After a few moments, all heads returned to their meals and conversations. She noticed that Nyla, Sarja and Vaxi had already left.

If there was one thing that made Kelia feel even more helpless than being unable to adequately divine Arantha's wishes, it was discovering that one of her people had been hurt and knowing there wasn't anything she could do about it. The world was a dangerous place, and the Protectress' ability to protect only extended so far.

The rumble of conversation resumed just as Runa entered the dining area. She removed her bow and quiver, setting them right inside the entrance before heading to a serving table where several plates of cooked meat and fruit were laid out. Grabbing a small portion, she made her way over to Kelia.

"Welcome back, Protectress," she said, sitting down in the seat Liana had just vacated.

Like their daughters, Runa and Kelia had been close friends since childhood. She was one of the tallest of the Ixtrayu, just over six feet tall, nearly five inches taller than Kelia herself. Her skin's hue was dark from a lifetime of being outside. Her legs were long and powerful, her senses were as acute as a non-Wielder's could be, and her dark brown eyes still bore a youthful exuberance.

Kelia had planned on getting more food, but after learning what just happened to Talya, her appetite had left her.

After a few moments of tense silence, Runa said softly, "I heard what happened. Talya will be fine."

"I know," Kelia replied, nodding glumly. "Lyala's an exceptional healer. She'll have Talya fixed up in no time." Between the previous night's sighting, her upcoming meeting with the Council, Vaxi's despair, and now the attack against Talya, she wondered what *else* the day had in store for her.

"Of course she will," Runa said, digging into a slice of meat. "Did you know Vaxi is responsible for today's meal?"

Grateful for the change of subject, Kelia met her friend's gaze. "Is she really?"

Runa nodded. "Her skill as an archer surpasses even my own. She felled the beast with one shot."

Kelia smiled. "She is fortunate to have a great teacher."

"Very true. She's every bit the huntress Ilora was. Maybe even better." Her face became serious. "I worry, though, that Susarra may be pushing her too hard. Vaxi sometimes takes risks that often put her in danger during the hunt. When I chide her about it, she apologizes, says it won't happen again, but it always does. I don't want to be too harsh with her, given her situation, but ... "

"I understand. Did you know Vaxi came to see me this morning?"

"Really?"

Kelia nodded. "She practically begged me to let her go on Sojourn."

"Susarra's doing, no doubt."

"No doubt." Kelia idly ran a hand through her hair, which desperately needed washing. "I certainly don't wish to cause Vaxi further consternation. It would bring me no end of joy to be able to tell her, and all the Ixtrayu, that Arantha has decreed the Sojourns may resume. But I can't, because that is not what

Arantha is showing me." Kelia sighed, staring at her plate like the answers could be divined by the bones that lay on it.

Runa exhaled. "Kelia, forget for a moment what Arantha is or isn't showing you. You are, and always have been, the most logical person I've ever known. I know you got that from Onara."

"Thank you."

"It grieves me that Arantha hasn't given you the answers we seek. I worry that unless things change, I'm going to have to give Sarja the same news you gave Vaxi."

Fifteen years earlier, a year before Kelia had embarked on her third Sojourn, Onara's health began to decline. Despite the healer's ministrations, her mother's strength waned a little more with each passing season. It eventually became clear that Onara was in the final weeks of her life, and Kelia, as the most powerful Wielder in the tribe, would soon succeed her.

One would have thought that Kelia's imminent succession would preclude her from undertaking any further Sojourns, but Onara proclaimed it was her destiny to produce a daughter and successor—especially as her first two Sojourns had produced sons. The day Nyla was born, Onara stunned the tribe by announcing no further Sojourns would be taken ... by anyone. Her spirit made the journey to the Great Veil soon thereafter.

"I worry that without answers, those supporting Susarra's notion that we resume the Sojourns without Arantha's approval will grow in number," Kelia mused.

Runa arched an eyebrow. "You know, on days like today, I'm glad my duties are so simple compared to yours: go out, kill kova, come back. As long as I keep Susarra sufficiently well-fed, I never have to deal with her."

Kelia rolled her eyes. "Want to trade positions? Just for one day?"

Runa gave her friend a look of droll amusement, and then laughed. "You? A huntress? I love you, *Protectress*, but you couldn't even catch a three-day-old nemza kitten with a lame paw."

Kelia's mouth dropped open. "You are *never* going to let me live that down, are you?"

Runa reached over and grasped Kelia's hand. Kelia noted, not for the first time, how strong her friend was. Even though she'd reached her fortieth year, she could still keep up with huntresses half her age. "Kelia, the Ixtrayu are your family. They respect and love you. Don't ever think otherwise."

"I'll try." Kelia popped the last slice of riverfruit into her mouth, chewing thoughtfully. "But with each girl I continue to deny the Sojourns too, the more difficult it becomes to justify my mother's decision."

Runa stood and made a move to depart. "I'm afraid I must cut our conversation short. The hunt is to resume shortly." She placed her hand on Kelia's shoulder. "I have faith in Arantha. But more than that, dear friend, I have faith in you."

Kelia glanced up to see Runa smiling down at her. She gave a slight nod, and walked away.

* * *

A few minutes later, Kelia left the dining area and strode down a stone staircase, her booted feet making soft slapping noises as she descended. The staircase merged into a winding path running alongside the River Ix, a freshwater stream meandering through the Ixtrayan Plateau. Her pace was deliberate, and though many of her tribe bowed to her as she passed by, she did not return the gesture as she normally did.

Runa was right: the Ixtrayu *were* her family, and the last thing she wanted was to be as standoffish as her mother was. Onara commanded respect with her every move, but her stern nature created a rift between her and the women she led. As a child, from the moment she knew she would succeed her mother as Protectress, she vowed to be more personable, to not set herself apart despite her title and abilities. Since Onara's death, she'd kept that vow.

Today, though, such pleasantries as acknowledging her people were the furthest thing from her mind. With everything currently occupying her thoughts, Kelia began to wonder if the chasm between leader and tribe was as inevitable as the changing of the seasons.

She reached the northern edge of the village, and was preparing to cross one of the bridges traversing the stream leading to the Council members' homes when she heard a high-pitched shriek. Turning her head, she saw a billow of smoke wafting up past the top of the plateau. More shouts sounded in the distance, and the acrid smell of scorched wood drifted past her nostrils.

Kelia cursed under her breath, retracing her steps and running down the path that led out of the village, toward the farmlands and fruit orchards.

What else *can go wrong today?*

Chapter Ten

"WATCH THIS," Nyla said, closing her eyes. Seated at her table in the dining area, Sarja and Vaxi kept their eyes focused on the wooden mug in front of her.

Nyla waggled her fingers, releasing her breath a little bit at a time. As the other girls watched, the water within the mug began to bubble, then to boil. Nyla opened her eyes and spread her hands wide, smiling triumphantly.

Sarja clapped Nyla on the back. "Wow, Ny, you've really gotten good at that."

"Thanks. Guess all those boring lessons are paying off."

"Has your mother let you touch the Stone yet?"

"Not yet." Nyla frowned, glancing across the room to where her mother sat with Runa. "It's so unfair. She was my age when Grandmother let her touch it for the first time. But, of course, no matter how many times I ask her, she says I'm 'not ready'. She says I 'lack control.'" She turned to face Sarja. "Seriously? I mean, I pass all her stupid tests, and I 'lack control'?"

Sarja raised her hands defensively. "Hey, I'm on your side, remember?"

"It just makes me mad, Sarja." Nyla's face relaxed a little, her eyes downcast. "I mean, it's not my fault Grandmother made everyone stop having kids after I was born. Do you know what it's like to spend your whole life being the youngest member of the tribe? Everyone treats me like a blagging baby."

Sarja replied with her most apologetic look.

Nyla noticed that Sarja, just over a year older and two inches taller than her, had put a lot of muscle onto her slender frame since her mother Runa increased her physical regimen. She had not yet matured enough to join the hunt like Vaxi, but both of them knew that time was rapidly approaching. Nyla hated thinking about that day; the day her best friend would be out in the wild and she'd be stuck inside her mother's study poring over dusty scrolls or practicing her boring Wielding exercises.

She turned to Vaxi, who hadn't reacted at all to her magnificent feat. Vaxi's eyes were vacant, as if she was lost in her own thoughts.

Sarja noticed it too. "You okay, Vax?"

She snapped out of her daze and turned to face them. "Sorry. I just have a lot on my mind."

"What's wrong?" asked Nyla.

"I don't want to talk about it." She took a nervous gulp of her water.

"Come on, Vax, we're your friends," Sarja said. "We won't tell anyone, promise."

She sighed heavily, considering their words. Finally, she said, "Have you ever thought about Sojourning?"

Nyla scrunched her face up. "What, finding some stupid man to put a baby inside me? No thank you."

"Yeah, I agree," Sarja said. "Mother explained to me what's involved in, um, mating. It sounds disgusting."

Vaxi turned away with a scoff. "You girls are just kids. You don't understand."

"Hey, you're only four years older than me," Nyla said, scowling.

"And only three years older than me," Sarja added. "Don't get me wrong, I understand why the Sojourns are necessary. Doesn't mean I'm in a hurry to go on one."

Vaxi didn't respond, instead turning away to stare out the window.

Something seemed to occur to Sarja, who leaned forward. In a low voice, she asked, "Vaxi, are you ... lonely?"

Vaxi met her gaze again. "What?"

"It's not a big deal," Nyla said, catching on. "I'm sure there's someone in the tribe who would love to be your companion. Maybe all you need to do is ask."

"Yeah," said Sarja. "A few days ago I overheard Gruta tell Jara she likes you."

Vaxi's face turned red. "Never mind. I have to go." She stood up.

Nyla looked at Vaxi's meal, which she'd barely touched. "You're not going to finish?"

"You have it." Without another word, Vaxi strode to the door, retrieved her own bow and quiver from the floor, and walked out.

The two girls stared after her for a few moments. "What's with her?" Nyla asked.

"No idea," Sarja said. "Hey, how much time before you have to go to your Wielding lesson?"

"Not sure. Maybe an hour." Her eyes widened. "Wanna go have some fun? At the overhang?"

"You mean –"

"Uh huh."

"Yeah!" Sarja drained her water, shoved the last piece of fruit in her mouth, and together the two of them ran from the dining area.

* * *

60

The northern overhang was Nyla and Sarja's favorite vantage point: a small ledge of rock jutting out from the side of the plateau, overlooking a large sectioned-off field in which numerous crops grew. Several women tilled the soil, and others watered the budding plants of various fruits and vegetables. Off to the left lay a similar field where a large patch of holmgrass, the Ixtrayu's main source of grain, grew. Through the plateau, the River Ix wound its way down to the forests that lay beyond the farmland.

Lying on their stomachs, the two girls looked down upon a large number of Ixtrayu women going about their daily routine.

"You sure about this?" Sarja asked, suddenly doubtful. "The last time we tried something like this, you didn't exactly have your abilities under control."

"*Pfft.* That was months ago. I've learned a lot since then. You'll be impressed." Seeing her friend's skepticism, Nyla added, "Come on, *huntress*, show some spine. It'll be fun. So who should we prank?"

"How about Yarji?" Sarja pointed at a young, fair-haired woman on the other side of the river. She was using her hands to direct a long ribbon of water directly from the stream to hover over a lengthy row of nearly-ripe riverfruit that clung to vines abutting the water's edge. As they watched, Yarji clapped her hands and the stream of water shattered into a fine mist, raining down upon the fruit. She then moved farther downstream to tend to the next waiting vine.

"No, not her. She's really nice. How about her?" Nyla gestured in the other direction, indicating a much older woman, Trula, who was directing her equally ancient chava, Gim, to plow a recently-cleared area of land designated for the harvesting of holm grain. In his prime, Gim was a magnificent animal, like most chavas were: hooved creatures with strong, powerful legs that could propel their thick, muscular bodies to tremendous speeds, and long, angular heads that ended in mouths full of squared-off teeth. Trula was one of the few Ixtrayu with the ability to communicate with animals. She bonded with Gim many years before Nyla was even born, and now both of them relegated themselves to their current roles as farmer and plow-puller.

"Tempting, but we'd better not," Sarja replied. "A good scare might stop her heart, or she could fall down and break a hip or something."

"Good point."

Just then, another figure came into view, waddling down the path that led from the forest, along the river and into the village. She was in her sixties, heavyset, with her graying hair knotted into a braid pulled up into a rather ugly bun. She walked with a pronounced limp, offset by the thick walking stick she carried in her right hand. Her gait retained a full measure of authority, as did the haughty scowl permanently etched into her face.

Nyla's mouth curled into a mischievous smile. "Oh, *yeah.*"

Sarja crouched down even further, as if afraid the big woman's eyes would somehow lock onto their location. "Are you crazy?" she blustered. "That's Councilor Susarra!"

"So?"

"You can't prank a Councilor!"

Nyla scowled at her friend. "Why not? She deserves it!" She crawled forward a few more inches. Susarra appeared to be scolding Yarji as she passed by the poor woman. "She always takes the best pieces of kova meat at every meal and she gets the ripest fruit. And besides that, all she does is yell at people, including Vaxi *and* my mother, who's the blagging Protectress!"

"I know, Ny," Sarja said, sliding forward on her stomach until her head was next to Nyla's. "I feel so sorry for Vaxi sometimes. Can you imagine having to live with her?"

Nyla shuddered. "So it's settled, then."

"It's just ... do you know how much trouble we'll get in if we get caught? The last time we tried to pull something like this, my mother made me spend a month cleaning out the chava stables." Her nose wrinkled at the memory.

"Relax, Sar." Nyla fixated her stare on the corpulent Councilor. "She'll never know it was us."

Sarja exhaled. "Um, I hate to disagree with you, but there is no 'us' here. This is all you." With that, she slithered backward until her feet made contact with the cliff wall. Then, pulling herself into a low crouch, she prepared to make the climb back down to ground level.

"You're not leaving me here, are you?" Nyla asked.

"Yes, I am. Have you *smelled* chava dung? It's the worst-smelling thing on Elystra! I am not going back to that!"

Nyla rolled her eyes. "Fine, go. You want to miss the fun, be my guest."

Sarja remained silent for a few moments, considering. Finally, she crawled forward again, rejoining Nyla on the overlook. "You'd better be sure about this."

"Just be quiet and let me concentrate," Nyla said. Her eyelids half-closed, she began making slight circular movements with her hands.

Sarja turned to face forward just as Susarra resumed her trek back to the village. The Councilor was near enough that they could hear her heavy footsteps as well as the soft *thump* of her walking stick on the dirt path.

Abruptly, Susarra halted her forward progress, reeling in surprise as if she'd been pushed backward by a wall of wind. Her scowl disappeared, replaced by a confused grimace. She turned her head left and right, but her sister Ixtrayu were going about their daily business. None had reacted to whatever freak squall she'd just experienced. Shaking it off, she continued walking.

"Not bad," Sarja said, her eyes glinting in admiration.

"Oh, I'm just getting started," Nyla said impishly. She moved her hands again.

A thin ribbon of water, much smaller than the one Yarji just created, rose from the stream right behind Susarra. It formed itself into a small fist-sized ball and floated through the air, hovering over the unsuspecting Councilor's head. Nyla waggled her fingers, and the water-ball dropped to the ground. However, her aim was slightly off, and it smacked the ground right behind Susarra, who whirled around at the sudden *splat*.

As they watched, Susarra backtracked to accuse a befuddled Yarji of playing a practical joke on her. Whether the rotund woman believed Yarji's denial or not, Nyla couldn't tell, but Susarra resumed walking again, her stick pounding the dirt with each step.

"Oh, she's really ticked off now," Sarja whispered. Susarra was now closer than ever. "Let's go before she passes by us."

"No, I've got one more thing to try." Nyla waggled her fingers, focusing once again on Susarra.

Down below, the upper tip of Susarra's walking stick began to smoke. A few seconds later, it burst into flame. Feeling a sudden wave of heat, Susarra shrieked in alarm and, not even realizing in her panic that she was near a body of water, began to beat it against the ground to put out the fire.

Nyla and Sarja both laughed into their hands, watching the old Councilor hop around as she beat her stick upon the ground.

Their celebration was cut short when Sarja let out a high-pitched squeal. She clambered to her feet, swatting at something on her leg. It was a rock spider, black and yellow in color with eight hairy, sticky appendages. Its bite, while not poisonous, caused a dreadful rash.

As Sarja swatted at the offending arachnid, she bumped violently against Nyla, who was still attempting to control the fire tormenting Susarra. Nyla squealed in surprise. Her concentration fractured, her elemental abilities spiraled out of control.

The fire at the tip of Susarra's walking stick immediately tripled in size and intensity as another wall of hot air appeared, forcing her off the dirt path. Flailing her arms to try to regain her balance, she toppled backwards into the shallow stream, a shrill shriek escaping her lips before the water enveloped her.

The fire, meanwhile, had other ideas. The same wall of hot air blew the fire in the opposite direction, striking a line of juva-berry bushes that had yet to be watered. Within seconds, the entire vine was ablaze.

Having batted the spider off her leg, Sarja turned back to survey the chaotic scene below. The flames consuming the bushes were bending, as if trying to reach the next vine over. Nyla, fighting for control, finally calmed the wind that was causing the flames to dance and stretch, thus assuring that the fire wouldn't spread.

A few Ixtrayu, overhearing Susarra's screams, made their way down from the village to see what was causing the commotion.

The two girls shared one more glance before Sarja moved to the down-slope of the overhang. With one final look at her co-conspirator, she said, "I was never here." Then she was gone.

"Oh, *blag*," Nyla muttered to herself. She was in for it now. Her only hope was to get as far away as possible, as fast as possible. She was about to follow Sarja down the rock-face when she saw Kelia run past the overhang. Nyla quickly resumed her hiding place.

Peeking over the ledge, she watched as her mother, having reached the flaming vines, stretched her arms out, palms forward. A large quantity of water lifted from the stream and poured over the burning, blackening foliage. Kelia continued this process until the fire was completely out.

The crisis over, Nyla once again prepared to make her descent. This only took a few seconds, and she hit the ground with an ankle-jarring jolt.

All of a sudden, her forward momentum stopped. It felt as if a giant invisible hand had wrapped itself around her body, dragging her backwards. Her arms windmilled as her feet lifted off the ground, and she was so disoriented she couldn't even cry out.

After a short but nauseating journey, her momentum stopped. The invisible hand turned her around to face her mother, whose arms were still extended, keeping Nyla's body hovering several feet off the ground. Behind Kelia stood a sopping-wet Susarra, spluttering with rage.

Before Nyla could utter a word of apology, Kelia shoved her hands forward, and Nyla flew backwards again. She prepared for impact, expecting to hit hard ground, but instead, she landed in a large, muddy pool the Ixtrayu used to clean their farming implements. The water was brown and brackish, and from its smell, it was entirely possible Gim had relieved himself in it.

Nyla emerged, her face and clothes covered in mud. It dripped from her hair and arms in a viscous, slimy mess. She sloshed her way to the edge of the pool and climbed out, her boots squelching.

She no sooner stood upright on dry land than a huge cascade of clean water dumped itself on her, washing the noxious mud from her face and hair. As the shower ended, she looked down at her clothes, which were still stained an ugly dark brown. Her hair was matted and stuck to her face, and she looked as bedraggled as a drowned nemza cat. She glanced up again to behold Kelia, standing a few yards away and glowering at her.

Nyla had gotten in trouble before, many times, but she'd never seen her mother look at her with such fury. Her guts tightened in shame under her mother's frown.

It wasn't supposed to happen this way. It was meant to be a harmless prank. How could I lose control like that?

Arantha help me.

"Mama –" she whimpered.

Kelia held her hand up, silencing Nyla, her unblinking gaze firmly fixed on her disobedient daughter. "Go ... home ... *now*," she hissed, her chest heaving in barely-controlled rage.

Lowering her eyes to avoid the furious glares from her mother, Susarra, and every Ixtrayu who left the village to investigate the commotion, Nyla began her walk of shame, muddy footprints marking her trail all the way home.

Chapter Eleven

THE SUN was well above the horizon, and a brisk breeze blew through the city of Talcris. Elzor stood, back rigid, eyes fixed on the two-story wooden building in front of him.

He'd slept well the night before, allowing himself the luxury of slumbering in an actual bed for the first time in many months. Such were the spoils that go to the victors.

This morning, however, he had business to attend to.

He ordered the castle's terrified kitchen maids to prepare for him, his sister and his commanders a king's breakfast of roast waterfowl, a loaf of chaska bread with juva-berry jam and a flagon of cider. After his meal, he washed and dressed himself in the trappings of his new station–a brand new leather jerkin that fit him perfectly, black pants, boots and a small cloak taken from King Morix's closet. Finally, he selected two of the finest merychs from the royal stables for himself and Elzaria, and he made the short journey from the castle to this building, which served as a school for many of the young children of Talcris.

Elzor's reverie was broken by Langon, who approached from the side. He bowed his head, awaiting Elzor's acknowledgement.

"Is everything prepared, Langon?"

On Elzor's orders, the school's front and back doors had been sealed shut, and a company of Elzorath had surrounded the building the previous afternoon. His scouts reported fifteen children and several adult women were still inside, having taken shelter there to hide from the previous day's fighting.

A crowd of terrified citizens stood and watched from a distance. Most of the able-bodied men died defending the city, so it was the women, the elderly and the children who gathered to wonder what their conqueror planned to do next.

"It is, my liege. All exits have been sealed, and the outer walls have been painted in napal grease, per your instructions."

"Excellent," Elzor said, meeting his general's gaze. "Elzaria will arrive any minute now, and then we can get on with it."

"Yes, my liege." Langon gestured to two soldiers, who brought forward their burden: a large metal chest. They set it down at Elzor's feet and then resumed their post, watching the crowd for any signs of resistance or dissension.

A series of whinnies from the direction of the castle caught Elzor's attention, and he gave a slight smile as he saw Elzaria approaching on the back of her merych, a regal-looking white mount that had likely been one of the queen's favorites. Eight feet from muzzle to tail, the four-legged beast sported a long-flowing mane, two floppy triangular ears and a mouth full of strong teeth. Bred for their endurance, merychs could travel at top speed for several hours without stopping.

Stumbling along behind her was a filthy, disheveled Morix, whose bound hands had been lashed to the back of the saddle Elzaria now sat upon. He was panting and wheezing as he finally came to a stop, casting his eyes to the ground as if unwilling to look any of his subjects in the eye. His face and his short white beard were grimy and caked with dried blood, some his, some belonging to his dead wife.

"Ah, Morix, so good of you to join us," Elzor said, as if he was inviting the old king to join him at the dinner table.

Morix glanced up, flashing Elzor a look with enough malice to level a city. Elzaria dismounted her merych, untying the rope from her saddle and pulling him onward, like an animal on a leash. With a hearty yank, she caused Morix to lose his balance. He fell forward, landing on his knees with a painful yelp.

"Easy, dear sister, easy," Elzor cooed. "He can hardly help us if he's too winded to speak."

Once again, Morix locked eyes with Elzor, his brow knitted in defiance, his grayish-brown hair matted and unkempt. "I will never help you, you traitorous *braga*," he seethed before spitting on Elzor's boots.

"Such language," Elzor said, unfazed. "I wouldn't think that a king as ... *respectable* as you would know how to curse so well."

In one motion, he stepped forward and cuffed Morix across the face with the back of his gauntleted hand. A gasp went up from the assembled crowd as Morix toppled to the dirt, rubbing his sore cheek. Elzaria just smiled.

"I am no traitor, old man," Elzor continued. "I am not your subject. I am your conqueror."

With some effort, Morix was able to regain a kneeling position, his eyes still ablaze. "I know all about you. *Elzor.* You're a deserter, and a coward, and a filthy little –"

Elzaria waved her hand, and blue sparks shot forth from her fingertips, striking Morix in the chest. His body shuddered and twitched, and he collapsed to the ground. His eyelids fluttered and his breath came in shallow, ragged pants. His tattered shirt began to smoke.

Just as it seemed that Morix was on the verge of death, Elzor nodded at his sister, who immediately released her hold on him. Morix began coughing and hacking as he sucked in a deep lungful of air.

"Pick him up," Elzor sneered to two of his soldiers, who grabbed Morix by his elbows and hauled him to his feet, supporting the old king's sagging body between them. Elzor took a step forward, moving his face to within a few inches of his victim's.

"You are clever, old man. Perhaps you think your defiance will somehow inspire these people," he waved his hand dismissively at the crowd, "to revolt. The thought ... amuses me. But your oh-so-mighty army fell to mine in less than a day. Do you really believe these pathetic peasants will stand against me?"

A weak smile broke out on Morix's wounded face. "All tyrants fall, Elzor. Very soon, my allies will be united against you."

Elzor chuckled, which then erupted into a raucous belly laugh. Morix just looked puzzled.

After his laughter subsided, Elzor straightened up again, fixing Morix with a steely gaze. "Perhaps you refer to your son Morak, whom you dispatched to rally aid from your neighbors in Darad and Imar."

The blood drained from Morix's face.

Elzor backed up until he stood next to the metal chest, but he never took his eyes off Morix. "I regret to inform you, neither your son nor his sow of a wife made it past the borders of Agrus." With a flourish, he used his foot to kick over the chest, its lid springing open as it upended, discharging its contents onto the ground in front of Morix.

The king's face froze in horror as two severed heads rolled to a stop directly in front of him. He had to choke back tears as he saw the dead eyes of his son and daughter-in-law staring back up at him. A chorus of screams rose from some of the assembled throng.

Morix closed his eyes, his tears mixing with the streaks of blood on his face. "In Arantha's name, I curse your every step, your every breath until the Great Veil claims you," he sputtered.

"Enough!" Elzor grabbed the old king by the front of his shirt, hauling him to his feet again and roughly turning him to face the school his soldiers had surrounded. "I'm sure you recognize this building."

Morix didn't reply, though his eyes flashed recognition.

"This school is one of several scattered throughout the city. However, I am told that this particular school is special."

"What do you –"

Elzor held up his hand, stopping the old king mid-sentence. "I have it on good authority that your granddaughter, Turalda, has, on your instructions, disguised herself as a commoner. And it just so happens that she is in this building right now."

For the first time, a crack appeared in Morix's resolve. "What … what are you planning to do?"

Elzor laughed. "Your sense of smell has dulled with age, old man. If you were younger, you'd no doubt have detected the odor of napal grease coating every outer wall of this building."

Morix gulped hard. "Napal?"

"That's right. Very useful stuff, as I'm sure you know. And highly flammable. All it takes is one little spark, and …" He directed the old man's attention to his sister, who turned her palms upward. As they watched, a tiny spark appeared, hovering in mid-air, which grew in size and intensity until it became a crackling ball of energy a foot in diameter. Elzaria moved her hands again, and the ball moved away from them, heading ominously toward the school.

"You can't!" Morix screamed. "There are defenseless women and children in there! What could you possibly want that would justify slaughtering innocents like this?"

Elzor held up his hand, and Elzaria stopped the ball's forward motion. It continued to hover a short distance away from the school building, as the assembled crowd held its collective breath. Moving his face only inches away from Morix, Elzor yelled, "What do I want? I want the Stone!"

"*That's* what this is about? You invade my home, massacre my citizens for a blagging *rock*?"

Elzor scowled. "Do not insult my intelligence, old man. I know far more about the Stone than you might think. I would wager I know more about it than even you.

"I find it curious that for centuries, rumors have abounded that the Stone exists within the walls of the Castle Tynal, seat of power of the region of Agrus ... and yet, it would seem that in all that time, not a single Elystran has laid eyes on it. But given what I now know about the Stone, I can certainly see why you would keep it deep underground, behind a machinite door that is impervious even to Wielding."

Morix's cheeks flushed, but he didn't respond.

Elzor took a menacing step forward, standing almost chest-to-chest with him. "That Stone, and two others just like it, are the keys to unimaginable power. I have invaded your home, and I will continue to massacre your citizens," he gestured at the school, "if you do not tell me what I want to know."

Elzaria smiled, and the crackling energy ball edged ever closer to the school, as if it was eager to begin a glorious conflagration.

"I must admit," Elzor continued, "a hulking great door in the bowels of the castle is the best possible place to hide the Stone from prying eyes. But it will take weeks, if not months, to break into that room, and believe me, if I have to whip what's left of your citizenry to make that happen, I will do it. But in the interest of saving time—and lives—I will make you an offer. You answer me truthfully, and I will instruct my sister to spare the life of your granddaughter, and the other innocents inside that building. You refuse ..." He pointed to the still-hovering energy ball, "... well, I think you can guess what will happen."

Morix's breath became shallow, but he didn't avert his eyes from Elzor's. "What guarantee do I have that you'll keep your word?"

Elzor's jaw set in a firm line. "I swear on the soul of my mother, they will come to no harm if you cooperate."

Morix stared deep into Elzor's face for several tense moments, and then exhaled, casting his eyes to the ground in defeat. "The Stone is there. Behind the door."

"Have you seen it? With your own eyes?"

"Yes. It is one of the King's duties to confirm its concealment upon ascending to the throne."

Elzor nodded. "Very good. Elzaria, proceed."

"With pleasure, my liege," she said.

Before Morix could utter an objection, she pushed her hands forward, and the energy ball splashed against the front door of the school. Within seconds, the fire spread around every wall of the building, sending great plumes of smoke up into the sky. From within, faint wails could be heard as its occupants became trapped by intense, searing heat.

The screams on the outside, however, were even louder and more terror-stricken. One woman, hysterical, broke through the line of guards and ran toward the school, screaming, "Hydar! *Hydar!*" She stopped short of the building, the heat too great for her to get any nearer. She fell to her knees, sobbing, as the school was engulfed in flame.

Morix turned back to Elzor, his face twisted in shock and disgust. "You … you swore … on your mother's soul …"

Elzor drew a small dagger from a sheath attached to his belt, the same dagger he used to slay the queen. "I'll let you in on a little secret: I never actually met her. From what Father told us, she was a whore of the lowest caliber. Isn't that right, Elzaria?"

Elzaria strode forward to stand at her brother's side. "'Tis indeed, my liege."

"I am grateful for your help, old man," Elzor whispered to his foe. "But I think it's time you were reunited with the rest of your family." And with that, he quickly drew his dagger across Morix's throat in a deep slashing motion.

He and Elzaria took several steps back, as did the guards, as blood gushed from the king's neck. Morix continued to stare at his murderer, conveying an eternity of retribution with one single glance. Then his eyes clouded, his breathing ceased, and he crashed to the dusty ground.

Just then, the woman who had pushed through the line of guards stood up, white-hot rage marring her tear-streaked face. With a primal scream, she ran at Elzor, but Elzaria immediately called forth another surge of energy and struck the woman with it. She froze in mid-step, jerking and shuddering, before crashing to the ground right next to Morix's body. Several wisps of smoke curled upwards from her clothes as her breath faded away.

Turning away from the two corpses, Elzor addressed the crowd. "Hear me, all of you! Your rulers are dead. Your soldiers are dead. Your lives now belong to me."

None in the crowd uttered a word. A few women were still sobbing into their hands.

He gestured at the burning school. The whimpers and screams from within had quieted, leaving only the crackle of fire as the wooden structure buckled and splintered. "If you wish to avoid any further ... *demonstrations* such as this, you will do exactly as I say for the foreseeable future. If I catch a whiff of resistance from a single one of you, what's left of your family will die. If you are caught trying to flee the city, many, many lives will be lost. Do I make myself clear?"

They all just stared at him.

"Good. Now return to your homes. If and when we have need of your services, you will be duly informed."

With still nary a word spoken, the crowd began to disperse. Several women had to be supported by others as they marched sullenly away from the scene of the day's tragedy.

Watching them go, Langon strode forward, addressing Elzor. "Do you think he was telling the truth, my liege?"

"For the sake of the citizens of Agrus, he'd better have been. Or I will tear this city down, inch by bloody inch."

Chapter Twelve

KELIA APPROACHED the Council Chamber, an open-air room with a view of the River Ix winding its way through the Plateau. The dwellings that comprised the village had been carved right into the rock, and most were connected via staircases, ramps or ladders. The thick rock of the Plateau that existed above the village provided shelter from any thundershowers that often marred the cold season, as well as any sandstorms the nearby desert couldn't contain during the dry season.

As Kelia entered the room, she noticed all three Council members were already present and seated.

Katura was the eldest, tall and thin, her curly gray hair hanging in knotted rings around her aged but serene face. She was the wisest woman Kelia had ever known, wiser in some regards to even Onara. In fact, many years before, Katura was one of Onara's teachers. An invaluable advisor to three different Protectresses, including Kelia, she was the only Councilor to possess a Wielding ability. She'd been the Ixtrayu's healer and apothecary for many years. In her dotage, however, those responsibilities passed to her daughter Lyala and her granddaughter Sershi.

Next to Katura was Eloni. She was almost a full head shorter than Katura, but her diminutive stature belied her strength. She was a master craftswoman and builder, and it was she who designed the irrigation system that allowed the Ixtrayu's orchards and vegetable patches to flourish. She used to spend hours entertaining children by singing ancient rhymes in her deep, rich voice, and playing on a wind instrument called an uska, another one of her inventions. Her short, dark hair bore streaks of gray, but her blue eyes still shone with fierce intelligence.

And on the right, round as a stone and about as cheerful as one, was Susarra. Once a huntress, she had to find a new role within the tribe after her leg was crushed by a charging kova. On most days, Kelia didn't find her unpleasant so much as irritating. Tonight, however, she was steaming mad from Nyla's antics, and Kelia knew before she even sat down that she would have to answer for her daughter's misdeeds.

"Greetings, Protectress," Eloni said.

"Greetings, Councilors." Kelia sat down in the large chair at one end of the room, facing the three women arrayed in a semicircle around her.

All four waited for a few moments before Katura broke the silence. "Protectress, when last we spoke, you informed us that Arantha instructed you to venture to the western outcropping. Had word not reached our ears about your return, we might have ordered Runa to go find you. However, since you have returned, we can only assume that whatever it was you envisioned came to pass."

Kelia nodded. "Last night, at right around midnight, a ball of light appeared in the western sky, as my visions foretold. It streaked across the heavens, disappearing somewhere in the Kaberian Mountains."

She watched the three women for a few moments, gauging their reactions. Katura and Eloni's brows were furrowed in deep thought, but Susarra was clearly underwhelmed by the news. "That's it?" she said with more than a hint of sarcasm.

"You shrouded the reasons for your departure in mystery. You refused an escort. And after three days of waiting, that's *all* you have to tell us?"

Kelia bit her bottom lip as she tried to keep her voice calm. "I'm afraid so."

"The Stone has shown you nothing else?" Eloni asked.

"Not at this time." Kelia took a deep breath. "But I will tell you what my instincts are telling me. It is vitally important that what I'm about to say will not leave this room. I would ask that you all swear an oath that you will remain silent on this matter."

"Is that really necessary?" Susarra asked, looking nonplussed.

"I'm afraid I must insist."

As one, all three women placed their left hands on their sternums and then their right hands over their left. Then, bowing their heads, they spoke in unison, "*My word is my bond, and to Arantha I swear my silence.*"

"Thank you, Councilors," Kelia said. "I believe the object I saw last night came from The Above."

Katura let out a short cough, Eloni's whole body stiffened up, and Susarra's mouth fell open. No one spoke. For once, all three Councilors could think of nothing to say.

After a few tense moments, Kelia continued. "As I said, this is just my belief. Arantha led me to that spot so that I may witness the arrival of … whatever it was."

" 'It'?" Susarra said in a hushed tone. "You do realize … it could be the return of Arantha herself."

Kelia regarded Susarra, whose face was a mixture of reverence and uncertainty, and Kelia hoped her earlier anger had been momentarily forgotten. "I admit that is a possibility. Now you understand why I had you speak the oath. But I must caution the Council to resist the temptation to jump to any conclusions."

Katura nodded, her wrinkled face conveying her years of experience. "Wise advice, Protectress. Indeed, we understand the importance of keeping this quiet. If word of this got out, it could throw the tribe into chaos. Centuries ago, when the Ixtrayu were far more prone to superstition, our people might have made a mass exodus to the mountains to find this object."

Kelia held up her hand. "Which is why I will not make such a journey until Arantha directs me to do so. Even if what I saw was the return of Arantha herself, I am not so reckless as to go charging into the unknown based solely on my own instincts. The Ixtrayu have not survived for centuries by abandoning all reason."

"Which brings me to my next point ..." Susarra said.

Here it comes, Kelia thought with a sigh.

"... how much longer will the Ixtrayu survive without the Sojourns? It's been thirteen years, Protectress! There hasn't been a child born to us since –"

"Since Nyla. I am aware of that," Kelia interrupted, fixing her with a stern glare. "You know I am aware of that, Susarra, and yet it does not stop you from bringing it up at *every* conclave."

Susarra bowed her head in acknowledgment, deflated. "I apologize for my brusqueness, Protectress. Please know that my concern is not merely as a Councilor, but as a grandmother."

Susarra's only daughter, Ilora, died twelve years earlier. While out hunting, she'd been bitten by a hugar, a venomous serpentine creature that stalked its prey by burrowing into the ground and waiting for its victims to walk within striking distance. Runa brought Ilora back to the village on their fastest chava, but by then, there was nothing even Katura could do.

Ilora and Kelia were in their early twenties when they chose each other as companions, and remained so even after Nyla was born. As the Ixtrayu's leader, Kelia was forced to temper her grief, but Susarra's bitterness did not abate after they laid Ilora's body to rest.

"Susarra, your frustrations are ones I share. Had I my mother's prowess, I could tell you why the Sojourns were stopped, when they will resume, and exactly what this object from the Above is. For years, I've been unable to answer the same nagging question that you pose so regularly. But consider this: Arantha gave my mother powers of divination far beyond any previous Protectress for a reason. Perhaps the exact same reason my own powers of foresight are so weak and my elemental powers are so strong. It's because this is how it was *meant* to be."

Susarra nodded, but her scowl remained.

Kelia continued, "All of it is connected, of this I am sure. Centuries ago, Arantha set the Ixtrayu upon a path, a path we have followed every day since. She has watched over us and kept us safe from the machinations of men who would seek to either destroy us or put us back in chains. I simply cannot believe that, after eight hundred years and countless Sojourns, Arantha would put us on a new path that will ultimately lead to our extinction. I *refuse* to believe that. I pray you don't either."

Susarra's face remained blank. "No, Protectress."

Kelia exhaled. "Regarding Nyla's behavior ... I offer my sincerest apologies, Susarra. I can assure you, she will be punished for her actions. It will not happen again."

"See that it doesn't," she said, sounding unconvinced.

"Is there anything else?" Katura asked.

"Only to say that if my next consultation with the Stone reveals a course of action, I will summon you all again. Until then, this conclave is adjourned. Sleep soundly, my friends."

The three women rose, bowing their heads. "Sleep soundly, Protectress," they said in unison.

Kelia watched as the Council silently filed out of the room. She remained behind, however, turning to face the window. A slight wind had picked up, a cool breeze that gently caressed her cheek. Staring up at the sky, she could swear she saw Onara's face staring down at her.

"Give me strength, Mother," she whispered. Then she, too, exited the Council Chamber.

* * *

After taking an invigorating and much-needed bath at the cistern, Kelia entered her home to find Liana stoking the fire, sending wisps of smoke up through the vent in the ceiling. She also detected the unmistakable scent of nipa wood, which she guessed Liana was burning to cover up the noxious smell of mud and chava dung.

Liana looked up, and Kelia met her gaze. Her aunt looked exhausted. She, Lyala, and the entire gathering party had returned two hours before, and Talya was taken straight to the Room of Healing.

"I spoke with Lyala a few minutes ago," Kelia said. "She tells me Talya will be fine."

Liana just nodded. "Thank Arantha."

"How is her mother dealing with it?"

"Hathi's as well as can be expected, I guess. She's been by Talya's side the entire time." Liana gave the slightest of smiles. "Probably driving Lyala crazy by now. I don't know how many times Katura wanted to throw me out of the Room of Healing whenever Hathi was injured."

Kelia glanced around. Next to the door of Nyla's room, she spotted her daughter's boots, which looked scrubbed clean of most of the mud that caked them earlier. "Is Nyla in her room?"

"Yes," said Liana. "I know you told her to come here and stay here, but that mud you threw her in was just ... foul, so I took her down to the cistern with a clean robe. The water was warm, but at least she's clean now. Yadra was kind enough to bring your evening meal here." She pointed at a tray of food and drink on the rim of the fire pit, which still held one portion of kova steak, an array of vegetables and a small loaf of holm-grain bread.

The smell of the freshly-baked bread filled the room, causing Kelia's stomach to rumble. She strode forward, picked up the bread and took a large bite. "Thank you, ama," Kelia said between chews. "If you need some time tomorrow afternoon to go see Talya, I will understand. I will be consulting the Stone right after breakfast."

"Oh," Liana said. "You told the Council about what you saw, then?"

"Yes. I also managed to persuade Susarra to let me handle Nyla's discipline." Kelia flumped into the nearest chair. "I assume Nyla's not too happy with the way I punished her in front of the tribe."

Liana moved to the other chair and sat down. "She's not your biggest supporter right now, if that's what you're asking."

Kelia idly tapped the armrest, chewing on her bottom lip. "You've helped see one daughter and two granddaughters through adolescence, Liana. How would you handle this? I don't remember Yadra or Talya ever being this much trouble."

"I suppose not, but they didn't have Wielding abilities. They weren't the daughter of the Protectress." She leaned forward. "*They* weren't the one destined to be the next leader of the Ixtrayu."

"I understand that, but, again, how would you handle this? If I go in there breathing fire, I may only succeed in pushing her further away."

Liana thought for a moment. "You said you were able to persuade Susarra to see things your way?"

"Yes. For the moment, anyway."

"I don't imagine you did that by breathing fire at her."

Finally, realization dawned, and a smile curled the corners of Kelia's mouth. "No, I just got her to see things from my point of view."

"Well, there you go." Liana stood up. "Nima, one does not have to look far to see your mother in you." She stretched her back, yawned, and circled the fire pit to stand at Kelia's side. "Seems even thirty years after my lessons, there are still things I can teach you. Sleep soundly, nima." She leaned down and planted a kiss on the side of her niece's head.

"Sleep soundly, ama," Kelia said, and Liana disappeared into her bedroom.

After finishing her long-overdue evening meal, Kelia made her way into Nyla's room. She was sitting on her bed of lyrax pelts, her back against the far wall, reading a scroll from Kelia's study by the light of several kova-tallow candles that surrounded her. She looked up as her mother entered. "Hello, Mama," she said with noticeable regret.

"Hello, duma," Kelia said, hoping the familial greeting would convey her calmer state.

"I ... I heard what happened to cousin Talya. Is she all right?"

"Yes. It's a good thing the lyrax was already wounded, or her injuries might have been a lot worse."

"I thought lyraxes only came out at night?"

"For the most part, they do. But according to Hathi, this one had a broken forepaw. It probably couldn't get back to its lair."

"Did they kill it?"

"Yes, they brought it back with them. Runa and Aarna have already harvested the beast for its pelt, meat and bones."

Nyla nodded, returning her attention to the scroll on her lap.

Kelia removed her shoes and sat down next to her daughter, crossing her legs in front of her. "What are you reading?"

"Some of your notes about the Stone. About what it was like for you the first time Grandmother let you touch it."

"Ah, yes. She prepared me for months for my first consultation. She made me read every word in the library on the subject of First Consultations until I could recite them in my sleep. Let me tell you, Nyla, reading about it and experiencing it are two vastly different things."

"Did it hurt?"

"Oh, my, yes," Kelia said, reliving the painful memory. "The Stone was dim at first, but after a few moments, the light within it grew to such a blinding intensity that I had to shut my eyes. And after that, it felt like I pulled a red-hot coal from the fire with my bare hands. I remember screaming my lungs out."

"And then?" Nyla asked, suddenly curious.

"Imagine every memory you've ever had in your life just ... flash through your mind in the blink of an eye. Images poured through me, so fast that I couldn't even make out a single one. It was all too much for me to comprehend, so much power that I couldn't even begin to control. Thank Arantha your grandmother was there to calm my mind. She lent me some of her power before the experience overwhelmed me. I don't remember anything after that. I woke up two days later in the Room of Healing."

Nyla gasped. "Two *days*?"

"That's right. I tried to remember some of the things I saw, but it was all a blur. I did feel something, though ... "

Nyla turned her body to face her mother. "What?"

"I'm not sure how to describe it. It felt like my mind had been ... expanded. Like a door had been opened, and Arantha herself had allowed me to pass through it. From that point on, I took my training a lot more seriously. And every consultation after that became less and less overwhelming. While it's true Mother's ability to interpret her visions was far greater than mine will ever be, I accepted that shortcoming. So did she."

Kelia put a comforting arm around her daughter. "I know you're upset that I haven't let you have your first consultation yet, but you must understand that I do that for your protection. Your elemental abilities are much stronger than mine were at your age, and, frankly, that scares me a little."

Nyla's eyes narrowed. "Really?"

Kelia had to fight back tears. She had spent the last thirteen years trying to protect Nyla from her own nightmarish concerns. "Yes, Nyla. I believe you have the potential to become the most powerful Wielder in the history of the Ixtrayu. Maybe even more powerful than Soraya herself."

"The first Protectress? The one who freed the Ixtrayu from the slavers?"

"That's right," Kelia said, smiling. "Looks like you've been paying attention to Liana after all."

Nyla's face reddened. "Some of it is actually pretty interesting."

"Glad you think so."

She met her mother's eyes again. "So ... what's going to happen to me?"

Kelia bowed her head. "Susarra wants you to be sent into the desert in the morning, blindfolded, shoeless, and hands bound. I was forced to agree."

"*What?*" Pure horror crossed Nyla's face, and she scooted away from her mother, knocking one of the candles over. A second later, the flame touched the corner of the scroll she'd been reading, and the parchment began to smoke.

Reacting quickly, Kelia waved her hands, creating a small gust of air that snuffed out the flame before it could grow. She looked to see Nyla, her face ghostly white, backed up into the corner of her room. Her eyes were wide with terror as she blubbered, "Please, Mama! I'm sorry! I'm so sorry! It won't happen again! Please don't send me into the desert!" She buried her face in her hands, sobbing.

After a few moments, Kelia said softly, "Nyla?"

Nyla looked up, her eyes thick with tears.

Kelia let out a short guffaw. "I'm kidding."

Nyla's face scrunched up in puzzlement, and then she realized she'd been pranked. By her own mother.

"Oooooooh!" she screamed. Grimacing, Nyla reached down at her feet, grabbed one of her spare shoes and flung it at her mother. Kelia easily deflected it, sending it flying against the near wall. "That was *not* funny!"

Kelia stood up, continuing to chuckle under her breath. "If you say so."

Finally, a smile seeped onto Nyla's face, and she began to laugh as well.

Kelia strode forward, gathering her daughter into a warm hug. "Nyla, I may be Protectress, but there is no one on Elystra that I love more than you." They met each other's gaze as they parted. "Your abilities are a gift from Arantha. An incredible, divine gift. They are not toys to be used for your amusement. Do you understand?"

"Yes, Mama," she said. "So what's my punishment?"

"Outside of your lessons and your training, you will spend three hours a day helping out in the fields. Starting tomorrow, you will be assisting Yarji with watering duty."

Nyla exhaled in relief. "For how long?"

"Until I say otherwise." She moved towards the doorway. "Treat this as a learning experience, Nyla. Yarji is extremely adept at controlling water. You could learn a lot from her. Plus, she's very fond of you."

"Thank you, mama," Nyla said. "You really scared me with that 'sent into the desert' thing."

Kelia gave a wicked grin. "Thank Arantha your grandmother's not here. I got it much, much worse when I pranked Councilor Preela."

Nyla's mouth fell open. "What did you –"

"Sleep soundly, duma." Kelia winked at her, and quickly left the room.

Chapter Thirteen

THANKS TO Sen's healing abilities, Mizar's headache had dulled enough for him to get a few hours' sleep. Come morning, his face was still sore from where it smacked the floor of the Crystal Cavern.

As he made his way through the courtyard of Castle Randar, his dark brown eyes drifted skyward, where an array of storm clouds inched closer. This was not unusual for this time of year in the north, but there was an unexpected chill in the air, so he pulled the hood attached to his thick, black High Mage cloak up over his head, enjoying its warmth.

A large set of wooden double-doors loomed before him, as did two rather large guards standing sentinel on either side of it.

Both were clad in leather armor. The Daradian emblem of a great bird, its wings stretching across the horizon of the land, was emblazoned on their shoulders. Both held axes at their sides and wore longswords sheathed in scabbards. They eyed Mizar as he approached, bowing their heads respectfully. With merely a nod of acknowledgment, he strode past them, into the castle.

Mizar walked into a vast hall where the King, the Queen, and their court feasted. He noticed many of the chairs lining the long tables were empty, remembering the monthly governors' council meeting had been adjourned the previous week. He clasped his hands together, realizing his timing was perfect: his request was best heard by as few ears as possible.

In a room that could seat thirty, Mizar counted eight people enjoying their meal. At the head of the room was the table designated for King Aridor, Queen Belena, and their four children. The seats belonging to the King and Queen's oldest sons, Warran and Agedor, were vacant.

Sitting in the center was Aridor himself. He was a broad-shouldered man with black hair, steel-gray eyes and a short yet distinctive beard that tapered to a point three inches below his chin. A smile crossed his face as he saw his High Mage approach.

"Mizar!" Aridor said, dabbing his face with a cloth. "I did not expect to see you today!" He turned around, waving at a nearby servant. "Fetch the High Mage a plate!"

Mizar held up his hand, staying the servant before he could scuttle out of the room. "No thank you, Your Highness. This morning, your inestimable cooks provided me with a breakfast so large I may not eat again for a week."

Aridor laughed. "As you wish. It is good to see you, old friend."

"You as well, Your Highnesses." Mizar bowed politely to Queen Belena and the rest of the royal family.

"Mizar," the Queen said in a rich, stately voice, "what's wrong?"

"Highness?"

"Your gait is heavy, and your face is creased with worry. Something troubles you."

Mizar nodded in admiration. Though the Queen wielded little or no power beyond the walls of the castle, she was still a woman of intelligence and perception, a winsome beauty with fair skin, long brown hair done up in an elegant chignon, and an aquiline nose. She was a staunch supporter of every decision Aridor made during his reign, and she was also the architect of some of the trade negotiations Darad was embroiled in since her marriage to Aridor, an event that corresponded exactly with his coronation. "You see much, Your Highness. I am here to make a request."

Aridor picked up his flagon of honey mead. "What is it?"

Mizar stepped forward, stopping when only the long dining table stood between him and Aridor. "I would like to ask permission to access the Forbidden Knowledge."

Aridor's eyes went wide, his flagon stopping halfway between the table and his lips. He returned his drink to the table and leaned back in his chair.

Mizar looked around. The Queen was suddenly occupied with their youngest son Lehr, who was playing with the hem of her dress underneath the table. Next to them, their sixteen-year-old daughter, Tyah, was paying even less attention. The rest of the room's occupants, mostly Daradian military leaders, were too far away, though a couple of them were eyeing him warily.

He turned his attention back to Aridor, who rose from his chair. He leaned over to say a few words into Belena's ear, followed by a kiss on her cheek, before gesturing for Mizar to follow him through a door on the side of the room. "Walk with me," he said.

Mizar strolled alongside the King down a long open-air corridor that eventually became a covered bridge overlooking the main courtyard. Merych stables ran down both sides of the enclosure. At the far end was a set of fifteen-foot-high wooden doors, further fortified by a metal portcullis. Above those, patrolling the battlements, two guards kept watch.

Aridor stopped at the halfway point of the bridge, fixing Mizar with an authoritative stare. "Before I consider your request, I would have you explain the vision that befell you yesterday."

Mizar blinked. "You know of that? I went straight to my chambers afterward. I did not inform anyone."

A sly grin appeared on Aridor's face. "Nothing happens in this castle that I don't know about. I know you had a consultation yesterday morning. Numerous guards reported your apprentice searching high and low for you, and the soldiers stationed outside the Cavern entrance informed me that you did not look at all well when you left its confines. It was not difficult to discern what had transpired."

Mizar bowed his head. Not for the first time, he had discounted his liege's deductive abilities. "It was … disturbing, to say the least. What I remember of it, that is. The crystals conducted more power into my mind than ever before, even more than my first consultation. I was unprepared for its ferocity. It rendered me unconscious for most of the day. Without Sen's healing abilities, I would likely still be flat on my back in my bed."

"It was that powerful?" Aridor took a step forward, examining Mizar's face and apparently noticing the strain that Belena noted.

"Yes, sire. I've searched my memories, but there is little I remember clearly."

Aridor took a step back, placing his hands on the sill of one of the arched windows looking out over the courtyard. "Tell me what you do remember."

Mizar closed his eyes, bringing the horrific images to the surface of his mind. "I saw entire villages ablaze. Smoke and ash filled the sky, and charred bodies littered the ground." He shuddered, wondering if he would ever be able to purge them from his memory.

"I don't suppose you can tell me exactly which villages it was you saw?" Aridor asked, turning to face him again.

"No, sire. The sky was dark, so I'm guessing it was nighttime. I did not see any mountains or landmarks that might help me identify the location."

His eyebrows furrowed. "That is a portentous image, to be sure, but it doesn't justify your request."

"There was one other image," Mizar said. "It was of a battlefield, where two armies were locked in mortal combat. At the center of this battle, I saw ... three women. Two standing together, facing the third. They seemed oblivious to the battle being waged around them."

Aridor's face blanched. "Three *women*? What general would be so foolish as to send *women* into battle?"

Mizar held up his hands. "It was more than that. These three women radiated power. Great power. There was an aura, an energy field surrounding them. There is no doubt in my mind this power came from Arantha."

The King's jaw dropped open as he took another step forward, standing almost chest-to-chest with the High Mage. "You're saying ... they were Wielders."

"Yes, sire."

Aridor turned away, snorting dismissively. "That's impossible. Never in the history of Elystra has there been a female Wielder. The only pathway to Arantha is the Crystal Cavern. It has always been thus. Only you and the scant few who discovered their abilities have done so by standing on the Nexus of Arantha. It's one of the reasons Darad has maintained its level of respect from our neighbors, for only Daradians are accorded the opportunity to become Wielders."

Mizar squared his jaw. "What of the Agrusian Stone?"

"Rumors," Aridor said, snorting again. "If anyone possessed such a Stone, why would they not use it? Why would they lock it up in the bowels of Castle Tynal for a millennium? Surely at some point one of Agrus's rulers would have used it to expand their borders. But there's been nothing. I have my doubts such a Stone ever existed, a myth to hold those who might sow dissension in sway."

"That may be true, but I've been studying the teachings of Merdeen the Sage all my adult life. He truly was the wisest of all the Mages, but there's next to nothing from the year leading up to his death. Everything from that period was deemed 'Forbidden Knowledge' by King Sardor and locked away."

"My great-grandfather," Aridor said with no small amount of bile, "was a drunk and a letch, who single-handedly started the first war with Vanda, a war that cost thousands of Daradians their lives, including three of his sons. Had my grandfather not been too young to fight at the time, our royal bloodline might very well have ended. That being said, I can imagine his position: to come home from a brutal war only to have your High Mage forecast even more death and destruction.

"My father passed along stories about Merdeen, told to him by my grandfather, that never made it into the official records. By the time the Vandan War ended, Merdeen had grown ... eccentric. His visions became ever more fantastical and unrealistic, and Sardor suspected he had become demented in his old age. After revealing his dark vision, a vision Sardor refused to accept, Merdeen lost what was left of his mind. Sardor had no choice but to lock him away for his own safety, and so his rantings would not cause a panic. Merdeen spent his final days in his room, writing. Much of it, I'm led to understand, is undecipherable nonsense. The rest is locked in the Archives vault."

"If King Sardor suspected Merdeen's doom-saying was the work of an unhinged mind, why would he lock it away? Why not just destroy it?"

"I do not know. Perhaps it was out of respect for Merdeen's lifetime of service. If our history is to be believed, despite our losses, we would not have won the war without him."

Mizar ran his fingers through his beard. "Maybe that is why King Sardor proclaimed that all Daradian boys stand on the

Nexus of Arantha–to increase the possibility that future generations might have the benefit of a High Mage to further advise them, just in case Merdeen's final prophecy had merit."

"That's certainly possible. But it is a question we will likely never know the answer to."

Mizar nodded. "Have you never perused the contents of the vault yourself?"

Aridor shook his head. "No need. With the exception of the Vandan uprising forty years ago, Darad has known nearly a century of peace. Obviously, Merdeen's final prophecy never came to pass."

Mizar had anticipated this. Choosing his words carefully, he said, "Forgive me, sire, but ... what if what he foretold a century ago is coming to pass right now?"

"Ahhhhh," Aridor drawled. "This is the reason you require access to the Forbidden Knowledge."

"Yes, sire. I do not think you would judge my visions to be the products of an addled mind. While it's true, I'm not the youth I was when first we met," he patted his slightly-protruding gut, "I am neither sick nor enfeebled. I have nothing to gain by telling you anything but the truth, as far as Arantha has shown me."

Aridor turned around and took a few steps forward, gathering his thoughts, kicking aimlessly at a few small rocks littering the stone pathway. After a few tense moments' deliberation, he turned to face Mizar again. "Mizar, I've never had cause to doubt your visions before, but what you speak of is ... beyond belief. There has never been a female Wielder in the entire recorded history of Elystra, and now, you speak of *three*."

He made sharp gestures with his hands as he spoke, as if trying to convince himself of his own words. "I mean, if even *one* female Wielder were to exist, it would be impossible to keep such a thing a secret. News would spread like wildfire. While I'll admit my influence does not extend to all four corners of our world, there is nothing of such overwhelming significance that could pass by unnoticed."

He stepped toward Mizar again, his face softening. "I am sorry, my friend, but the only evidence you have of this possible future is one erratic vision that even you admit you cannot recall in its entirety. If future visions give you greater insight, or if new evidence comes to light that gives credence to your claim, I will reconsider the matter. Until then, however, I must deny your request."

Mizar felt his chest tighten. "Sire, with respect, you did not see what I saw. In my forty years as High Mage, I have never beheld such horrific images. Arantha would not have shown them to me were it not of the utmost importance. We must not react to his message with complacency."

"Take care, Mizar," said Aridor, a hard edge tinging his voice. "Arantha may be all-seeing, but it is I who rule Darad, not him. My decision is made."

Mizar considered protesting further, but thought better of it. "Yes, sire, forgive me. My only concern is for our people." He moved to the central window, overlooking the courtyard as Aridor did before.

Casting his eyes upward, he noticed a flurry of movement. Several guards were shouting and pointing at something just outside the gates. One of them turned toward the interior of the castle, cupped his hands to his mouth and shouted, "Merychs approaching! It's Prince Warran!"

Aridor ran to the end of the bridge, descending a stone staircase that led down to the courtyard in four leaps. Mizar was right behind him. "Open the gate!" Aridor yelled.

Several uniformed guards immediately manned the large pulley-wheel, cranking it to raise the portcullis, jamming a wedge into the wheel when it was ten feet off the ground. Three other guards slid back the large wooden plank that made the heavy door impregnable from anything less than an equally large battering ram.

As both doors swung open, two white merychs dashed into the courtyard. Atop one was a young man in his late twenties, holding the reins of the merychs in his gloved hands. He had short dark hair, green eyes, and a handsome, clean-shaven face, and was the spitting image of a young Aridor. He was as broad-shouldered as his father, and his prowess with a sword was unmatched.

Slouched across the back of the other merych like a sack of grain was another man, clearly unconscious. His clothes, which looked like they were of fine quality once, were burned and blackened in many places.

Warran called to some of the on-looking guards, "Help me with him! He's badly wounded!"

"Bring a stretcher!" called Mizar to two other guards standing behind them. "And fetch my apprentice!" They turned and disappeared through the arched doorway into the adjacent courtyard.

Leaping off his mount, Warran joined the guards in pulling the unfortunate man's body down off the other merych, laying him on a nearby pile of hay. Mizar saw that much of the man's face and arms were in the same condition as his clothes: the whole right side of his face was charred, one eye had swollen shut, and much of his fair hair had been singed away. Similar burns could be seen on his lower right arm and leg.

"Father!" Warran said, striding up to a waiting Aridor.

"What's the meaning of this?" the King said. "Who is this man, and why have you brought him here?"

"I was patrolling the western border, when I received word that this man had arrived, half-dead, at Promontory Point," Warran answered. "When I arrived, he could barely speak. We gave him manza cider to dull his pain and applied some herbal poultices, and he regained his senses enough to say he had a message for you and you alone. He claims to be Prince Zendak of Agrus."

There wasn't much left of his clothes, but Mizar could just make out the Agrusian emblem on the left breast of his tunic. There was also a brilliant sea-blue gemstone set on a signet ring that adorned his left hand. Seeing this as confirmation, Aridor knelt at the wounded man's side. "Zendak?" he asked, gently grasping the man's unwounded shoulder.

Zendak's eyes fluttered open, and they locked on his. "King Aridor," he said weakly.

"I am here," Aridor said.

"King Morix ... sent me and my cousin Morak to warn you and King Largo. We had no time ... to prepare. It happened so quickly."

"What? What happened?"

"We came under attack. By an invading army." Zendak coughed violently, as if his lungs were as blackened and scorched as his skin.

"Led by whom?" The King's voice deepened, and now carried a sharp edge.

"Elzor ... of Barju." He began another violent coughing fit, and both Aridor and Mizar had to hold his shoulders down.

Mizar looked up in alarm. "Sen! Where is that boy?"

As if on cue, Sen ran through the entrance to the inner courtyard, a small satchel in his hands. Aridor graciously stood to allow Sen access to Zendak.

"Forgive me, sire," he said, pulling a pair of aromatic leaves from his satchel. He rubbed them on his hands before placing them several inches over the burned man's face and chest. Closing his eyes to concentrate, he called upon his abilities. Zendak also closed his eyes, accepting Sen's healing touch. After a few seconds, the wounded man's breathing became steadier and less labored.

Mizar nodded in approval. "Good work, Sen."

"Master," he acknowledged. "I've done what I can to ease his pain, but I do not possess the knowledge to treat wounds this severe. He needs the court physician."

"Not yet," Aridor said, moving Sen aside. "Zendak?"

The Prince's eyes opened into narrow slits as he met the King's gaze.

"Tell me of the attack," Aridor ordered.

"We were ... riding for the northern forests, when we were intercepted. By ... a woman."

Aridor was thunderstruck. "A *woman* did this to you?"

Zendak nodded.

Aridor cast a quick glance at Mizar before returning his focus to Zendak. "Describe her."

He thought for a moment. "Tall ... long dark hair. And she ..." he paused, his breath quickening, "... she burned us. With blue fire. From her hands."

Aridor straightened himself up to his full height, looking down in disbelief. "From her *hands*?"

"Yes, sire. It felt like my blood was boiling inside my skin. I was sure I was going to die." He coughed again. "When I came to, she was gone. Everyone was dead, and Prince Morak and his wife ... their heads had been cut off. My cousin ..." He stifled a sob. "I was able to mount one of the merychs. I've been riding for days. Thank Arantha I made it." He choked back another sob. "My home, my family ..." He closed his eyes, his shoulders shaking. A tear fell from his good eye.

Mizar put his palm on the man's forehead, speaking soothingly. "Rest now, Prince." He stood up, turning to two soldiers who had arrived with a stretcher. "Take him to the Physician, quickly! Sen, you go with him."

"Yes, Master," Sen said, helping the soldiers lift Zendak onto the stretcher.

As the injured prince was taken away, Warran turned to his father, looking somewhat dubious. "A female Wielder? Clearly the man's mind is gone."

Aridor's face betrayed none of the incredulity his voice expressed mere moments before. "Go see your mother, Warran, and then grab yourself a meal. We'll speak more of this later."

"Yes, Father. High Mage," Warran said with a bow. Then he turned on his heel and left the courtyard.

Watching him go, Aridor reached inside his shirt and pulled out a thin cord with a pouch on it. Removing it from around his neck, he tossed it to Mizar, who deftly caught it.

Loosening the pouch's drawstrings, Mizar upended it. Into his waiting palm fell a key. His eyes widened as he looked at his king's face.

"Return it when you're done," Aridor said, and he, too, walked out of the courtyard.

Chapter Fourteen

ODAY WAS Davin's fifteenth birthday, so Maeve decided to mark the occasion by doing something she never did: sing. She belted out, "Happy birthday to you!" at the top of her lungs, as she placed the cake in front of him. His smile was so wide she feared he might swallow the entire thing in one gulp.

"Thanks, Mom." Davin used a knife to cut a thick slab of mint chocolate cake and put it on his plate. "… I think."

"You *think*?" Maeve did her best to look offended. "Well, sorry, Your *Majesty*, I tried to get a chorus of angels to sing for you, but gosh darn it, they went and canceled on me at the last minute. Stupid angels."

He laughed. "Well, Mom, your body may be covered in birds, but you don't sing much like one." He stabbed at the cake with his fork and shoveled a big bite into his mouth. "Oh, man, that's good," he said as he chewed.

"Hey now," she said indignantly, pointing to her stomach. Beneath the cloth, he knew, was a tattoo of a sparrow hawk, wings and talons outstretched as it swooped down on its unseen prey. "In case you've forgotten, mister, my flock is comprised of some of the most badass birds to ever roam the Terran skies. There isn't a bloody *songbird* in the bunch."

"Okay, okay." Davin cut a second slice from the cake onto another plate and held it out to her. "Here ... peace offering."

She continued frowning for a few moments, and then her face cracked into a smile. "Fine, you got me." She sat down, picking up her fork. "But just for that crack about my voice, you get first shift on the excavator."

His face fell. "Really? I can't claim Birthday Boy privilege?"

"Sorry, kiddo. A couple of the motion sensors I put on the perimeter have stopped sending signals. I have to go check 'em out. And it'll give me a chance to try out the personal transporter your father created before we left."

He nodded. "How's it work again?"

"Pretty much like the Jegg's quantigraphic rift drive, only on a much smaller scale. You just attach it to your belt, program its location with this thing." She showed off a small computer console now attached to her left forearm. "And *poof*, you're there."

"Is it safe?"

"Should be. Gaspar and your father tested it extensively before we left. It helps if you've actually been at the location you're zapping yourself to, though, as it helps to program the exact coordinates. If you try to transport to a location, say, a hundred miles away that you've never seen, you may end up in mid-air over a chasm, or at the bottom of the ocean."

"Can't we program it with the topographical data from the long-range scanners?"

She looked at the small, silver, tube-shaped device on her belt, and then at the console. "That's a damn good question, Dav. That would certainly help, wouldn't it?"

Davin took another bite. "I'll program it, see if I can make long-distance travel safer. Would that be all right?"

Concern tinged her voice. "This is a dangerous mix of technologies we've cobbled together. I know you're better at stuff like this than I'll ever be, but ..." She sighed. "Okay, you can tinker with it in your spare time–not that we have much of that. Do *not* use it until I say it's okay, you got that?"

"Got it." Davin brightened. "How many devices do we have?"

"Four."

His brows knitted in puzzlement. "Four? What happened to the rest of them?"

"No idea. I remember Mahesh saying he wanted to do some last-minute tests on them. I guess they never made it back into the box."

"Well, four is better than zero, I suppose. At least that means we can spare one."

"Excellent." She forked the last piece of cake into her mouth and placed the empty dish in the synthesizer's drawer. "So, if you're done satisfying your sweet tooth, it's time to get back to work."

Davin made a face. "Yeah, yeah. Anything else?"

"Just one thing." She tapped lightly on her console, and with a barely audible *poof* of displaced air, Maeve vanished.

Before Davin could react, he felt his mother's arms fold around him from behind, where she'd instantly transported herself. Her violet hair fell into his eyes as she nuzzled him and planted a wet kiss on his cheek. "Happy fifteen, Little Bug."

"Thanks, Mom." Davin turned his head and returned the kiss on her cheek. "That was really riff, by the way."

Maeve grinned, straightening up. "It was, wasn't it? Now you see me ... " She tapped the console again, and transported away.

Maeve reappeared about a half-mile away, and was immediately thrown off-balance when one of her boots slipped on a small rock. Flailing her arms, she was able to regain her balance without toppling over. "Okay," she said to herself. "That would've been embarrassing."

Getting her bearings, she quickly located the malfunctioning motion detector. It was nothing more than a polycarbonate rod shoved into the ground, roughly four feet tall with a collection of micro-fiber optical sensors clustered around its tip. This one, however, was not standing vertically; it had been broken in half, the fractured top half lying on the ground with a few indentations that looked disturbingly like teeth marks along its length.

She pulled her pad from the pouch on her belt, tapped a few buttons, and brought up the last images the sensor recorded. According to the computer data, it went off-line around midnight the night before. Pulling up the last five minutes of video, she switched the feed to night-vision and played it.

A gasp escaped her lips as she watched a blur of movement zoom past the sensor. Then, a few moments later, she froze the screen on the image of a large paw with some alarmingly sharp claws, milliseconds before it destroyed the sensor.

Her eyes wide, she glanced up at her surroundings. She looked around the barren, rocky landscape, with peaks jutting up from the ground, closing around her like a large, broken cage. She felt paranoia creeping over her. Instinctively, she drew her pistol, holding it in front of her as she scanned the area in a 360-degree circle.

Nothing. Only a faint stir of wind to break up the silence.

Maeve was not one to easily give in to fear. She'd fought in and survived numerous space battles, recon missions, and one particularly psychotic ex-boyfriend. Her back bore several ugly scars as mementos, including a six-inch slash across her shoulder blade from a piece of shrapnel she caught when crashing her disabled fighter into a rocky outcropping on Denebius IV.

"Farking shite," she spat, gathering up the broken sensor. Tapping furiously on the console, she teleported again.

* * *

A few minutes later, she reappeared at the exact spot she'd departed from, right next to the dining table. Hearing the raucous sound of the excavator coming from down the tunnel a hundred yards away, she ran for the *Talon*.

Sprinting up the entrance ramp, she made her way to the cockpit, plopping down into the pilot's chair and activating the onboard computer. As an afterthought, she removed the transporter from her belt and placed it next to the console. Despite her near-panic, she took a moment to be thankful that the unit seemed to be working perfectly. Apart from almost falling, the transport itself was instantaneous and flawless. There were no side-effects like nausea or dizziness, and the only hiccup was a slight sense of disorientation due to the abrupt change in location and elevation. *Have to remember to close my eyes next time,* she thought.

The second malfunctioning sensor had been mangled even more than the first, and it took no time to determine that both broken sensors were irreparable. And they didn't have many to spare.

For the next hour, she scanned the optical feeds from every sensor she'd set up, hoping to catch a better view of whatever had destroyed two of them. Even with the night-vision, there wasn't much to see. A couple of the sensors showed a long, fast-moving shape zooming by, but even magnifying and enhancing the images failed to reveal the nature of this silent threat.

"I don't understand," Maeve muttered to herself. "The sensors are supposed to notify us immediately if they're malfunctioning or if they go offline, so why didn't they?"

She tapped the computer a few more times, and her eyes closed as she pounded her fist on the console. Then she covered her face with her hands.

I am without a doubt the stupidest person in the history of history.

Fark me.

Chapter Fifteen

AVIN SMILED as his Mom vanished. He couldn't wait for the chance to use the transporter himself. He placed his plate into the synthesizer, stood up, wiped his mouth with the back of his hand, and headed for the entrance to the tunnel they'd created.

They'd been digging for three days now. The mountain range they now called home was made from a type of sedimentary rock resembling shale, according to the scanner. It wasn't tough to dig into, and because there was no seismic activity on Castelan VI—this part of it, anyway—they didn't have to spend as much time and energy shoring up their tunnels as much as anticipated.

That didn't change the fact that this whole operation, which would ideally have been undertaken by a team of twelve to twenty, was instead being performed by two people with no real experience in this type of work. They'd both been schooled on how to operate the excavator, as well as the safety protocols they'd need to obey while tunneling into a mountain on an alien planet; even so, it was slow going.

Donning a set of form-fitting, one-size-fits-all blue coveralls and a pair of sound-cancelling earplugs, Davin climbed into the excavator's cab, where he fastened a dust-mask and goggles over his face. Flipping the ignition switch, he smiled as the powerful motors whirred to life, feeling the vibrations it sent through his body. Turning on the powerful lamps on both sides of the cab, he maneuvered the hulking vehicle into the opening.

When the excavator reached the point where they stopped digging the night before, Davin flipped another switch. Harshly bright lasers shot from the vehicle's front, disintegrating the rock into fine powder. The powder was then sucked up by powerful vacuum tubes jutting out near ground level and collected in a huge compartment in the back. When the tank was full, he would turn the excavator around and drive it a few hundred yards down the wadi to dispose of it. They'd already created several six-foot-high mounds of dirt.

He grimaced. *So this is fifteen. It sure is everything I thought it would be.*

* * *

An hour later, Davin trundled the excavator down the wadi to their designated dumping zone. After emptying the dust compartments, he parked the machine back by the tunnel entrance and turned off the ignition. It was hot again today, and though the coveralls' built-in thermal regulators kept his body cool, he'd worked up quite a thirst.

He dismounted the cab and removed his facemask and earplugs before making his way to the purifiers for a drink of water. Glancing at the *Talon*, he was surprised to see his mother, sitting at the bottom of the entrance ramp, staring into space. She was rocking back and forth, and Davin gulped. He knew that sign, and it wasn't a good one. Forgetting his thirst, he sprinted toward the ship.

Maeve didn't even look at him as he ran up. She just sat there, glassy-eyed, and at her feet were the destroyed remains of two motion sensors.

"Mom, what's wrong?" Davin asked, kneeling down in front of her.

The sound of his voice snapped her out of her trance, as her eyes focused on him. "I screwed up, Dav," she said, so softly he almost didn't hear it. "I screwed up *bad.*"

His eyebrows knitted. "What do you mean?"

She picked up her pad from beside her and handed it to him. He tapped a button and replayed the incident, his guts tightening as he saw the cause of the sensors' destruction. "What is this? Some kind of animal?"

"Yeah," Maeve said drily. "A big, honkin', scary one. I've checked all the feeds, and that's the best image of the bunch."

Davin's eyelid twitched in alarm. "I thought these mountains were uninhabited!"

"So did I."

"Why didn't you scan for hostile life-forms, Mom? Isn't that what you're supposed to do when you land on a strange planet?"

Maeve cast her eyes to the ground. "I set the scan for humanoid life only."

"You –" Davin shook his head, dumbfounded. "That's great, Mom. That's just great."

"I've had so much other shite going on, I just ... " She sighed, looking him in the eyes again. "I'm sorry, Dav."

Davin took a few steps back, his mouth dropping open in shock. "You're sorry? You're *sorry*? Oh my God, Mom! What if this ... this *thing* decided to come into our camp? It could have destroyed our machines, even killed us in our sleep!"

Maeve grabbed him by the shoulders, steadying him. "But it didn't. We've been here for four days, and nothing's happened until now."

"Yeah, well, we arrived in this great big farking spaceship," he gestured at the *Talon*, "and we've had the excavator going practically sunup to sundown since then. That thing makes enough noise to scare anything off."

"But not at night, Dav. We've been ceasing our digs at sundown. It would seem this creature is nocturnal."

Sensing his rapidly growing anxiety, she spread her arms out, gesturing at the nearby mountain peaks. "It's just an animal, Dav. Animals need food. We've been a half-mile in every direction, and apart from a few insects and some rodents, we've seen nothing. Not much of a menu for a carnivore."

"That we know of, Mom," he replied. "It's not like we had a chance to do a complete work-up of this region's biosphere. The plan was to be in and out in two weeks, tops."

"That was when there were ten of us," Maeve said softly.

Davin bent down to examine the broken sensors. "Which two sensors are these?"

"Six and fourteen."

His eyes went wide. "What? Those were a mile apart! One creature couldn't have done this, unless ... "

She nodded. "Yeah. There are more." Her shoulders sagged.

Davin's breath caught in his throat. "How many more?"

"I'm not sure. If I had to guess, based on the readings, I'd say somewhere between five and ten."

He tried to process it all; a whole pack of creatures who came out at night to hunt, who were too fast or too stealthy for the sensors to pinpoint, and strong enough to break a polycarbonate rod in half. "Fark," he whispered.

"Yeah," Maeve said, sitting down on the entrance ramp again.

Davin turned away, not wanting his mother to see the pained expression on his face.

He always thought of himself as an easygoing person, not easily ruffled, preferring to meet life's problems head-on with a smile instead of a frown. Even living under Jegg occupation for five years hadn't crushed his spirit. No matter how bad things got, he still had his parents by his side: his father, who never stopped looking for solutions to the Terran Confederation's problems, and his mother, who was quite simply the toughest person he'd ever known.

Over the last few days, though, it had all come crashing down. This was their last chance to free humanity, and fate seemed determined to block their every attempt at success. Terrans had lost their world; all their worlds. His home, his friends, his father. All gone. And now, their very last hope was circling the drain because of … wild animals. It was ridiculous, and Davin might have laughed if tears hadn't been forcing their way to his eyes.

If only Dad was here. He'd know a way out of this.

But he's not. We're here, and he's not.

Davin began walking toward the lake, his pace quickly becoming a jog, and then a full sprint. Maeve watched him go for a few moments before she stood up and followed him.

When Davin reached the shore of the lake, he was out of breath, bending over and grasping his knees as he fought to fill his lungs with air. His vision was blurred with tears. Unable to stand any more, he balled up his fists and screamed.

The sound of his cry reverberated off the walls of the basin, echoing back in a recurring chorus. Davin continued to scream until his vocal chords were raw and scratchy. His legs gave way and he collapsed on the ground, covering his face with his hands.

Maeve reached the lake's edge. "Dav?" Her voice quavered.

"We're done," Davin sobbed, picking up a stone and chucking it into the water. "It's all over." His chest looked like it was caving in, and he was shaking all over.

She put her hand on his shoulder. "Dav –"

"It's over, Mom!" He finally turned to look at her. "We're on an alien planet, a gazillion light-years from Earth, we don't know what we're searching for, we don't know what to do with it *if* we find it, and we can't go home anyway! And to top it all off, we're about to be eaten by animals!"

Maeve said nothing. He'd been bottling this up since finding Gaspar's body, so she just let him vent.

He picked up another stone and threw it in the water, with a lot less force than the first one. "We have to go, Mom."

She edged her body forward, coming to rest right beside him. In barely a whisper, she replied, "Go *where*, Dav? We have nowhere to go."

"You can't possibly think we can win this fight." He still wouldn't look at her.

Maeve put an arm around him. "As a matter of fact, that's exactly what I think."

"How can you say that? How can you look at me and *say* that? Dad's ..." Tears overwhelmed him and he finally broke down, falling into Maeve's arms.

She clutched him tightly to her chest, closing her eyes and rocking him gently back and forth. "I know, baby, I know," she whispered into his ear.

After a few minutes, his breathing normalized again, but he didn't let go. "What do we do, Mom?"

She brushed his hair away from his face. "We keep going."

"How?"

"Any way we can, Dav. It's what your father would do. It's what our friends would do. It's what *we* have to do. We give up now, and they died for nothing."

They both stared at the lake for a long time. Finally, Davin released himself from his mother's arms, straightened up, and turned back to look at the *Talon* again. Sniffling, he asked, "Do you know where these creatures are?"

"Not precisely. They must make their lairs underground, so the scanners are having a hard time pinpointing their location. They appear to group together in packs of four or five, and based on the sensor data, there are at least two packs that hunt in this area."

He let out a deep, cleansing breath. "So what you're saying is that this lake is in the middle of their territory."

"Pretty much."

Davin stood, scratching his chin as he surveyed the campsite. Apart from their various machines, a few tables and chairs and a couple of unopened crates, the area was clear. Then he turned around and looked at the *Talon*, scanning it from stem to stern.

"Can we fly the ship into orbit? Come back in the morning?" he asked.

Maeve considered this. "We don't have a surplus on fuel, kiddo. We could do that three, maybe four times, but we'd have to keep coming back here. At the rate we're going, it could be a few more weeks before we strike gold, or whatever it is. No, we're gonna have to deal with this problem here and now."

"I don't suppose sealing ourselves in the ship for the night is an option."

"Oh, it's an option, just not one I like. If one of these things is strong enough to snap a sensor rod in half, imagine what a bunch of them could do if they concentrated their efforts."

"What about that cache of machine guns we got last week?"

"Useless. Those that hadn't rusted through, the firing pins were shot to shite. We never got a chance to replace them."

"I'm guessing we don't have any energy weapons."

"Nope. Jegg had 'em all destroyed. The Underground tried to get the parts to build more, but they couldn't swing it. Those black market bastards wouldn't give you a bucket of water if your house was on fire."

Davin snapped his fingers. "I've got it! I could take one of the lasers off the excavator –"

She shook her head. "Thought of that. Those things get super-hot, and we would have to remove the entire cooling system along with it. That's like a hundred and fifty pounds of machinery."

His face fell. "Do we have anything more ... basic?"

"We're out of D34Z, and don't have any spare fuel to use as an explosive. I did find three concussion grenades in Calvin's footlocker, though."

"Figures. He always did love blowing shite up. Anything else?"

"Ji-Yan packed two short swords and a tritanium baseball bat. We also have a few knives, and I suppose we can also use our hand-operated digging tools as clubs if we have to." She then looked down at her sidearm, a refurbished pistol, which she'd once told him was standard issue for soldiers before energy weapons were developed. "And this."

"How much ammo you got for that thing?"

"Just shy of six full magazines, I think."

He rubbed his temples. "Well, it's better than nothing, I guess."

Maeve sighed. "I'll have to break out some more motion sensors and place them around the site. Lights, too. Then, once the sun goes down, we can take turns keeping watch."

"Can I execute Birthday Boy privilege now?" Davin asked, a crooked smile cracking through.

Seeing his grin, Maeve's face softened, and she chuckled. "All right, all right, I'll take first shift. Sorry to give you such a sucky birthday, Little Bug." She moved forward, enfolding her son in a warm embrace.

"Sorry for the meltdown," Davin said, returning the hug.

"It's okay, kiddo. Sorry I messed up. My sarge back in Basic would've kicked my arse."

"Hey." They faced each other again, and he placed his hand on his mother's shoulder. "You're not Major Cromack anymore. You're just Mom. You're allowed to be human."

"Thanks. You sure you're all right?"

He shrugged, and his smile widened. "Hey, we got mint chocolate cake and wild animals. All we need is some beer and a few girls and it'll be a party."

She smiled, and playfully mussed his hair. "Back to work, lover-boy. The clock's ticking."

* * *

By mid-afternoon, they'd unpacked the remaining motion sensors from the *Talon*'s hold and placed them around the campsite, a hundred yards in every direction where they could find even terrain. Davin disconnected one of the ship's audio speakers and hooked it up to the sensors, programming it to sound a loud, obnoxious siren if anything larger than a mouse breached the perimeter.

With just over an hour before sunset, Maeve took the final turn of the day on the excavator as Davin carried two large canisters of water back from the lake. A more in-depth analysis revealed the lake was fed by a large underground spring, and while it contained no harmful microorganisms, it still had to be fed through the purifiers before they could safely drink it. This was essential, as the dry air provided little condensation.

As soon as he got the purifiers going, he grabbed a handful of organic nutra-pellets from the canister on the work table and poured them into an aperture on the top of the synthesizer.

Davin was perusing the synthesizer's list of possible dinner choices when the noise of the excavator's motor echoing up through the mouth of the tunnel abruptly ceased. A quick glance at the sun confirmed that twilight was just over an hour away. It had only been twenty minutes since Maeve had started her shift, so there was no way the dust compartments could be filled already.

He grabbed a wrist-communicator from the work table and switched it on. "Mom, everything okay?"

He waited a few seconds, but no reply came. "Mom?" he asked again.

Still no answer. A sense of dread crept over him.

He walked toward the tunnel, his stride becoming more urgent with each step. "Mom!" he shouted into the communicator, but there was still no answer.

Breaking into a full sprint, he dashed into the cave, passing by a series of small portable lamps fastened to the cave walls at regular intervals. Taking care not to trip on any of the loose rocks that littered the cave floor, he maintained a quick pace until the tail-lights of the excavator loomed into view. The dust had settled, thankfully, and his heart rate jumped when he saw his mother sitting sideways on the driver's seat, her legs dangling out of the cab. She was holding her head in obvious pain.

"Mom! Are you all right?" he said as he ran to her side.

She looked up at him, and under the harsh glare of the excavator's lamps, he could see the stress on her face. "Dav?"

"Yeah, it's me," he said, kneeling down to get a closer look at her. "Why didn't you answer me?"

She looked down at the communicator on her wrist, which was completely dark. She pushed a button on the side and tapped the screen with her finger. Nothing. "Must be malfunctioning. Sorry, Dav." She moved her hand back to her temple, rubbing it gently.

"Mom, are you hurt?" Davin asked.

"It's nothing," she said, waving him off. "Just a little headache."

She reached out her hand, which he took, and she got to her feet. Almost immediately, she doubled over, clutching at her head again, moaning in pain.

Taking her shoulder, he helped her down until she was able to sit on the ground. " 'Little headache', my arse. How long have you been in pain?"

She looked at him wearily. Her crow's feet appeared to have sprouted talons. "It started a couple hours ago. At first it wasn't too bad, but it's been getting steadily worse ever since." She let out a long, painful breath. "It feels like a Chethran wamzu is howling inside my brain."

"Yikes. We are having a shite day, aren't we?"

"Don't start."

Davin looked up the tunnel, which sloped upward at a fifteen-degree angle. He imagined the sun creeping ever closer toward the horizon. "I think it's time we called it a day, Mom."

"No argument here." Maeve reached her hand up to her son. He hauled her to her feet and wrapped his arm around her shoulder.

"Come on," he said. "You need a good meal and a good night's sleep."

"Dav –"

"No, Mom. You're not gonna do either of us any good if you drop dead from exhaustion."

"Fine," she muttered, stumbling forward, using her free hand to brush a lock of hair, which had come free from its rather shabby ponytail, away from her eyes. "But I'm still taking night watch."

"Bloody hell, you are. You're hitting the sack right after dinner." He gave a grim smile. "That's an order."

She quirked an eyebrow, a slight smile playing at the side of her mouth. "Um, pretty sure you're not my C.O., and you're damn sure not my father."

"No, but it's still my birthday, so I'm officially pulling rank."

She chuckled, despite the pain. "Don't think it works that way, but I'm in too much pain to argue. You're waking me at midnight to take over for you, and that is *not* negotiable. You got it?"

"Got it, Mom," he said, thankful when the last of the day's natural sunlight came into view.

Chapter Sixteen

INSIDE THE small cave at the southern edge of the Ixtrayan Plateau which had housed the Stone for more than eight centuries, Kelia fought to maintain her patience as she relived the same, unhelpful vision she'd experienced every day since seeing the mysterious object in the night sky.

In her mind, she was flying. No, not flying: gliding. Gliding across the desert floor, the distant Kaberian Mountains looming ever closer. As she neared the closest peaks, which stretched as far as the eye could see in both northerly and southerly directions, she heard something strange. She concentrated on this sound: a sound unlike any she'd ever heard before. It was like a thousand metal swords striking hard stone simultaneously, but with no interruptions or pauses in between strikes. Whatever secret the mountains held was something foreign to Elystra, which only solidified Kelia's belief that the mysterious visitors had come from the Above.

With each consultation, her mental journey to the mountains seemed to bring her a little closer to revealing the source of the noise, to the nature of the visitors. Each time, though, the vision ended before she could get the answers she sought, and it frustrated her to no end. She briefly considered that Arantha was teasing her, goading her, but dismissed this notion.

Today, she hoped, was the day she would finally *know*.

The pounding, grinding noise increased in volume as, in her mind, Kelia reached the base of the mountains and soared upward, skimming the tops of the smaller peaks as she glided between the larger ones. Looking down, she beheld a lake just on the edge of her sight. Arantha seemed to be directing her there. She suddenly dove downward, heading straight for the lake, and she knew this was her final destination.

One more peak to clear, and all would be revealed. The grinding noise was now at a fever pitch, and it sounded to Kelia like someone—*something*—was tearing the heart out of one of the mountains. She was concentrating so hard on the sound, she didn't realize her vision was breaking up until moments before it happened. The last image she saw was that of the lake, surrounded on three sides by walls of rock. A short distance from the water's edge on the southern side were several objects that at first glance appeared strange to her, but before she could focus on them, the image dissipated.

As Kelia's mind rejoined her body, she became aware that she was holding the Stone so tightly, her knuckles were white. Short of breath and mildly disorientated, she released her grip, shaking her hands to rid herself of the pins-and-needles sensation.

She groaned in frustration. *So close. So ... blagging ... close.*

She stared at the Stone, embedded on top of a flat altar-shaped slab of rock that stood at waist-level along the far wall of the small cave. Closing her eyes and clenching her fists, she momentarily gave into her frustration. Several layers of dust coating the cave floor jumped and swirled around her, flying to and fro in a pattern of pure chaos that reflected her mindset.

Why do you do this, Arantha? Why do you bring me so close to understanding your wishes, only to pull me back?

The Ixtrayu are restless. They want answers only I can give them, and yet you tell me nothing. For thirteen years, you've

*tested our faith. With every breath I have taken as Protectress,
I have tried to reinforce that faith. And in return, what have you
given us? More tests, more questions, no answers.*

Is this our reward for centuries of devotion?

Opening her eyes, Kelia realized she was in the middle of a
dust-storm, somehow encapsulated within the cave in which
she now sat. She retreated inside her mind again, calming her
maelstrom of doubts. She made her breathing more regular,
and her heart rate slowed to normal. When she opened her
eyes again, she exhaled in relief. Most of the dust had settled,
and only a thin haze remained.

She climbed to her feet and dusted off her robes, taking a few
extra moments to comport herself before leaving the cave. It
would do no good for the tribe to see her in such a frantic state,
assuming none of them had witnessed the miniature storm she
just created. Her face blank, she strode out of the cave and into
the midday sun.

* * *

Her throat dry, Kelia made her way to the cistern, where
two vats of drinking water were available for the Ixtrayu to fill
their water-skins.

Kelia always made it part of her daily routine to lower the
temperature of the drinking water for all. Whether the women
she protected toiled in the fields or the orchards, whether they
wove cloth or crafted objects from wood, whether they cooked
or laundered or hunted or gathered, if providing them with
cool water helped them quench their thirst, then it was a service she happily provided.

Today felt like the hottest day of the dry season thus far, and
a crowd of about twenty women eagerly filled their mugs and
skins, bowing and smiling to Kelia before returning to their du-

ties. She smiled back, momentarily forgetting her earlier frustration.

Kelia strode along the path leading east from the village to a wide, flat area set up as an archery range. This was where huntresses and gatherers would practice their skills with a bow and arrow. She heard the sound of several arrows piercing their targets, bags of thick cloth stuffed with grass, as she approached.

Only one Ixtrayu was training at this time: Vaxi. Kelia marveled as the girl fired three more huxa-wood arrows in rapid succession, striking the distant target in nearly the same spot every time. After the final shot, Vaxi realized she was being watched, and bowed her head. "Protectress," she said.

Kelia beamed as she closed the distance between them. "Runa's right; your prowess with a bow is phenomenal. It's like Arantha herself guides your aim."

"Thank you, Protectress." Vaxi's eyes were still cast to the ground.

Kelia had asked Nyla several days earlier if she knew what might be troubling the young huntress beyond her inability to go on Sojourn. Nyla said she suspected Vaxi might simply be lonely. At nearly eighteen years of age, Vaxi had fully blossomed into womanhood, and she was now at an age where choosing a possible companion might be foremost in her thoughts. Kelia could only wonder if Vaxi's troubles ran deeper than that, and she suspected the undue pressure being put upon her by Susarra was the cause of her fragile temperament.

Kelia put a reassuring hand on her shoulder. "Vaxi, look at me."

Vaxi lifted her head, and for the first time, Kelia saw that one side of the girl's face was abnormally red. Kelia moved to touch Vaxi's cheek, but she just shied away, embarrassed.

"Vaxi, what happened?"

"It's nothing," she said, turning away from her. She moved a few paces away, staring absently at her archery target and the collection of arrows sticking out of it.

Kelia felt her anger rising. "Did your grandmother do this to you?"

Vaxi didn't respond. Despite the heat, Kelia could swear she saw the girl tremble.

"Vaxi, tell me what happened. And please be truthful."

She turned to face Kelia, a tear forming at the corner of her eye. "I failed her."

"How could you possibly have done that?"

"I–I put myself right in the path of a charging kova. I killed the beast, but Runa was so angry with me. And Grandmother …" She sniffed, and the tear rolled down her cheek.

Kelia recalled the day Ilora gave birth to Vaxi. It was such a beautiful time in their lives, and Susarra was as happy as Kelia that Ilora's first Sojourn produced such a perfect, healthy daughter. How things had changed since then.

Overcome by memories, Kelia enfolded the young huntress in her arms. Vaxi returned the hug as her tears continued to flow.

After Vaxi calmed herself and her breathing returned to normal, Kelia faced her, placing both palms on the girl's shoulders. "You are so much like your mother. I look at you, and it's like I'm looking at her."

A tiny smile appeared on Vaxi's face. "She loved you. So much."

"And I loved her. And I know …" Kelia caressed Vaxi's uninjured cheek, "… I *know* she would be so proud of you."

Vaxi tried to lower her head again, but Kelia put her fingers under the girl's chin, forcing her to keep eye contact. "I'm not so sure," Vaxi said.

"She would, Vaxi. There's no doubt in my mind. But you can't endanger yourself like that. It would not do anyone any good if you were hurt or killed. Not the tribe, not Arantha, and not me."

Vaxi just stared, continuing to blink away tears.

"You're a skilled huntress, Vaxi," Kelia continued. "I know it, Runa knows it, your sister huntresses know it. You don't need to prove yourself to anyone."

Her breath became shallow again. "But Grandmother –"

As if on cue, the telltale *thunk* of Susarra's walking stick entered Kelia's ears. Kelia turned her head to see the portly Councilor approaching. As usual, she was not smiling.

Before she could come within earshot, Kelia whispered to Vaxi, "Go get yourself some water. Midday meal will begin shortly, so once you've sated your thirst, head for the dining area. I'm sure Nyla and Sarja will be there waiting. They'll be serving a fresh batch of honey-bread, their favorite."

Kelia's heart warmed as Vaxi's smile widened. "Yes, Protectress. Thank you." Snatching up her bow, she shot a glance at the target. "My arrows –"

"I'll get them," Kelia said. "You run along."

Vaxi nodded, and bounded down the path to the village. She gave her grandmother a wide berth, noticeably avoiding eye contact with Susarra as she ran past.

Susarra moved to follow Vaxi, but Kelia stayed her with a commanding, "Stay, Susarra. I would like to speak with you."

Susarra didn't move, no doubt hoping Kelia would be the one to close the distance between them. When she did not, Susarra snorted and began walking.

As she drew near, Kelia straightened her spine, giving Susarra a look of thinly veiled contempt.

"How may I serve you, Protectress?" Susarra said.

Kelia jabbed her finger at the archery target. "Take a look at that."

Susarra followed the direction of Kelia's finger, noting the tight cluster of arrows protruding from the cloth bag. "She is quite proficient, isn't she?"

"Yes she is. I've rarely seen such accuracy."

"You are most kind, Protectress."

Kelia met Susarra's gaze. "So why is it Vaxi feels compelled to endanger herself for your benefit? And more importantly, why is it that she feels she's a failure?"

Susarra didn't even blink. "Children should always be motivated to improve themselves."

"Yes, but at what cost?" Kelia's eyebrows knitted together.

"Protectress?"

"That girl has achieved more in her short life than most Ixtrayu. She's one of our best huntresses, she's loved and respected by the tribe, and yet, instead of rewarding her accomplishments, you diminish, belittle, and abuse her. And I will not stand for it."

Susarra's face reddened. "I am responsible for Vaxi's upbringing. This includes her education *and* her discipline. You ceded that responsibility to me after Ilora's death, did you not?"

"I did," Kelia replied through clenched teeth. "Had I known this would be the result, I would have spared you the burden."

Several beads of sweat appeared on Susarra's plump face. "But you did not. That child is my responsibility, and yours is –"

Finally, Kelia's anger broke loose. "Do not speak to me of *my* responsibilities, Susarra! I am Protectress! It is my duty to protect those within the Ixtrayu, my *family*, our family, from harm!"

Susarra's glare was pure ice. "Like Ilora?"

Had Kelia not trained her mind to maintain control over her abilities, she might have set Susarra on fire at that moment. Quelling a sudden buildup of power within her, she spat, "Don't you *dare* blame me for her death! What happened to her was a tragic accident! I loved her more than you could possibly know, and I would have given my life for her in a heartbeat!"

Susarra shuffled her feet, leaning heavily on her walking stick.

"I am sympathetic for your loss, Susarra. You have lost more than most. But you have made Vaxi the scapegoat for your grief and your bitterness, and that cannot continue. You call her a child, and yet you push her to produce one of her own."

"What are you going to do?" Susarra spluttered.

"I am going to make it clear to Vaxi that her path, and her happiness, are hers to determine, not yours. She is of age, and not beholden to you anymore."

Susarra opened her mouth to protest, but Kelia held her hand up. "And before you challenge my wishes further, let me make it equally clear that your position as Councilor is as much mine to determine as it was my mother's. Don't force me to take that away from you as well."

Susarra averted her gaze and lumbered away. Her lungs heaving and her back turned, she finally muttered, "Yes, Protectress." Then she picked up her pace, striding away as quickly as her crippled body would allow.

Chapter Seventeen

MIZAR ENTERED his personal library to find Sen sitting at the long work table piled high with many unrolled scrolls, all pressed flat with expertly-placed weights. His head lay atop his crossed arms, his short, dark hair askew, and he was snoring and murmuring in his sleep. A thin, unbroken chain of drool connected his bottom lip to the sleeve of his beige tunic.

After placing his burden of three bound tomes on the end of the table, Mizar crept over to the basin in the corner, filled a wooden mug with fresh water, and promptly poured it over his apprentice's head.

"Gaaaaah!" Sen shouted. He was so disoriented he flung himself backwards, which was enough momentum to topple his chair.

Mizar grabbed the towel sitting next to the basin and threw it at Sen as the young man clambered to his feet. He looked up just in time to catch the heavy cloth right in the face. Mizar couldn't quite suppress a chuckle. "I thought I told you to sleep in your room."

"Sorry, Master," Sen said, dabbing the water from his eyes. "I noticed something interesting last night, and I wanted to research it further. I guess I fell asleep."

"Yes, I heard your resounding snores from all the way down the corridor."

Sen blushed.

"I brought the translation texts we need," Mizar continued.

Mizar and Sen had been poring over the scrolls deemed "Forbidden Knowledge" for the past three days. Much of what they found was as Aridor said; indecipherable nonsense, meaningless scribbles from the obviously unhinged mind of Merdeen. However, some of Merdeen's musings were legible, though those were written in Ancient Elystran script, a crude set of symbols that hadn't been used in centuries and was impossible to translate without a cipher text. It took the palace archivist, Binro, two days to locate the proper volumes.

"I'll get to work on translating Merdeen's notes right away, Master."

Mizar once again filled his cup from the basin, this time downing the contents in one gulp. "That must have been some dream you were having."

Sen's face flushed. "I was dreaming of my father."

"Pleasant, I hope."

"No, not really."

Mizar's brow furrowed. "You do not speak of your family often. Why is that?"

Sen stared into space, his shoulders stooped. "My father is a great man. A successful man. He owns one of the largest farms in Thelwyn province. He has more havsu, gurns, and billocks than any in the region."

"… But?"

Sen resumed his seat with a heavy sigh. "He's never been the fatherly type. To me, anyway."

Mizar sat in the chair opposite Sen. "I am sorry to hear that."

"He sired three other sons before me, you see. Three muscle-bound idiots who could tear down a huxa tree with their bare hands. But when their mother died, Father took it hard. When my own mother came into his life, I think he was hoping to produce similar offspring. And then I was born."

He held out his skinny arms, which probably would have been hard-pressed to even lift a longsword, much less swing one. "As you can imagine, I was the runt of the litter since before I could even walk. Even though I learned to read and write at a much earlier age than my brothers, they treated me with nothing but contempt. So did Father. No matter what I did to please him, it wasn't enough. It was never enough."

A wisp of a tear formed at the corner of Sen's eye. "Thank Arantha for King Sardor's decree that all Daradian men must journey to Dar to be tested for Wielding abilities when they come of age. That was my salvation. All through childhood, I counted the days until my sixteenth birthday, the day I could enter Mount Calabur and stand on the Nexus of Arantha." He sniffed. "Even had I not discovered my healing ability, I doubt I would have returned home. Anything would have been better than that.

"Even though my family wasn't as devout as most of our neighbors, I would pray nightly to Arantha that I may find a destiny beyond the fields of Thelwyn. And I have thanked him every day since my first consultation that I am your apprentice, Master." Finally, a smile broke through the sadness.

Mizar put a reassuring hand on Sen's arm. "As High Mage, my duties were such that I was unable to find time to marry and raise a family of my own. If I ever were to have a son, though, I do not think I could do better than you."

Sen bowed his head. "Thank you, Master."

"Whatever became of your mother?" Mizar asked.

"She left my father before I was born." He scoffed. "She probably couldn't wait to get away from him. He searched all of Thelwyn, but didn't find her. Then, nearly a year later, he found me on his doorstep."

Sen cast his eyes to the ceiling. "I constantly ask myself why, if my mother thought she was better off without my father, she felt it necessary to return just to leave me in his hands. He probably only kept me around so he could have someone to vent his bitterness and anger upon."

A sympathetic smile came over Mizar's face. "And yet, by the grace of Arantha, two farmer's sons who never knew a mother's love now walk the halls of Castle Randar, serving their king and country in ways few Daradians have."

"Indeed, Master."

"My own mother died giving birth to me. It broke my father's heart. He said Areca was his one true love. He ended up never marrying."

Sen sniffed. "At least you knew your mother's name. My father never told me. I was forbidden from the age of six to ever speak of her in our house."

"Again, regrettable." Mizar raised his hands, calling an end to this particular conversation. "Now, tell me what is of interest in these scrolls."

Sen brightened, and grabbed the stack of scrolls to his left that he'd been working on the night before. As he flipped through them, searching for the right one, he asked, "Did you consult Arantha again, Master?"

Mizar nodded. "Yes, early this morning." Anticipating Sen's next question, he continued, "It went fine. I was not overwhelmed as I was last time. I made sure to strengthen my mental defenses before the consultation began."

"Did you learn anything new?"

"Later, Sen," Mizar said impatiently. "First, tell me what you found."

Sen pulled a scroll out of the stack and turned it around so Mizar could read it. "Thank Arantha for the thoroughness of Daradian record-keeping. This is a list of all in our history who have discovered Wielding abilities. There are nine total, not including you and me."

Mizar scanned the list, which included the names of the three previous High Mages: Durkin, Jerril and Merdeen. The other names, accompanied by their dates and regions of birth, belonged to individuals who discovered they possessed minor Wielding abilities: enough to be of service to the Crown, but not enough to wear the mantle of High Mage. Nearly all the non-High Mages had been born in the last century. Were it not for King Sardor's edict, they would not have realized their potential at all. Try as he might, though, Mizar couldn't figure what had gotten his apprentice so worked up. "Whatever it is you've discovered, Sen, please enlighten me."

Sen walked around to Mizar's side of the table, tugging another scroll from the stack and placing it next to the other one. "It would seem every single Daradian who has manifested Wielding abilities has three things in common."

Mizar leaned forward over the documents, intrigued, trying to determine what his apprentice had deduced. After scanning them for a few moments, he said, "They were all born in the outer regions of Darad, to fathers who, while not lavishly rich, were not paupers either: farmers, ranchers, merchants, even an innkeeper."

"Yes, Master. A great many of these Wielders' fathers were also brought to Dar to see if they, too, were Wielders. To a man, they were not."

Mizar straightened up, his eyebrows raising. "These scrolls are not from the vault."

"No, Master. They were in your cabinet."

"Why were you looking in my cabinet?"

Sen nervously rubbed behind his ears. "After you retired for the night, I started thinking about this female Wielder Prince Zendak mentioned. I began to wonder just how a woman could become a Wielder in the first place. As far as we know, the

Crystal Cavern is the only way that a person may unlock their abilities, and women are not permitted entry there … not even the Queen or Princess Tyah."

"That is correct."

"So I got to thinking: if we can figure out what *we*," he gestured to himself, Mizar, and the list of names on the scroll before them, "have in common, then maybe we can discover this female Wielder's origins as well."

Mizar gave Sen a hard glare. "The priests in the High Temple would state that we were chosen by Arantha himself. Do you not believe this?"

Sen shuffled his feet nervously, looking abashed. "Forgive me, Master, I do not mean to speak heresy."

Mizar shifted his glance to the library door, making sure it was closed and no prying ears had overheard Sen's admission. After confirming this, his face relaxed. "Those priests would likely have both our heads if they knew we were speaking of this, Sen, but you've made me curious."

Sen glanced at him in dubious wonder.

"Fear not, lad, my upbringing was much like yours: my cousins and I were taught to have faith not only in Arantha, but in ourselves as well. I have spent the last forty years wondering why I was accorded this honor and not other, more worthy men. I'm rather astonished that you have discovered a line of reasoning I had not previously contemplated."

"You honor me, Master," Sen said, bowing his head.

"So." Mizar returned his attention to the scrolls. "You said all Wielders had three traits in common. They were all from the outer provinces, and all were born to successful but otherwise unremarkable fathers. What is the third?"

"All of them grew up without a mother."

Mizar's gaze returned to Sen, his jaw hanging open in shock. "*All* of them?"

"Yes, Master."

Under the weight of this revelation, Mizar was forced to sit back down at the work table, his mind awhirl. Eleven men—including Sen and himself—all born to fathers with no Wielding abilities at all, and to mothers who either died or left under mysterious circumstances. "This … this cannot be a co-incidence."

Sen, too, resumed his seat. "What do we do now, Master?"

Mizar rose again, striding toward the door. Grabbing and donning his black High Mage cloak, he turned to face Sen again. "*You* are going to get some breakfast, wash, change clothes, and be back here in two hours. Then you are going to start translating Merdeen's final prophecy."

"Yes, Master."

"I am going to speak with the King. You and I will be journeying to Ghaldyn very soon."

"Ghaldyn?" Sen inquired. "Your home province?"

Before Mizar could answer, there was a series of loud thumps on the door. He opened it to see a thickset guard standing just beyond the threshold, head bowed. "Sorry for the intrusion, High Mage," he said, "but the King requires your presence in the courtyard immediately."

Mizar fastened the clasp of his cloak around his neck. "That cannot be a coincidence either," he said, winking at Sen before walking past the guard and down the corridor.

Chapter Eighteen

MAEVE TOSSED and turned in her cot aboard the *Talon*. For the second night in a row, she was wracked by nightmares.

A giant explosion engulfed the hangar in flames. Sirens blared, and there was the muffled sizzle of energy weapons being fired. This was followed by the clang of the airlock door closing, the violent thud of the engines roaring to life, and the whoosh of air as they climbed into the sky, leaving their world and everyone they loved behind.

Their faces ricocheted around her mind: Ji-Yan, Calvin, Suri, Mahesh, Kacy, and Manny.

Gaspar.

Richard.

In the week since making planetfall, Maeve had experienced these nightmares. She wanted to scream at them to get out, to stop tormenting her. She had a job to do, and she couldn't honor their sacrifice if she was consumed with guilt and grief. Didn't they understand that?

And, just like that, the horrific images were replaced with new ones: strange, disjointed images she couldn't explain.

Somewhere in space, a supernova scattered its broken remnants in every direction.

Planets flew by her vision, too fast for her to make out any details.

And then, the cosmic kaleidoscope abruptly ceased, and one lone planet locked itself into position inside her mind.

Castelan VI.

The ground rushed up at breakneck speed, but just as it seemed she would crash into it, the image slowed down again.

She saw a sprawling, tree-covered mountain range stretching as far as the eye could see. Nestled in between several mountains was a vast lake, and branching off from that lake was a wide, crystal-clear river, winding downward across a grassy plain and through a plateau. On either side, carved into the very rock comprising the underside of the plateau, was a village. At the far end of this village was a cave, the mouth of which grew larger and larger, finally swallowing her up.

She found herself in a small room, dark except for the light seeping in through the narrow entrance. On the far side of the cave, standing before a rocky altar, was a woman. She was dressed in a simple, reddish-brown robe, and her long hair was swept up in a complex braid that dangled down her back. She appeared to be praying.

Maeve wanted to call out, to announce herself. But though Maeve made no sound, the woman seemed to have registered her presence. She turned around, and in her hands, she held a glowing stone, pulsating with warm, beatific energy.

Maeve moved closer, basking in the stone's radiance.

And then all went dark.

Jarring awake, Maeve immediately sat up and swung her legs off her cot, feeling the comfort of the cold metal of the *Talon*'s hull beneath her bare feet. As she sat upright, her head began to throb with pain.

"Ugh," she groaned and rose to her feet. After throwing on a clean pair of socks, work-pants and a black tank top, she moved to the bathroom. She relieved herself and ran a quick brush through her hair. She then reached into a drawer for the derma-hypo, which she loaded with an ampoule of clear liquid before jabbing it against her neck and pressing it down.

Maeve sighed with relief as the pain-blockers entered her bloodstream. She hated resorting to such measures, but none of the analgesics they'd brought provided a respite from the intense pain. The downside to the pain-blockers was that she could slash her wrist, and she'd just smile blissfully as she bled to death. But she had a mission to complete, and she couldn't do it with her skull threatening to explode.

After putting on her work boots, she walked down the exit ramp to find Davin, her pistol cradled in his lap, staring down the length of the wadi. "Morning, Dav."

"Oh, is it morning?" he said sleepily. "Ah. Sun's out. So yeah, I guess it's morning."

"Any more prowlers in the night?"

"Nope," he said, as cheerfully as he could manage given how little sleep he'd gotten. "My eyes were glued to the scanners the whole time. A couple of the beasties came pretty close, but a few strobe lights and a blast of the siren sent them back into hiding. For badass predators, they seem to be pretty skittish."

"Well, that's good news for us."

"How'd you sleep, Mom?"

"Pretty well, I guess," she lied. She hadn't told Davin about the nightmares, nor about her dreams of the strange woman in the cave. She dismissed the vision as being a product of her exhausted brain. "Ready for another exciting day at the Castelan VI Resort and Wildlife Park?"

"Yeah, sure." He made a sour face.

The last few days had been frustrating as hell. In addition to their animal problem, the excavator recently developed a bug: the cooling system that kept the laser-drills from overheating was on the fritz, and they lacked the knowhow to fix it. As a result, instead of continuous drilling, they could only operate the excavator one hour before they risked blowing the thing completely, followed by two hours of cool-down time.

They'd used some of their spare time to shore up their defenses. Rather than leave the functioning sensors out on the perimeter, Maeve and Davin collected them and put them anyplace an animal attack might come from: the rim of the basin, down the far end of the wadi, and everywhere in between. The personal transporters, which worked so well earlier, were now unreliable: they only worked about thirty percent of the time. The rest of the time, nothing would happen when activated.

Once that was done, they laid out everything they could use as weapons on the floor of the *Talon*'s hold, which wasn't much. Their lookout chair at the base of the exit ramp seemed like the best place to keep watch: if the creatures attacked *en masse*, they could hide inside the ship. At least they'd be safe. Hopefully. But just in case, Calvin's concussion grenades and Ji-Yan's short-swords were always kept at arm's length once the sun set.

That was their routine: they ate, they slept, they dug, they swam, they kept watch. That was it. Every time it seemed like they were on the brink of discovering a lode of the energy source they'd come to find, they would drill through rock only to find … more rock. The scanners were damn near useless in this regard now, and they had no way of knowing whether they were even drilling in the right direction.

Maeve and Davin were determined not to give up, but as they plowed on, day after day, they grew increasingly desperate. They barely spoke over meals, and all the jokes they knew weren't funny anymore. They were tired and cranky, and even Davin was starting to get headaches now. But they kept going. They had no choice.

* * *

By midday, Maeve, having filled the purifiers with water from the lake, strode down the tunnel to see if the excavator's motor had cooled down enough to be used again. She'd already taken two shifts on the machine that morning, which meant that it would be Davin's turn once he woke up.

Satisfied, she walked back through the tunnel and up to the surface. As she passed through the mouth of the cave, she saw that Davin was indeed awake. He was walking toward her, and he was grinning.

Maeve smiled back, out of reflex. Whatever he'd found on this benighted planet to make him happy made her happy as well. He was beaming as he approached her, his long, curly red hair spilling over the collar of his white shirt.

"What're you smiling at?" she asked. "Not that I'm complaining."

"Look," he said, pointing at his face, his grin widening even further.

Maeve leaned forward, and sure enough, the tiniest wisp of stubble poked through the skin on Davin's chin and upper lip.

"Well, look at you, all grown up!" she said, beaming.

"Not bad, eh?" He flicked his hair back dramatically, a look of pure masculine pride on his face. "If only Emma Donnelly could see me now."

"Yeah, if only." Maeve strode forward, wrapping him in a brief but warm hug and kissing his cheek. "Time to break out the razor, I guess."

"No way," he replied, stroking his infant facial hair. "Girls love a young guy with a man-stache. I'm sure there are plenty of medieval lasses on this planet that would die to get a piece of this."

Maeve lifted her hands up to her collar, unfastening the snaps that kept her blue coveralls in place. Working downward, she eventually undid enough for her to step out of them.

She handed them over, and he immediately began putting them on.

"Sorry, Romeo," she said. "The people on this planet may look like us, but I don't think we'd blend in very well." She gestured to her purple hair and tattoos. "They'd probably call me a witch and burn me at the stake or something."

"Killjoy." Davin did up the snaps on the coveralls' collar and tugged on the fabric so that it stretched over his frame perfectly. "What time's lunch?"

"I'll have it ready for you by the time the dust compartments are full, promise. But right now, I'm going for a swim."

He scrunched up his face in disgust. "Fine. Just wait for me to go down the tunnel before you start showing off your goodies, okay, Mom?"

"Get your butt to work," she said drily, "and give yourself a dose of anti-UV medicament, will ya? Your face looks redder than your hair." Then she walked toward the lake.

She rubbed her temples with her hand. The pain-blocker she took earlier was wearing off, and her head was starting to throb again. But first she needed to soak her body in the cool water.

Thankful for the thick clouds that had just arrived to block the sun, Maeve approached the water's edge. She'd enjoyed several swims since their arrival, and it always did wonders for her energy.

Behind her, the sound of the excavator drifted from the cave mouth as Davin began his shift. She'd come to hate that sound, as it invariably made her headaches worse.

Maeve used her feet to remove her work boots and socks. Then she unfastened the belt at her waist and stripped off her pants. Finally, she pulled off her black tank top. Standing on the shore of the lake in nothing but her underwear, she dipped a cautious toe into the water and smiled. The temperature was perfect.

She stretched her back muscles, staring at the natural beauty of the high-walled basin that held the magnificent lake.

This planet may suck sometimes, but there are much worse places we could have ended up.

Drawing in a deep breath, she slid out of her underwear and, with a girlish squeal, bounded forward into the water, diving headfirst when she reached waist-deep depth.

She dove downward, touching the lake bottom that sloped toward the center of the basin. Then she swam up to the surface, breaking through with a satisfied smile.

The water had clumped her hair together in front of her face, so she whipped it back behind her head with a flourish. Wading back to the shore, she looked up at the sky, which was a beautiful shade of blue. She could make out the sound of birds cawing in the distance.

As the droplets of water cascaded back to the lake, Maeve suddenly became keenly aware of her body. She used her hands to trace the shape of her breasts, admiring the white-tailed kite and the harrier hawk tattooed on her sternum. She loved her birds, as each tattoo marked a special occasion in her life. Unable to resist, she gave her left nipple a squeeze.

And then the strangest thing happened.

Something that sounded like a breath of wind swept across the lake, filling her ears. But there was no wind. Just the sound, as if God himself had exhaled on their little corner of the universe.

She looked up, incredulous, hoping to locate the source of the sound. But there was nothing. Her eyes scanned the rim of the basin above her.

There, on a high ridge to her right, stood a figure.

Maeve blinked her eyes as several drops of water trickled down from her hair. Wiping them away with the backs of her hands, she focused on the spot where she saw the mysterious apparition.

It was still there: someone standing on the rim of the canyon, staring down at her.

But something was wrong. As Maeve shaded her eyes from the sun, she found herself unable to focus. The figure was indistinct, as if it were both there and not there.

Maeve stepped out of the lake, water falling off her naked body as her feet found damp dirt. She never took her eyes off the figure.

It was a woman.

Saints alive, it's her. The woman from the cave. From my dreams.

She wore the same reddish-brown robe, and her dark hair was done up in a similar braid. She had beautiful, tanned skin and a regal bearing.

It was her. It had to be.

Warm air pricked at Maeve's skin as the cool water continued to drip from her body, and she felt a tiny insect land on her shoulder. She absently swatted at it, and it flew away with a buzz.

Maeve quickly looked back toward the spot where she'd seen the woman, but she was no longer there; evaporated like a mirage.

Still uncomfortable, she began putting her clothes back on.

Who is this woman? Why am I seeing her?

Am I going insane?

Chapter Nineteen

AFTER MIDDAY meal, Kelia paid a visit to the Room of Healing, where Lyala was brewing several herbal teas over a small fire. In addition to being a wonderful healer and apothecary, much like her mother Katura, she was also a master of tea-brewing, a job made much easier thanks to several kettles she'd procured on the second of her two Sojourns. Her first produced a daughter, Sershi, whose healing abilities seemed to improve with every season. On her second, however, she'd borne a son.

For Lyala, giving up her infant son to his father was extremely difficult, as it often was for Ixtrayu mothers who bore male children. It took a long time for her to accept it, but this had been the tribe's way since the days of Soraya. Lyala, unlike her mother, was quite delicate in disposition and in manner. She was tall and slender, with long, dark hair, narrow cheekbones and very little muscle on her frame. Sershi, if it was even possible, was even more willowy.

Kelia was glad to be informed that, thanks to Sershi's ministrations, Talya's leg was now healed, and she would resume her gathering duties immediately. Kelia thanked the two healers, chose two sachets of jingal-root tea from a table in the corner and placed them in a pouch on her belt before exiting.

She strode down the path toward the fields, heading for the section where the juva-berry bushes grew. It pleased her to see Nyla, deep in concentration as she maneuvered a ball of water three feet in diameter from the belly of the river. As Kelia watched, Nyla thrust her elbows outward, splaying her fingers. The water flattened and elongated into a straight line, moving steadily over its target: a nearly-ripe row of bushes. Nyla then clapped her hands together, and the ribbon burst into a fine mist, which rained down in small droplets upon the bushes.

Kelia was all smiles as she closed the distance between herself and Nyla, who finally noticed her. "Mother! Did you see that? Did you see what I did?" She was practically jumping for joy.

"I saw," Kelia said, giving her daughter a brief hug. "That was quite impressive. I don't think I could have done better myself."

Nyla beamed. "Thank you, Mama."

Kelia tapped Nyla lovingly on the chin with her thumb. Then she turned her attention to an attractive, fair-haired, blue-eyed young woman standing about five yards away. "You've done well, Yarji. Nyla's water-wielding abilities have never been better."

"Thank you, Protectress," she said, bowing. "I know sending her to me was meant as punishment, but ... " she glanced at Nyla, "... we've gotten along well. We've turned watering duty into a game, of sorts."

"Really?" Kelia quirked an eyebrow. "Who was the victor?"

Nyla raised her hand. Her grin still hadn't gone away.

Kelia laughed. "Well, then, it seems you've found a duty you enjoy. If you like, you may keep doing it."

Nyla cast a glance at Yarji. "What do you say? Think you can beat me next time?"

"Let's find out," Yarji replied with a half-grin, half-glare.

Kelia produced the two sachets of tea from her belt and handed them to Yarji. "Here. Two bags of jingal-root tea. The perfect remedy for fatigue."

Yarji took the tea, and her face became sad. "I've—I've been meaning to apologize, Protectress. When the fire started, I should have been the first one to react. But I ... I panicked. It all happened so fast. Thank Arantha you came along."

"What of the bushes themselves? Were they destroyed?"

"Not completely, Protectress. The berries were consumed by the fire, but the roots remain. With luck, they will bear fruit again by this time next year."

Kelia nodded. "That is good."

"So ... am I forgiven?" Nyla asked.

"You are forgiven, duma. Both of you are forgiven." She placed a hand on Nyla's shoulder. "One more hour, and then back to Liana for your history lesson. All right?"

"Yes, mama," Nyla said. "Where are you going?"

She gestured down the path alongside the river to the tree line, where the expansive forest began. "To the clearing. Runa said she had something to show me." She faced Nyla again. "Keep up the good work. See you at evening meal."

As Kelia walked away, her mouth morphed into a radiant, maternal smile.

* * *

Over the next several hours, Kelia walked the length and breadth of the Ixtrayu's territory, speaking to many tribe members as part of her daily routine. Many of them smiled and bowed respectfully in greeting, but there was an underlying tension in the air, which she attributed to the escalating concern over the Sojourns. Other than that, though, all was well: the fruit and grain crops were proliferating, they had enough preserved kova meat to last them three months, and Nyla had apparently found something to occupy her time that she enjoyed more than studying scrolls or causing mayhem.

As the sun began its descent below the crest of the plateau, Kelia decided to bathe herself in the cistern. The water was, again, as warm as the dry air, but she was able to cool it down so she and several of her sisters could enjoy a nice cool bath as the afternoon came to an end.

Having done up her hair into a simple braid and donned a clean robe, Kelia trod the southern path leading back to the village. Suddenly thirsty, she contemplated returning to the apothecary for another sachet of tea to go along with her evening meal. As she passed the entrance to the cave where the Stone was housed, however, she stopped.

She shuddered, ever so slightly, as a wave of strange energy rippled through her. Facing the cave entrance, she noticed the faintest of glows emanating from within.

As the only living Ixtrayu—apart from, eventually, Nyla, she presumed—with the gift of foresight, the Stone usually only became luminescent when she laid her hands upon it or when she was near enough to do so. The Stone had not glowed on its own during Kelia's entire reign as Protectress. In fact, it had only occurred once in Onara's lifetime.

Several years before Kelia was born, a monstrous sandstorm—the most violent in Ixtrayu history—blew in from the desert. The Stone warned Onara only hours before the storm hit. The food packed into the plateau's storage room survived, but most of the crops were destroyed. Two Ixtrayu and three chavas lost their lives.

Kelia walked, mesmerized, into the cave, making her way over to the pedestal of rock that formed the base upon which the Stone sat. The glow intensified with every step she took, illuminating the cave in a gentle white hue. Her breath caught in her throat.

Arantha is calling to me. Could this ... could this be the moment where she reveals the answer we've been waiting for?

Stepping forward, she recited a brief prayer: "I bask in your divine presence, O Arantha, for I am your humble servant." Then she clasped her hands around the Stone, and the light radiating from within it became so bright, she was forced to close her eyes. She also felt the Stone become warm, almost hot, as images poured into her mind.

The first images, though blurred at the edges, were familiar, as she felt herself gliding across the desert floor, faster than any animal could run, faster than any bird could fly, towards the Kaberian Mountains. As with her previous vision, she reached the base of the easternmost peak and then soared upward, flying low over the hills and valleys of this inhospitable, largely unexplored region.

After a few moments, she spied the same mountain lake she saw that morning. Her heart pounded as she approached the threshold, the farthest she'd ever gone. At long last, the nature of the object she'd witnessed from the western outcropping would be revealed to her.

She cleared another peak, and then her speed slowed as she glided down to ground level. The sight was breathtaking, marred only by the same crunching, grinding noise she'd heard before.

The mountain lake lay beneath her, clear blue water lapping against the rocky walls of the enormous basin that held it. As picturesque as it was, however, it was what lay near the western edge of the lake that stole Kelia's attention.

A short distance from the lake were a table and two chairs, right next to two square-shaped devices whose function she couldn't begin to imagine. Further away, nestled between two peaks, sitting on a riverbed that looked to have gone dry centuries ago, was ... she didn't have words to describe it. It was gigantic. Black and silver in color, it resembled a bird. An enormous bird, to be sure: it had to be almost a hundred feet from end to end.

And it was made of metal. *Metal.* Forging ten thousand longswords would require less metal than this object.

Great Arantha. This thing . . . did *come from the Above. It must have.*

Kelia considered for a moment that the thing might be alive. After all, who knew what form beings from the Above might take? Still, the thing did not appear to be moving, and as her vision brought her even closer, she saw someone exit the belly of the thing and walk towards the mouth of a nearby cave.

This . . . person—for it appeared to have the size and shape of an Elystran—was tall, with pale skin that looked like it bore a rather unhealthy sunburn. Its hair was long, dark red in color, and its clothes were unusual. It wore neither robes nor a tunic, but dark pants of a material she'd never seen before, and a loose-fitting white shirt.

The vision shifted slightly, and Kelia caught her first sight of the mysterious being's face.

It was a man.

No, not a man; a boy. His face was youthful, freckled and handsome. She guessed that he could be no more than a year or two older than Nyla, assuming his kind aged the same way Elystrans did. And he looked to be quite tall, almost as tall as Runa.

She followed the boy as he neared the mouth of the cave. He smiled as a second person exited, wearing a blue outfit that hugged her body from the neck down. From her face, she appeared to be considerably older than the boy. They exchanged a few words as they neared each other, but Kelia couldn't hear them. The boy pointed at his face, and the woman laughed and gave him a hug and a kiss on the cheek. The boy's mother, perhaps?

The woman stripped the blue outfit off of her body and handed it to the boy, who immediately stepped into it, putting it on over his own clothes. To Kelia's amazement, the fabric seemed to stretch to fit his frame as perfectly as it did the woman's. The pair exchanged a few more words, and then the boy disappeared into the cave. A few moments later, the grinding, crunching sound resumed.

What are they doing? Why have they come to Elystra? Are there others?

Kelia watched as the woman approached the lake. Her face looked haggard, exhausted. When she reached the water's edge, she unfastened the belt at her waist and tugged her pants down. Then, using both hands, she peeled off her sleeveless, tight black shirt, baring her breasts.

Even though the woman resembled that of an Elystran female in every noticeable way, her body was quite unlike any Kelia had ever seen. Her arms, her back, her torso, even her breasts bore strange bird designs drawn upon her very skin. She also had numerous scars marring her voluptuous frame, the largest being a diagonal-shaped scar, a hand-span in length, on her back and shoulder blade. It made Kelia wince to see it. And her hair ... it was purple, a deeper purple than even the wildflowers that grew in the forest.

The woman dipped her toe into the water, testing the temperature. She then removed her final undergarment and sprinted into the water, diving in head-first after a few paces. A few seconds later she emerged again with a smile on her face.

Kelia felt her breath become shallow. This woman was fascinating. Beautiful. Exotic.

As Kelia watched, the woman ran her hands over her breasts, fondling them.

Kelia felt her heart start to pound as desirous thoughts flooded her mind. Unable to contain it, a deep, cleansing, almost wanton breath escaped Kelia's lungs.

In that same instant, though, the woman's smile vanished. With a look of dismay, she cast her eyes skyward.

Kelia followed her gaze, but saw nothing. She then glanced at the alien woman again, and was shocked to see that she was no longer looking upward.

The woman was staring directly at her.

Though she was still locked within her vision, Kelia felt her hands shaking.

No. The woman couldn't be looking at her. It was impossible. And yet, the woman's gaze remained fixed in her direction. Kelia saw utter surprise on her face, which gently morphed into one of ... recognition?

And just like that, the vision ended. Kelia removed her hands from the Stone, breathing heavily as the light within diminished and faded. She was distressed to find her whole body was trembling and her face was drenched with sweat.

Suddenly unsteady on her feet, she sat down on a ledge of rock a few paces away from the Stone.

She saw me.

This woman ... saw me.

How is this possible?

Chapter Twenty

As HE made his way to the main courtyard, Mizar pondered the ramifications of Sen's findings and how it all tied into the events of the past few days.

The morning after Zendak's arrival, Aridor dispatched Prince Warran, along with a full contingent of soldiers, to relay the wounded Agrusian prince's message to King Largo, who ruled Darad's nearest neighbor, Imar. Word reached Mizar that a messenger had returned early that morning with a letter from Warran stating that Largo was requesting a meeting with Aridor so they could discuss strategies for dealing with Elzor and the female Wielder. Viceroy Callis of Barju had also been summoned to explain how Elzor could create an army without him knowing.

As for Zendak himself, thanks to Sen and the court physician, his condition had improved to the point where he was no longer in pain, but he would bear the scars of his encounter with the female Wielder for the rest of his life. That, along with the knowledge that his homeland had been invaded and his family butchered, made Mizar wonder if the poor man would ever recover.

By the time Mizar reached the courtyard, the space was filled with merychs, saddled and shoed, upon which fifteen members of the King's personal guard sat. They were all decked out in full battle gear, leather armor covering their bodies from neck to shins, with longswords dangling at their sides and shields slung over their backs.

Taking care not to step on anything malodorous, he sidled through the throng until he spied Aridor. The King was giving Queen Belena a warm kiss, causing Mizar to turn away, feeling guilty at having invaded their privacy. Only a moment later, the couple parted and Belena, with only a respectful nod and a smile to Mizar as she passed, walked regally past the riders and through an interior door.

Mizar turned his attention back to Aridor. At that moment, he flashed back to the day the two of them met for the first time, the day his life changed completely.

Sixteen-year-old Mizar, accompanied by his father, Deegan, made the two-day journey from Ghaldyn province to Mount Calabur in accordance with King Sardor's edict. Darad had been without a High Mage since the death of Merdeen fifty years prior, and though the kingdom was able to survive without the benefit of a High Mage in the interim, the rulers never stopped their search for another that might assume that role.

The entire Cavern thrummed with energy, which coursed through Mizar's veins like water through a conduit. When it was discovered that he could manipulate the elements—air, earth, fire and water—he was vigorously trained to take his place at the side of Aridor's father, King Armak. There were none alive to teach him the art of Wielding, but Armak provided many instructors to help him strengthen himself both mentally and physically in order to facilitate controlling his fledgling abilities.

Saying goodbye to Deegan was difficult and tearful. With no siblings, Mizar worried that his father wouldn't be able to maintain the family farm. King Armak, however, generously allowed Mizar to provide his father with more than enough coin to compensate for his absence, and when Deegan became too infirm to manage, Mizar's two cousins graciously moved their families to the farm to take over for him.

Aridor was a lad of ten when Mizar first met him, a stout-hearted boy determined to prove himself worthy at every turn: practicing swordplay, archery and merychship until he dropped from exhaustion. He grew to be a warrior of monumental repute, and was right alongside King Armak when they won the final battle against the lawless region of Vanda; a battle that, sadly, Armak did not survive.

Since assuming the throne, Aridor had reigned with a firm yet just hand, hammering out trade agreements with the neighboring kingdoms of Imar, Barju and Agrus. Darad was rich in precious metals and crop-producing farmland, it enjoyed a healthy population of cattle, and it boasted the largest and best-trained army on Elystra, ten thousand strong. Their borders had not been encroached upon, and Aridor's sovereignty had not been challenged, in decades.

In the blink of an eye, Mizar's ominous vision of death and devastation returned to his thoughts. Though he'd experienced hundreds of visions, most of them were mild, almost innocuous. Since that fateful day nearly four decades ago, he'd been High Mage of a country that hardly needed one.

Until now.

"Mizar," Aridor said, striding over. "I am leaving to meet with King Largo. I expect to return in ten days. Possibly longer, knowing how much that old windbag likes to hear himself speak."

"Yes, sire," Mizar replied with a surreptitious grin. "Who will be in charge during your absence?"

"I sent word to Prince Agedor, who is commanding our forces along the southern border. He will be returning later today."

Mizar's jaw twitched. Unlike Warran, Prince Agedor's arrogance was often difficult to deal with. "Do you not wish me to accompany you, sire?"

"I appreciate the offer, old friend, but your presence in Imar would likely do more harm than good. Viceroy Callis has never been adept at hiding his jealousy that the path to Arantha lies within our borders and not his. Not to mention your ... other limitation."

They locked eyes, not speaking. After a few moments, Mizar nodded again. "Understood, sire."

"Did this morning's consultation give you any more insight as to what travails we might face in the near future?"

"Regrettably not, sire. Though the images did not cause me the same distress as before, they were no less opaque. I made it a point to try to deduce which villages were the sites of the massacre I saw, but it was no use. I then tried to concentrate on the female Wielders, hoping to gain some insight as to their identities."

The King waved to a nearby servant, who came forth and fastened a thick black cloak emblazoned with the Daradian emblem around his neck and shoulders. He tugged the clasp into place just below his Adam's apple. "And?"

Mizar exhaled. "As before, there were two women standing together, facing the third. The light that clothed the two was bright and warm, and it completely obscured their faces. The third, however, I saw much more clearly. Her appearance matches that of the Wielder Prince Zendak ran afoul of: tall, slender, with long dark hair. Her countenance was one of pure malice, as was the blue energy that sparked and crackled around her."

"Elzaria," Aridor said knowingly.

"Sire?"

"Her name is Elzaria. Several refugees from Agrus sought sanctuary in Barju. With most of the Barjan militia in shambles thanks to Elzor, Callis has had his Black Guard close his borders until further notice."

This did not surprise Mizar in the least. The Barjan ruler's penchant for paranoia was common knowledge among the royals. Elzor's defection, to some degree, seemed to justify that paranoia. Even so, to bar refugees from entering his country was cold, even for him.

Aridor continued, "Thankfully, he had the foresight to send his own envoy to Imar to inform them of Agrus's fall. The mastermind behind the invasion was indeed Elzor, a former captain in the Barjan militia. Elzaria is his twin sister."

Mizar averted his eyes, staring at the throng of soldiers attempting to keep their merychs still as they awaited the order to move out. "I don't suppose these refugees were able to shed some light on the nature of the fe ... of Elzaria's power."

Aridor shook his head. "I'm afraid not. I have also heard that the army Elzor commands is not large, barely six hundred men, though I am loath to trust that number. Regardless, there is no way they could stand against the combined might of Darad, Imar and Barju."

"Your Highness –"

Aridor held his hand up. "I will not underestimate the power of this Wielder, I assure you. The Agrusian army, though skilled and well-trained, was caught off guard. We will not make the same mistake."

He waved at a waiting stable boy, who brought forth Aridor's mount: a tall gray merych with a patch of white hair on its forehead that closely resembled a sword. In one motion, Aridor placed his foot in one stirrup and swung his body over the beast's back. Grasping the reins, he turned to face Mizar again. "Accelerate your studies. Whatever knowledge lies locked within Merdeen's scribblings, you have until I return to find it."

"Yes, sire." Mizar bowed his head. "If I may, I would ask permission for my apprentice and I to travel to Ghaldyn once our studies are complete."

Aridor fixed his High Mage with a steely glare. "We may be on the brink of war, Mizar. Now is not the time to surrender to homesickness."

"With respect, sire," Mizar said, unblinking, "My father has been unwell for some time now. If dark days are indeed ahead of us, this may be my last chance to see him." Not to mention, it would keep him from having to deal with Prince Agedor, who had never approved of his ascension to High Mage given his common upbringing, but he didn't want to admit this to Aridor.

The King considered this for a few moments, rubbing his bearded chin with his thumb and forefinger. "Very well. But you'd better be back by the time I return. I strongly suspect my mood will not be as jovial as it is now."

Without waiting for a response, Aridor shouted, "Open the gate!"

Three men drew the wooden plank from its housings and two others pulled the giant doors open. As the morning sun poured in through the entrance, Aridor kicked his merych's flanks, and it immediately bolted through the opening, his personal guards kicking their mounts into motion and following right behind.

Chapter Twenty-One

D AVIN WORKED two shifts on the excavator, and Maeve decided to take another nap after they finished lunch and she gave herself another shot of pain-blocker. At the rate she was using the stuff up, they would run out in a week, perhaps ten days. If it was this energy source that was causing her headaches, they needed to find it and get it into a containment unit before it killed her. *Thank the Saints there doesn't seem to be any radiation.*

With the sun beginning to set, Maeve pulled two bowls of stew from the synthesizer and set one in front of Davin, right next to his cup of water. He immediately started eating, making a satisfied face after the first spoonful. "Oh my God, thank you. After two shifts in that damn tunnel, this is what I need." He licked his lips. "Did you program it to add extra thyme?"

"Of course," Maeve said. "Just like Grandma used to."

He took another heaping spoonful. "Thanks, Mom," he said around a mouthful of potatoes.

She took a similarly large bite. "No problem. How's your head?"

"It's okay, I guess. Not as bad as yours, thank God. The blockers still working?"

"Yeah. I may need one more dose before I start night watch. Any luck with the PT's?"

Davin spent most of his free time trying to fix the personal transporters, but so far without much luck. "Not yet. And if I'm being honest, I don't know what else I can do. But something else occurred to me today."

"What?"

"Well, Banikar sent us here to find something that will help us defeat the Jegg, right?"

"Right."

"The PT's are Jegg technology, and the closer we seem to get to this energy source, the more it seems to affect them negatively. Which makes me think we're on the right track after all."

Maeve nodded. "That makes sense. At least we didn't come all this way for nothing." She took a swig from her cup. "Now all we need to do is find the bloody stuff. Of course, with good news comes bad news."

"Yeah," Davin said gloomily. "How're we gonna get back home if we can't use the quantigraphic rift drive? Even if we had the fuel, it would take a hundred years to get home using the supralight engines."

"Ninety-seven years, three months, fourteen days," Maeve said.

Davin chuffed under his breath. "Oh, well, that's *much* better. I wonder if there'll be anything left of the Terran Confederation by the time we get there."

"One problem at a time, Dav," she said before tilting her bowl up to her mouth, draining the last few scraps of stew. "So far, everything Banikar told your father has been correct."

"Mmm hmm. Wish he could've thrown in a bit about dealing with the local wildlife." He looked thoughtful. "I was wondering: do you think taking a turn on the excavator after sunset would be worth it? We would increase our productivity, and the cave is pretty well lit. The noise might even keep them away."

"That's true, but one of us would still have to keep watch all the time. Think you're up to another round on that thing?"

"Sure. We can take turns until one of us needs to sleep."

"Sounds like a plan."

Maeve deposited the empty bowl and spoon into the synthesizer's drawer and stood up. "Sun's about to set. I'm going to check the sensors, make sure everything's still functioning."

"Okay. I'm going to take a dip before we lose the light."

"Make it quick. Be right back." She activated the PT and tapped the console on her arm. It was a crapshoot whether it would work or not, but if it saved time, it was worth it. She relaxed slightly when she heard the familiar whir, and just like that, she was gone, transporting down to the far end of the wadi.

They still hadn't had a visual of the beasts, and Maeve was grateful for that. She made it a point to make sure the sensors at this location were a hundred percent operational. If an attack was going to come, it would most likely come via the riverbed, as the mountain lake was a bottle-neck with only one way out. The only other way in would involve an eighty-foot jump from the rim of the basin. She couldn't imagine any animal, alien or otherwise, escaping that fall uninjured.

She checked each of the five sensors, and they were all working properly. Farther back were some powerful floodlights, which were programmed to activate if the sensors picked up any movement at all.

Directly west of the wadi was another enormous mountain, taller than any in the vicinity, and Maeve looked up to see the Castelan sun nearly completing its descent. If the PT didn't cooperate, she would have to leave now to make it back to the *Talon* before the wadi was completely dark.

She hadn't taken two steps back toward the camp when the floodlights suddenly activated, illuminating the rocky riverbed. Just as she turned to face in that direction, she heard another sound. A deep, guttural growl. And then another. And another.

Maeve's breath caught in her throat as three dark, sleek shapes sprang from the shadows, each landing on four enormous paws about a hundred yards away.

The sirens blared into raucous life, causing Maeve to clap her hands over her ears. The beasts took a half-step back, but they didn't run away. Instead, they continued their march forward. Towards her, towards Davin.

Maeve's battle-hardened nerves barely held together as, for the first time, she beheld the creatures whose territory they'd invaded. Sharp, pointed ears jutted from a narrow, tapered skull ending in a black nose. Beneath their noses were mouths that bore some nasty-looking fangs that could rip the flesh from her bones in a heartbeat. But more fearsome than their savage appearance was their size. Though they resembled feral wolves, they were the size of lions.

Shite.

Doing her best to ignore the siren, she activated the PT device, stabbing furiously at the console. This time, however, she heard no whir, felt no field of energy surround her. She cast a quick glance at the console screen, which bore the words "Transport Failed."

Double shite.

Maeve stabbed at the console several more times, but the PT obstinately refused to activate. Panic rising, she drew her pistol from its holster and took aim at the nearest creature, who she guessed to be the pack leader. She hated to kill a wild animal merely defending its home, but it was either her or it. Maybe she'd just wound it, and that would be enough to chase it away.

She pulled the trigger. Nothing happened.

She pulled again. Still nothing.

Jammed.

Are you farking kidding me?

With no other options, she turned on her heel and sprinted back to the camp as fast as her legs could carry her.

She felt more than heard the creatures following her. If the video images she saw were any indication, they would catch her long before she reached the ship.

She was about halfway back when she heard one of the floodlights topple and shatter behind her, obviously knocked over by one of the creatures. They were after her, all right. And if they caught her, they would go after Davin next.

No.

She didn't dare turn around. She had to run. She had to keep running. If by some miracle she made it to the *Talon*, and the box next to the exit-ramp that held the concussion grenades, she'd teach these creatures a thing or two.

Only fifty yards away. Fifty yards to safety. Could she possibly make it?

Her heart, which felt like it was going to burst from the long, panic-fueled sprint, lifted when she saw Davin cross her field of vision. He'd reached the *Talon*'s ramp, and was rifling through the box, no doubt looking for a grenade to throw.

The growling noises were close, and Maeve imagined the wolf-creatures were within pouncing distance behind her. She heard the sound of their padded paws as they connected with the dirt. They were close. Too close.

She wasn't going to make it.

Ignoring her instincts, she turned her head to glance behind her, but before she could discern how far away she was from certain death, she felt a massive paw swipe at her back. Its claws grazed her skin, and she felt the back of her tank top being torn away. The sudden shift in momentum caused her to trip over a rock that protruded up from the dry riverbed. Unable to right herself, she pitched headfirst onto the dirt, hitting the ground with a thud that knocked the breath from her body.

Immediately, she turned over onto her back, silently praying to every Saint she could think of that she would somehow survive the next few minutes.

"Mom!" Davin cried from behind her.

Then, the largest of the creatures sprang, straddling her body with its enormous frame, knocking the gun from her hand. She locked eyes with the thing. It had dark, savage eyes, tinged yellow by the miniscule light provided from the lamps set up around the encampment. Saliva dripped from its fangs as it hungrily eyed its next meal.

Fear gripped Maeve's heart, forcing its way through her chest and up into her brain.

As a pilot, she'd faced death many times. She'd conquered her fear then, but this was different. She wasn't afraid of dying so much as she feared she'd led her own son, the only thing she had left in this universe, to his doom as well. And with their deaths, humanity's last hope died with them.

No. It can't end like this.

Unable to escape her fate, she stared into the creature's lupine face.

We mean you no harm, she thought at them, hoping they could understand her. *Please don't kill us.*

Please.

Don't.

Kill.

Us.

She closed her eyes, waiting for the creature to end her life, to rip her throat out with its massive fangs and feast on her flesh and bones.

Moments passed, and the beasts' snarls faded to a low rumble. She felt the creature back away, lifting its massive weight off of her.

"Mom!" she heard Davin scream from behind her.

"Stay back, Dav!" she hollered at him. "Don't come any closer!"

She opened one eye, then the other, and lifted her head.

The giant wolf-thing was sitting down on the dusty ground, several yards away. Its two pack-mates were also sitting, their forepaws held together in front of them. They were no longer snarling or growling. They were just ... staring at her. Like obedient dogs, awaiting their master's command.

What the farking fark?

She gingerly climbed to her feet. They hadn't moved a muscle.

Did they hear me? Understand me?

These creatures could have killed her. They *should* have killed her. But they didn't. Why?

Maybe...

Every instinct told her to run away and get herself and her son to safety, but something else, something deeper, told her to do the exact opposite.

She took a cautious step forward, then another, and then another.

"Mom, what are you doing?" Davin screamed.

She turned to see him, grenade in hand, about ten yards away from the nose of the *Talon*. His hand was on the pin, ready to pull it and toss the grenade in their direction at a moment's notice.

"Stay back," she called, as calmly as she could.

"Mom –"

"I said, *stay back!*"

He nodded, but didn't take his finger away from the pin.

Turning her attention back to the wolf-things, she inched her way toward the leader, which was now near enough for her to touch. Moving as non-threateningly as possible, she reached out her right hand. She waited for the creature to pull back, to bare its teeth, to snarl at her. But it didn't.

Her fingertips made contact with the beast's head, and Maeve was surprised at how soft it was: much softer than the fur of a creature living in the wilderness should be. It still hadn't moved. It just watched her, with those big, unblinking yellow eyes. Eyes that no longer looked vicious or feral.

As she laid her palm upon the creature's forehead, she felt a surge of energy rush through her. It was like adrenaline, but not quite. In a flash, she felt the sensation of running, faster than any human being could run. She felt hunger, hunger that could only be sated by the meat of other living animals. She felt warmth, as it fed its young.

This creature was a female. With pups of its own.

How did I know that?

Somehow, she'd bonded with it. On some level, she'd become one with it.

It listened to her.

It obeyed her.

"We mean you no harm," she said, barely above a whisper.

If she expected a vocal answer, she didn't get one. The wolf-thing merely lowered its head, as if in acknowledgment.

"You are hunters. Go hunt somewhere else."

The creature lifted its head and locked eyes with her again. Then, quite unexpectedly, it stood up, turned around and bounded away, back down the wadi. The other two beasts immediately rose to their feet and followed their leader.

She watched them go, and within moments, the darkness swallowed them up. A few seconds later, the sirens ceased their droning wail.

Maeve's heart felt like it was going to jump right out of her chest. She barely felt it when Davin came up from behind her, putting his hand on her arm.

"Mom, are you all right?"

She placed her hand on his, drawing strength from his touch. Calming herself by breathing through her nose, she nodded. "I'm all right."

He stared into the darkness as well. The soft pads of the creatures' paws upon the ground had faded into nothingness. "What just happened?"

Maeve was at a loss. "I–I don't know. It–it spoke to me, somehow. Or it listened to me. I have no idea." She noticed that the left strap of her tank top had been torn off, and became aware that her shoulder blade now ached, more and more as the adrenaline rush wore off. The creature's claws hadn't just grazed her after all. Her mouth opened in pain, and she let out a yelp.

"You're bleeding, Mom," said Davin, surveying the damage.

"It's just a scratch. I thought it would be much worse."

"No shite. You have a gash. It's small, but it looks deep. Let's get that taken care of."

With his arm around her, they made their way back to the ship. After sitting her down on the exit-ramp and placing the grenade back into its box, Davin ran inside to fetch the med-kit. He was back in seconds, sitting next to her.

"Mom, I never thought I'd say this, but ... take your shirt off."

Too stunned to even make a snarky comeback, she turned her back to him and pulled off the remains of her tank top, using the tattered fabric to cover up her bare breasts. "How bad does it look? Did it get any of my birds?"

He checked. "You lucked out. It missed your spotted owl by about an inch."

"That's good," she breathed. "Guess if I have to have another scar, it might as well be on my back. It won't look out of place with all the others."

Davin cleaned her wound and applied their antiseptic salve. She waited for him to put on a dermaplast bandage, which would regrow the skin and prevent infection. But it appeared he'd stopped.

"Dav, what's wrong?"

When he didn't answer, she turned to face him. His eyes were wide, and his jaw hung open. She'd never seen him looking so shocked. "Dav?"

He closed his mouth with a loud gulp. "It's your scars."

Her eyebrows raised. "What about them?"

"They're ..." He trailed off, too dumbfounded to even finish his sentence.

"They're *what*?"

Davin shook his head in incredulity. "They're gone."

Chapter Twenty-Two

ELZARIA STRETCHED out on the former Queen's bed, reveling in the comfort it brought her. She'd slept most of the week since they conquered Talcris, and Elzor had not objected. She replenished her power somewhat by holding her Stone, but her body needed rest after expending so much energy, and there was no substitute for restful slumber in that regard. Every now and then, a terrified servant came by to drop off a tray laden with food and drink for her. After relieving them of their burden, she dismissed them with a condescending wave.

She smiled as she bathed in her memories of decimating the Agrusian army. Seeing so many heavily-armored, sword-wielding men rendered immobile by the energy she commanded was something she would always remember. It reminded her of the day she used her abilities for the first time.

Her and Elzor's father was an ogre of a man. Once, in a drunken stupor, he told them their mother was a selfish whore who tried to escape his clutches when she was still pregnant with them. She would always recall his smile when he regaled them with the story of how he cut her throat immediately after she gave birth to them. Elzaria exhaled in disgust at the memory.

The only person who ever showed them kindness was a man named Ramson. While their father worked in the mines, Elzor and Elzaria spent their days at Ramson's smithy, where he forged all sorts of items from machinite ore: weapons, armor, merychs' shoes, and more. They would help him do his chores, and in return, he not only gave them food, but he also taught them to read. He even gave Elzor his first lesson in swordplay.

When they were eight years old, however, disease swept through their village of Orme, killing half its residents, including their father and Ramson. With no other living relatives, they were relegated to an orphanage in the nearby town of Bruck. They spent four miserable years there, their only hope being that when they came of age, Elzor would become an apprentice blacksmith and earn enough coin to take care of both himself and her. *Such are the dreams of children.*

Though Barjan law stated that children under the age of fourteen could not be forced into crushing servitude, there were many who flouted this law with impunity. Just before their thirteenth birthday, Elzor and Elzaria were sold to a mining foreman named Rogin, one of the most brutal and repulsive individuals to ever walk the face of Elystra.

The Mogran mining camp was run much like a prison. Most of its labor force consisted of the orphaned, the downtrodden, the unwanted. They were forced to live in deplorable conditions and barely given enough food to perform their duties, which was to mine for machinite ore. Two-thirds of those sent to Mogran died within a year.

When they first arrived, they quickly learned it was safer to keep their heads down and ignore everyone around them. Workers dropped dead from exhaustion, malnutrition, and disease on a daily basis, and those that attempted escape were tracked down and whipped to death in front of everyone, usually by Rogin himself.

Countless times, Elzaria wanted to give up, to surrender to death, reasoning that whatever lay beyond the Great Veil had to be better than what they were forced to endure here, but Elzor possessed an inner strength she never had. Whenever one of the bigger boys tried to steal their meager helping of food, he fought them off. She remembered one instance when he actually snapped the neck of a boy nearly twice his size. The rest of the workers left him alone after that.

There were times, however, that even Elzor's strength wasn't enough to protect them. One of Rogin's favorite hobbies, apart from getting drunk on manza cider, was having his way with the female workers, and for him, the younger the better.

Remembering the several instances when Rogin dragged her into his quarters made her skin crawl. He was a large, pot-bellied man, whose stink alone was enough to make her gag. When he was on top of her, inside her, all she could do was close her eyes and pray for death.

For two years, they survived this horrific routine. And still, Elzor refused to give up. His will to survive remained steadfast. He seemed to draw strength from his anger, his hatred for all that had led them to this place. He hated their father for dying, their mother for letting herself be slaughtered, and Rogin for stealing the innocence of children to satiate his own drunken lust.

Ramson tried to teach them as children that Arantha watched over all of Elystra and protected the righteous. By the time Elzor and Elzaria turned fourteen, however, they'd renounced all of their former mentor's beliefs. No benevolent deity would allow such atrocities to flourish. They could only depend on themselves.

One day, deep in the mine, they snuck away during a rest period. Elzaria had grown ever more frail and sickly, and Elzor decided that the time had come to attempt escape. With only a small lantern in hand, they followed a closed-off shaft that had been mined out. Elzor had overheard a whispered rumor among the workers that this particular tunnel led up to the surface, a hidden exit from the mountain. He had no idea if the rumor was true, but he and Elzaria were out of options.

They followed the passage for about half an hour when Elzaria collapsed, clutching her head in pain. Elzor had to clamp his hand over her mouth to prevent her from screaming, as its echo would likely be heard all the way to the surface. The pain eventually overwhelmed her, and she lost consciousness.

When she woke, though, she felt rejuvenated. Where her sudden strength came from she had no idea at the time, but as Elzor guided her farther up the shaft, she felt her pain recede. They reached a steep rock-face, twenty feet high, that they needed to climb to continue. And climb they did. Elzaria, much to Elzor's amazement, scaled the wall in no time.

After helping him up onto a flat ledge, they rested. They couldn't wait for long, though; they had neither food nor water, and their lantern would soon burn out. They had no way of knowing how close they were to the surface, and the only path left to follow was a narrow tube just wide enough to accommodate their thin frames.

They crawled, foot by foot, up the tube. Twenty minutes later, their lantern went out, plunging them into darkness. Elzaria began to sob, but Elzor kept her moving. Her newfound strength was ebbing, but he staunchly refused to let her give up.

For hours more they climbed in total blackness, until they lost all sense of time and place. And then disaster struck again, as they felt the entire mountain tremble.

Tremors were common in Barju, and though most of them did little more than shake a few layers of dust from the ceiling, this one was far worse. Dozens of tiny pebbles and chunks of stone rained down, but just as it felt like the entire mountain would collapse on them, the shaking stopped.

The two of them huddled together, breathing in the thick, stale air, coughing and choking on the dust. When they lifted their heads, they had to blink their eyes from the light pouring down the shaft. It took them several moments to realize the light wasn't coming from the sun. It was coming from a small, fist-sized lump of stone that had fallen from the roof of the shaft and now lay, illuminating them in an eerie blue light.

Mesmerized, Elzaria crawled forward and grasped the stone tightly in her hands. Within moments, her body was wracked with an indescribable pain, as power the likes of which she could never have conceived coursed through her. Through the pain, though, Elzaria felt something come over her: a knowledge that she would be safe. She was given a gift, a gift she would use to escape their vile prison.

With a stupefied Elzor behind her and the stone's blue glow lighting their way, they were able to make their way to the surface. They had to push through a series of narrow openings and tear through some gnarled roots and scrubby bushes, but they'd never been more relieved in their lives than when they tasted fresh air.

It was pitch dark outside, and they were a good distance away from the camp, so they did the only thing they could think of: make a break for it through the forest. Elzor had to tear off his shirt and wrap it around the stone lest it become a beacon for their captors to see. Eventually, they emerged into a small clearing, starving and dehydrated. The surge of strength the stone gave her had waned, and they collapsed on a patch of grass on the edge of the clearing.

They woke to find rough hands twisting their arms behind their backs by several large men whom Elzaria recognized as Rogin's hired thugs. Once bound, the thugs threw them into the back of a merych-drawn cart and drove them straight back to Mogran.

Rogin was quite pleased to see them. Smiling his broken smile, he promised to torture Elzor to death in front of her, right before cutting her throat. First, though, he planned to have his way with her one last time.

With Elzor bound and gagged in the corner of Rogin's bedroom, the sadistic foreman started by smacking Elzaria's face so hard the redness was easy to see in the dim light against the paleness of her skin. Then, holding her down, he used a knife to cut her clothes off, one piece at a time. As she lay naked on the floor, sobbing, with her brother powerless to do anything but watch, Rogin stood over her, his eyes flitting between her body and the stone they found.

He rolled it around his grimy, meaty hands, puzzled as to what it was and what it was doing inside a machinite mine. For it certainly was not machinite. It was like nothing he'd ever seen before. "Oh, the coin I'll fetch for such a rare and precious item!" he boasted.

As he continued to fondle the stone, dreaming his squalid dreams of wealth and power, Elzaria felt her strength grow again, and a surge of energy pulsed through her weakened body. The stone's glow returned, dim at first but with increasing intensity, and with it, the power within her began to manifest.

The blinding light forced Rogin to drop the Stone. It fell to the floor as he shielded his eyes. When he opened them again, they widened in terror as he beheld Elzaria, on her feet and surrounded by a field of crackling blue energy. Tiny bolts of lightning flew out from her naked body, randomly striking the walls of Rogin's cramped hovel. Elzor, out of self-preservation, curled into a fetal position to avoid the deadly discharges.

Elzaria couldn't remember exactly what she said, but all her hatred and pain and hopelessness poured through her at that moment. As if guided by an unseen force, she held out her hands in front of her. Rogin didn't have time to react before a massive bolt of lightning shot from her hands and into his body. The wispy strands of hair that remained on his head stood on end, his back arched and his arms and legs twitched in a dance of death. His mouth opened, but he couldn't even cry out.

Lightning continued to shoot from her body, striking the walls and ceiling. One bolt flew into a pile of dirty, grubby clothes Rogin had piled up in one corner of his bedroom, and within moments, they were ablaze. Elzaria obliviously kept her focus on Rogin, pouring surge after surge into his body until there was nothing left but a charred, twisted, smoking corpse. By the time she regained self-awareness and the power within her abated, one side of the room was on fire.

Thinking quickly, she used Rogin's knife to cut through Elzor's ropes. He ripped a filthy sheet off of Rogin's bed and wrapped it around her. They exited the hovel to be met by Rogin's gang of thugs: five loathsome men with pockmarked faces handpicked by Rogin for their greed and cruelty. Each man brandished a sword, and all were pointed at them.

Elzor immediately leaned in and whispered in Elzaria's ear, "Kill them, sister. Kill them all."

At his words, Elzaria's rage grew once again, and the blue crackling energy reappeared around her body. Without taking her eyes off the thugs, she whispered, "Take cover, brother."

Elzor, having backed away at the reappearance of the blue energy surrounding Elzaria, retreated around the one corner of Rogin's house that hadn't yet caught fire.

The looks of terror on the faces of Rogin's men fed her hunger, her desire for vengeance even more. They began to backpedal, and three of them even turned to run away. They had only taken a few steps before blue threads lanced out from Elzaria's hands, striking each man in turn. Their faces twisted in pain, their eyes rolled back into their heads, and they fell to the ground, dead.

Elzaria, consumed by the raw power that coursed through her, continued to emit the deadly energy. It was liberating. So much power to be controlled at her whim.

She turned left and then right, her dark eyes falling upon the buildings that made up the Mogran mining camp, the hellhole that had been their prison for two years. She hated every inch of it. It was a place of sorrow and despair; of torture, rape, and death. It was a blight upon the world, a scourge that had to be destroyed.

Yes, she remembered thinking. *I will destroy it. I will burn it to the ground. The smell of death will be so potent, all of Barju will retch. The scent of its very existence will mar the land for years to come.*

There were times when Elzaria regretted killing all of the workers that had slaved away in the Mogran mine, but she always dismissed these rueful thoughts. Those people, those pathetic people, were dead the moment they set foot in that place. They were lifeless souls, accepting their fate and doing nothing to change it. She did them all a favor by putting them out of their misery.

Only she and Elzor, along with one merych they used to escape, had survived Mogran. And now, nearly twenty years later, they were on the brink of omnipotence. Not once had she questioned his judgment in that time. He was the only one on Elystra who loved her. He protected her, cared for her, and kept her alive when she was inches from death.

Elzaria never had a problem deferring to her brother. He was cunning, charismatic, and ruthlessly intelligent. While she mastered her ability in secret, he joined the Barjan militia, covertly recruiting soldiers who would follow him. He raised an army that, with her help, would soon become the most feared army in Elystran history. And thus the Elzorath were conceived.

A loud knock on the door brought her back to the present. Only one person besides the servants dared disturb her while she was in this room, and the forcefulness of the knock dismissed any notion that it could be one of those mewling toadies. "Enter, my liege."

Elzaria heard the knob twist, and the door opened to reveal her brother, standing on the threshold. His face, usually so impassive, curled into a slight smile. "Sister, I've told you before, you need not refer to me by my title when it's only the two of us."

She sat up and swung her legs out of the bed, letting her feet slide into a pair of slippers. She stretched her back muscles as she stood. While she was doing this, Elzor crossed the room, grabbed a silken robe off of the former queen's massive clothes-chest, and moved to stand behind her.

"Thank you, brother," she said, slipping her arms into the robe and pulling it over the nightgown she looted from Turalda's closet. It felt good, wearing luxurious clothes, growing up wearing nothing but rags.

"Are you well rested?" Elzor asked.

"I am indeed. I do believe I'm strong enough to join you for supper, though with your permission, I would lay my hands upon the Stone one more time first."

With a quick glance at the metal box, about eighteen inches in length, that sat on Elzaria's night table, Elzor reached into a small pouch that hung from his belt and brought forth a key. He handed it to her with an exaggerated bow. "But of course."

She took the key with a bemused smile. "Any progress with the door?"

He sighed. "When we began our labors, progress was painfully slow. The rock is dense, and the door is nigh impregnable. Solid machinite." He gave a wry chuckle. "There are no machinite mines in Agrus. This must have come from Barju."

"How ironic that the metal from that door might have come from the same mine we toiled in as children, and now it blocks us from completing the next stage of our quest."

"At this rate, it will likely take us months to break through it. But I have found a way to speed things along."

"Oh?" She looked expectantly at him.

"Yesterday, I spent several hours in the royal apothecary's workshop, and I made a fortuitous discovery: it would seem that a combination of several ingredients can produce a substance known as sargonic acid. When applied correctly, it can eat away stone and corrode metal, even one as durable as machinite."

"That *is* indeed fortuitous."

He nodded. "Needless to say, I set the royal chemist to creating as much as he could straight away."

"He didn't object?"

"Not after I cut off two of his fingers," he said, smirking.

Something that had been bothering Elzaria occurred to her. "Elzor … what will we do if the Agrusian Stone is not behind that door?"

"I do not know," he said. "Many believe the Agrusian stone to be an unsubstantiated myth, a fiction created and upheld for centuries by the aristocracy. But I believe it exists. If it is not within the bowels of this castle, it is somewhere else. Someone must know of its location, and if I have to tear this world apart to find it, I will."

She put a hand on his arm. "What makes you so certain?"

"Just an instinct, dear sister. When we were slaves, I wanted nothing more than to destroy those who wield power they neither earned nor deserve, those who grow fat on the labors of others. Finding the Stone was an unexpected happenstance; it gave me an innate sense of purpose, a path to follow that I was previously unaware of." He met her gaze. "And it gave you the power to eliminate all who stand in our way."

"I hope it's enough," she said, almost to herself.

He gave her a withering look. "What does *that* mean?"

She bowed her head. "Forgive me, brother, but ... if I may speak plainly?"

He nodded.

"I have trusted your instincts my entire life," she said. "But by this time, word of our conquest will have spread to Imar and Darad. They will likely ally themselves with the Viceroy's forces and come looking for us. Their combined might would be formidable, brother, and I'm not sure I'm capable of defeating them on my own."

"Which is why it's imperative we locate the Agrusian stone with all due haste."

"Agreed, but I repeat: what if it's not here? Do we have the time and the resources to scour the length and breadth of Elystra before our enemies bring the battle to us?"

"Our path will take us where the fates lead us."

She quirked an eyebrow. "I didn't think you believed in such things."

He waved his hand dismissively. "Don't mistake my fervor for belief. Arantha may be a false deity, but that doesn't mean there aren't forces greater than ourselves influencing us. The fact that I'm standing in a room with the first female Wielder in Elystran history is proof enough of that."

"In that case, I hope those forces remain on our side. If the Prophecy is true, then we still have a long way to go before our quest is complete."

He closed his eyes briefly and smiled. "One thing at a time, sister." He turned with a whoosh of his cloak and headed for the door. "The servants have prepared a fine repast for our evening meal. You will join me once you are suitably refreshed and attired?"

"Of course."

"Then I will expect you shortly." Without looking back, he exited the room, closing the door behind him.

After Elzor's footsteps faded into nothingness, she stared down at the key in her hand. Moving over to her night table, she slid it into the keyhole of the ornate box that sat upon it. With a click of the tumbler, the lid popped open. There, on a bed of crushed velvet, was the Stone. Exposed to the light as well as her proximity, a blue glow began to emanate from within its depths, as if anticipating its imminent union with her.

She sat on the bed and reached for it. As she scooped it up with both hands, the soft glow increased to a blinding intensity. Energy more potent than she was prepared for poured into her, and her sight faded out as she retreated into her own mind.

All was dark. She wondered if she'd gone blind. Or mad. Or perhaps she had overestimated her strength, and the surge of power had killed her outright.

Then an image flashed through her mind. She saw Elystra from a great distance, as if she were floating high above the surface. She wasn't sure how she knew it was Elystra she was looking at; she just knew.

What's happening to me? Am I having a vision?

It was common knowledge that the High Mage of Darad, Mizar, was the only living Elystran to possess this ability. It had never happened to her. Until now.

Something sped by her, a fiery object streaking toward the surface, leaving an incandescent trail in its wake. And then another, and another, and another. She watched as they struck solid ground, hitting three different parts of the continent.

Before she could contemplate the meaning of what she just saw, her aspect changed. She was no longer looking at Elystra from high above, but from much closer to the ground. She skimmed the surface of the land, gliding across it like a low-flying bird. Miles of desert terrain flew by in a matter of seconds, and she beheld a vast mountain range looming in front of her.

Straight through the mountains she flew, her velocity not ebbing until she burst through the wall of a high rock-face. Below her was a serene mountain lake, surrounded on three sides by vertical cliffs. But her journey wasn't over yet. On the far side of the lake was –

Had she control over her body, she would have gasped in astonishment.

What ... is ... that?

* * *

An hour later, clad in her favorite emerald-green outfit, she made her way toward Castle Tynal's dining hall. She entered the large room to find Elzor, General Langon and several other high-ranking Elzorath finishing up their meal. Most of them were leaning back in their chairs, with one hand grasping a flagon of honey mead and the other on their full bellies.

As she approached her brother, she saw out of her peripheral vision several of his men ogling her. There was a time when such leers made her uncomfortable, but not anymore. These men knew that the penalty for crossing the line of "look but don't touch" was less than desirable.

Elzor glanced up as she approached. "Ah, so good of you to finally join us, Elzaria," he said with a sneer. "I expected you quite some time ago. It is fortunate that you arrived before I was forced to come get you."

She bowed her head as she absorbed his reproach, which she knew he only made in order to look authoritative in front of his men. "Forgive my tardiness, my liege, but ... something has happened."

He tore the last bite of meat off the havsu leg he was gnawing on, swallowed, and wiped his face with a cloth. "Well?"

She cast a surreptitious glance to her left and then to her right. Upon closer inspection, several of Elzor's men appeared to be dozing. Langon was still concentrating on his meal. The man could put away food like a ravenous chava.

Leaning in close to Elzor, she whispered, "I had a vision."

His eyes widened, and for a moment he looked at her like she was insane. "If this is some puerile jest, Elzaria, I'm not laughing."

"It's no jest, my liege. The Stone showed me something. I scarcely have the words to describe it."

He put down his napkin and leaned closer to her, lowering his own voice to a whisper. "Try."

Chapter Twenty-Three

THE COUNCILORS' faces went slack as Kelia related every detail she could remember from the vision she experienced the night before. When she told them about the alien woman with the strange designs on her skin, as well as the mysterious mental bond Kelia shared with her, the Council members were aghast.

"Great Arantha," Eloni finally said. "I always suspected we were not alone in the Creation, but to actually have proof of it ..."

"Agreed," Katura said. "Arantha created all things. These beings may be her emissaries."

"What if they're not?" Susarra asked in a coarse voice. "You maintain that their appearance, their presence is the will of Arantha. Have you considered the possibility that it may be a warning?"

Kelia frowned. "A warning?"

"Yes. We know nothing of these beings. Maybe they are the first of many, sent to destroy our world. Maybe Arantha alerted you to their presence so that we may prepare for battle."

"I concur with Susarra," said Eloni. "We cannot know these beings' true motives. Until we do, we must exercise extreme caution."

"What is your plan, Protectress?" asked Katura.

"I will make the journey to the Kaberian Mountains to make contact with these beings. Alone."

Katura gasped. "Alone? Protectress, is that wise?"

"Katura's right. It could be dangerous," Eloni added.

"I realize that," Kelia said, her voice bearing a confidence far greater than she actually felt. "But I am the most powerful Wielder in the Ixtrayu. I can take care of myself, as I'm sure you would all agree. I am also Protectress. If these beings are indeed hostile, I would not have anyone else imperil themselves."

"How will you travel?" Eloni asked.

"I will travel on Fex. She is the swiftest chava on Elystra." Kelia cast a glance out the large window, where the sun was beginning its ascent. "On her back, I should be able to reach the mountains by sunset. I shall leave within the hour. Liana is already busy packing me some provisions."

"Forgive me, Protectress," Susarra chimed in. "But I've heard those mountains are home to many dangers. Should something happen to you, what would you have us do?"

Kelia looked at Susarra, whose face remained blank. This was her first conversation with the Councilor since their argument on the archery range. She hadn't had the chance to tell Vaxi about her decision to liberate the young huntress from her grandmother, and now that conversation would have to wait.

"I will leave the fate of the Ixtrayu in your capable hands, Councilors," Kelia said. "Our people look to you for guidance, and so it will be up to the three of you to provide one united voice until such time as you deem Nyla worthy to succeed me." Again she looked at Susarra, convinced her pronouncement would be met with disdain or, at the very least, resistance, but Susarra did not object.

Kelia suddenly found herself becoming suspicious. *What is Susarra up to? She's never this cooperative!*

Katura rose to her feet, and the other Councilors followed suit. "We will do as you command, Protectress," she said, bowing her head. "May Arantha speed you on your journey, watch over you and keep you safe from harm."

Kelia also stood. "I will endeavor to return as quickly as possible. Let us pray that we will all be more enlightened when I do."

She strode forward, looking each of the three women in the eyes, one at a time. In Katura's and Eloni's eyes she saw both concern and confidence; confidence in her, and Kelia drew strength from them. Susarra's face, however, might as well have been carved in stone for all it revealed.

As one, the Councilors bowed their heads, and Kelia walked out of the Council Chamber.

* * *

"You're leaving again?" Nyla asked, biting her bottom lip.

Kelia fastened a belt around her tunic and met her daughter's gaze. "I'm afraid so."

"Why do you have to go this time?"

Though Kelia had explained her previous day's vision to Liana as best she could, they had both thought it best that Nyla not be told. If she knew her mother was heading for a dangerous mountain range to converse with aliens, there was no telling how she might react. She pulled Nyla into a warm hug, feeling her daughter's arms encircle her waist. "Because Arantha wills it," she said.

Nyla tightened her grip on Kelia. "How can you be so sure this is what she wants?"

"Hey," Kelia said, facing Nyla again and placing a hand on her cheek. "One day, you will understand what it means to be Protectress. Having Arantha speak to you is the highest honor one can have. I will admit there have been many instances that her wishes have been difficult to discern." She cast a quick glance at Liana standing right behind Nyla. "But this is not one of those occasions. More than any time in my entire life, I am certain this is what I must do."

Nyla's cherubic face scrunched up. "When will you be back?"

"I don't know, duma. Two days, maybe three."

Liana held out a thick, reddish-brown robe to Kelia, who slipped her arms into it. She shrugged the garment over her tunic and pulled up the cowl until it covered her hair, which Liana helped her do up in a simple braid. Kelia grabbed her satchel from where it sat on the chair next to the fire-pit. Testing its weight, she slung it over her shoulder.

"I need you to do something for me, Nyla," Kelia said. "I need you to keep an eye on Vaxi for me."

"Why?"

"Susarra's up to something. I can feel it. And I'm willing to bet it involves Vaxi."

"I'll watch her, mama. You be careful."

"I will, I promise," Kelia said.

She gave her aunt and daughter one more embrace, and then exited, heading for the chava stables.

* * *

Fex's hooves pounded the sand as Kelia sped across the desert.

Kelia kept her eyes focused straight ahead, trying to ignore the heat from the sun. Today was the hottest day she could remember, and she knew the fact that there wasn't a single cloud in the sky or a breath of wind would make her journey that much more arduous. She'd already perspired through her tunic.

She absently reached down and patted Fex's neck, and she chuffed and snorted in response. Gray in color and with two short horns protruding from her snout, Fex had always been

180

Kelia's favorite mount on the rare occasions she had to travel away from the village. Though her Wielding abilities didn't include being able to communicate with animals, the two shared a good rapport.

Most of the kingdoms of Elystra preferred to travel by merych. While those creatures were indeed majestic and durable, no animal could match the speed and stamina of a chava. Whereas most merychs were unable to run much more than a hundred miles in a day, a well-rested, healthy chava could far surpass that number. They could cover the three-hundred-mile distance in six hours, meaning Kelia would reach the base of the range well before sunset. Finding a traversable route through the mountains, however, would take some additional time.

Kelia had spent a lifetime poring over maps previous Protectresses had drawn from centuries of visions, and was quite familiar with the landscape of the Kaberian Mountains. The region was dry and inhospitable, and there were few safe routes through those mountains, so anyone who had cause to cross the continent circumvented the range by travelling to the northernmost edge of the range, several days' journey away.

She hoped she would be able to find the visitors' encampment before sundown. Susarra was correct: the mountains held many hidden dangers. A ravening pack of lyraxes was at the top of that list, and she was not eager to encounter one.

* * *

Kelia slowed Fex to a halt as the desert sand gave way to the rocky detritus sloughed from the Kaberian Mountains. She climbed off the chava's back to stretch her legs after the long journey. Bringing out two skins of water, she took a sip from the first and poured the contents of the second into Fex's large, panting mouth. Fex nuzzled Kelia's hand with the side of her head as she gave a low guttural grumble.

"You're welcome, girl," Kelia said, patting the massive creature's nose. "We're not quite there yet, though."

Kelia scanned the area, looking north and south at the mountains that stretched in a jagged line all the way to the horizon in both directions. If her vision had been accurate, she was still an hour away from her destination. She would have to take a winding path through the mountains to reach the dry riverbed that led to the spot where the aliens were encamped. It would be slow going, as chavas were not particularly adept at climbing, but she was confident they would reach the encampment before the sun set.

How the aliens would react to her was a different matter entirely.

She took a few deep breaths, as well as another quenching gulp from her water-skin. Resuming her seat on Fex's back, she urged the beast in a southerly direction, looking for the path that would lead into the heart of the mountains.

* * *

The path had been even more treacherous than Kelia had thought, tapering at several points to a width barely sufficient for Fex's substantial girth. On one occasion, Kelia had to use her air-wielding abilities to help the chava climb a steep rock face, which left her even more physically drained. By the time they hit the riverbed, fatigue had nearly overtaken her.

The mountain lake was now only half a mile away. Kelia hoped the aliens were friendly, if only so they could have a place to rest and replenish their water supply. If the aliens weren't friendly, they had enough water for the return journey and no more.

Kelia considered the best way to approach the encampment. She would definitely have to do it before sunset, as they would likely have some form of defense-system in place to guard against intruders. It had been more than a week since their arrival on Elystra, and if they hadn't yet encountered lyraxes, it was only a matter of time before they did.

She contemplated riding in on Fex's back, but then thought better of it. Though chavas were tame creatures once domesticated, their appearance was intimidating, fearsome even, and Kelia needed to appear as non-threatening as possible. Better to keep Fex out of sight and make the final approach on foot. She prayed the connection between herself and the alien woman was not only real but went both ways. Would she recognize Kelia, or would she just kill her on sight?

She dismissed the thought. Arantha would not lead her to this place only to be slaughtered.

Kelia stood up, moving over to where Fex was standing. She looked her travel companion in her large round eyes. "You stay here, girl."

Fex gave a plaintive growl.

"I'll be all right." She gave the creature a tired smile. Then, turning away, she added, "I hope," under her breath.

Pulling her cowl over her head, she walked around the bend of the riverbed.

The first thing she noticed was the giant, bird-shaped metal thing. She couldn't help but stare at it with childlike wonder; even from several hundred yards away, it was an impressive sight. Now that she'd laid actual eyes upon it, however, she knew it was not a living being. It had to have been the object she saw from the western outcropping.

In the foreground, arrayed across the length of the riverbed, was a series of thin black sticks. At the tips of these sticks were blinking red lights that seemed to flash faster the closer she got. Behind them were two more objects, also resembling metal sticks but taller and with a circular appendage at the top. Before she could determine their purpose, however, they illuminated. Kelia had to avert her eyes.

Moving cautiously, she walked between the line of small sticks and past the two large metal light-things. Nothing jumped out at her, and she saw no sign of the alien woman or the boy.

Kelia was a hundred yards away when the crunching, grinding sound she heard in many of her visions assaulted her ears. It was some distance away, and she could see the mouth of a cave at the base of the larger of the two peaks dominating the area. The edges of the mouth of the cave were round and smooth, too perfect to be natural. *What are they doing?*

The magnitude of what was about to happen felt like a weight upon her shoulders.

These ... people are from the Above. Not since the time of Arantha's first coming has anything like this happened. Whatever form she took all those centuries ago has been lost to the winds of time. This is something unknown to this world. And I will be the first Elystran in history to take part in it.

Arantha protect me.

Step by step, Kelia closed the gap between her and the giant metal object. Off to the left and around another bend, she beheld several more artifacts, the same devices she saw in her last vision, as well as a table and two chairs. Just past them was the edge of the mountain lake.

She smiled at the idea that these beings used such things as tables and chairs just like the people on her world did. Funny that something so mundane would give her comfort.

A slight movement in Kelia's peripheral vision caused her to focus once again on the giant metal bird. She was only thirty or so yards away now.

A pair of legs appeared, walking down the metal ramp leading from the belly of the object. A few seconds later, a figure stepped out onto the dirt of the riverbed. She wore black pants and a dark brown sleeveless garment that covered her breasts, back, and torso. On her arms and shoulders, partially obscured by the garment, were colorful drawings of several unfamiliar yet majestic birds. Her shoulder-length, straight hair flowed down the back of her head like a purple waterfall.

It was her. The woman from her vision.

At that moment, the raucous noise coming from the mouth of the cave cut off. A deathly calm swept over the area, as if the entire world had suddenly stopped.

Kelia felt her heartbeat quicken.

The woman continued walking toward the lake, her thick black boots crunching on the dirt and gravel of the riverbed. She was tapping her fingers on a square black object that Kelia couldn't see clearly. She appeared to be lost in thought.

Kelia watched as the woman continued her trek toward the lake. She held her breath, waiting to see if the woman would notice her. Her feet shuffled slightly, creating the softest of scraping sounds. There wasn't a breath of wind, and the sound seemed to magnify itself a thousand-fold.

Time slowed to a crawl as the woman stopped in her tracks. She slowly turned her head in Kelia's direction. Her eyes went wide as she faced Kelia full-on.

The black square thing slipped from her fingers. The woman didn't even notice, keeping her gaze fixed on Kelia.

Kelia raised her hands to her head, preparing to remove her cowl and identify herself.

Before she could utter a single word, however, the woman averted her gaze, looking at another black square, smaller than the one now lying in the dirt at her feet. This one was attached to her right arm. She rapidly tapped it a few times and turned to face Kelia again while reaching behind her back for something.

Kelia grasped the edges of her hood, pushing it back and revealing her face. "I am –"

The woman vanished.

Into thin air.

Kelia gasped.

Great Arantha. Where did she –

Suddenly, Kelia felt the presence of someone standing immediately behind her. Before she could react, an arm snaked around her neck, followed by something sharp pressed against her throat.

"Dohnt muuv," a female voice said in her ear.

Chapter Twenty-Four

WHEN SHE woke up the morning after her confrontation with the wolf-creatures, the first thing Maeve did was rush to the *Talon*'s restroom's mirror. Last night's surprise development had really happened: her back was scar-free, something it hadn't been since she went through Space Corps training. She'd scanned herself with a medcorder, and sure enough, the tissue had completely regenerated. There wasn't even a trace of the cut she sustained the night before.

Neither she nor Davin could explain her sudden healing. That alone was cause for concern, but when she factored in her equally sudden and inexplicable ability to communicate with the wolf-creatures, all they could theorize was that she was somehow empowered by the energy source they were mining.

On another positive note, her headaches had abated, and for the first time since her initial migraine, she woke up pain-free. Davin, however, was still having headaches, but they weren't too severe, and a mild dose of pain blocker was enough for him to perform his duties.

Her nightmares were also lessening. Though she found the waking vision—*hallucination?*—of the native woman disturbing, she also came away from the encounter with an innate sense of peace, like she was exactly where she was supposed to be, doing what she was meant to do.

After breakfast, Maeve took two shifts on the excavator while Davin caught up on sleep. Even though they'd made some kind of truce with the beasts, they thought it prudent to keep watch in case they returned. She also decided to disconnect the sirens, as it appeared to no longer have the desired effect. They would still have the floodlights to warn them of intruders.

In the early afternoon, while Davin took his first turn of the day on the excavator, Maeve had another swim, continuing to scan the rim of the basin for any further signs of the woman from the cave. She was almost disappointed when the woman didn't appear. She wondered if the whole thing really *had* been a hallucination, and was glad she hadn't told Davin about it.

With another day of digging nearly behind them, both she and Davin were in good spirits as they sat down to dinner. Maeve took a big whiff as he set a plate of corned beef and cabbage in front of her, but her spirits sank when he gave her a rousing mug of purified lake water to accompany it.

"Saints," she said, grabbing the mug and taking a swig. "What I wouldn't give for a shot of whiskey right now. Or at least a beer."

"You and me both," Davin said. "It's too bad we can't synthesize something with a little more kick to it." He jerked his thumb at the synthesizer.

Synthesizers could rearrange the molecular structure of the organic matter from the nutra-pellets into thousands of possible combinations—within reason, of course. The invention had effectively ended world hunger in the 25th century. Engineers over the last two hundred years had improved the actual taste of the synthesized food immensely, but they'd never been able to reproduce alcoholic beverages effectively. Synthesized alcohol, at best, tasted like water. At worst, it tasted like rocket fuel.

"I hear you," Maeve said. "How're you feeling?"

"Not bad. Would it be all right if I turned in after my next shift? I'm still running a little behind on sleep."

She smiled. "Go ahead. I'll wake you at midnight. Possibly earlier, if Roisin decides to show up."

"Roisin?"

"Our lupine friend. I decided to give her a name."

He chuckled. "That's pretty riff. Why'd you pick that name?"

"Roisin Malone. Girl I went through pilot training with."

His brow furrowed. "Don't remember you ever talking about her before. Were you two friends?"

She shook her head, "Oh, hell no, she was a complete slag. Her mission in life was to outdo me at absolutely everything. If I aced a sim-flight, she had to do it better. When I ran the obstacle course, she had to have a better time than me. And if I showed even the slightest interest in a guy, she'd be all over him two seconds later."

"Yeesh, really?"

"Yup. But I got her good."

"How?"

"I started a rumor that I had the 'mones for Jack Stonestreet. Big, dumb guy, built like a quadranium shite-house, and if you had boobs, you were a potential notch on his belt. I couldn't stand the arsehole. But I told my two best friends at the time that I was going to let him have a turn with me, and two days later, I caught him sneaking out of Roisin's quarters."

"What happened then?"

She grinned. "She washed out right after he knocked her up."

Davin burst out laughing. He tried to control himself by lowering his head and smacking his palm on the table. "Well, I guess you showed her, huh?"

"Yup. I named our four-legged friend Roisin because they have the same snarl."

He laughed again. "Nice."

Maeve waved at Davin as he disappeared into the cave to begin his final shift. They had a little time left before sunset, so she made her way to the *Talon*'s cockpit to check the scanners. The wolf-creatures were still ensconced in their lair, and Maeve hoped they would take her suggestion and hunt somewhere else for the time being.

Davin had continued tinkering with the PTs, but if anything, their ability to transport had gotten worse, not better. There was no doubt the proximity of the energy source was affecting them. After a little experimenting, they'd determined the best way to improve their functionality was to keep them in a containment crate until they needed to be used. Even so, there was still only a moderately slim chance they would work.

She chose one of the PTs from the box and attached it to her belt. Then she attached a small console to her right arm and synched them up so she could hopefully transport at a moment's notice if need be. She grabbed one of Ji-Yan's short swords and stuck it through one of the back belt-loops of her pants. She wasn't sure if she would need it, but it made her feel safer.

Finally, she picked up her computer pad and tapped on it a few times, bringing up a readout of the weather forecast for the area. Though the air was still warm and dry, she'd observed several thick cloud formations to the north. If the data was accurate, this part of the planet, which seemed to be near the equator, would soon be transitioning from summer to autumn, which meant cooler temperatures and a fair amount of rain.

She strode down the *Talon*'s ramp, listening to the crunch of her boots upon the dusty, rocky ground. She felt the warm sunlight on her skin as she walked towards the lake.

Behind her and to her right, the sound of the excavator cut out. It had only been forty-five minutes or so since Davin started his shift, and Maeve hoped that the overheating problem with the excavator wasn't getting worse, or they would be digging with hand-operated tools next.

Maeve took several more steps forward. And then, off to her left, she heard something. With the background rumble of the excavator having faded away, this noise, a soft scraping sound, resonated like a bell in the all-pervading silence.

She turned her head to look down the wadi. Someone was there, staring back at her.

Maeve's body tensed and the hairs on the nape of her neck stood on end as she turned to face the figure. Unlike Roisin, this, whatever *this* was, was alone. And it wasn't a four-legged animal this time. It was humanoid.

With the sun nearly hidden behind the high peak directly west of them, Maeve didn't need to shade her eyes to make out what it was. Only forty yards away, it looked to be about her height, clad in a reddish-brown robe with a hood that obscured its face.

Maeve's mind raced. *Could it be ... her? The woman from my vision?*

She continued to stare at the figure, which hadn't moved or spoken. The body hidden underneath the robe was of average build with only the hands visible. The figure was too far away to determine whether the hands belonged to a male or a female.

Maeve's computer pad slipped from her fingers.

What do I do? If I let this one go, he or she might tell others, and then we'll have half the planet breathing down our necks. We'd have to abandon the mission.

No. I can't let that happen.

Maeve reached toward the PT device on her belt and flipped a small switch, hearing a tiny surge of energy as it activated. Then she cast her gaze to the small console on her arm, which had also activated. Watching for movement out the corner of her eye, she set the device to transport her to a position just behind the figure. With any luck, she could catch whoever it was by surprise.

The PT device started to hum. Her eyes firmly locked on the figure, Maeve slowly reached behind her back, her fingers closing around the hilt of the short-sword.

The figure's hands raised, making a motion to pull back the robe's hood. In a distinctly feminine voice, the figure said, "Ee sha –"

At that exact moment, Maeve felt the invisible field surround her body. She closed her eyes and transported.

She reappeared six feet behind the figure. Turning quickly around, she saw that the figure had pulled back the hood's cowl, revealing a head of thick brown hair done up in a braid.

Drawing the short-sword, Maeve closed the distance between her and the native woman in no time flat, grabbing one of her shoulders with one hand while holding the fifteen-inch blade against her throat with the other.

"Don't move," Maeve whispered into her ear.

'Don't move'? What in God's name made me think she can understand a word I say?

The woman's body tensed, but Maeve kept the edge of the blade firmly pressed against her neck.

"Com vala so nee spira," she said softly. "Kashat veh." The last two words were spoken with conviction.

Maeve didn't budge.

"Kashat veh!" she repeated, much louder this time.

What am I going to do now? I can't just kill this woman!

Maeve had an idea.

Shoving her prisoner forward with her left hand, she reached for her pistol with her right, reasoning that the loud report of a gunshot or two might get the primitive to surrender. Thank goodness she'd properly cleaned the gun to prevent another jamming disaster like the previous night.

As Maeve's hand touched the cold hilt of her gun, however, she felt the sudden sensation of invisible tendrils snaking around her body. Before she could even react, she was flying backwards, as if thrown by the concussive blast of an explosion. She landed flat on her back, knocking the wind from her lungs.

What the fark? Did she just throw *me?*

Her breath ragged, Maeve scrambled to her feet immediately, drawing her gun and holding both it and her short-sword in front of her in a defensive posture. The woman had turned around, and Maeve saw her face clearly for the first time.

It *was* her.

The woman from the cave. The woman she'd formed a mental connection with.

The woman she'd just held at knifepoint.

Shite.

Maeve and the woman stared at each other in silence for a few moments. Neither moved.

The woman looked to be about her age. The image Maeve had seen in her mind didn't do this woman justice. She was beautiful. She had bronze skin, piercing brown eyes, a regal nose and full lips. She had the bearing, the demeanor of a warrior queen.

"Nee shala tovum se cala Arantha?" she asked in an inquisitive tone.

"What?"

Great. Language barrier. This is gonna be so *much fun.*

"Nee shala tovum se cala Arantha?" she repeated, much louder this time.

"I don't understand what you're saying!" Maeve replied, still holding the gun on her.

The woman raised her hands, and in a moment of panic, Maeve assumed she was going to use whatever magic she seemed to possess to hurt her again, perhaps even kill her. Maeve's finger squeezed the trigger.

A loud bang disrupted the serenity of the landscape. The woman's face contorted in pain as the bullet grazed the upper part of her left arm, and she used her right hand to cover the wound.

Maeve gasped.

What did I just do?

Maeve looked on with a mixture of relief and horror as the woman removed her hand to reveal only a few drops of blood. The bullet had barely nicked her, but the shoulder of her robe was now a darker shade of red.

She turned to look at Maeve again. Her face was livid.

Oh, f-

Before Maeve could even utter a half-assed apology, she felt her body lifting off the ground as if plucked by an invisible hand. A hand that was closing into a fist and rendering her immobile. She could see everything in front of her, but struggle as she might, she couldn't move. Unable to control her hands, Maeve dropped the gun and the short-sword.

The woman took several steps forward, glaring up at Maeve, who dangled like a puppet in mid-air. Powerless to do anything else, Maeve made her face as apologetic and contrite as she could, hoping she could stave off death just like she did with the wolf-creatures.

Just then, the woman's body began to shake, and her eyelids fluttered. Maeve felt the invisible fist loosening its grip. Seconds later, it disappeared altogether, and Maeve crashed to the ground in a heap.

She looked up at the woman, whose eyes had closed. Her hands had dropped to her sides, and she was swaying unsteadily. Then, before Maeve could climb to her feet, the woman toppled over, landing on her side with a thud.

Maeve ran to her, turning her face-up, and grasped her hand. The woman's face, so full of anger mere moments ago, now looked drawn and haggard, as if she hadn't slept in years. Her eyes fluttered open again, and she stared up at Maeve. Their eyes met, and Maeve's guts clenched.

I played this all wrong. This woman is not my enemy. This is her world, not mine. I curse the Jegg for their brutality, and then I prove I'm no better than them.

Maeve exhaled. "I'm so sorry," she said, knowing full well the woman wouldn't understand her.

The woman released Maeve's hand, moving her own hand up to Maeve's face. Maeve wasn't sure what the woman was going to do, but she wasn't going to resist. If there was any chance she could keep this cock-up from escalating further, she had to take it.

Without flinching or resisting, the woman touched her fingertips to Maeve's forehead.

There was a blinding flash of white light, and then blackness.

* * *

Davin exited the cave just in time to see his mother, kneeling next to a strange woman in a reddish-brown robe, keel over when the woman touched Maeve's forehead.

He was about to cry out when he felt his legs go numb and his vision fade.

He was unconscious before he hit the ground.

* * *

Within the walls of the castle Tynal, Elzaria's legs wobbled and collapsed under her. She fell to the ground in a heap, right outside her bedroom door.

On a wide dirt road leading from Dar to Ghaldyn province, Mizar felt his head start to throb. He doubled over, trying to stay atop his merych and somehow stave off unconsciousness, but it was no use. The last thing he heard was Sen's cry of "Master!" and then darkness overtook him.

Chapter Twenty-Five

ONE THING Nyla hated was the way most of the older Ixtrayu looked at her out of the corners of their eyes whenever she walked past. She knew it was only because she was Kelia's daughter that they chose not to make their disapproval obvious. Her mother, despite all the reasons they had to doubt her, had earned their respect. Nyla hadn't, and for the first time in her life, it bothered her.

She'd spent her entire childhood not caring what others thought. She didn't care that she was the Protectress' daughter, destined to follow in her mother's footsteps. All she wanted was to have fun, enjoy her childhood, and put off for as long as possible the responsibilities she would one day need to shoulder. When, at age eleven, her Wielding powers began to manifest, she saw it as just another way to enjoy herself.

Seeing her mother leave the village under mysterious circumstances for the second time in as many weeks, coupled with the subsequent murmurs from her tribemates about the possible reasons behind her departures, set Nyla to thinking about the society she lived in. She thought about all the thankless tasks her mother performed every day, trying to keep the tribe unified, happy, and safe. Even when everything seemed to be going well, like now; the crops were plentiful, the hunt was bountiful, and apart from Talya, no Ixtrayu had been severely injured in many months. A thousand little things always seemed to crop up that Kelia had to deal with in order to maintain the fragile tranquility.

Then there were the Sojourns. She had been the last daughter born to the tribe, and she could sense the anger in many of their eyes whenever they looked at her: resentment at Onara for stopping the Sojourns, at Kelia for having had the special privilege of being the last Ixtrayu to go on Sojourn, and, by extension, at her for being the product of that Sojourn. The tribe had called untold generations of her family "Protectress," and now it all threatened to end.

The blazing heat beat down on Nyla as she worked in the fields with Yarji. The bushes and vines needed extra water, and Nyla was more than willing to spend an additional ninety minutes helping Yarji with watering duty. Keeping cool was both easy and fun, being so close to a river they could both manipulate and cool at their whim. By now, Nyla had earned Yarji's trust to take care of the riverfruit and juva-berry bushes on one side of the River Ix unsupervised while she took the other side. Her trust made Nyla happy. It gave her fulfillment, and Yarji was always kind to her. She had come to love Yarji like a big sister.

All afternoon, Nyla pondered her mother's departing words regarding Susarra and Vaxi. It was true: Vaxi had been quite distant of late, but Nyla figured it was the usual depression at having to live with her impossible-to-please grandmother. Kelia had asked her to keep an eye on Vaxi, but how was she supposed to do that? During the day, Vaxi was out with Runa's hunting party. The rest of the time, Susarra almost never let Vaxi out of her sight.

The sun had already set when Nyla finished her Wielding training session with Liana. By the time she entered the dining area, she was famished, and she was pleased to see Sarja already there. Runa was sitting on the opposite end, eating her meal with a group of her sister huntresses. Nyla quickly filled a plate with kova meat and fruit and sat down across from Sarja. It didn't look like her friend had much of an appetite, though, as her plate was only half-full, and she was barely nibbling at the meager portion she'd taken for herself.

"What's wrong, Sar?" Nyla asked, tearing into the juicy flesh of a slice of riverfruit. "Not hungry?"

"Not really," she replied, her eyes hooded. "I, um, got my ..." She leaned forward, lowering her voice to a whisper. "My blood."

Nyla swallowed hard. "Oh," was all she could say. Ixtrayu girls usually started having their regular bleedings at around Sarja's age, and though Kelia told her many times that it was part of growing up, she wasn't looking forward to it. "Sorry, Sar."

"It's okay," Sarja said. "It's the third time for me. I'm starting to get used to it."

They ate in silence for a few minutes. After picking a kova bone clean of meat, Nyla looked up to see Sarja staring at her. "What is it?"

"Do you think you and me will end up being companions?"

At that moment, the piece of meat Nyla was chewing on went down the wrong pipe. After a brief but noisy fit of coughing, she swallowed the offending bite and chased it down with a long gulp of water.

"Sorry, Ny," Sarja said, lowering her eyes to avoid the stares of several Ixtrayu who were looking in their direction. Her face had gone scarlet. "Didn't mean to blurt that out."

Nyla took another sip, followed by a deep breath. "Are you serious?"

She gave the slightest of nods. "Ever since we had that talk with Vax, I've kind of been thinking about it."

Nyla blushed as well. "Why? It's not like we have to choose our companions right now."

"I know, Ny, but think about it. We're the two youngest girls in the tribe, right?"

"Yeah."

"And how many other girls are close to us in age? Six?"

Nyla shrugged. "Sounds about right."

"Everyone knows Bika and Zarina will be companions; I mean, they can barely keep their hands off each other now. You can bet they'll have their bonding ceremony by the time the cold season's done."

"I'm sure," said Nyla. "I would also be surprised if Jara and Lami didn't choose each other. They're a lot better at hiding their feelings than Bika and Zarina are, but even I can tell how much they love each other."

Sarja nodded. "Which just leaves Eleri and Cassia. I honestly can't see myself choosing either one of them. Can you?"

Nyla thought for a moment. "Not really. Eleri's really nice, but she's been infatuated with my cousin Talya since she was twelve. And Cassia … well, she's just mean. We haven't gotten along a single day in our lives."

"Exactly," Sarja said. "Which means we'll either have to choose companions that are at least three years older than us, or –"

"Or each other," Nyla finished her sentence.

"I mean, maybe by the time we're old enough to choose, the age difference won't matter as much. But by then, we might have even fewer choices than we do now."

"I see your point." Nyla pursed her lips. "If you could choose someone else right now—you know, besides me—who would you choose?"

Sarja thought for a moment. "Ebina, I suppose." Her face flushed.

"Ebina?" Nyla pictured the two of them together. "I guess I can see that. You're both huntresses. And she's gorgeous."

"Yeah, she is. But she's twenty-two, Ny. I'm only fourteen. And I don't really know her that well. I doubt she's going to wait for me."

An idea came to Nyla. "What about Vaxi? You're already friends with her, she's also beautiful, and she's only eighteen. Almost."

"That's true, but choosing her would mean having to deal with Susarra every day. I'm not sure I could take that. And besides, Gruta already likes her, remember?"

Nyla sighed. This conversation was becoming more awkward by the moment. "I know our options are limited, Sar, but if I choose a companion, I want it to be with someone who wants me for who I am. Someone who doesn't care that I'm not tall and sexy and gorgeous like Vaxi or Ebina, or that I'm going to be Protectress someday." She cast her eyes to the table. "That kind of narrows the field down to zero, doesn't it?"

She looked up again. Sarja's large, pale blue eyes were open wide, and her brow was furrowed. "So you're saying that if I was available, you wouldn't want me?"

Nyla became lost in thought. *Me and Sarja, companions? I haven't even started having my bleedings yet! Why does she have to bring this up now?*

Seeing the hurt look still plastered on her friend's face, she said, "It's not that, Sar. You've been my best friend since I was four years old. In fact, for the most part, you've been my *only* friend. Most of the other girls stay away from me because I'm the Protectress' daughter, but you never have."

Sarja's shoulders relaxed, and a happy smile returned to her face. "Our mothers have been best friends since they were children, so I guess it makes sense that we are too."

"Yes, Sar, best friends. But companions? I've never thought about you in *that* way." Nyla's eyes widened as a thought struck her. "Are you thinking about *me* that way?"

"No!" Sarja retorted, her face reddening.

The expression on Nyla's face didn't change. "Really?"

"Okay, maybe a little," she said, her shoulders slumping. "I mean, I know a lot of people end up not choosing companions, but I don't want to be one of those people, living your whole life with no one to –"

"Sarja!" Nyla interrupted.

Sarja looked shocked, as if she'd read Nyla's mind. "I wasn't going to say *that*, Ny. I just meant that it would be nice to know there's someone waiting at home who ... *loves* you. I mean, someone besides our mothers. You know?"

"I guess." Nyla suddenly became aware that her heart was racing, and a bead of sweat was trickling its way down her neck. She took a deep breath, pushing several strands of hair back behind her left ear. "Can we *please* talk about something else?"

"Sure," Sarja said, exhaling. "You want to tell me what's going on with your mother?"

"Wish I could," Nyla said, thankful for the change in subject. "She's consulted the Stone a bunch of times since she got back from the western outcropping, but if she had any visions, she didn't talk about them with me. And then last night, when she came home, she had this crazy look in her eyes that I've never seen before. Then this morning, she met with the Council, and an hour later, she took a chava and left. The Stone had to have shown her something."

"Where was she going?"

"Across the desert, to the Kaberian Mountains. That's all I know."

"She didn't say *anything* else?"

Nyla shrugged. "Just that it was Arantha's will. And to keep an eye on Vaxi."

Sarja's brow furrowed. "Vaxi? Why?"

"I don't know. She thinks Councilor Susarra is up to something, and Vaxi is involved."

"Susarra's *always* up to something, and it's never good," Sarja mused. "What are you going to do?"

"I don't know. I don't even know where Vaxi is right now."

Sarja cast a quick glance over Nyla's shoulder before facing her again. "She's right behind you," she said, smirking.

Nyla turned around to see the tall huntress standing at the serving table, talking to Aarna, the tribe's head cook. Neither one was smiling. After a brief conversation, Aarna disappeared into the back room where the kitchens were. While Vaxi awaited her return, she scooped up several large slices of riverfruit. But she didn't put them on a plate; rather, she wrapped them in a piece of cloth that she retrieved from a large satchel hanging over her left shoulder. After placing the wrapped fruit in her bag, she brought out another cloth and set it on the table. A minute later, Aarna returned with a small bundle bound tightly in kova leather. Vaxi took the bundle, wrapped it in the second cloth and deposited it in her satchel as well. She and Aarna then exchanged cheerless nods, and Vaxi headed for the exit.

"Hey, Vax!" Sarja called, waving her arm.

Vaxi stopped in her tracks, turning her head to look at Sarja and Nyla. Then she glanced at the exit again, as if unsure whether she should stop to chat with her friends or keep going. After a few seconds, she still hadn't made up her mind, so both girls rose from their table and approached her.

"You okay, Vax?" Nyla asked.

Vaxi didn't look at them, instead keeping her eyes focused on the exit. "I'm fine."

"You're not going to eat with us?" Sarja sounded hurt.

"I can't," Vaxi said softly. "I have to bring Grandmother her dinner tonight. She's, um … she's not feeling well."

Nyla and Sarja exchanged glances. "Sorry," Sarja said, even though all three of them knew she didn't really mean it.

"Do you need our help with anything?" Nyla asked in her most congenial voice.

"No," Vaxi quickly replied. "I'll be all right. I just want you to know that I'm … I'm honored to have you girls as friends."

Nyla cocked an eyebrow. *Huh? Where did* that *come from?* she thought.

Again, Nyla and Sarja looked at each other. "Uh … thanks?" Sarja said.

A jarring *thunk* came from the doorway, and all three girls turned to see Susarra standing there, scowling at them. Nyla scanned the Councilor's face for signs of illness, but couldn't see anything out of the ordinary. Just that horrible glare.

"Did you get it?" Susarra asked Vaxi.

"Yes, Grandmother," Vaxi said, bowing her head to avoid Susarra's stare.

"Then come." Susarra gestured for Vaxi to follow her. "We have much to do."

"Yes, Grandmother," Vaxi repeated. Without a goodbye or even another glance their way, Vaxi walked past Susarra and out the exit, heading in the direction of their home.

Nyla made a move to follow her, but Susarra blocked her way with the walking stick. "I'm sure you two have other things to do right now," the Councilor said.

Nyla didn't want to appear cowed, but a few seconds as the recipient of Susarra's icy frown was enough for her to back down. "Yes, Councilor," she said.

"You just stay away from her, you hear me?" Then, without waiting for a response, she limped out the exit, following Vaxi down the path.

Once the *thunk* of Susarra's walking stick faded away, Nyla whispered, "I'm going to follow them."

Sarja opened her mouth to object, but then closed it again. "Want me to come with –"

"Sarja!" came a voice from across the room. Both girls saw Runa beckoning to them. "Come over here. I need to speak to you."

Sarja nodded at her mother, letting out a silent groan. "Sorry, Ny, guess you're on your own. Be careful, okay?" With a wry smile, she reached out and grasped Nyla's hand. "Don't want anything to happen to my future companion."

Nyla rolled her eyes, extracting her hand from Sarja's. "Thanks, Sar. You just *had* to make it weird again." But she gave her friend a smile of her own before turning and heading out into the night.

* * *

Nyla always enjoyed walking through the village at night. It was quiet and peaceful, and seeing the thousands of lights in the sky almost always brought her joy.

Most of the tribe's homes were lit from within by fires, and placed alongside the path next to the river were a series of torches set alight once the sun set. As she neared the edge of the plateau, however, the light became dimmer and dimmer. Not that it mattered; Nyla had trod this path since she could walk, and she could make her way from one end of the village to the other with her eyes closed.

Most of the village's homes were on the west side of the river, but the Councilors' homes were located on the east side, carved into the plateau near ground level to accommodate their age and lack of mobility. Nyla stole across the narrow bridge that spanned the river, confident her footfalls wouldn't be heard over the water tumbling over the stones.

When she reached the other side of the bridge, she bore to the right. The home belonging to Susarra and Vaxi was only a short distance away, and she could see the dance of shadows created by firelight through the window.

Hugging the wall, she edged closer to the window, grateful the torchlight lining the river didn't stretch all the way to her location. No one on the other side would be able to see her unless they were looking directly at her.

With the window only a foot away, Nyla finally made out two voices, though she could barely hear them over the noise of the river.

"… certain about this, Grandmother?" said a young voice that Nyla recognized as Vaxi's. "I don't want to anger Arantha by defying her wishes."

Susarra's raised voice came next. "Certain? Don't you question my judgment, girl! Following Kelia's path has led us to the brink of destruction. We must force the Ixtrayu down another path. *That* is your destiny. Your return will show her, and the rest of the Council, that we need not fear Arantha's wrath just because the *Protectress…*" she practically spat the word out, "… tells us to."

Nyla's ears pricked up, and she edged even closer, trying to hear more.

"Nyla?" said a voice from behind her.

Startled, Nyla whipped around to see Katura standing in the entrance to her home, which was right next door to Susarra's. She was clad in a long night-robe that covered her thin frame, and her long, curly white hair was tied back in a knot behind her head. The old Councilor was not glaring at her, but rather looking at her with bemusement.

Abandoning her spot next to Susarra's window, Nyla quickly ran over to where Katura was standing. "Councilor," she said, trying not to look shamefaced but probably failing.

"What were you doing just now?" Katura's voice was even, much like it was every other time Nyla had spoken to her. Nyla loved the kindly old woman, but she wasn't sure whether Katura would approve of her eavesdropping.

Nyla glanced back at Vaxi's door, hoping Susarra wouldn't walk through it and discover her there. Turning back to Katura, she whispered, "My mother is worried about Vaxi. So am I."

Katura, seeing Nyla's need for secrecy, also lowered her voice. "And why is that?"

Nyla looked blankly back at her. "I–I don't know. But Mother asked me to keep an eye on her, so that's what I'm doing."

"Did she now?" Katura drawled. "When did she do that?"

"Before she left."

"I see." Katura drew herself up, leaning on her doorframe for support.

"I'm sorry, Councilor. I know I shouldn't spy, but ... " She trailed off, casting another worried glance back. "Please don't tell Susarra ... I mean, Councilor Susarra I was here, okay?"

Katura leaned forward. "You know, when you get to be my age, your mind often plays tricks on you. You look like Nyla, and you sound like Nyla, but in this light, I can't be sure." She gave Nyla a toothy smile. "So I'm going to rub my eyes, and when I open them again, I expect to find that I'm talking to myself."

Nyla broke out in a wide grin. "Thank you, Councilor."

Katura made a show of stretching out her arms, yawning, and rubbing her eyes with the backs of her hands. Taking the cue, Nyla ran back across the bridge. When she reached the western bank, she turned back to see Katura had reentered her home. Neither Susarra nor Vaxi had shown any signs they'd heard their conversation.

Sighing, Nyla ran back to her home.

Chapter Twenty-Six

KELIA'S HEAD pounded as she struggled to sit up. She still lay on the dirt between the lake and the metal bird. She turned to her left, where the alien woman also lay, unmoving. In a moment of panic Kelia thought she might have killed her, but the rise and fall of the woman's chest relieved her of that notion. She turned to her right, noticing a body lying prostrate on the ground near the mouth of the cave.

She staggered to her feet and stumbled over to the body. Catching sight of a shock of curly red hair atop his head, she realized this must be the boy she saw in her visions.

Kelia knelt down, turning the boy so that he lay on his back. His breathing was shallow but steady, and she exhaled in relief. She took in the details of the boy's face. Though he was tall and quite muscular, his boyish face betrayed his true age, as well as his resemblance to the woman.

She then turned her attention to the cave itself, which was illuminated from within. There were none of the flickering shadows usually cast by torches or candles, and the light was more intense. Beyond that, though, Kelia sensed something else from deep within the cave. A feeling of something tugging at her, not unlike the pull she felt from the Ixtrayu Stone. The gentle waves emanating from within the cave felt strange and familiar at the same time.

Kelia stood, warily approaching the mouth of the cave, feeling the invisible energy penetrate her body. It gave her strength.

Her mind whirled as she worked out the day's remarkable events. She'd been physically drained by her daylong journey across the desert, and using her Wielding abilities on both Fex and the woman had sapped all her remaining strength, causing her to collapse.

On only three previous occasions had Kelia traveled this far from the village: her three Sojourns. She, like all Ixtrayu with Wielding abilities, was vigorously warned before making those journeys to not, under any circumstances, use her powers while in foreign territory. In kingdoms where no one possessed such abilities, to do so would have serious repercussions, and Kelia had refrained from revealing her true nature on all three Sojourns. She remembered feeling physically weakened after reaching her destinations, but she assumed that had just been normal fatigue from traveling. She'd never before used her abilities this far from home, from the Ixtrayu Stone. Could this be the reason for her collapse?

She always knew the power that flowed through her came from Arantha, via the Stone. She'd always assumed she could go anywhere on Elystra, and the power would follow her. Now she could only wonder if the Stone's power waned the further away she was from it.

Kelia's mind jolted back to the here and now. She shrugged the heavy robe off her body and folded it as neatly as she could before placing it beneath the boy's head. Then she turned and strode back to where the woman was just beginning to stir. With every step, more of the images she first saw when she touched the woman's forehead crystallized in her mind. They were fantastical.

Images of exotic alien worlds, of beings she could not have imagined in her wildest dreams. Images of the Above, the lights of the Creation that she'd gazed at since she was a child.

After that came images of a beautiful blue-green world, of green forests and vast metal cities home to thousands, millions of people.

And then ...

Images of death and devastation. Pyramid-shaped objects dropped from the sky, laying waste to those vast cities, reducing them to twisted, lifeless rubble. Images of bodies, everywhere. Unhonored, unburied. The young, the old, and everyone in between.

Kelia's eyes widened, and tears welled in them.

This woman and this boy have lost their entire world. Stolen by a race stronger than them. She lost her mate, the person she loved more than any, save ... her son.

She turned to where the boy still lay. He hadn't moved.

He is *her son.*

A groan interrupted Kelia's thoughts. The woman pushed herself into a sitting position. She rubbed her temple and coughed slightly before looking up at Kelia.

"What did you do to me?" she croaked.

Kelia gasped. Though the woman was still speaking in her own strange language, Kelia could understand every word.

Thank you, Arantha.

"It is called 'the Sharing'," Kelia said. "A brief joining of minds, where we share experiences and knowledge through images."

The woman's mouth fell open, and she climbed unsteadily to her feet. "You ... you just spoke English."

Kelia shook her head. "I did not speak ... *English*, as you call it. I spoke in my own tongue."

"But I can understand you."

"Yes." Kelia touched her own forehead. "Our Sharing has allowed us the ability to understand each other." She strode forward, stopping only a few feet away from the woman. "I apologize for my actions. I was determined to present myself as a peaceful emissary for my people, and I failed."

The woman looked behind her, at the spot of ground where Kelia had thrown her, before turning back. "It's all right. I'm sorry I shot you." She nodded at the wound on Kelia's arm. "Does it hurt?"

"Yes." She, too, looked at the wound, which had stopped bleeding, but a nasty burn mark marred the flesh where the bullet grazed it.

The woman's mouth turned up at the corners. "I guess we both farked up, huh?"

Kelia just stared blankly at her.

"We both made errors in judgment," the woman said.

"Ah. Agreed."

Several metal sticks with the circular appendages set up around the encampment activated, bathing the area in a soft white glow that chased away the growing darkness. Turning to the west, both women saw that the sun had almost disappeared behind the tall mountain peak.

"Mom?" said a voice from behind them.

Kelia turned to see the boy staggering toward them. He was clutching his head, having obviously just woken up.

"I'm okay, kiddo," the woman said. Two more steps, and the boy almost fell into the woman's arms. She wrapped her arms around him, supporting him while he regained his equilibrium. "Are you okay?"

"Just a massive headache," he mumbled. "I had the most bizarre dream just now. What the hell happened?"

"We're getting to that."

He disengaged himself from her arms and turned, shuffling his feet as he registered Kelia for the first time. "Who are you?"

Kelia straightened her back, speaking in a practiced, measured voice. "I am Kelia, daughter of Onara, vessel of Arantha, Protectress of the Ixtrayu."

The two aliens just stared at her for a few moments. They turned to each other, exchanged a look, and then faced her again. "That's ... very impressive," said the woman. "I haven't a clue what it means, though."

"Um, Mom?" the boy said. "How does she know English?"

The woman opened her mouth, but nothing came out. Finally, she said, "I'll explain later."

"And by what name are you known?" Kelia asked.

The woman straightened up to her full height, much as Kelia just did, and spoke with the same prideful cadence. "I am Major Maeve Cromack, daughter of, um, Helen," she said. "Retired Space Corps pilot, commander of the 308th Antares Squadron." A self-satisfied smile wormed its way onto her face.

"That is also quite impressive," said Kelia, "and I am equally ignorant of what that means."

Both women stared at each other for a moment, then their shoulders relaxed.

"And I," said the boy, puffing his chest out, "am Davin." He grinned from ear to ear, and Kelia couldn't stop herself from returning one of her own.

Kelia bowed her head. "It is agreeable to meet you, Davin." She turned to the woman. "And you, Major Maeve Cromack."

Davin chuckled, and the woman said, "Um, you can just call me Maeve."

"Then I shall," Kelia said.

"Dav," Maeve said, "get the salve. Kelia's been hurt."

Davin peered at the wound on Kelia's arm. "How'd that happen?"

"Maeve shotted me," Kelia said plainly.

He turned to Maeve. "You shotted her? Way to go, Mom."

She smacked him on the shoulder. "Don't start. Just get the med-kit. And bring another chair from the hold, will you?"

"On it." He strode away from them and headed up the ramp into their ship.

"Would you like to sit down?" Maeve gestured at the table and chairs set up about twenty yards away.

"I would, but first I have to get Fex. I don't want to leave her alone in the dark. She's just down that way." Kelia pointed down the wadi. "With your permission, I would like to bring her into your encampment. She needs water, and so do I."

"Fex?"

"My chava."

Maeve's brows furrowed. "Which is what, exactly?"

Kelia smiled. "You'll see in a moment. I assure you, she's harmless. Do I have your permission to call her?"

Maeve mulled this over for a moment. "Yeah, go ahead."

Kelia took a few steps forward, cupped her hands to her mouth, and let out a loud, trilling call. Within moments, the sound of something moving their way reached their ears. Something very large and very heavy.

At that moment, the metal lights down the wadi flared into life, shining their bright glare further down the riverbed. Kelia smiled as Fex's enormous bulk came into view, moving toward them at a brisk pace.

Dust flew up from Fex's flanks, her hooves seemingly beating the ground into submission. Kelia cast a glance at Maeve, who stood in awe at her mount's approach and smiled to herself. To Maeve's credit, she remained still, though she did keep her hand close to the weapon she'd wounded Kelia with.

Fortunately, Fex made her approach without knocking over any of the lights, but as soon as she saw Kelia, she broke into a full run.

Out of the corner of her eye, Kelia saw Maeve back up a few more paces. Off to the left, Davin ran down the ramp with a small satchel in one hand and a chair in the other. Hearing the loudening hoof beats, he dropped both as he saw the chava run towards Kelia and his mother.

Kelia stepped forward, raising her hands. "Stop, Fex!" she commanded.

The beast didn't slow down. It was now only fifty yards away.

Kelia increased her volume. "Fex, *stop*!"

No effect.

Kelia looked at Maeve, suddenly afraid for her new … *friend? Ally?* She raised her arms, preparing to use her Wielding abilities to slow the charging chava's progress.

At that instant, Maeve also raised her arms, holding her hands out in front of her. Her eyes were locked on Fex. Then, just barely loud enough for Kelia to hear, she said, "Stop."

Kelia whipped her head around to look at Fex, who finally broke stride, slowing her pace and coming to a halt only five yards away from them. Fex looked up at Maeve expectantly, as if acknowledging her new master.

Without another word, Kelia moved over to Fex, placing both hands on the beast's nose. She was calm now, panting as she nuzzled Kelia's hands. A low grumble came from her throat, a sign Kelia recognized as contentment.

Kelia turned around to look at Maeve, who still had her hands raised. As Kelia watched in astonishment, Fex curled her four limbs inward, lowering her massive body down until it rested on the dirt of the riverbed. Once settled, she grumbled in acquiescence again.

Maeve was panting as well. The threat over, she lowered her hands and walked slowly forward.

Kelia looked deep into Maeve's eyes. With as much reverence as she could muster, she stammered, "You're … you're a Wielder."

Chapter Twenty-Seven

I CAN'T BELIEVE *that worked,* Maeve thought.

Saints alive. I can talk to animals.

I ... can talk ... to animals.

Davin ran over, giving Fex a wide berth. "Mom, what happened?"

"I just told Kelia's ... rhinoceros-looking creature to stop, and it did. Just like the wolf-things last night." She turned to Kelia, having just registered what the woman said. "What's a Wielder?"

Kelia stared at Maeve as if she'd witnessed a miracle. "You wield the power of Arantha."

Maeve waited for her to say something else, but Kelia obviously thought this cryptic statement was self-explanatory. "Arantha? You mentioned that name before. What is it?"

"Arantha created all things. She watches over all of the Creation. She is our guide, from the moment of our birth until the day we journey to the Great Veil."

Davin retrieved the med-kit from where he'd dropped it and moved over to Kelia. Removing a small aerosol can from the satchel, he said, "So, Arantha is your god."

Kelia regarded his kind, inquisitive face. "Yes. Do the people on your world not believe in a godly being?"

"Yes," Maeve said. "They give Him many names. Some on my world call Him 'Allah', others call Him 'Jehovah'. We," she indicated herself and Davin, "just call Him 'God'."

Kelia considered this, then nodded. "It makes sense that in all of Creation, she would have many names. It is not unusual that you refer to Arantha as 'Him'. Though Arantha is beyond such trappings as gender, the Ixtrayu prefer to think of Arantha as a female, for it is she that helped free my ancestors from the tyranny of men."

Davin led them over to the table next to the purifier and synthesizer, where they all sat down. "This is going to sting a little." Davin said, spraying the salve onto Kelia's wounded shoulder. She winced and gritted her teeth, but did not cry out.

A short distance away, Fex clambered to her feet and lumbered forward. She didn't break into a run this time, but rather, walked right past their table to the water's edge, lowering her massive head for a drink.

"Would you like something to eat?" Maeve asked as Davin applied a small bandage to Kelia's wound. "I'm not familiar with the delicacies of Castelan VI, but I'm sure we can find something you'd like."

Kelia gave her a puzzled look. "Castelan VI?"

Davin put the finishing touches on the bandage. "That's what we call this world. What do you call it?"

Kelia looked at his handiwork, running a finger over the bandage. "We call our world Elystra." She smiled at him. "Thank you, that feels much better. You are most kind."

His eyebrows knitted together. "You sound surprised."

"In my experience, men do not tend to treat strangers, especially women, with kindness. For the most part, women are treated as inferior beings. It has always been thus." She smiled at Maeve. "You said you were a commander?"

"That's right."

"And there were men under your command?"

"Yes. Twelve men and women that I went through hell and back with."

A regretful look crossed Kelia's face. "In the kingdoms of men, Elystran women are not permitted to fight. In fact, in some countries, they are not even allowed to learn how to read or write."

"It was like that on our world too. Many, many centuries ago," Maeve said. "But now, women may perform any task men can."

"It would be wonderful to live on such a world," Kelia said.

Maeve stood up, walked over to the synthesizer, and entered her passcode. Then she opened a compartment on the top, grabbed a handful of nutra-pellets and fed them into the aperture. Selecting something simple for their dinner, she tapped the screen a few times, and thirty seconds later, the door popped open on the side, revealing three steaming bowls of pinkish-red soup on top of a tray. Davin removed the tray and placed one bowl in front of Kelia.

Kelia sniffed at the unfamiliar aroma, and a smile broke out on her face. "It smells amazing. What is it called?"

"Lobster bisque," said Maeve, grabbing three spoons from another compartment and handing them out.

Kelia took it, turning it over in her hand, unsure what to do with it.

"It's a spoon," Davin said, using his to scoop a small amount of soup and bring it to his mouth. "Oh wait, you're not allergic to shellfish are you?"

Kelia knitted her eyebrows together, "I'm sorry, allergic to what?"

Davin smiled and shook his head. "Never mind." He picked up his spoon and showed her how to hold it properly, and before long, Kelia had mastered its use.

After swallowing her first mouthful of bisque, she gave a satisfied sigh. "This is delicious. What is it made from?"

"On Earth, there are creatures that live in the sea called lobsters," said Davin. "Their meat is very tasty. You chop them up along with some vegetables, add some broth, heat it up, and ..." he pointed at the bowl in front of her, "there you go."

Kelia stared blankly at him. "I did not see you chop anything."

Davin looked at Maeve, who smiled. "That would take a little longer to explain."

Maeve poured three cups of water and handed them out. Kelia took a cautious sip, but did not comment on it. Maeve's eyes went to Kelia's other hand, which had moved up to touch a small, lump of metal hanging from a thick leather string around her neck.

"What is that?" she asked, gesturing at the lump. "Is that a symbol for your tribe or something?"

Kelia looked at her quizzically, as if wondering what she was talking about. She looked down, and instantly discerned what Maeve meant. She smiled. "No, nothing of the sort. It was a gift from my daughter Nyla. When she was very young, she loved crafting things with her hands. With nothing but a leather string, a handful of beads, and this token of farewell my mother gave me before she died, Nyla gave me the best gift a mother could receive. A gift of love."

"What kind of metal is it?" Davin asked.

"I do not know. My tribe does not have much in the way of metal. The only metal objects we have are what we brought back from centuries of Sojourns."

"I see," said Maeve. "I would love to hear more about the Ixtrayu."

Over the next hour, Kelia relayed the entire history of the Ixtrayu, from the days of Soraya up to the present. She told them of the Stone and the Wielding abilities it gave certain members of the tribe. She also spoke of the Sojourns, and how her mother had, without explanation, called a halt to them.

While she spoke, Fex chose a spot at the lake's edge to lie down. She hit the ground with a loud flump and quickly dozed off, its deep-throated snore resounding through the night air.

Maeve hung on Kelia's every word, so much so that it took the entire hour to finish their soup. "Wow," Davin said. "You actually had a vision about us coming here?"

"In a way," Kelia replied. "Arantha showed me where to go, and I went. Two days later, I saw a light streak across the sky. I did not know what it was at the time, of course, but further visions led me here." She smiled at Maeve. "I am gratified that my instincts about you were correct. Though one of the Council feared you may be hostile, I know now that you are not."

Maeve was about to respond when Kelia reached across the table and grasped her hand. "During the Sharing ... I saw into your mind. I was overwhelmed by much of what I saw, but ... " she trailed off, her face becoming sad. "I grieve for your loss, Maeve. Your presence here is a wondrous thing that I cannot even begin to understand, but I regret the circumstances that brought you to Elystra."

Maeve was taken aback by the show of tenderness. She suddenly thought of Richard, and of all her friends that hadn't been able to fulfill this mission with her. "Thank you, Kelia," she said, her voice choked with unwanted sobs. "I–I saw things, too. Much of it was a blur, but what I remember clearly was beautiful. You lead a simple life, off the land, and the bonds you share with your family are as strong as ours. Thank you for letting me experience it."

Kelia bowed her head.

In a typical Davin moment, he let out an obnoxious belch, causing Kelia to retract her hand and Maeve to look at him with a maternal glare.

"Sorry," he said. "Mom, if it's all right with you, I'd like to take another turn on the excavator. I meant to tell you when

I came up last time, I think we're getting close to finding the energy source. I assume you'll be up for a while?"

"Yeah, Dav, go ahead," Maeve said. "How's your head?"

"It's all right. It was spinning for a while, but now it doesn't even hurt anymore."

"What about this dream you said you had? Do you want to talk about it?"

He thought for a moment, then shook his head. "Nah. It's already starting to fade, like most of my dreams."

"That's good. You got the coveralls?"

"Uh huh. They're in the cab." He pointed at the mouth of the cave.

"Okay," Maeve said. "Let us know if you find anything."

"I will." He and Kelia exchanged nods, and then he walked away from them, disappearing into the cave. A minute later, the noise of the excavator resumed, but it wasn't as loud or raucous as before. If they were close to a breakthrough, Davin was likely only using one-half power to proceed.

Kelia turned to face Maeve again. "The way you stopped Fex—how did you know you could do that?"

Maeve shrugged. "I don't know. I just knew. It worked last night with the wolf-creatures, so I thought it would work with your chava."

"Wolf-creatures?"

"Yes. Huge, four-legged animals with gray fur, long fangs, pointy ears and yellow eyes. Not as big as Fex, but darn close."

Kelia's mouth fell open slightly. "Lyraxes."

"Is that what they're called?"

"Yes. They generally live in mountainous regions, feasting on smaller animals. How many did you see?"

Maeve recounted the events of the previous night, when the three lyraxes had her pinned and helpless yet spared her life. She also explained the mental bond she'd formed with the creature, as well as the mysterious disappearance of twenty years' worth of scars.

Kelia was amazed. "You can heal? That is another Wielding ability. There are few in my tribe's history who possess this power. It is a rare and precious gift that is generally handed down from mother to daughter."

"That's what I don't understand. How did I just suddenly get these abilities? What I can do, what I've done, it's like ... magic. Such things do not exist on my world, nor on any other world I've ever been to."

Kelia placed her palms in her lap and lowered her eyes. "Arantha chose you. Or God, as you call her. Of that I have no doubt. You were brought to Elystra for a reason."

Maeve tore her eyes away, and her voice began to quaver. "I came here to find a way to free my species from the Jegg."

"This is the race that enslaved your people?"

"Yes."

Maeve once again met Kelia's confident brown eyes. "If that is your future, Major Maeve Cromack, then Arantha will see you through it. But I think the true reason you've come to our world is only beginning to emerge."

Without warning, the image of Richard's face forced itself into Maeve's mind, and she had to avert her gaze. It had been ten days since they escaped Earth; ten days since Richard and the rest of her friends died. She'd tried to put his death out of her mind. She had a mission to complete: come to Castelan VI, no, *Elystra*, find the energy source, and return with it. The chances of succeeding were infinitesimal, but she came anyway, out of duty and desperation.

The enormity of it all crashed down on her like a tidal wave. All the death she'd seen and experienced over the last five years flooded over her at once. Her husband's handsome, beautiful face, the way his stubble scratched her when they kissed, the way his hand felt on the small of her back. She would never see him, never experience those things again. She was taught to be tough, to conquer emotion, to ignore pain. But this was too much to ask of anyone.

Unable to dampen her roiling emotions, Maeve stood up and walked a few paces away. Her shoulders slumped as the weight of her situation pressed down on them. Her lungs heaved as they struggled to push air out.

"Maeve?" came Kelia's concerned voice behind her. "I know this must be overwhelming to you –"

"You don't understand!" Maeve cried. "I'm not trained for any of this! I'm not a savior! I'm just a soldier! A soldier and a mother! I keep telling Davin we can still win, we can somehow get home and beat the Jegg and free humanity, but …" Her eyes brimmed with tears, and she was powerless to hold them back. "I'm not even sure I believe it anymore. My husband was the brilliant one, not me. I was just trained to fight, to defend Earth, and I couldn't do that. They're all dead, and I couldn't save them. I couldn't …"

Bitter tears spilled out of Maeve, and she felt her knees give way. She expected to hit the ground, but two strong hands held her up. Hands that twirled her around, and she found herself facing Kelia's beautiful, wise, regal face. A tear trickled down her cheek as well, and Maeve realized that through the Sharing, Kelia had experienced the same pain, the same loss.

"Kelia …" Maeve sobbed.

Kelia brought Maeve into a warm embrace, folding loving arms around her.

Maeve returned the hug, placing her hands between Kelia's long brown tresses and her tunic, as she let it all pour out of her. All the grief she'd been holding in came out in an avalanche of tears.

Had she been in a calmer state, she would have realized the peculiarity of her situation: here she was, standing on a dry riverbed on another world, a hundred years from home, sobbing onto the shoulder of an alien woman she'd only known for a few hours.

No. Not an alien. A mother. A daughter. A leader.

A friend.

"I feel your pain, Maeve," Kelia's soothing voice whispered in her ear. "But you can Wield. Heal yourself."

Kelia was right, Maeve realized: though her physical scars were healed, the scars she bore internally ran far deeper. The soldier part of her told her to persevere, but that part was giving way to the part that wanted to fall into a dreamless sleep and never wake up. To join her husband in death.

She hadn't realized until that moment just how broken she was inside. She'd put on a brave face for Davin, creating a shell of false bravado and snarky humor, but it was all a lie. Two days ago, when he lost control, she'd wanted to lose control with him, but she couldn't. She didn't want him giving into the despair that haunted her sleep and plagued her waking mind.

Maeve felt a surge of incredible warmth come from Kelia, cocooning her in invisible filaments of power. She gasped as the energy seeped into every pore, every molecule of her body.

"Yes, Maeve," Kelia whispered, tightening her hold. "Let it in. Embrace it."

Maeve closed her eyes, and her last stubborn defenses crumbled. She gave in to the wave of energy, letting it suffuse her, permeate her. It calmed her roiling thoughts, repaired the cracks in her heart. Whether this energy, this sense of peace, came from within her, or from Kelia, or Arantha, or God, or the Universe, Maeve didn't care.

I am human. I am Terran. I am a wife, a mother, a pilot, a warrior, a resistance fighter, a survivor. I have survived. I will survive. I will not give in to despair ever again.

With every beat of her heart, Maeve's sobs faded away and her breathing returned to normal. Finally composed, she withdrew her arms and took a step back.

Sniffling, Maeve wiped the remnants of her tears with her hand. Regarding Kelia, she said shakily, "Kelia ... I don't know what to say."

Kelia bowed her head. "When I set out from my village to find you, I had no idea what you would be like. You are, after all, from the Above."

Maeve sniffed again. "Based on what little we knew of your world, I thought you would all be, well, savages." She gave a sad smile. "Not the first mistake I've made."

Kelia smiled as well, putting a comforting hand on Maeve's shoulder. "I guess we both farked up, then."

Maeve felt a peal of laughter coming, and she couldn't stop it even if she wanted to. She laughed like she hadn't laughed in ... well, maybe ever. Kelia joined in. Together, their laughter echoed off the walls of the basin, drowning out even the noise of the excavator.

Their laughter had barely died down when the excavator's motor abruptly shut off. Only the faint hum given off by the floodlights provided audible noise. Within moments, however, the sound of Davin's rapid footsteps echoed up to the surface.

Hearing the urgency in his footfalls, Maeve strode in that direction, with Kelia right behind her.

Davin burst from the opening and ran over to them. His face was flushed, beads of sweat dotting his forehead. "Mom!" he panted, bending over to catch his breath.

"What is it, Dav?"

Davin took a few deep breaths, then straightened again. "The energy source—I think I found it."

Maeve looked over at Kelia, whose face remained impassive. "Show me," Maeve said.

Davin led the women down the gently sloping tunnel at a brisk pace, anticipation building within Maeve. Finally, the ground leveled out and the excavator came into view. Beyond that, where the lights fastened to the tunnel walls began to dim, something else was providing illumination, bathing this part of the tunnel in a distinctly yellowish hue.

Maeve watched as Kelia sidestepped the excavator, eying it warily as if it was a sleeping beast. A few paces later, they both laid eyes on what Davin had found.

Embedded in the rock wall, about four feet off the ground, was a chunk of mineral unlike any Maeve had ever seen. It was incongruous with the rock that surrounded it, the rock that had presumably been its home for untold millennia. Though its surface was opaque, it looked almost crystalline in nature. Threads of yellow light danced upon its surface, back and forth, like small fish swimming in a tiny pond. The sudden rush of blood in her own ears made Maeve wonder if it was alive, and had actually registered their presence.

Kelia fell to her knees, crossing her arms over her chest and bowing her head in reverence. Maeve and Davin tore their eyes away from the stone to watch Kelia as she began to chant under her breath. "I bask in your divine presence, O Arantha, for I am your humble servant." She repeated this phrase again, and then again.

Maeve turned her attention back to the Stone, wondering if Kelia's litany would provoke a response. None came. It continued to pulsate as it did its luminous dance.

Davin's eyes, meanwhile, flicked from his mother to the Stone and then back again. "Mom?" he whispered. Maeve turned to face him. "We did it, didn't we?"

Still on a high from her emotional healing, she simply nodded. "Yeah, kiddo, we did."

Kelia climbed to her feet and took a cautious step toward the Stone, speaking with hushed reverence. "I don't understand."

Maeve was unsure whether Kelia was speaking to them or to herself. "What?"

Kelia halted, turning to look at them. Maeve saw utter confusion on her face. "Eight hundred years. Thirty-five generations of my family. All of them possessed the gift of foresight far greater than mine, and yet, none of them foresaw this." She shook her head in disbelief. "Why? Why would Arantha keep the existence of another Stone from us?"

Rather than attempt a reply to this unanswerable question, Maeve turned to Davin. "Dav, bring me the small pickaxe and some gloves."

Davin nodded and strode the short distance to the excavator, reaching inside the cab. A few moments later, he returned with a pair of thick gloves and a two-foot pickaxe in his hands.

Before Maeve could take the items from him, Kelia took her gently by the wrist. "Come," she said. "Let us lay our hands upon it together."

"Are you sure that's a good idea?" Davin piped up.

"Ask her, she's the expert." To Kelia, she asked, "Do you think it's safe?"

She nodded. "It is no coincidence that you, a visitor from the Above, and I, a Protectress, are together to witness this finding. Though our paths started so far apart, they have converged at this spot. It was our destiny. It has always been our destiny."

Maeve's faith had always been a tenuous thing, and had grown even more so since she joined the Space Corps. It had all but disappeared after the Jegg invaded Earth. In her mind, there was no such thing as destiny, only what people made for themselves. Even though she was raised in a family that believed in such things as fate, she never fully embraced that philosophy.

Until now.

"Stand back, Dav," Maeve whispered.

"Mom –"

She looked at him, giving him her warmest smile. "It'll be okay."

Davin nodded, retreating until he stood next to the excavator again.

Maeve turned to Kelia, who was still holding her wrist. "Won't it?"

Kelia gave an ironic smile. "I have been wrong before."

"Great."

They stepped forward. Kelia raised Maeve's hand, interlocking their fingers before hesitantly positioning their hands a few inches above the Stone.

Suddenly, the spiraling swirls within the Stone began to spin faster and faster and the yellow light intensified.

The two women cast one more glance at each other. Their eyes locked, and they nodded. They simultaneously drew in a deep breath and brought their hands down on the Stone.

Chapter Twenty-Eight

NYLA DECIDED not to tell Liana what she overheard outside Susarra's window. If what she suspected was true, she had almost no time to stop it from happening. Having Liana get involved would only slow her down.

Based on what little Nyla heard, it seemed her mother's suspicions about Susarra were correct. She was taking advantage of Kelia's absence by sending Vaxi on Sojourn. Against Vaxi's wishes, her mother's wishes, and Arantha's wishes. Vaxi was going to sneak away from the village in the middle of the night. *Tonight.*

It was moments like these that Nyla was grateful for her years of geography lessons under Liana's tutelage. She knew the names and locations of each of the kingdoms that lined the western, northern and eastern coasts of the continent. Assuming none of said kingdoms had vigorously expanded their borders since she was born, the nearest populated area was over four hundred miles away. There was no way Vaxi would make that journey on foot. She would travel the same way every Ixtrayu going on Sojourn would travel: by chava.

Nyla used her Wielding to brew some herbal tea for Liana, which her great-aunt graciously accepted. As Nyla hoped, Liana retired to her bedroom immediately after finishing the tea. Within minutes, she heard Liana softly snoring, and was out the door a heartbeat later.

Nyla's mind raced as she crept through the silent village. It had to be near midnight, and just about everyone was asleep by now. She descended the hill leading down to the farmlands, cutting to the right once she reached the bottom.

Here's where it gets tricky, she thought. Though she knew the terrain, she wasn't as familiar with every rock and stone outside the village as she was within it. She hadn't brought a torch to light her way, and the lights in the Above did little to guide her. Hoping she wouldn't fall and break something, she trudged carefully along a trail she couldn't see.

The dirt beneath her feet eventually gave way to grass, and as she crested another small hill, she rejoiced when she saw a campfire in the near distance, illuminating a large part of the huge corral where the chavas were kept.

Though she couldn't see the beasts, Nyla knew there were roughly forty of them, males and females, of various sizes and ages. They preferred to sleep outside, on a comfortable patch of grass. The stable, a wooden building off to the left, was large enough to house ten chavas, and this was where the keeper, Olma, not only worked but slept. She was the only member of the tribe who didn't live within the confines of the village, preferring to be near the creatures she tended.

Nyla couldn't see any lights on in the stable as she approached. However, this abruptly changed when a door at the far end of the building opened and a tall figure stepped out, leading a saddled chava behind her. The figure was holding a small, lit torch, and Nyla immediately knew who it was.

"Vaxi!" she shouted, running the last twenty yards.

Vaxi gasped at the sudden appearance of her friend. "Nyla!" she said in a choked whisper. "What are you doing here?"

Nyla drew in a deep breath, trying to block out the offensive odor of chava dung that thickened the air around the stables.

One whiff, and she could already feel her eyes watering. Olma had to have lost her sense of smell decades ago. "I might ask you the same question."

Vaxi kept walking, leading the chava out into open ground. Just ahead was a closed gate, and beyond that, the vast Plains of Iyan: thousands of square miles of open grassland.

"Don't try to stop me, Nyla. I have to do this."

"Do what?" Nyla whisper-shouted. "Go on Sojourn? Just because your grandmother told you to?"

"You don't understand." Vaxi's voice became choked. Whether that was because of the foul-smelling air or her own roiling emotions, Nyla couldn't tell. "This is my destiny. My responsibility."

"You don't believe that! Please, Vaxi, don't go. Just come back with me, and we'll wait for my mother together. She'll know what to do, I promise."

Vaxi patted the chava's nose, and the beast obediently stopped walking. They had reached the gate. Striding forward, Vaxi undid the three leather straps that held the gate fast, swinging it open so the chava could move through it. She didn't respond to Nyla's plea.

Nyla felt her guts clench. What was she supposed to do? Vaxi was one of the strongest, most athletic girls in the tribe. There was no way she could win in a physical fight. If she screamed for help, Vaxi would still be long gone by the time Olma could do anything.

She would have to use her Wielding to stop her. But how? The last thing she wanted to do was hurt her friend. But she couldn't just let her go either.

Thinking fast, she ran in front of the chava just as Vaxi lifted herself up into the saddle. She raised her hands as threateningly as possible, sending small ripples of air Vaxi would feel in the poor light. "I'm not moving, Vax."

"Nyla, go home. Please."

"I'll stop you!"

"No, you won't." She gently kicked the chava's flanks, and the beast began to lumber forward.

Her bluff called, Nyla quickly slipped to the side to let the chava pass by.

From her mount, Vaxi turned to face Nyla one last time. "Tell your mother I'm sorry." Then, holding the torch to one side, she spurred the chava into motion again. Within moments, it burst into full gallop.

Nyla could only stand there helplessly, listening as the chava's hoof beats faded into nothingness. Her heart sank at the thought of what she was going to tell her mother upon her return.

Chapter Twenty-Nine

MAEVE WOKE, finding herself on her own bunk in the *Talon*'s crew room. She turned her head from side to side, puzzled, grasping the blanket that covered her from the waist down.

How did I get here? she thought. *The last thing I remember is …*

The stone. I—no, we, Kelia and I—touched the stone. Together. And then nothing.

She blinked a few times and sat up, feeling the welcome coolness of the metal floor against the soles of her feet. She stood, half-expecting to be overcome by a wave of dizziness like the last few mornings, but there was nothing. No disorientation, no pain.

She let out a deep, cleansing breath, and a smile crept over her face. There was no pain whatsoever. Even her heart, once weighed down by despair and melancholy, beat with renewed hope. She felt strong. Powerful.

Alive.

Her silent celebration was interrupted by a low snore from a few feet away, and Maeve turned to see Davin, sprawled out on a nearby bunk. He was lying face-down, with his hand dangling over the side and his mop of red hair covering his eyes.

After standing and stretching her back muscles, she walked over and gently shook Davin's shoulder. "Dav? Wake up."

He stirred, but didn't open his eyes. "Please, Mom," he slurred. "I just went to sleep, like, an hour ago. I was up all night keeping watch."

"Okay, okay," she said. "Just tell me what happened. I don't remember anything."

He moved a lock of hair away from his eyes, which stared up at her. "After you two touched the Stone, you just passed out." He used his mouth to simulate a *splat* sound. "I had to use the excavator to bring you back up to the surface."

"Really?" Maeve asked, impressed at her son's resourcefulness.

"Yeah. I gave you both the once-over with the medcorder, and it said you were fine. So I brought you in here, covered you up, and took night watch."

Maeve smiled, cupping the back of her son's head. "Thanks, Dav."

He smiled back. "Well, I couldn't leave you down that tunnel, could I?"

"I guess not." She looked around the crew room, noting that they were alone. "Where's Kelia?"

Davin faced his pillow again as he lazily pointed across the room. "Over there."

Maeve followed his finger, which was aimed at a bunk with nothing on it but a tousled blanket. "Um, no she isn't."

"What?" Davin sat bolt upright, suddenly alert. After confirming the bunk's emptiness, he stuttered, "She was there when I went to bed. What time is it?"

She checked the wall, which bore a clock Maeve had synchronized to the planet's twenty-two-point-five-hour day just after they landed. "It's just past seven in the morning."

"Oh, shite, I hope she's okay," Davin said, scrambling clumsily to his feet. He was fully clothed, having flopped into bed that way.

They walked out of the crew room and down the exit ramp, blinking as the morning sun hit them. Shielding their eyes, they scanned the campsite for Kelia. She wasn't down the wadi, and she wasn't near the cave. They made their way toward the lake.

Maeve was relieved when she saw Fex. The giant beast was awake, rubbing her massive bulk up against a nearby boulder, scratching one enormous itch. Satisfied, she collapsed onto the ground again, turning her head towards the lake.

Kelia was there, the water coming up to her knees. She was using her hands to wring out her long tresses. Her skin, which the day before was covered in a thin layer of dust from her journey across the desert, now glistened as droplets of water fell from her body.

Her *naked* body.

Davin's footsteps ground to a sudden halt, and Maeve turned to see her fifteen-year-old son staring in goggle-eyed amazement at the sight of what was—she *hoped*—the first naked woman he'd ever seen in the flesh.

"Whoa," he whispered.

Having finished wringing her hair out, Kelia turned to face them, and Maeve's breath caught in her throat, taken aback at her new friend's alarming lack of modesty. There she stood, stark naked, in front of two people that until yesterday were complete strangers.

Maeve knew she should say something, *do* something. Turn away, and make Davin stop ogling her like some lowlife creepazoid. But there she was, doing the same thing. And she couldn't turn away.

If Kelia's face was beautiful, her body was even more so. Despite being in what Maeve guessed was her late thirties, Kelia didn't seem to have any fat that came so unwelcomely to women approaching middle-age. Her skin was covered in an even, impeccable tan. And her body … it was gorgeous, like that of a bronzed goddess ancient artists used to make statues of. Try as she might, Maeve couldn't stop staring, with no more decorum than the teenage boy standing right next to her.

Maeve's daze was interrupted by Kelia's voice. "Good morning," she said with a smile.

"Good morning," said Davin, grinning gleefully. Kelia had still made no move to cover herself up.

"I didn't want to wake you." Kelia strode forward until her feet emerged from the water. "I hadn't bathed in two days, and I thought … " she trailed off, noting Maeve's and Davin's slack-jawed faces. "Is something wrong?"

"Not at all," Davin said. His smile remained, and his cheeks had gone hot pink.

Finally, Maeve regained her composure. "It's just, um, we don't usually … *exhibit* ourselves so freely." She cast a maternal glare at Davin. "Dav, why don't you go get some more sleep."

"I'm good," he said, not meeting her gaze in the slightest.

"Davin Padraig Cromack, get back on the ship, *now*."

At the sound of his full name, Davin finally tore his eyes away. He fixed Maeve with a hangdog look, snorted, and walked back toward the ship, casting the occasional glance back at Kelia.

When his feet disappeared up the ramp, Maeve turned back to face Kelia, who was donning her tunic again. She approached the Elystran woman, finding herself still tongue-tied by Kelia's display. "Kelia," Maeve said, "I know this is your world and all, but, um … "

"Yes?" The look of naïve innocence in Kelia's eyes threw Maeve off-balance.

"It's just … I don't want Davin getting any … ideas."

Kelia stared at Maeve for a few moments before moving her glance to the ship. "Ah," she said. "You do not wish me to disrobe in front of your son."

"Yes," Maeve said. "I understand if it's your way, but …" She shuffled her feet. "I don't want to offend you, but I'm his mother, and …" She shrugged.

"I understand," Kelia said. "After all we have shared, I forgot that you are strangers to Elystra." She bowed her head. "Please forgive my indiscretion."

"It's okay," Maeve hurriedly replied. "Would you like some breakfast?"

"That would be wonderful. But I must see to Fex first." She gestured at the lounging chava, who continued to stare at them from her shady resting place.

Kelia brought out something bound in leather from her saddle-bag and unwrapped it, revealing a bundle of leafy green plants. With a smile, she set them on the ground next to Fex's head.

Fex gave Kelia a look of what Maeve could swear was gratitude, and began grazing.

"That's all you're giving her?" Maeve asked as Kelia approached. "That doesn't look like much food for such a large animal."

"It will suffice," Kelia said. "Chavas can store food in their bodies for many days after eating. I assure you, she will eat most heartily when we return to the village."

Maeve programmed the synthesizer to create a light breakfast of scrambled eggs, sausage links and wheat toast with strawberry jam. Feeling extravagant and wanting to impress her guest, she decided against pouring another boring cup of purified lake water and instead synthesized two rousing cups of grapefruit juice. After explaining to Kelia the minute difference between a fork and a spoon, they set down to eat.

"Do you remember anything about last night?" Maeve asked.

"No," Kelia replied. "I touched the Stone, same as you. And then I woke up on your ship." She looked sideways at the *Talon*. "It was a little strange at first, but when I saw you and Davin sleeping nearby, my anxiety went away. Do you know what happened?"

"According to Davin, we touched the Stone, and then we hit the dirt. The end." She flexed the fingers of her right hand in front of her. "When I woke up, I felt good. Really good. Like I could run for miles."

Kelia smiled. "Once you get used to it, Wielding becomes as easy as walking. Physical contact with the Stone often produces renewed vigor for those who Wield. It's not a substitute for actual sleep, though, especially if one uses their abilities excessively."

"Fascinating." Maeve forked a sausage link into her mouth, chewing thoughtfully. "I wonder what else I might be able to do."

"You mean like disappear and reappear?" Kelia asked. "It was quite surprising to me when you vanished right before me. In the history of my tribe, none have ever possessed such an ability. It was remarkable."

Maeve chuckled. "That actually wasn't me. Well, it was, but it isn't quite what you think. Your abilities, people on my world would call them 'magic'. This –" she pointed at the small console still attached to her arm, "–this is what we call 'technology'. It's a machine. It's a PT, or personal transporter. It can take us from one place to another in less than a second. When it works, that is."

"Tech–no–logy," Kelia said, sounding out the unfamiliar word. "People on my world would call *that* magic." She took a sip of grapefruit juice, and smiled. "This is quite good. It reminds me of riverfruit juice."

Maeve pointed to the bandage that still covered Kelia's bullet wound. "How's your arm?"

"It still hurts, though not as much as before. I'll have our healer fix it upon my return."

"I am so sorry about that." Maeve cast her eyes to the table. "I panicked. I thought you were going to, well, do something bad to me."

Kelia just nodded, taking a bite of toast.

"You know," Maeve said, "we've already determined that I can heal myself. I wonder if I can heal others too." She pointed at Kelia's shoulder. "Would it be all right if I tried?"

Kelia smiled. "Of course."

Maeve stood up and moved over to Kelia's side of the table, sitting down next to her. She held her hands in front of her face, unsure what to do next. "You said you have healers in your tribe, right?"

"That is correct."

"How do they heal? I mean, I don't remember doing anything special to heal myself. It just happened."

Kelia shrugged. "I do not know. As I am not a Healer, I was never trained in the art. However, when I began my Elemental training, the first thing I was taught was how to calm my mind. It was not a lesson easily learned in my youth, but without it, I could not have learned to harness the power of Arantha. I would imagine being a Healer is no different."

Maeve exhaled, and pursed her lips. "It sounds a lot like combat training. My instructor at the Academy was a master of shodokan aikido. He was the most unflappable S.O.B. you'd ever want to meet. But damn, he could dole out a beating." Seeing Kelia's puzzled expression, Maeve continued, "Never mind. Let's give this a shot."

Kelia leaned in closer to Maeve, who used her hands to encircle Kelia's arm, taking care not to touch the wound beneath the bandage. She closed her eyes and concentrated, trying to empty her mind of extraneous thoughts. Then she focused on the sounds around her. The faint whisper of a breeze, the buzz of tiny insects as they flitted to and fro, the rasp of her own breathing.

Focus, Maeve thought. *Focus. Focus.*

Nothing.

Calm. Serene. Placid. Quiet. Relaxed.

Nothing.

Shite. Shite. Shite.

She let go of Kelia's arm, shaking her head. "I'm sorry. It's not working."

Kelia smiled, placing a reassuring hand on Maeve's shoulder. "Don't worry, no one gets it to work the first time. When my daughter Nyla first manifested her abilities, it took everyone by surprise." She chuckled. "She nearly set my hair on fire."

Maeve's eyes widened. "Ouch."

"I soon discovered that asking an eleven-year-old to quiet her mind is like asking the sun to stand still."

"Ain't that the truth," said Maeve, laughing.

"Try again."

Maeve obeyed, replacing her hands on Kelia's arm.

"This time, don't try so hard," Kelia advised. "Focus on me." Their eyes met, and Maeve put her thumbs over Kelia's wound. "When we had our first shared vision, I saw a large scar on your back."

Maeve felt her cheeks flush. "You saw a lot more than just my scar. If I recall, I was wearing about as much as you were a little while ago."

"Yes," Kelia said with a cheeky grin. "That was one of the more interesting visions I've ever had."

Maeve shifted in her seat, silently willing the blood not to rush to her face as she focused on the bandage. *Saints, what is wrong with me? I'm a grown-arse woman, and I'm acting like a giddy teenager!* "You asked about my scar," she said, gratefully changing the subject. "I thought you had all my memories through the Sharing?"

Kelia shook her head. "It has been my experience, from helping others perform this ritual, that not all memories are shared; only the most vivid ones."

"How do you help others do it?"

"Most Ixtrayu are not Wielders. The Sharing generally occurs when two perform a Bonding ceremony. I act as a conduit between them, allowing them to share their thoughts with each other. It only lasts a few minutes. To Share *all* of one's memories would require the contact to last for many hours. Ours was much briefer than that."

"I see. Well, how I got my scar is a good story; I'm just not sure I can tell it in a way you'll understand."

"Just do your best," Kelia said soothingly.

"All right." Maeve took a deep breath. "Some years ago, before Davin was born, we received signals from the Denebian system, a collection of worlds circling a sun much like yours. Anyway, we thought the race who sent the signals, the Vaal, were sending out a message of peace. So my squadron was sent in to accompany an ambassador to make first contact."

"I gather it didn't go well."

"No. It was an ambush. Little bastards set a trap, and we waltzed right into it. We had them outgunned in every conceivable way. They were like … a little kid in the schoolyard, trying to take the big kid down. Does that make sense?"

Kelia nodded. "I believe I understand. Continue."

"I was unlucky enough to be the first one hit. I lost control of my fighter, and I ended up crash-landing on the fourth planet in the system." She paused, inhaling and looking deep into Kelia's eyes. "Does this world have lightning storms?"

"It does," Kelia said. "Their arrival marks the end of the dry season."

"Well, imagine the worst storm you've ever seen, multiply it by a hundred, and that's every single day on Denebius IV. The technology that allows my ship to fly just stopped working, and I crashed into a mountain. I'm lucky I survived at all.

"When I regained consciousness, my back felt like it was on fire. A piece of metal had torn itself free and ripped right through it." She winced. "I was lucky enough to find a cave where I could take shelter. Thank the Saints I had enough oxygen and medicine to keep myself alive until the rescue teams found me. It took them an hour to beat the Vaal into submission, and two days to find me. They told me it was a miracle we survived."

"We?" Kelia asked.

"Yes. I was four months pregnant with Davin at the time. Another month, and I'd've been put on restricted duty. But those little shites damn near cost me and my unborn son our lives. I've been in fights, lots of them, but I'd never come that close to death before. I was proud of that scar. It reminded me of how I fought to stay alive." Maeve chuffed under her breath. "And now it's gone. All my scars are gone. I'm not sure whether I should be thankful or not. Those scars were part of who I am."

She looked at Kelia, who had her eyes closed and was breathing deeply. Maeve became aware that she was still holding Kelia's arm. Just then, Kelia's deep brown eyes opened, locking on Maeve. "Remove the bandage."

Anticipation building, Maeve used her fingernails to peel up the edge of the dermaplast bandage. It came off, to reveal a patch of nearly-clear skin. There wasn't a single trace of the bullet wound from the previous night except for a tiny scar barely an inch long.

Maeve's eyes nearly leapt out of her head. "Bugger me." Then, smiling broadly, she faced Kelia. "I did it!"

Kelia smiled warmly, rubbing her palm over the healed skin. "Well done, Maeve. Even Katura couldn't have done it better."

Maeve was still reeling from her accomplishment. "Wow. Thank you, Kelia. You're an excellent teacher."

Kelia bowed her head. "I enjoyed your story."

"Wow," Maeve repeated. "This healing power sure would've come in handy a week ago. The headaches I was having were some of the worst I'd ever had. It would've been nice to ... " A thought struck her, and she stood up, turning her back on Kelia and walking several paces away.

"Maeve?" Kelia said, standing up. "What is it?"

She wasn't listening. Her mind was going at the speed of light, as something Richard said a week before his death chose that moment to flash through her mind. "Denebius IV," she murmured. "Holy farking shite."

Maeve realized Kelia was staring at her. "We came here looking for an energy source that we were told would help us beat the Jegg. This energy source turned out to be the Stone we found.

"We had several other planets to choose from. Two were gas-planets that we didn't have the means to search. One was deep in the heart of Jegg territory, and the other was Denebius IV. That can only mean ... there's a Stone on Denebius IV."

Kelia gasped. "A Stone of Arantha?"

"Yes. If what Banikar said was correct, maybe there are Stones littered all over the galaxy. If there really is one on Denebius IV, maybe I came into contact with it without knowing it. It ... changed me, somehow, someway that I didn't even realize, and that's why this is happening to me now. All I remember besides the crash are the horrible headaches I suffered during those two days on that awful planet. When I woke up, I was back on Earth and the headaches were gone."

"Until you came here," Kelia offered, "and you found another Stone." A knowing smile crept across her face. "It is as I said: you were chosen by Arantha. She was shaping your destiny, even before you knew her name."

A small, black bird with a curved beak and a tuft of red feathers jutting from its head flapped down and landed on the dining table. It gave out a high-pitched trill as it folded its wings into its side.

The women watched as the bird studied the remnants of their breakfast, no doubt wondering if they were edible. Then, it picked up a small crumb of toast in its beak and swallowed it in one motion. Apparently satisfied that it wasn't poisonous, it set about picking more crumbs off the plate.

An idea struck Maeve. Holding her hands out in front of her, she concentrated on their winged guest. "Come to me," she said, just above a whisper.

The bird, bobbing up and down as it fed, jerked its head around to look at Maeve. A few seconds later, it spread its wings and took off, flying the short distance to Maeve and perching on her outstretched wrist. It trilled again, looking at Maeve as if seeking approval.

"Fly in a circle," Maeve whispered, using the index finger on her other hand to make a circular motion.

Without a moment's hesitation, the bird spread its wings again and flew from Maeve's wrist, but it didn't go far. Keeping low to the ground, it flew around them in a tight circle, never more than ten yards away. It trilled as it flew, clearly pleased to be doing Maeve's bidding.

Maeve lowered her hands and nodded her head silently, and the bird flew up into the morning sky. The two women watched it go.

As it disappeared over the rim of the basin, Kelia turned to Maeve. "Do you believe in Arantha now?"

Maeve stared at her hands, looking at them as if for the first time. Turning back to Kelia, she said, "I'm getting there."

Chapter Thirty

WHILE DAVIN slept on the ship, Kelia and Maeve spent the whole day talking. The Stone was now a centerpiece on the makeshift dining table. They conversed about the wonders of technology on Maeve's home planet of Earth, and of the Terran Confederation. When the topic turned toward the Jegg, Kelia saw Maeve's entire body go rigid and her eyes become haunted. Not wanting to broach such a sensitive subject, Kelia steered the conversation to that of the Ixtrayu and Wielding. Kelia even gave her new friend an impressive display of her water-Wielding ability, twisting and shaping a large volume of lake water into various geometrical patterns. She sent one stream of water corkscrewing over the lake's surface, from one end to the other and back again, before dumping it on top of Fex, who snorted gratefully for the impromptu shower.

Immediately thereafter, Fex relieved herself. A lot. A vast mound of green, semi-solid foulness that wasted no time infecting the air with its stench.

While Maeve ran to get a hand-shovel, Kelia used her earth-Wielding ability to create a large hole in the ground. Maeve arrived in moments to shovel the noxious dung into the hole and cover it with dirt. By the time they finished, Fex had resumed sleeping.

"Saints," Maeve said after they resumed their seats at the table. "That shite smells as bad as a Chethran wamzu during mating season."

Kelia quirked an eyebrow. "What is that?"

"An animal that lives on the planet Chethra. They like to wallow in swamp mud, and when you combine the mud with their sweat, it gives off an odor that attracts female wamzus. It's one of the foulest-smelling things in the known universe. And if that isn't bad enough, when they're done mating, they emit a howl that will split your eardrums in half." Maeve grinned. "Don't get me wrong: Fex is a magnificent animal, but I hope I never smell what comes out of her arse ever again."

Kelia laughed. marveling at how incredible the last day had been. True, her first face-to-face meeting with Maeve had been disastrous. True, these beings did not have the answers she sought. Even so, she would not trade this experience for anything. She was among people from the Above who, though they were centuries beyond the denizens of Elystra, they were just people at their heart. A mother and son, who valued family and friends as much as Kelia's people did.

In only a day, despite their initial difficulties, she and Maeve had become friends. A Terran and an Elystran. A soldier and a Protectress. Two leaders. Two mothers. Two Wielders.

But it was more than that. Ever since her first vision of Maeve, Kelia felt something stir within her that she'd not felt since Ilora's death. Glimpsing Maeve's naked body had Kelia thinking thoughts she had not dared think for more than twelve years.

In her lifetime, she'd only ever had passionate, lustful feelings for Ilora. She'd never wanted to be with anyone else, not even Runa, her best friend. She'd intended to grow old with Ilora, to share her bed and raise their daughters and granddaughters together. But when she was only twenty-four years old, Kelia's companion was taken away from her, and out of respect for Ilora's memory, she couldn't bring herself to choose another companion from within the tribe.

Despite being born on another world, Maeve possessed many of the same qualities that Ilora had. Maeve was not a huntress but a soldier, and like most soldiers Kelia had met on her Sojourns, their personalities were tinged with hardness, by a life spent training to fight and die for their king. Maeve possessed such a hardness, but it was a shell that hid a vulnerable and fragile soul. So much like Ilora. And like Ilora, Maeve was also beautiful, and strong, and womanly.

Kelia imagined what it would be like to make love to Maeve. To kiss her full lips. To feel her body pressed up against her own, their arms and legs entwined. To caress her light-skinned face and stare into her deep, violet eyes as they succumbed to their roiling passions.

She harrumphed. *This is the height of foolishness. I just met this woman, and yet I feel myself almost uncontrollably drawn to her. Why? Has the Sharing created a deeper connection than I originally thought? Am I just ... lonely? I am a strong, healthy woman, in the prime of my life, and yet I have denied myself the pleasures of the flesh for twelve years. Do I feel this way because Maeve is the first non-Ixtrayu I've encountered in all that time? Or am I just fascinated with her because she's alien to this world?*

Kelia knew a relationship between herself and Maeve was impossible. They were, literally, from different worlds. Eventually, she and her son would leave Elystra, never to return. On top of that, Maeve had chosen a man as her companion. Having never been close to a man in that way, she could only wonder if Maeve's connection to him lasted even after his death. She also wondered if it was part of Terran culture for a woman to be intimate with another woman.

She would give anything to find out.

Kelia realized she was staring. "May I ask you a question, Maeve? If it's not too personal, I mean."

Maeve smiled warmly. "Go ahead."

"Do many of your race have purple hair?"

A chuckle, accompanied by a broad grin. "Really? I'm from the other side of the galaxy, and you want to know about my hair?"

"I am merely curious. Some Elystrans have fair hair; others have hair as dark as the night. Some in the country of Rhys even have red hair, not unlike Davin's. But I never imagined a person could have hair in such a vibrant purple."

Maeve grasped a strand of her hair in her hand, then met Kelia's gaze. "I was actually born with black hair, just like my mother and father. However, on my world, we can manipulate our genetic code so we can choose whatever hair and eye color we want."

Kelia's eyes widened. "That is … astounding."

"I once knew a girl who changed her colors every couple of months. Every color of the rainbow. You name it, she tried it at some point. Once she even made her eyes white. Which was just creepy, if you ask me. I mean, white on white? She looked like an albino zombie."

"I see … I think." Kelia grinned. "Why did you choose purple?"

"I just like the color. It's the same color as the flowers that used to grow near my parents' house in Cork. That's the name of their, um, village."

"It is one of my favorite colors as well."

"May I ask you a question?" Maeve asked, placing her arms on the table.

"Of course."

"Can you fly?"

"Fly?"

"Yes. I mean, you made me do it, I was wondering if you could do it yourself."

Kelia quirked an eyebrow. "Oh, you mean my air-Wielding. I controlled the air surrounding you, using it to keep you off the ground."

"I see. It certainly was intense to experience."

"I have used this technique on my daughter, but then, she does not weigh very much. The more something weighs, the harder it is for me, and the faster it drains me." Kelia nodded toward Fex, who was still dozing. "I had to lift Fex up to the top of a rock she couldn't climb on her own. I'd never had to lift anything so heavy before."

"Yeah, she is a heavyweight," Maeve agreed. "Have you ever tried it on yourself?"

"When I was younger, I had dreams of flying over the Ix-trayu's territory like a great wingless bird. However, I quickly discovered that the strength to accomplish such a feat is beyond even the most powerful Wielder."

"That's too bad."

"Indeed. But I think I would be willing to attempt it again."

"Really?"

Kelia gave a mischievous smile. "I don't see why not."

They stood up, and Kelia walked a few yards to an open spot. After a few deep breaths, Kelia closed her eyes and lowered her head, calling upon her abilities.

The cloth of Kelia's tunic rippled in the brisk breeze that seemed to come from nowhere. The wind encircled her, light at first but with more and more force. She felt her forehead crinkle in concentration, and within seconds, her feet lifted off the ground. Slowly, majestically, she rose into the air.

Kelia opened her eyes to see Maeve gawking at her. Kelia smiled back, and the slight lapse of concentration caused her to momentarily lose focus. She slipped and fell, bracing herself for impact.

And then, just like that, she was floating again. The strain Kelia felt a moment ago was gone. She looked up to see Maeve, holding her hands out in front of her.

Kelia felt a surge of energy pulsate through her body, exactly as it had the previous night when she'd consoled Maeve. They were sharing something. Not thoughts or memories, but energy. Kelia had never considered the possibility of one Wielder sharing their own power with another. Not only did Maeve possess the ability to heal *and* communicate with animals, but she could augment other Wielders' abilities.

This was unprecedented. But then, never before had two such powerful Wielders undergone the Sharing.

"Maeve!" Kelia shouted over the fiercely-blowing wind, unable to keep the joyous smile from her face.

"Oh my God!" Maeve screamed, as if just realizing her part in this revelation. "Am I doing this?"

"Yes!" Kelia waved her hands slightly, and she found she could move herself through the air with ease. She went up, down, forwards, backwards, side-to-side. It felt natural. Exhilarating. As easy as breathing.

Concentrating once again, she watched her sister Wielder's face light up as, with another slight movement of her hands, Maeve lifted off the ground as well.

Maeve let out a squeal of excitement. "Kelia!"

"Relax, don't struggle," Kelia said, smiling mischievously. The two of them floated, at arm's length, in a rotating circle, five feet off the ground.

Kelia held her hands out, and Maeve did the same. Their fingers interlocked as they continued their aerial dance, their hair whipping wildly in the fierce breeze of their own creation. But the childish grins never left their faces.

Never in Kelia's entire life had she felt such liberation. To laugh at gravity was one thing, but to do it jointly, with a remarkable woman she'd already come to admire, was something else entirely. She fed off the energy Maeve supplied her. It was intoxicating.

She gazed into Maeve's deep, violet eyes, which shined with the same exuberance she was feeling with every fiber of her being.

And then the ground came up and hit them as they crashed to the dirt, finally breaking their contact, and with it, the feeling of euphoric glee.

Both women quickly sat up. "Are you all right?" Maeve asked.

Kelia checked her hands and arms, which had taken the brunt of the fall. "I appear to be uninjured."

They locked eyes again, and burst into laughter. This went on for many moments.

Maeve, gasping for breath, panted, "Wow, Kelia. That was ... incredible. Just incredible. Thank you."

Kelia edged her body forward, placing a gentle hand on Maeve's shoulder. "Thank *you*, Maeve. I don't know that any Ixtrayu in history has ever experienced what I just did." She gazed deeply into the Terran woman's eyes, and wondered if Maeve shared the desires that were all but consuming her.

Could it be true? Kelia thought. *Dare I hope ... ?*

Kelia leaned forward in anticipation.

Maeve leaned forward as well.

Their breath held.

Their eyes closed.

Their lips met.

Chapter Thirty-One

WITH A final pull on the ropes by eight of the burliest men in Elzor's ranks, the enormous metal door fell outward and into the wide corridor. The resulting crash caused all present to cover their ears. They had to turn their backs to avoid the billowing clouds of dust thrown up by the door's fall.

It had taken the terrified chemist only a few hours to produce a large amount of sargonic acid. Elzor wasted no time having one of his trusted lieutenants apply it to the door's massive hinges. As advertised, the acid quickly ate through both the machinite of the hinges and the rock edging the door frame, creating enough space for grappling hooks attached to strong ropes to be inserted. A few hefty tugs, and the giant door obediently fell to the ground.

Brushing the residual dust from his face and beard, Elzor beckoned to several of his men further down the corridor. "Torches! Now!" Four men with lit torches immediately came forward with Langon's massive frame towering right behind them. Elzor snatched one from a soldier's hand and approached the gaping hole in the wall of the sub-dungeon.

The musty smell of death assaulted Elzor's nostrils as he neared the entrance, but he ignored it. He'd smelled far more rancorous odors at Mogran, and now that the object of his quest was quite possibly within his grasp, he wasn't going to let any foul stench deter him.

He entered the dank room, which was much smaller than he imagined it to be. As the torch-light swept into every corner, his exultation turned to frustration, then to seething rage. Apart from a two-inch layer of dust on the floor and the remains of a skeleton in the corner, the room was empty.

"Well, go on, search the place!" he bellowed, using his head to indicate the floor. "Search every square inch of this room!"

He stepped back out into the corridor as the soldiers fell to their hands and knees, searching the dusty floor for anything that might resemble the storied Agrusian Stone. His fists and teeth were clenched as he approached his general. "That old braga! Even with the lives of children at stake, he lied to me! If he weren't dead, I would kill him!"

Langon's face remained impassive. "I don't understand, my liege. If the Stone is not here, why lie about it? Could he have been unaware?"

"Unaware? Of course he was aware, Langon! He, like every King of Agrus for the last eight centuries, chose to maintain this absurd lie even at the cost of the lives of his citizens! His own granddaughter!"

"But why, my liege?"

He gave Langon a withering look. "To plant a seed of doubt in the minds of any who might choose to invade Agrus, of course!" He clenched his fists, and gave an exasperated sigh. "According to legend, it was a stone that channeled untold power. Normally, I would not be swayed by such superstitious nonsense, but the letters I read in the Viceroy's library indicate that not one, but *two* stones exist on Elystra ... besides the one my sister and I found in the mines of Barju."

"Yes, my liege." Langon bowed his head. "I'm no expert, but it seems clear that no one has been on the other side of this door for centuries. The Stone is long gone ... if it was ever here at all."

Elzor locked his hands behind his back and took a few purposeful paces down the sparsely lit corridor. His breathing had quickened, and he hung his head. "I have spent my entire adult life working for this moment, Langon. I have pored through every musty scroll, in every repository of knowledge I could find, on the subject of the Stones. It exists, and I *will* find it."

Langon followed Elzor's footsteps, placing a meaty hand on his liege's shoulder. "I, and the rest of the Elzorath, will follow you wherever you may lead us, even unto death."

Elzor turned to look at Langon, his face an emotionless mask.

"You should know, my liege," Langon continued, "that in the past week, several hundred men, believing Elzaria's abilities to be a divine gift from Arantha, have shown up at the castle gates, ready to swear their allegiance to you. We have more than replenished the losses we sustained when we sacked the city." He paused. "But even with your sister's help, our numbers are not sufficient to withstand the combined might of all our enemies' armies."

"I am aware of that," Elzor said. "I trust you have personally vetted these men? We wouldn't want an Imarian or Daradian spy to infiltrate our ranks."

"Of course, my liege. You now have a thousand men at your disposal. But even blind loyalty will wane if it is not given direction. The good news is, we have availed ourselves of the land's resources: our men are now outfitted with the best armor and weapons this side of Darad. And not only that, but we have nearly enough merychs for every Elzorath to ride."

"That is good," Elzor said.

"Has your sister awoken from her sleep, my liege?"

Elzor shook his head. "Not as of yet, but I have men stationed outside her bedroom door who will inform me the moment she does. I would have probably attributed her collapse to exhaustion if not for the fact that she seems to be having visions."

The previous evening, he'd allowed his sister access to the Stone, only to be told that it had shown her images of a great metallic bird somewhere within the vast Kaberian Mountain range. She'd also seen two beings, much like Elystrans in appearance, moving about their tiny camp on some unknown task. Elzor asked Elzaria to provide more details, but the otherworldliness of the images had utterly baffled her. After their meal, he sent her back to her room to consult the Stone again, but she'd lapsed into a comatose state before she could do so. Nothing they did for her succeeded in waking her up, but her heart was strong. All they could do was wait.

Langon's dark, beady eyes narrowed, but he didn't respond. Elzor faced him full on. "What is it?"

"None on Elystra have experienced visions outside the High Mages of Darad," he said. "At least, not that I'm aware of. I am bothered by the timing of this development. The appearance of this 'metal bird,' as she described it, at nearly the exact moment that we discover the Agrusian Stone missing, cannot be a coincidence."

"I'm inclined to agree with you. Let us hope that when Elzaria wakes, she provides us with our next destination. It will take weeks for our enemies' armies to combine forces and make the journey to Agrus. We must be well on our way long before they near the border."

"Yes, my liege." Langon bowed again.

The soldiers assigned to search the small room emerged with torches in hand, approached Elzor, and knelt at his feet.

Elzor addressed the one in front. "Speak, Nilrem."

"We searched every inch, my liege." He raised his head to meet Elzor's gaze. "There was no Stone. However, we also studied the skeleton. Most of his bones and clothing crumbled to dust when we entered, but from what we could salvage, we don't believe they belonged to an Agrusian."

"Explain," Elzor said, straightening his spine and holding his arms akimbo.

Nilrem held out a handful of ancient coins and a small, sheathed dagger, which Elzor took. "If I had to guess, I'd say he was a thief or a raider."

Elzor turned the objects over in his hands. The coins were definitely ancient, and not made of metal at all. It felt like polished stone. The dagger was equally devoid of metal, as it must have come from a time that predated metalworking on Elystra. The hilt of the dagger was wooden, and the blade itself was sharpened stone.

"Very good, Nilrem. You and your men, get some breakfast and rejoin your regiment. Spread the word to remain alert and at the ready, for we may be moving our army out soon."

"Yes, my liege." As one, the men rose to their feet, saluted by placing a closed fist against their left breast, and moved up the corridor, past Elzor and Langon, heading for the stairs leading up to ground level.

After their footsteps faded away, Elzor held the objects out to Langon. "What do you make of these?"

Langon grabbed an additional torch from where it had been anchored to the wall, bringing the light as close as he dared to the objects in Elzor's hands. "I am unfamiliar with ancient currency, my liege." He cautiously took the dagger and unsheathed it, holding the stone blade close to the light. After a few moments' studying, he said, "If I didn't know better, I'd swear this stone was echorite."

"Echorite?" Elzor said. "That's volcanic, isn't it?"

"Yes, my liege. And the only volcano I know of is Mount Vaska, on the eastern coast. It marks the beginning of the southern wastelands, and is only a day's ride from the border of –"

"Vanda," Elzor interrupted. "The man was a Vandan raider."

"It would appear so."

Elzor, in a sudden rage, reared his arm back and flung the coins into the darkened vault. "The Vandans stole the Stone! Those blagging barbarians!"

Langon took several steps backward, not daring to utter a sound.

Elzor took a few deep breaths, trying to calm himself but not succeeding. "No wonder the royals lied all this time! It wouldn't do for the people of Agrus to know that Vandan raiders had absconded with their precious Stone, now, would it?"

"Will we be leaving for Vanda, then, my liege?" Langon piped up, his voice trembling with more than a little trepidation. "If we wish to avoid the borders of Barju, Imar and Darad, not to mention the Kaberian mountains, we will have to cross the Praskian Desert and the Plains of Iyan. It will take many weeks to make the journey, even by merych."

Elzor nodded. "Have the men begin preparations, Langon. We will move out within the next few days, assuming Elzaria is able to rouse herself in that time. We will want to maintain a steady pace, so have the men pack no more than we need. We may need to hunt for our food in addition to our provisions. I will plan the most direct route for us."

Langon bowed once more. "I will relay those orders, my liege." Then he turned on his heels and followed the soldiers to the stairs leading upward.

Elzor stared at the stone dagger in his palm. "Vandans," he spat. "I will rid Elystra of those ignorant savages once and for all." Then, eager to breathe fresh air again, he made his way back to the surface.

Chapter Thirty-Two

WHAT THE *bloody FARK, Maeve?*
The excitement, the adrenaline rush from being the first Earth-born human to actually *fly* without artificial means, added to the unexpected, sudden attraction she had to Kelia, had led to this.

It hadn't even been two weeks since her beloved husband, the father of her son, sacrificed himself so they could escape. The man she vowed to honor and cherish as he slipped the ring onto her finger. His body, if there was anything left of it, had barely had time to grow cold, and here she was, in the arms of another. A woman, no less. Holding her. Embracing her. Thinking wanton thoughts of her.

How could I do this?

What does this say about me?

I am so going to Hell.

After only a few moments, Maeve broke the kiss, scrambled to her feet, and backed away like she'd been stung. She felt her whole body tremble as she realized the line she'd just crossed.

Maeve turned her head, unable to look at the woman who had tempted her so. "I–I–I'm sorry. I–I–shouldn't have done that." Maeve cast a frantic look at the *Talon*, uttering a silent prayer of gratitude when she confirmed Davin hadn't seen her massive indiscretion.

After several deep breaths, Maeve sat down at the table again, her eyes locking on the Stone. In the light of day, the yellow glow it gave off was much more subdued, but still noticeable. She heard Kelia's footsteps as the Elystran woman moved away from her.

Maeve glanced up. Kelia was leaning on Fex, her hands grasping the beast's saddle for support. Guilt washed over Maeve as she observed Kelia's posture; her shoulders sagged, as if an invisible weight were pressing down upon them.

Maeve quickly made her way over. "Kelia?"

"I have acted shamefully," Kelia said. Maeve noticed she was trembling. "I let my feelings of exhilaration sweep away my inhibitions like a child. I should know better than that." She sighed heavily, her body still shaking. "In all my time as Protectress, I have never let my base desires dictate my actions." She looked askance at Maeve. "I have no excuse. I beg your forgiveness, even though I do not deserve it."

"Kelia." Maeve grasped her shoulder and turned her until they faced each other. "I am as much to blame as you. Don't beat yourself up about it."

"Last night you called me 'enlightened,'" Kelia said, her face pinched into a haunted frown. "That is how I wanted to present myself to you, who have traveled from one end of the Above to the other, who have endured so much and whom I have come to venerate in our brief time together." She exhaled again. "I'm not feeling particularly 'enlightened' at the moment."

Maeve took another cautious step forward, keeping her voice low. "We have a saying back on Earth: you're only human."

"I am not human."

Maeve felt her eyes moisten. "Yes, you are. In every way that matters, you are. You have strength, so much strength. And you have weakness, just like us." She cast another glance at the ship. "But that ... *cannot* happen again," she said with as much conviction as she could muster.

"Agreed." Kelia knelt down and patted Fex's neck. The chava's leg twitched, but she did not raise her head.

Maeve returned to the dining table, taking her seat again. Within a few moments, Kelia rejoined her. Still in a state of agitation, Maeve drained the last few drops of grapefruit juice from her cup. "You know, we've spent most of the last day talking, but we've conveniently avoided asking the biggest question of them all."

"Which is?"

"What are we going to do now?"

"You came to Elystra looking for this." Kelia indicated the Stone in between them, "And now you've found it."

"Yes, we have." An alarming thought struck her. "If I tried to take this away from Elystra, would you ... stop me?" Before she could answer, Maeve quickly added, "I mean, this is your world, and I don't want to plunder something that rightfully belongs to you –"

Kelia held her hand up, cutting Maeve off. "This is a Stone of Arantha. It belongs to her, not me. It's been here for centuries and we never knew. If she had meant for my people to have it, she could have led me or any one of my ancestors to it. But she didn't. She led *you*. I've never been adept at interpreting her wishes, but in this case, it couldn't be more clear: she wants you to have it. Should you wish to depart with it, I will not stop you."

Maeve nodded, relieved.

"This being that sent you here –"

"Banikar. I never actually met him. Only my husband had that honor. If any other person but Richard had come to me with a story about a strange, glowing alien who just showed up out of the blue, with precise instructions about what to do and where to go, I would have said they were stark raving mad.

But Richard was the most level-headed man I ever knew. And besides, it's not like the rest of us had a better plan."

Maeve gestured to the Stone. "According to what Banikar told my husband, finding this Stone was the first step in defeating the Jegg. Judging from these freaky powers I've suddenly developed, I can certainly see the potential. But the Jegg are *everywhere*, Kelia. They've conquered nearly one-third of our entire galaxy. I'm only one woman, with one Stone. I can't possibly take on an entire race by myself. That is, if I could even get back."

Kelia reached over the table and grasped Maeve's hand. Maeve's body tensed, but she didn't pull away. "I know you may not accept this, Maeve, but I meant what I said before. It is Arantha that guides you along your path, even though you may not see it."

Maeve squeezed her eyes closed, her mind a seething cauldron of indecision. "What do you think I should do?"

"Come back with me."

Maeve opened her eyes, fixing Kelia with a puzzled look. "Back? To your village?"

"Yes. For centuries, Protectresses have chronicled their visions in written form. I have spent my life studying them. I don't remember any specific reference to a second Stone, but that doesn't mean it isn't there. It's certainly worth checking."

Maeve nodded. "What about your people? How would they react to me?"

"I do not know," Kelia said, retracting her hands. "I believe I can convince them that you are no threat to the Ixtrayu, or to Elystra, but we may have to engage in subterfuge."

"What do you mean?"

Kelia's brows knitted. "I've told you of our current difficulties. There have been no Sojourns for thirteen years. For the first time in our history, my sisters are questioning whether or not the path we are on is the right one. I was certain that when I envisioned beings from the Above, they would bring with them the answers we seek."

"But I have no such answers."

"I realize that. I also believe that if I present you to my tribe as an emissary of Arantha, it will allay their fears long enough for us to determine our next course of action."

Maeve stood up and walked a few paces away, placing her hands on her hips. "I can't get involved in the politics of your world, Kelia. No good can come of it. I am glad you do not fear me, but people tend to fear what they don't understand. Some may accept me, but others will surely be terrified of me. And then there's Davin."

Kelia also stood up. "I assure you, I will do everything in my power to protect him."

Maeve spun around, her volume increasing. "According to you, no male has ever set foot in your village. You teach your daughters to hate and fear men from birth. Once you put him in front of them, it won't matter that he's from another world. It won't even matter that he's just a boy. They won't trust him, and they'll probably try to hurt him. Will an order from the Protectress be enough to keep him safe?"

Kelia thought for a few moments. "Tensions are high right now, and his presence would assuredly make things more precarious."

"Precarious," Maeve repeated. She felt her guts tighten. "That's one way of putting it. Frankly, I'm surprised the Ixtrayu have survived *this* long."

Kelia looked as if she'd been slapped. Her face morphed into a scowl. "What does *that* mean?"

"I saw the life you live," Maeve said, "during our Sharing. I think it's remarkable what your people have achieved. But it can't last forever, and I suspect you know that."

Kelia's frown had intensified, but no response came.

"The fact that you've remained undiscovered while living right under the noses of the kingdoms, the *men* you hide from, is nothing less than a miracle. What would happen if a scout, or a hunting party, or an entire army just happened to pass within sight of your village? What would you do? How far would you go to protect your secret?"

"We would do whatever we must," Kelia said coldly. "The men of this world would not entertain even the notion of a tribe of independent women. They would see us as a threat, and wouldn't hesitate to destroy us or enslave us, lest their own women get ideas above their station."

Maeve took a step forward, pointing at a convenient horizon. "And what makes you better than them? What makes your way of life so superior to theirs?"

Kelia straightened her back, each word flicking off her tongue. "We live in harmony with nature. Men war with each other. They fight, and steal, and kill, and squabble over every scrap of land they can get their fingers on. This is how it's always been."

"Maybe so, but there's another saying we have on Earth: if you're not part of the solution, you're part of the problem. And this system you've created *will fail.* It's inevitable."

Kelia's even-tempered countenance fell away, and she exploded in anger. "You have been here a week! Do not pretend you know us!"

"But I *do* know you," Maeve retorted. "My planet went through exactly the same thing. We were ruled by bigotry and prejudice and ignorance. For centuries, people were discriminated against because of their gender, or their lineage, or their religion, or even the color of their skin. We fought wars over these things, and millions died. *Millions*, Kelia! Every single lesson the human race learned was paid for in blood! You say the men of this world see women as inferior? You teach them otherwise! You don't hide from them, you don't hoodwink them into becoming sperm donors, and you *certainly* don't abandon your sons just because they weren't born girls!"

Kelia's chest was heaving, stunned by Maeve's tirade. She looked like she was going to respond in kind, but instead she quietly said, "This is our way."

Maeve took several more steps forward until she was standing right before Kelia. "Your way is wrong. Men cannot survive without women. Women cannot survive without men. How many hundreds of boys have the Ixtrayu forced to be raised by jilted fathers who no doubt told them that their mother didn't want them? You think any of *them* grew up respecting women?"

Kelia's voice was a taut whisper. "You believe you have all the answers to this world's problems. What would you have us do?"

"Change it. Raise your sons the same as your daughters. Teach them to respect and honor women as equals."

"I cannot do that."

Maeve threw her hands up in frustration. "*Why*? Why can't you? You are their leader, Kelia! Lead your people out of this ... this Dark Age. Before it's too late."

Kelia glanced up, looking at the sky. It was now mid-afternoon. She turned to the side, staring at Maeve. The look of pain on her face tore Maeve's heart in half. "At first light tomorrow, I will return to my village. Will you accompany me?"

Maeve squared her shoulders. "No. I will not endanger my son."

Kelia nodded, almost imperceptibly. "So be it. I thank you for your ... hospitality. Take the Stone and go. Leave Elystra."

So that's it, Maeve thought. "Kelia –"

Kelia faced her again. The harshness had gone from her face, and in its place was grim, sorrowful resolve. "No. There is nothing more to say."

The sound of feet upon metal came from the ship, and both women turned to see Davin descend the exit ramp. Upon hitting solid ground, he stretched, working the stiffness out of his arms and back, punctuating it with a big yawn.

"Don't say anything. I will explain it to him tomorrow," Maeve whispered.

Kelia nodded. "I wish you well, Major Maeve Cromack. May Arantha speed you on your journey." Then she returned to Fex's side.

The conversation now over, Maeve went to greet her son. She smiled warmly at him as she approached, but on the inside, she felt like a part of her soul had just died.

* * *

The three of them ate a sumptuous dinner of barbecued spareribs, corn on the cob, and spinach salad. For Davin's benefit, no words were spoken about Maeve and Kelia's tandem flight, their kiss, or their disagreement. When the sun set, Davin agreed once again to take night watch.

Kelia eventually fell asleep on the same bunk she slept on the night before. Maeve, however, couldn't sleep. She felt queasy, and deeply regretted vocalizing her judgments so poorly. But she'd spoken the truth, and as much as she'd grown to care for Kelia in their brief acquaintance, it needed to be said. Kelia was part of a system based on discrimination, deception, and prejudice. She was just so engrained in that system she couldn't see it.

What Maeve found more disturbing than the thought she might have offended Kelia was the realization that after tomorrow, she would likely never see her again. They'd been given a chance to explore one of the most unique relationships in human history together. The moment her abilities joined Kelia's, twining like invisible tendrils around each other until they became one, was indescribable. But the clash of cultures, of philosophies, was just too great to overcome.

The last thing Maeve saw before surrendering to sleep was Kelia's beautiful, serene face, only yards away from her own. She would miss this woman. A lot.

Her final thought was a jarring one: *Am I sending her away because of who she is, or am I just covering up my own guilt at what I did? And what I still feel for her?*

The next morning, Maeve woke to find Davin asleep and Kelia's bunk empty. The clock read 6:30 am, which meant the sun had risen less than an hour ago. It took less than ten seconds to determine that Fex was nowhere to be found, and neither was her rider.

Maeve moved to the dining table, where the Stone still sat. Right next to it was a collection of small round rocks that Kelia must have gathered from the floor of the riverbed. They were arranged into three symbols that Maeve recognized thanks to the gift Kelia gave her through their Sharing. Three words: *Farol Dama Ven.*

Goodbye, Dear Friend.

A fist of regret closed around Maeve's heart as she replayed every word of their argument in her mind. Her legs felt suddenly unsteady, so she sat down in the nearest chair.

Through moist eyes, she read Kelia's farewell note again.

"Way to go, you dumb slag," she chided herself. "Way to go."

Chapter Thirty-Three

MIZAR'S NOSTRILS twitched as the scent of cooked meat floated into them, and he snorted as he roused into wakefulness. He'd fallen asleep with his head atop his High Mage cloak and his interlocked fingers resting on his chest.

He opened his eyes. The sun was sinking behind the treetops of the Celosian Forest, which marked the border of Darad. Sen was nearby, turning the stripped meat of a small creature on an improvised spit. Their merychs were tethered to a nearby tree, grazing on a patch of grass growing in tufts at its base.

"Sen?" he croaked, rising into a sitting position.

"Dinner's almost ready, Master," Sen said curtly.

Mizar rubbed his temples, recalling the awkward moment when he woke up two days before, after blacking out and tumbling from his merych. Much like the moment Sen shook him awake in the Crystal Cavern, he had to assuage his apprentice's fears that he was all right and had sustained no injuries beyond the bruises from falling to the ground, which Sen had expertly healed.

"Smells wonderful, Sen," Mizar said. "Your skill at trapping jarveks is a constant source of amazement to me. How did you acquire it?"

"Thank you, Master." Sen nodded in Mizar's direction, but didn't smile. "Jarveks were a big problem back on my father's farm. From the age of seven, it was my job to make sure his croplands were free of them. A nearly impossible task in Thelwyn."

"I imagine so, given how much they reproduce."

"If even one got by me and Father found out about it, I was ... *punished.*" Sen spat out the last word. "So it was worth my while to become an expert at trapping them."

Mizar stood, stretched his legs, and walked over to the campfire, sitting down on a small boulder that lay nearby. With the sun setting, the temperature was starting to drop, so Mizar warmed his hands by the fire.

Sen hadn't spoken much in the last day. After getting back on his merych following his collapse, Mizar had led them to this spot, a verdant glen with a narrow, slow-moving river meandering its way into the forest. In that time, he'd given Sen no reason for his blackout, mainly because he had none to give. Sen gave him the occasional inquisitive glance, which Mizar ignored.

Mizar could tell that Sen was irked by the unannounced detour they'd taken to this spot. The boy's movements were rough and jerky, and he was clearly doing his best to not look his master in the eye.

"Sen, what vexes you?" Mizar asked.

"It's nothing, Master," he said after a short pause. He didn't lift his gaze from the cooking meat.

"*Sen.*"

The young man stopped rotating the spit, shifting from a kneeling to a sitting position. He let out a loud breath, then turned to face Mizar. "I am merely your apprentice, Master. It is my sworn duty to obey your commands without question."

Mizar's brows knitted. "I thought I taught you better than that."

"Master?"

"There are times, yes, when I have had to be rather cryptic about what Arantha reveals to me and, in turn, what I reveal to others, up to and including the King. I may be High Mage, but that hardly makes me infallible. After two years, I would think you'd feel comfortable speaking your mind. I have come to trust your insights, Sen. I may not always show it, but I consider your opinion important."

"All right." Sen cleared his throat, and out came the question that had obviously been on his mind for the past two days. "Why are we here? In this place?"

Mizar stood and put his hands behind his back. Instantly, he changed his approach from that of a concerned Master to an engaged teacher. "Why do you think we're here?"

"I don't know, Master. When we left the castle three days ago, I was under the impression we were riding to Ghaldyn province." He gestured to their surroundings. "I've never been in this part of the country, but I've studied enough maps to know this is not Ghaldyn. By my reckoning, we should've bore east at the Shardyn Crossing. Instead, we bore south."

"Very good," Mizar said, smiling. "So where are we now?"

Sen pointed at the trees in front of them. "This is the Celosian Forest. If we were to travel through it, we would emerge upon the Plains of Iyan. If we head south, it would lead us straight to the Vandan border. Neither option is desirable."

"Why do you say that?"

"I've heard some of the guards' murmurings of Vandan incursions into the forest. Many travelers who venture into that forest are never heard from again."

Mizar nodded. "I've heard those rumors as well." Seeing Sen's apprehension, he added, "Fear not, lad. We are but thirty minutes' ride away from an encampment where an entire garrison of King Aridor's best are stationed. They patrol this section of the Daradian border vigilantly."

The meat of the jarvek was starting to blacken, so Sen lifted the spit away from the fire, setting it down on top of a large cloth. "That's reassuring, Master, but it doesn't explain what we're doing here. Are we still going to Ghaldyn?"

"Yes. As soon as our business here is concluded."

Sen removed a small knife from his belt and began cutting the meat from the jarvek's bones. "Business?" he asked incredulously. "What sort of ..." He trailed off, and Mizar could almost see the wheels turning inside the boy's mind.

A smile curled the corners of Mizar's mouth as Sen worked it out.

"You had a vision. Arantha led you here," he said in a hushed tone.

Mizar nodded. "Yes."

"Why?"

No response.

Sen's shoulders sagged. "Do you have any idea how long we'll be here?"

Mizar gave a wry smirk. "Arantha's instructions are rarely *that* specific."

"I see." Sen brought out two small wooden plates from his satchel, portioning out the jarvek meat and a hunk of chaska bread onto each and handing one to Mizar.

They ate their meal in silence, enjoying the jarvek meat, which was tough but tasty. By the time they finished, the sun had disappeared behind the trees.

Swallowing the last morsel of food, Mizar handed his plate back to Sen and clapped the crumbs from his hands. "Tell me of your progress in translating Merdeen's prophecy."

Sen lowered his head, failing to mask his shamefaced expression. "I regret that I haven't made much, Master. Unfortunately, whoever created the cypher text you acquired was even less organized than the palace archivist. Matching the symbols to

Merdeen's hand, those that are even legible, has been a slow, tedious process."

The fire had ebbed to a few smoldering coals. Mizar stood, grabbed a few sticks from a pile that Sen collected earlier, and threw them in. A wave of his hand later, the fire had rebuilt itself. Satisfied, he reclaimed his seat. "Don't be too hard on yourself, Sen. Those documents were locked up for good reason. Nothing worth doing is ever easy. Now, tell me what you have translated."

"Well, the first few pages dealt with the end of the Vandan War, and the death of King Sardor's sons."

"No wonder Sardor locked it up. That would have been a painful reminder of what a hollow victory that war was." Mizar picked up another stick and idly poked the fire with it.

Sen nodded. "I had only just begun the second set of documents when we had to depart. He mentioned something about a tree."

Mizar's ears perked up. "Tree?"

"Yes, an ancient tree, its roots spreading all over Elystra." He chuckled. "That would be one enormous tree, to be sure. Do you know of any trees of such size, Master?"

Mizar was barely listening, instead gazing into the far distance. "Many years ago, right after I became High Mage, I read a text regarding some of the prophecies of High Mage Jerril. I seem to recall him mentioning a great tree as well."

"Jerril?" Sen inquired. "He was High Mage, what, three hundred years ago?"

"Three hundred fifty." He met Sen's gaze again. "What you just said matches Jerril's prophecy almost exactly."

Sen's eyebrows raised. "Do you remember anything else from the text?"

"No," Mizar said, running his fingers through his beard. "It was right before he died. Many historians have tried to interpret its meaning. Most agree that Jerril was not referring to an actual tree, but a metaphorical one."

"Merdeen called it the 'Mother Tree'," Sen said. "There's even an ancient word for it, which he graciously provided, as there likely wasn't an Elystran symbol in existence to represent it. It was written at the bottom of the page in regular Daradian script."

"Mother Tree?" Mizar asked. "That also sounds familiar. And I think I remember the word you speak of. What was it ... Ix ... Ixtro –"

"Ixtrayu," said Sen.

"Yes, that's it." He glanced sidelong at his apprentice. "Nothing about female Wielders, I take it?"

"Not so far, Master. But like I said, I have a long way to go."

"I understand. Keep on it Sen, you have my faith."

"Thank you Master," Sen said. "There was one other thing: I found several letters hidden, rather poorly I might add, in the back binding of one of the volumes. It would seem that Merdeen corresponded regularly with a scholar from Barju. His name was Miro. They spoke at length about many of Merdeen's visions, but nothing that included female Wielders. If there were letters regarding that subject, I haven't found them yet. Perhaps it was at that point that Sardor had Merdeen locked away, thus ending his communications with Miro."

"That's certainly possible." Mizar smiled. "You've done well, Sen. That's more than I was hoping for in such a short time. When we return to Dar, I will help you with the rest of the translation. I'm convinced the answers lie within."

At that moment, a deep rumbling sound drifted through the darkness of the forest. Both men turned in its direction. "Master?" Sen asked fearfully.

"I hear it too," Mizar said, rising to his feet. He waved his hands at the fire, reducing it to mere embers. He strode forward, scooped up two handfuls of dirt and tossed them onto the coals. "Hurry, Sen, help me put this out."

Sen joined Mizar in shoveling dirt on the campfire until it was reduced to nothing more than a few wisps of smoke. Their task completed, Mizar pointed to a large rock that jutted out of the ground twenty yards away, behind which the merychs had been tied. "Sen, go hide behind that boulder," Mizar said. "And don't come out until I tell you to. If things go badly, take your merych and head for the garrison as fast as you can."

All the blood drained from Sen's face. "Master?"

"Just do what I say, Sen!"

Sen gave no further objections. Gathering up his belongings, he made his way behind the boulder, disappearing from sight.

Chapter Thirty-Four

Vaxi slowed her chava, Tig, to a halt, glancing furtively to both sides of the forest path they now occupied. She hopped off and led her mount to the side of the road. Tig immediately began to snack on the narrow-leafed plants growing at the foot of the trees that towered hundreds of feet above their heads.

After leaving the village, she rode through the night and part of the morning before stopping for sleep and food from her saddlebag. Susarra told her to put as much distance as possible between her and the village before the tribe discovered she was missing, and she'd done that. Vaxi was confident she was far enough away now that they wouldn't catch up with her. Only Susarra knew where she was heading, and she assured Vaxi she would keep that knowledge secret no matter what.

Over the centuries, Ixtrayu women had Sojourned to all six of the other countries since their tribe was founded. Political climates changed, often without the Ixtrayu's knowledge, but even so, Susarra knew where to send Vaxi with the best chance of completing her Sojourn and returning unharmed.

On the eastern coast was the land of Vanda, whose men were known to be crude, rough, barbaric anarchists with little or no regard for the welfare of the women they bedded. The Ixtrayu had deemed Vanda off-limits centuries ago.

Also off-limits was Barju, a mountainous land due north of the village whose people were, in one way or another, involved in the country's mining industry. The men there were hard-working and known to be excellent breeding stock, but Susarra explained that Onara had forbidden any further Sojourns there when, thirty-two years ago, an Ixtrayu named Proda journeyed there and never returned.

Susarra eliminated the lands of Rhys and Imar from contention because, in her words, the men there were "sluggards and ruffians." The point of the Sojourn was to mate with a man whose strength and vitality was worthy of adding to the Ixtrayu, and her grandmother assured her that the best chance of finding such a man was either in Agrus or Darad. In the end, Susarra chose Darad for the simple fact that she'd Sojourned there herself forty years before, a Sojourn that ended up producing her mother, Ilora.

It would take two or three days to travel from the village to the Daradian border, Susarra had explained. First Vaxi would traverse the Plains of Iyan, which would likely be mostly devoid of life as the herds of kova had migrated to the south by this time of year. Men rarely ventured outside their borders to hunt, as they generally bred cattle and other animals for the purposes of supplying their food and leather. Besides, the Plains of Iyan were governed by no kingdom, which meant anyone who traveled through it did so at their own peril.

Tig was a strong, healthy chava, only ten years old according to Olma, and had enough food stored in her body to give her the energy to run for two days without eating. As they reached the point where the Plains of Iyan ended and the forest began, however, Tig began to complain from hunger, as evidenced from the loud gurgling sound coming from her stomach. Thankfully, there was plenty of plant life within the forest that she could feast upon.

"Okay, girl, we can rest here for a while," Vaxi said, patting Tig's neck. Tig acknowledged her with a grunt before continuing her meal.

Vaxi reached into her saddle-bag and brought out the bundle of food Aarna gave her the night she left, which was a goodly amount of dried, salted kova meat. She selected two large strips for herself, and returned the rest to the bag.

She sat down by the side of the road, wrapping one arm around Tig's thick foreleg as she ate. A soft, cooling breeze blew through the forest, raising gooseflesh on her arms. It was pleasant to be out of the hot sun, but she wondered how cold the evenings would get. Her ears perceived the rustling of the branches of the reesa trees, which were the largest living things she'd ever seen, nearly three times the height of the huxa trees that grew in the forest just north of the village. Apart from the wind and the calls of distant birds that nested in the uppermost branches, she heard nothing. It unsettled her.

As a huntress, Vaxi possessed a heightened sense of self-awareness, and for the first time since leaving the village, the full scope of how alone she was hit home. She was farther, *much* farther, from everything and everyone she'd ever known and loved than at any other time in her life.

Her grandmother had prepared her for the dangers she might encounter, but knowing the perils of traveling alone in a strange land and being able to overcome them were two different things. She could die out here. If she did, her people would never find her. They probably wouldn't even look for her, after what she did.

The thought turned to acid in her stomach. She'd disobeyed Onara's directive, maintained for the past thirteen years by Kelia. The Protectress, Arantha's vessel. She was disobeying the divine, generous being that had watched over the Ixtrayu for eight centuries.

She closed her eyes, remembering the look on Nyla's face when she rode past her and away from the village, sneaking away in the dark of night like a coward. She imagined the same pained look on the faces of Sarja, of Runa and her sister huntresses, and of Kelia, who had been her mother's companion and who had watched over Vaxi since she was a little girl.

Vaxi had let herself be dominated, bullied by her grandmother. But why? Susarra was old, overweight, and crippled. She was no match for Vaxi physically. But Susarra was her family. She was the only blood relative she had left. She was also a Councilor, and Vaxi felt obligated to listen to Susarra's voice over everyone else's, even Kelia's. Like she was no more than a scared little girl.

What would happen if she turned back right now? When word got out that she'd gone on Sojourn, her grandmother would be questioned. Maybe Susarra would be removed from the Council. Maybe she'd even be shunned, forced to live out her days as a pariah. And perhaps, Vaxi thought with a shudder, the same fate would befall her. Even if she returned to the village, safe and with child, would her people welcome her back into the fold?

Vaxi stood up, swallowed her last morsel of meat, and took a swig from her water-skin. Then she led Tig, who had also apparently sated her hunger for the time being, back onto the road.

Susarra said it was Vaxi's destiny to usher in the newest generation of Ixtrayu. Whether she believed it at the time, or whether she believed it now, didn't matter anymore. She'd made her choice. She had to go on.

She climbed back into the saddle, nudging Tig into motion. The road ahead was long, but if she kept a good pace, she could reach the border of Darad by nightfall. Another kick to Tig's flanks, and her chava burst into a full gallop.

* * *

Though the canopy of leaves above her head was thick, there were plenty of spots where the sun shone through, providing ample light for Vaxi to continue her journey. However, as the afternoon wore on and the trees' massive shadows grew longer and longer, she realized there was a chance she might not reach the forest's edge by sundown. She had no way of knowing just how far away the border was, as the winding path through the forest seemed to have no end. There were several other smaller, narrower, more overgrown paths that intersected with the one she was on, but she was confident she was going the right way. The path widened the further she went, to the point where three chavas could travel side-by-side on it without wandering into the undergrowth.

The sound of a distant branch snapping echoed through the trees, causing Vaxi to slow Tig to a canter. It had come from somewhere ahead of her but still distant, based on the clarity of the sound. Vaxi gripped the handle of her bow, unslinging it from around her body. Then, she reached over her shoulder and grasped the fletching of one of the many huxa-wood arrows in her quiver. She expertly nocked the arrow between the second and third fingers of her left hand, but didn't draw back on the string; instead, she kept the arrow pointed at the road as Tig ambled forward. Vaxi's eyes darted from left to right, scanning the forest on both sides of the road and wondering if this forest, like the one near the village, was home to packs of large nemza cats that would tear her apart if they had the chance. Nemzas generally preferred to live in the lowlands where it was warmer, so it was unlikely they inhabited this particular stretch of forest, which was at a much higher altitude. Still, there was always the chance. Hopefully Tig's size would intimidate any predators into thinking twice before attacking her.

Progressing down the trail, Vaxi felt some reassurance that the trees seemed to be thinning out. She hoped this was a sign that the forest's end was drawing near.

She forged ahead, keeping a vigilant eye all around her. She had seen nothing more threatening than a group of burrowing rodents scampering through the trees. No large animals, or people to fear. Once again, the loneliness of her situation crept in on her.

As Vaxi rounded another bend in the path, she heard another twig snap. This one was much closer than the previous one, and it was behind her. Vaxi whipped her head around, catching a flash of movement behind a cluster of trees to her right. Then she heard more movement to her left, and she saw something. It looked like a person, atop a large, four-legged animal. They were riding through the trees, parallel to the road she traveled.

Keeping her hands securely fastened on her bow and arrow, she gently nudged Tig into quickening her pace. With a snort, Tig obliged.

Tig continued around another bend in the path, and Vaxi had to call, "Stop, girl!" There was something in the road ahead of them. Several somethings.

Standing still, facing her, were four people, each one sitting atop a saddled animal that Vaxi assumed, based on its appearance, was a merych. The beasts, much like their riders, had colorful marks upon their bodies, streaks of blue and red that looked to be made from some form of dye.

These riders were men. The first men she'd ever seen.

Susarra had taught her the physical differences between men and women. She'd even shown Vaxi some rather crude drawings of the male anatomy. Vaxi now knew what needed to happen for her to become pregnant, and she wasn't relishing the idea any more than the pain she would feel the first time it happened.

She was prepared to endure this pain for the good of her tribe. One look at these men, however, and she knew it wasn't a pain she wanted to experience at their hands. She suddenly became very afraid as the men silently eyed her, scanning her body as if it was their next meal. Their looks made her feel dirty, soiled. She knew she was not in the company of friends.

All her life, she'd been taught that Elystran men would not hesitate to victimize a woman, particularly a young one riding alone through the woods. Vaxi found it hard to believe that *all* men had such callousness in their hearts. If that were true, far more Sojourns would have ended in disaster. But it would seem these riders were exactly the type of men she'd hoped to avoid.

When she began her journey, Vaxi was confident that her strength, her archery prowess, and Tig's ability to outrun any merych would carry her through. She prayed it would be enough.

All four men bore beards of different lengths, along with pieces of metal that pierced the skin of their cheeks and ear-lobes. Their clothes were various shades of brown, and from their smell it appeared they didn't bathe much. She silently cursed the wind; had it not been blowing in the same direction she was riding, she would have picked up their stench a mile away.

She searched their eyes for even the faintest trace of amicability, but saw none. Two of the men, upon seeing the weapon in her hands, produced bows of their own.

The leader, a short, burly man with beady eyes, a ragged black beard and a nose that looked like someone had squashed it against his face, spoke. "Well, look 'ere, boys, at what's come'n delivered itself right to us." The other men's faces cracked into ugly, toothy smiles, and Vaxi felt her stomach churn.

"Let me pass," Vaxi said, showing them her weapon but not pointing it at them yet. She hoped her voice wouldn't betray her anxiety. "I am on my way to Darad."

"Oh, izzat right?" the man said. "An' where izzit you're from, gell?"

Vaxi had anticipated being asked this question, as it was one that was regularly asked of Ixtrayu going on Sojourn. The story they'd told for centuries was that they were members of a nameless tribe of nomads who eked out a living in an area close to the southern wetlands. This would dissuade men from attempting to locate them once the Sojourn ended.

Vaxi had practiced this cover story for hours. However, these men were most assuredly not potential mates, so she didn't feel like wasting her time telling it. "Where I'm from is none of your concern. Let me pass."

She heard more movement behind her, and turned to see two more riders emerge from the forest behind her, cutting off any possible retreat. They, too, had bows with nocked arrows in their hands.

"Be my pleasure, gell," the leader drawled. "But first ya gotta pay a toll."

"Toll?"

"Yeah. We'll start with any coin or valuables ya got on ya."

Tig began to stamp her hooves nervously, and Vaxi gently patted her neck in an attempt to calm her. "I have no such things."

A flash of annoyance crossed his face. "What'cha got in yer bags, den?"

"Just food and water."

The large man on the leader's right broke out in an ugly, lascivious grin. "We'll be takin' dat too." He ran his eyes over her body again, making her skin crawl.

She'd had enough of this. "I have no quarrel with you," Vaxi said, a tremor entering her voice. "I will ask you one more time to step aside. I will not ask again. Do not force me to kill you." She raised her bow, aiming it at the leader.

He didn't seem the least bit fazed. The large rider on his right turned to face him. "Well, dat's jus' rude, innit, brudda?"

"Sure is. Mebbe we'll jus' take the toll in some other way." He gestured with his arms, and the two archers riding along-side them pulled back on their drawstrings, the arrows pointed right at her.

"Ya thinkin' what I'm thinkin', Voris?" the big man asked.

"Sure am. She looks young 'n healthy. I bet she could go for hours."

Vaxi knew exactly what he meant, and she knew equally well that she would die before she'd let herself be subjected to such treatment. She felt the hair on the nape of her neck rise as she calculated the best possible ways to escape. There were six men in all, and four of them were armed with bows. There was no way to know if they were as skilled as she was, or if they were skilled at all. The other two, the leader and the grinning man, wore swords at their sides as well as a couple of bone-handled knives stuck into their belts. If she could get past them, Tig would easily outdistance them. She just needed to survive the first volley of arrows.

"Dis' your last chance, gell," Voris said. "Get offa your beast and come wit us, and mebbe you'll live to see mornin'," the leader said. "Though ya might be a bit sore. My brudda tends ta be rather rough wit his women. Ain' dat right, Steff?"

The grinning man nodded. "Yeah, Voris. Though dey always thank me after'ards."

"Over my dead body," Vaxi said with as much defiance as she could.

Voris smiled, as if this was how he wanted the encounter to end. "Whatever ya say, gell." He nodded his head at Steff. "Have fun, brudda."

The man called Steff urged his merych forward, drew his sword from its sheath and charged at her. He'd only covered half the distance between them when she fired.

The arrow flew straight and true, embedding itself into Steff's eye. The impact flung the big man off his mount, and he hit the ground with a loud *thump*. His merych continued to trot past her as well as the two men behind her.

Vaxi looked down at Steff. His one remaining eye was wide open, staring up at the hidden sky, with a three-foot arrow lodged in his skull.

Despite her warnings, Voris obviously hadn't expected a mere girl to threaten a company of men, let alone fire upon them. He looked down at Steff's body, spluttering and choking muted, coarse words she couldn't understand. When his eyes met hers again, they were blazing with hatred. His chest heaving with anger, he bellowed, "Kill her!"

Vaxi kicked Tig's flanks as hard as she could. Like a coiled spring, the chava charged forwards, rushing at the three men and their merychs. She lowered her body onto Tig's back as she quickly drew another arrow from her quiver. One arrow whizzed by her head, and then she heard the sickening sound of a second arrow embedding itself into Tig's flank.

Tig roared in pain as Vaxi nocked and fired again, hitting one of the archers square in the heart before he could loose his own arrow. He tumbled off his merych, dead before he hit the ground. The fourth archer fired, and Vaxi saw it too late to dodge it. She nudged Tig slightly to the right, and the arrow stuck itself deep in her thigh.

The pain was overwhelming; unlike any she'd ever experienced. But she couldn't see to it now. Tig was now upon Voris and the remaining archer. Voris's eyes widened in fear as he tried to spur his merych into motion, but he was too late.

Tig squeezed herself into the small space between the two merychs, her wide girth knocking both of them off balance and causing their riders to fall to the ground. With another burst of speed, Tig raced down the forest path, away from the riders.

Vaxi dared not turn around to see if they were following. Doing her best to ignore the pain in her leg, she used her feet to steer Tig down the path. The arrow in Tig's flank had gone deep, and it was affecting her speed. If Vaxi didn't lose her pursuers quickly, Tig would continue to tire until they caught up to her. And then they'd both be dead. The gallop of hoof beats behind her filled her ears as the reesa trees continued to thin out.

She couldn't help but wonder if this was Arantha's punishment for defying her wishes. Her grandmother was wrong. This wasn't her destiny. She'd disobeyed the Protectress, betrayed her friends and her tribe, and now she would die, miles and miles away from home.

Arantha forgive me, her frantic mind thought. *Please don't abandon me, great Arantha. I will serve you faithfully from this day forward, I swear to you! Please don't forsake me!*

Another arrow shot past her head. Turning back, she saw that Voris and the other archer had remounted their merychs, joining the other two men in pursuit. Trying to steady herself, she pulled a series of arrows from her quiver and fired them in rapid succession, but the intense pain in her leg threw her aim off, and she missed her targets.

The archers' aim, however, was not as amateurish as she'd hoped, and another arrow pierced Tig's hindquarters. Vaxi felt the vibrations in her body as her mount's muscles tensed and contracted, and she felt her chava's cry of anguish as if the arrow had penetrated her own body.

The next one did. Vaxi turned to fire another volley of arrows, and one of the archers' shots found its mark, piercing the leather that covered the left side of her torso. She couldn't hold it in this time. The ghastly pain coursed through her, and she screamed in agony.

She resumed looking at the road ahead when the last of the reesa trees shot past, and she burst from the forest into an open area, a narrow strip of treeless land bisected by a shallow, slow-moving stream. Straight ahead was a large, steep hill leading to another row of trees. She didn't want to stay out in the open if she could, but climbing that steep a hill would no doubt slow Tig enough for the men to catch her, so she banked to the right. Tig jumped into the stream, which was less than a foot deep and only a few yards wide, and reached the other side within seconds. With nowhere else to go, she spurred Tig alongside the river, looking for an escape.

She heard the riders exit the forest behind her, and the merychs' hoof beats echoed through the darkening twilight. She reached for another arrow, but her hand came up empty. She was out of ammunition, Tig was noticeably laboring, and she had no idea where she was going. They would soon catch her. But she would not give them what they wanted. They would not violate her while she was alive. She would fight them to her last breath.

Chapter Thirty-Five

I T TOOK far less time for Kelia to make her way from the lake to the passageway leading out to the desert than it did on the way in. She didn't need to use her Wielding this time either, as Fex was more than capable of making the six-foot jump off the same rock Kelia had to help her ascend before.

She was thankful Maeve allowed her to fill her water-skins from the purifier the night before; while she disliked the strange metallic taste the purification process infused the water with, it was still cleaner than drinking water taken directly from the lake.

Before beginning her trek back across the desert, Kelia finished off the few strips of kova meat and riverfruit from her satchel, and gave Fex the last remaining leaves from the bundle. Satisfied they had more than enough nourishment to sustain them, Kelia gently nudged the chava into motion. Within seconds, they were racing at top speed across the dusty, barren landscape.

Kelia spent several hours with her head buried in the folds of Fex's neck. Traveling at high speeds put her at risk of getting sand in her eyes. It wasn't like there was anything to see anyway. She trusted Fex's instincts that they were traveling in a direct line back to the village.

For the first few hours of the journey, however, tears constantly pricked at Kelia's eyes, and she knew it wasn't from the dust.

What wonders she'd seen. She'd met, eaten with, and engaged in civilized conversation with beings from the Above; two people who had redefined her perception of life, her world, and all of Creation. Arantha herself deemed an alien woman worthy of her divine gifts, and led her to a Stone. She'd Shared with Maeve, Wielded with her, flew with her.

Kissed her.

And now she was returning home, alone, with no more solutions to their problems than when she first set out from the village. Their questions remained unanswered. She had nothing to present to the Council, and her people, but an interesting story.

She used the cloth of her cowl to wipe the tears from her eyes. Her chest was tight, and her nose felt clogged. This was also not from the dust.

What we could have achieved together, Maeve and I. We could have used our combined abilities to build a community, a nation the men of this world would dare not challenge. We could have shown all of Elystra how truly powerful women can be. But no. She chose her son over fulfilling her destiny.

She pictured Davin in her mind's eye. A kind, respectful, intelligent boy.

Had she been in Maeve's place, would she have acted any differently?

Kelia's thoughts turned toward the two sons she'd birthed. The first was to a fisherman named Seelan, who called a small coastal town in southern Agrus home. He was a kind enough man, good-looking and strong, but a little rough-natured at times, and with a wandering eye. Definitely not the monogamous sort.

Her second Sojourn led her to mate with an Imarian pelt merchant named Krast. He was considerably older than she, nearly fifteen years her senior. His wife had passed away the year before, and he was starving for companionship when they crossed paths. She found him a pitiable man, but it was obvious to her he'd been a good, if overly possessive, husband to his late wife. The son she'd left on his doorstep, she realized, would now be exactly the same age as Davin.

For much of the second half of her journey, Kelia wondered what became of her two sons. Was her eldest a fisherman like his father? Did Krast's son fill the void in his father's heart?

Maeve's stinging words echoed in her mind. The moment Kelia's sons were born, it was clear what had to be done. They couldn't stay within the Ixtrayu. It did not matter that they had grown within her womb, nor how great her personal desire to stay with them was. She was Protectress: how could she expect her sisters to follow her if she flouted her tribe's most important tradition?

So many boys born to Ixtrayu mothers. Given up, never to be seen again.

What if we hadn't given them up? What if we'd raised them to share our values, our beliefs?

No. They were boys, and boys grew into men. Men did not abide by women's rules.

But what if they could?

Kelia's introspection was interrupted by a familiar sight that appeared in the distance: a long line of huxa trees that stretched across the horizon.

She smiled. Fex had gone a little off course because of her inattention. They were too far north, but not alarmingly so. Within the hour, they would reach the trees, and not long after that, home.

She slowed Fex's pace to a gallop. She needed the extra time to figure out what she was going to tell the Council, who surely waited with bated breath for her return.

* * *

Riding through the forest, along the banks of the River Ix, refreshed Kelia, every stone and boulder along its edge a welcoming friend. She half-expected to encounter at least one or two of the huntresses along the way, but concluded Runa must have employed them elsewhere.

When she emerged from the forest, gaining her first full view of the Plateau, as well as the fields and the orchards of her home, she heaved a sigh of relief. All seemed calm and normal.

She'd no sooner had this thought than she saw Yarji sprinting down the path towards her. The mixture of tension and worry on her face instantly set Kelia's teeth on edge. She nudged Fex into a faster pace, finally bringing her to a halt as Yarji ran up.

"Protectress!" she said, panting. "Thank Arantha you've returned!" She doubled over, grabbing her knees as she fought to get her breath back.

"Yarji, calm down," Kelia admonished. "What's wrong?"

After several more deep exhales, Yarji said, "It's Vaxi, Protectress."

An icy terror gripped Kelia's heart. "Vaxi? What's happened?"

"She's gone."

"Gone?"

"Yes, Protectress. She went on Sojourn."

Kelia's jaw fell open. "She *what*? When?"

"Two nights ago."

Kelia cursed under her breath.

Susarra.

Thinking fast, she offered a hand to Yarji. "Get on. Now."

Yarji swung herself into the saddle, right behind Kelia. Moments later, Fex resumed her gallop. They passed several more Ixtrayu working the fields and vines, but did not stop to converse.

When they reached the northern edge of the Plateau, Kelia slid off Fex's back, handing the reins to Yarji. "Take her to the stables. I must speak to the Council immediately."

"Yes, Protectress." She pulled the reins to the left and urged Fex to the east, toward the chava corral.

Many Ixtrayu hailed her as she passed through the village, but she didn't have time for pleasantries. She had just reached the stairway leading up to her home when Runa came running up. "Protectress!" she said, looking both alarmed and relieved.

"I heard," Kelia said before Runa could continue. "What happened?" She began her ascent, and Runa fell into step behind her.

"Susarra sent Vaxi away. She left in the middle of the night. Nyla tried to stop her, but couldn't."

Kelia scowled at her. "Nyla knew about this?"

"No, I don't think so. Don't be too hard on her. She says she did everything short of using her Wielding on Vaxi. She didn't want to hurt her friend."

"Any idea where she went?"

"I'm afraid not. There are so many chava tracks heading away from the village, it's nearly impossible to tell which ones are fresh. And besides, I taught her everything I know about covering her trail." She snorted. "Never thought I'd regret that."

They'd reached the top of the stairs, and were now on the threshold of Kelia's home. "I must change. Summon the Council immediately, Runa. Especially Susarra. Drag her if you have to."

"I will." She turned to move away, but then paused. "Did you find anything? In the mountains? The entire tribe has been speaking in whispers ever since you left. I'm loath to believe unfounded rumors, but ..." She trailed off, looking at Kelia expectantly.

Kelia met her friend's gaze. "I have a great deal to tell you, the Council, and the entire tribe. But one thing at a time, Runa. I must deal with this crisis first."

"Yes, Protectress." She gave a humorless smile. "Welcome back." And then she ran down the steps.

* * *

It only took Kelia five minutes to change into a clean tunic, explain to a frantic Liana that she was fine and would spell out her last two days' adventures in due course, and grab a snack from the dining area before heading for the Council Chamber. Nyla was nowhere to be found, and Liana could only surmise she was off with Sarja somewhere.

Once again, she had to pass through a throng of Ixtrayu on the way to the Council Chamber. Their faces bore a mixture of curiosity and repressed anger. Kelia's sense of dread increased with every face she beheld, and wondered if the tide she'd spent the last thirteen years trying to stem had finally broken through. The whole Sojourn situation had reached a boiling point, and if she hoped to contain it, she would have to act quickly.

She climbed another stone staircase to the Chamber, but turned around halfway up to see a crowd of fifty Ixtrayu milling around, waiting for answers. Their murmurs blended together to make one incoherent voice, rapidly increasing in volume.

Kelia held up her hands. "My sisters! Calm yourselves! I have returned, unharmed. I know you seek answers, and I promise I will provide as many as I can. But first, I must speak to the Council."

The crowd, momentarily silenced by Kelia's commanding voice, nodded their assent, and began conversing amongst themselves. Kelia turned and strode up the stairs and into the Chamber, where all three Councilors were waiting for her.

"Protectress!" Katura said, rising unsteadily to her feet. "Thank Arantha –"

"Be seated, Katura," said Kelia, striding to her appointed chair. She sat down and faced the Council, her eyes locking on Susarra, whose self-satisfied smirk told her all she needed to know.

"You must know, Protectress," Eloni said, her eyes pleading, "We had no idea what Vaxi was planning."

"Eloni speaks the truth," Katura added.

Susarra snorted at them. "How ironic that your first words are to shift the blame away from yourselves, when you three are, in fact, the reason this had to be done."

"Be silent, Susarra!" Katura growled, in as angry a voice as Kelia had ever heard the old woman use. "You have defied the will of Arantha, and of not one but two Protectresses, all to serve your own selfish needs."

"Selfish?" Susarra spat. "I have done this for the good of the Ixtrayu!" She glared at Kelia. "Because of your inaction, we are poised on the brink of extinction. Since your last Sojourn, *Protectress,* we have lost nearly one-fifth of our population. How many more have to die before you act?"

"Before *I* act?" Kelia retorted, gripping the armrests of her chair. "I am Arantha's vessel, Susarra! We follow the path *she* decides for us! You dare insinuate that I have acted counter to her wishes? Or do you suggest that Arantha no longer has our best interests? Which is it? Has Ilora's death weakened your faith to such an extent that it has led you to defy her so blatantly?"

"This isn't about faith in Arantha," Susarra said, her tone now cold and emotionless. "It's about faith in ourselves."

Kelia's brows furrowed. "Explain yourself, if you can."

She straightened up, addressing Kelia. "When Onara called a halt to the Sojourns, it took us all by surprise. But she journeyed to the Great Veil before she could provide us with a satisfactory explanation. Since that day, we have waited for Arantha to reveal to you her reasons, but Arantha refuses to tell you. And I can only ask myself, 'Why'?"

"Just say it, Susarra," Kelia seethed. "You deem me unworthy of my position. You've never made a secret of that."

"Then you have misjudged me. I do not believe Arantha has withheld the answers we seek because you are unworthy. I believe she wants us to find those answers for ourselves."

Katura visibly trembled. "You think she's abandoned us?"

"Not abandoned. Released. For eight centuries, we have held her hand. Back then, we were but children, trying to survive in the wilderness. But look what we have become: a strong community of women, who have survived and thrived without the help or supervision of men. We teach our daughters logic and reason, not superstition. We have *grown*, my sisters, as all children do. We are all mothers, and we know there comes a time in our children's lives when we must let them go, let them find their own way."

"Profound words," said Kelia, "which would carry far more weight were they not laced with such hypocrisy. You speak of letting children find their own path, and yet you have pushed Vaxi to follow no other path but *yours*."

"What I have done," Susarra continued, "I have done for the benefit of all. Vaxi is the strongest, the most capable of all our youth. She will complete her Sojourn, and she will return. You will see. Arantha will protect her, not punish her."

Kelia rose to her feet, taking several menacing steps forward. "As I have told you repeatedly, Susarra, Arantha's will is not always ours to understand. You think you know her wishes, but the truth is, you only *hope* you know. I am Arantha's vessel for a reason, and it is not your place to substitute your judgment for mine. Whether you believe your own words or not, it doesn't change the fact that you sent your own granddaughter into danger the moment my back was turned."

"It was the only way. You would certainly not have allowed her to go otherwise."

Kelia grasped the arms of Susarra's chair, leaning over her. "Where did you send her?"

Susarra glared, unblinking, back at her. "I will not tell you. All I will say is that I have been preparing her for this for a long time. She knows what to do."

"If that girl comes to any harm," Kelia said through clenched teeth, "So help me, you will pay dearly."

She looked away, snorting dismissively. "Do what you will."

"I shall." Kelia straightened herself up and returned to her chair. "Susarra, daughter of Veeta, you have violated my trust, and my orders, for the last time. Whether you were motivated by egotism or altruism is unclear. It is also irrelevant. I regret that I have no choice but to remove you from this Council. Return to your home, and remain there until I decide what is to be done with you."

Katura and Eloni let out a long, slow breath, bowing their heads in acceptance of Kelia's judgment. They did not look up as Susarra stood, grabbed her walking stick, and limped towards the door, exiting without another word or even a glance back.

Kelia rubbed her temples before burying her face in her palm.

After a few moments of silence, Eloni spoke up. "Such an unpleasant business."

"Agreed," said Katura. "What's to be done now?"

"Regrettably, there's nothing we can do," Kelia said wearily. "Runa has been unable to determine in which direction Vaxi traveled. We could send search parties after her, but I fear it would be in vain. She's in Arantha's hands now." She sighed. "I will consult the Stone later today. Pray Arantha gives me some insight as to Vaxi's well-being."

"Yes, Protectress," said Eloni. "Are you in a proper state to inform us of your journey?"

Over the next hour, Kelia told them of her experiences in the mountains. At first they were astounded to hear of the advanced beings from the Above, but soon they became drawn into the story of Maeve's and Davin's origins. She briefly spoke of their technology and its wonders, including—with wry amusement—their ability to change their own hair and eye color. When she mentioned the existence of a second Stone, the two elderly women couldn't hold in their amazement.

"A second Stone," Eloni said softly, her eyes glassy. "Buried in the mountains only a day's journey from here. I can scarcely believe it's true."

"I was as shocked as you, Eloni," Kelia said. "Nowhere in our written history is there mention of a second Stone; at least, not that I'm aware of." She turned to Katura. "Katura, if there is anyone who has spent more time than I perusing the recorded visions of past Protectresses, it's you. Do you recall any such mention of another Stone?"

Katura shook her head. "I do not, I'm afraid. Granted, my memory is not what it once was, but I think I would remember something like that. Unless the reference was so cryptic I just missed it." She fixed Kelia with a sharp glare. "What could it mean?"

"I don't know," Kelia said. "Anyway, the question is moot. By now, the aliens will have taken the Stone and left. And if not, they will soon."

"And you just let them have it?"

"Yes, and I would appreciate it if you didn't spread news of this Stone around. It would only cause further distress. These beings," she paused, her mind filling with images of Maeve, "came to our world to save theirs. I am convinced not only was it Arantha's will that they find it, but that they have it. They were—*are*—good people, and I cannot begrudge them that chance any more than I can lay claim to a treasure that may never have been found without their help."

"I suppose not," Eloni said. "What a shame we could not have forged an alliance with them. To learn from beings from the Above ..."

"Yes," Kelia said, standing. "Most unfortunate. But our destinies, it would seem, lie along different paths."

Kelia regretted not informing the Council of her Sharing with Maeve, and of the remarkable symbiosis their Wielding abilities seemed to have. But doing so would have been pointless. Maeve was gone. All Kelia had left were memories of the most incredible two days of her life, memories she would hold onto for all her remaining years.

"We will need to fill Susarra's spot on the Council as soon as possible," Kelia said. "I can think of no one more suited for the position than Liana. Any objections?"

"I would not object," said Katura, "but do you not think there is a conflict of interests? Replacing your biggest detractor with a member of your own family?"

Kelia considered this for a moment, then shook her head. "We need to restore unity. Everyone in the tribe knows Liana is not one to hold back her opinions. Not even from me." She gave a wry smile. "She is knowledgeable, wise, and fair. She has done a remarkable job training Nyla. I believe she's earned it."

"Then it's settled," said Eloni. "I trust you will inform her straightaway."

At that moment, a great clamor came from outside the Council Chamber. Raised voices, some in anger, floated through the doorway. All three women rose to their feet, but Kelia was the first one to pass through the door.

There, at the foot of the staircase leading from the Chamber, the crowd of discontented Ixtrayu had tripled in size since she entered. Upon seeing her emerge, many of them raised their hands, shouting questions at her.

"Will Vaxi be safe?"

"Is Arantha displeased?"

"Will the Sojourns be resuming?"

"Where did you go, Protectress? Has Arantha returned?"

"Did you really remove Susarra from the Council?"

"What's to be done?"

Kelia raised her hands, quieting the cacophony of voices before they became deafening. "Sisters, please! Enough of this!"

No effect. The voices just became louder, angrier.

Kelia drew upon her Wielding abilities, creating a small cyclone of air that lifted her off the ground. She spread her arms out and floated majestically down the stairs. The crowd could only stare, wide-eyed, unable to find their voices.

Kelia landed several steps up from the bottom, and the air around her dispersed, ruffling the clothes of those nearest her until that, too, calmed and died. Only an awed silence remained.

"To answer your questions," Kelia said in her most strident voice, "Susarra has been removed from the Council. Vaxi's Sojourn was not sanctioned by myself, the Council, or Arantha. We do not know where she has gone, and Susarra refuses to tell us, which means we cannot go after her."

A few murmurs came from the crowd, but no one else spoke.

"I know you all want the Sojourns to resume. Believe me, I want that too. But I cannot authorize that at this time. I maintain what I always have: Arantha has done this for a reason she has chosen not to reveal to us yet."

"Protectress?" said a voice from the middle of the crowd. "May I speak?"

Kelia identified the source of the voice, a dark-skinned woman from Hathi's group of gatherers. "Speak, Uleta."

"I was seventeen when Protectress Onara called a halt to the Sojourns. I just recently celebrated my thirtieth year," she said.

"I am aware of that," Kelia said.

"I lost my mother last year. I have no sisters, no blood relatives. If I do not produce a daughter, my family's line will end. Please do not let that happen, I beg you." She stared up at Kelia with mournful eyes.

Kelia felt as if her heart was being torn asunder. Her mother's order had produced many ripples, many consequences within the tribe, but Uleta's circumstances were perhaps the most tragic. "You come from a strong family. I would never wish to see it end," she said with a tightened jaw.

Aarna, the head food preparer, put her arm around Uleta. "We do not want to oppose you, Protectress, but Uleta is not the only one who has had to wait for far too long. My own daughter, Ryta, is in the same position. She has more years of fertility behind her than ahead of her. Would you force upon her the dishonor of not producing at least one daughter to carry on our traditions?"

Before Kelia could answer, there were nods and shouts of assent from the crowd. The situation was close to boiling over, Kelia realized. She had thought the Ixtrayu's faith in Arantha, in *her*, was enough to dispel their doubts, but she had severely underestimated how troubled her people were … and with Susarra adding fuel to the fire, they were on the brink of revolt.

Could Susarra be right? Is this what Arantha had in mind for them all this time? If so, why couldn't she have made this clear to Kelia, as she did with Onara? Why send her all the way to the Kaberian Mountains for a meeting that ultimately amounted to nothing?

Kelia sighed, self-doubt washing over her. *Maybe Susarra is right. Maybe Maeve is right as well. It's time things changed.*

She held up her hands again, attempting to quell the rising tumult. "My sisters! Please, compose yourselves!"

After a few moments, the crowd became silent, and all eyes were upon her.

"Much has happened in recent days," she announced. "Events have transpired that will require much contemplation between myself and the Council, after which, I can assure you, you will be informed. Regarding the Sojourns: while I believe Vaxi did not make this journey of her own free will, the fact is that it has happened. All we can do is pray for her safe return."

"And if she returns?" Uleta asked.

"If she returns, we will welcome her back, and any baby she carries," Kelia said. "If she is successful, and her child is born healthy and strong, we will take that as a sign that Arantha favors resuming the Sojourns. If, however, Vaxi does not return, we can only interpret it that Arantha is displeased with us, and we will continue to wait for a direct sign from her. Is that acceptable to you?"

No one responded directly. They cast furtive glances at each other, at their feet, or at nothing in particular.

"I cannot reveal all of the details yet, my sisters, but I believe we are at a critical point in our tribe's history. We dare not anger Arantha at a time when we will need her guidance the most. What say you all?"

Many remained stock-still, but many others slowly nodded their assent. Aarna bowed her head, as did Uleta. "We will pray for Vaxi's safe return, and for Arantha's continued guidance, Protectress," Aarna said.

"Thank you, sisters," Kelia said, the knots in her stomach loosening. "Please return to your duties. I will inform you of any developments should they arise."

A final chorus of nods, and the throng began to disperse. At the back of the crowd, Kelia locked eyes with Liana, who nodded her approval. Next to her were Nyla and Sarja, who couldn't hide the worry on their faces.

Kelia ascended the stairs again, only to find Eloni and Katura waiting for her at the top of the landing.

"Well spoken, Protectress," said Katura. "I regret that it was necessary. It would seem that I have become appallingly disconnected from the tribe, or I would have seen this coming."

"As have I," said Eloni. "I knew Susarra was disgruntled, but this ... I had no idea she had this much support."

"Do not fret, Councilors," Kelia said. "And do not dwell on this. What's done is done. We must redouble our efforts to keep our voices, and our tribe, unified, however this situation resolves itself."

"Agreed," said Katura. "You will indeed consult the Stone again?"

"Yes. After the confusion this past week has brought, I hope Arantha will finally bring clarity."

And if she doesn't, may she at least give me the strength to endure.

Chapter Thirty-Six

THE DISTANT sound had now increased in volume, and seemed to be coming from the forest's edge just south of their location. Seconds went by, and the rumble morphed into hoof beats. A whole horde of them, and they were headed in his and Sen's direction.

Mizar realized he'd forgotten to put his High Mage cloak back on after his nap. At that moment, he had nothing to identify himself as the High Mage, except for his Wielding abilities.

With a roar, something large burst through the tree line several hundred yards away. Mizar couldn't make out any features, but he knew immediately that it was far too large to be a merych. It appeared to be running for its life.

Mizar tried to calm his mind as the beast veered to its right and ran straight through the shallow river. It was heading his way, and fast. As it drew near, he could better make out some details: a wide torso, four thick, powerful legs, and an elongated nose that sported two horns of different lengths. A chava.

Even more surprising than the presence of a beast that generally roamed the Plains of Iyan was the fact that it seemed to be equipped with a saddle. Someone was riding it. He was shocked to see the chava had several arrows sticking out of its body.

Seconds later, the forest disgorged four merychs, one right after the other. They also forded the stream with ease and pursued the wounded chava. Atop the steeds were men riding like the wind, and two of them were firing arrow after arrow at their prey. One arrow embedded itself in the chava's hindquarters, and it roared with pain, slowing its pace even further. The merychs would soon overtake the wounded beast and its rider.

Keeping low to the ground, Mizar watched as the pursuit neared his position. His breath caught in his throat when he saw that the person riding the chava was not a man, but a girl. She wore an outfit made from some kind of tanned leather that revealed long legs and muscular arms. She clutched a bow in her left hand, but judging from the way she was slumped over in the saddle, she lacked the ability to fire back at the men hounding her. Like her mount, two arrows protruded from her body, one in her leg and the other in her side. Blood flowed freely from both wounds.

One of the two pursuing archers pulled up alongside the weakening chava, took aim and fired another arrow into the neck of the creature. It gave another gurgling roar, and its knees buckled, causing it to lose its balance and fall face-first to the ground. The girl was thrown from the saddle, landing several yards away on a patch of thick grass that grew near the bank of the river.

All four men brought their merychs to a quick halt and dismounted them. Three of the men had bows drawn. Two of them covered the chava, whose breath had diminished to a hollow rasp, and the third pointed his arrow at the prone body of the girl.

Mizar took a good look at the men: rough, dark brown skin, and faces adorned with thick beards and metal pins stuck through them. Vandans.

The rumors were true: Vandan raiders roamed the woods, preying on unsuspecting travelers, and this girl had been unfortunate enough to cross their path.

The one man not armed with a bow drew a short knife from his belt as he approached the girl, using his free hand to turn her over onto her back. Mizar faintly made out her shallow gasps. He was relieved that she wasn't killed by the fall, but it didn't look like her situation was about to improve.

He stealthily approached the men, all of whom had their backs to him. The chava now lay unmoving. Three raiders stood back, watching the fourth as he crouched down next to the girl, grabbed a hold of her tunic and held his knife right in front of her eyes. "Good," he said, panting. "Ya ain' dead yet." With a snarl, he closed his fingers around the arrow protruding from her thigh and gave it a twist. Her mouth opened in a muted scream, as if she didn't have the air in her lungs to support the sound. Her back arched, and he shoved her back to the ground again.

He straddled her, leaning over until his face was right next to hers. "You killed my brudda," he snarled. "And yer gonna stay alive jus' long enough to feel me cut ya ta small pieces, ya manky whore." Then he stood up, brandishing his knife. He shifted it in his hand, as if preparing to plunge it downwards into the girl's bleeding body.

Mizar strode forward, feeling the rush of adrenaline as the power of Arantha surged through him, waiting to manifest and teach these heathens a lesson. One of the archers must have heard the sound of his footfalls, as he spun around and saw Mizar approaching. "Voris!" he cried out.

As one, all three men turned to face him. One of them was so startled by Mizar's sudden appearance he let loose his arrow, the shot going wide. Mizar didn't even have to move to dodge it. The man, realizing he'd just wasted his last arrow, dropped his bow to the ground and drew his sword. The other two archers, who possessed cooler heads, kept their aim on Mizar.

"What's dis?" said Voris. "Whaddaya want, old man?"

As he normally did when he traveled back to his home province, Mizar dressed in the trappings of a commoner: a simple brown tunic that came down past his knees and a pair of thick riding boots. Though he was proud to serve his King, he never felt comfortable having the citizens of Darad bow to him. It was out of respect, he knew, but even forty years after becoming High Mage, he still thought of himself as nothing more than a farmer's son who'd been called upon by Arantha to do his duty.

"You have crossed into Daradian territory," said Mizar authoritatively, "and I would wager you don't have permission to do so."

Voris sneered, pointing his knife at Mizar. "Oh yah? What'cha gon' do 'bout it, old man? Arrest us?" He gave a coarse laugh, eliciting smiles and chuckles from the other three men.

"Something like that."

Voris laughed so hard it turned into a hacking cough. "Der are four of us, ya old braga. I don' see no sword, no bow 'n arrahs on ya."

"I need no such devices to deal with scum like you," Mizar said, knitting his brows. He felt his anger rising, but he somehow kept his voice even.

Mizar considered himself a man of peace, and he was loath to condemn an entire country of men based on the actions of a few, but he had yet to hear of any Elystran encountering a Vandan and describe them as anything but sadistic, barbaric animals. He'd heard tales of how Vandan raiders treated their victims that would make even men with the strongest constitutions nauseous.

"Dis ain' yer bus'ness, old man," Voris spat. "Dis gell killed my brudda, and I mean to take my revenge. Walk away now, or ye'll be joinin' her."

"Maybe you didn't understand me, Vandan," Mizar said, raising his voice to a yell. He held his hands out from his sides, splaying his fingers. "It is you that needs to walk away."

Voris scoffed. "Why would I do that?"

"There is most assuredly a patrol not far from here, and if you leave now, you might just avoid being captured and executed." Mizar moved his hands in front of his body, holding them palms-down. His eyes were still locked on Voris. "But if you touch that girl again, I'll save them the trouble."

Voris's face scrunched up in anger. Turning to the Vandan who'd drawn his sword, he yelled, "Kill him!"

Holding the hilt of his sword with both hands, the man rushed at Mizar, who didn't move. With a primal scream, the man swung his sword in a wide arc, intent on separating Mizar's head from his body.

With a quickness belying his age, Mizar ducked under the sword as it sliced through the air. Calling upon his abilities, he directed a powerful bolt of compressed air right at the swordsman's gut. A moment later, the man was flying backwards, his limbs flailing as he flew past his cohorts. He hit the water of the stream, but didn't stop there. His body bounced across the surface like a stone being skipped, coming to an abrupt halt when he crashed head-first into a large rock that stuck out of the ground on the other side. There was a sickening crack of bone upon stone, and the man's head fell limply under the water. It did not rise again. Only his feet and chest protruded above the surface, right next to a large red stain that now decorated the stone.

The stupefied look on the faces of the three men was almost comical. Composing himself, Voris gestured to the two archers, whose bows dangled slackly in their hands. Gibbering with rage, he spluttered, "Shoot him!"

The archers were only ten or so yards away from Mizar. At this close range, anyone with even moderate skill would be able to hit their mark. In one motion, both men raised their bows, pulled back on the drawstrings, and fired.

Mizar only had a second to react as the two arrows split the air on their way to him. With a slight wave of his hands, he changed the flow of air around him, thereby directing the arrows to zip past his head, continuing on their harmless trajectory.

Before they could hit the ground, Mizar turned in the other direction and waved his arms in a circle. As if they'd developed a mind of their own, the arrows changed direction, one banking left and the other right, sweeping around in a wide arc and climbing high into the air.

Mizar whirled around to face the Vandans again, moving his arms in a practiced, precise series of gestures, bending the air to his will. The raiders watched, goggle-eyed, at the arrows that seemed to defy gravity. Mizar thrust his hands forward, and the two arrows decided on a new direction. Before the archers could even react, the arrows embedded themselves in their throats.

Voris's jaw dropped, his knife hand shaking visibly as he watched the last of his men topple to the ground, blood gushing from their necks and staining the grassy earth.

Satisfied, Mizar fixed Voris with his steeliest glare. "Only you and me now, Vandan."

Voris didn't move. He could only croak out a barely intelligible, "Wh-what are ya?"

"I am Mizar, High Mage of Darad." He dropped his hands to his sides, but didn't take his eyes off Voris.

All at once, Voris found his courage again. "Yer a dead man!" he screamed, charging at Mizar with his blade held high.

Mizar didn't even wait for Voris to get within striking distance. He raised his hands, and a violent gust of air appeared from nowhere, lifting the enraged Vandan off the ground. Mizar thrust his hands upward, and up Voris flew, higher and higher until he was above the level of the reesa trees, his screams growing fainter and fainter.

Forming his hands into fists, Mizar made a downward tugging motion like he was pulling on the rope of a bell. Voris's rapid ascent stopped, and was instantaneously followed by an even more rapid plummet. The raider's screams grew louder and more frantic until he hit the surface of the stream with the same impact as if he'd been thrown from a two-hundred-foot cliff. There was a bone-jarring crack, a loud splash, and then silence.

Mizar looked around at his handiwork, at the four corpses that now littered the countryside. It was not the first time he had killed; the last time had been many decades before, when King Armak ruled Darad. Like now, he'd been forced to kill Vandans. As much as he wanted to condemn his own actions, he just couldn't. Vandan raiders took what they wanted, and they never spared their victims. If these men had been captured, they would have been executed per King Aridor's orders. They deserved no less, and he had given them fair warning.

His reverie was disturbed by a plaintive call from behind him. "Master?" came Sen's voice. "Is it over?"

"It is," Mizar said, striding over to where the unconscious girl lay. "Quickly, Sen, before she dies."

Sen ran out from his hiding place, bringing his satchel with him. He less-than-gracefully hopped over one dead archer and nearly tripped over the other before kneeling at the girl's side. As Mizar watched, Sen felt the girl's forehead before putting his ear to her mouth. "She's breathing, but just barely," he said.

Without waiting for a reply, he reached into his satchel and brought forth a small bag held tight with a drawstring. Unknotting it, he dug out two thin leaves that Mizar recognized as carmista, an herb that promoted blood coagulation. Sen pressed the leaves between his palms and closed his eyes, absorbing their healing properties.

"I need your help, Master," Sen said shakily. I can't heal her with arrows sticking out of her body. We need to pull them out."

Mizar was not a healer, and knew little of the art, but he knew this was a dangerous gamble. "Are you certain?"

Sen nodded. "The arrows are deep inside her. If I help her blood clot without removing them, it may kill her."

"And if you remove the arrows, she could die anyway."

Despite the bad light, Mizar could see Sen's pained expression. "I know," the boy said.

"Very well," Mizar knelt down next to Sen. "Which one first?"

"The one in her side." He brought out the knife he used to clean the jarveks, rinsing it as best he could in the stream and wiping it off with a clean cloth. Then, casting an embarrassed glance at the girl's face, he carefully cut the leather of her tunic, exposing her bare skin. Both men winced at the sight of the arrow, its head submerged inside her body. The tissue surrounding the wound was red and swollen. Mizar was thankful the blood hadn't adhered the leather to her skin.

Sen placed his palms on either side of the arrow, looking up at Mizar. "Pull it out as cleanly as you can."

"I will try."

"On your count, Master. Whenever you're ready."

"Alright. On three." Mizar drew in a deep breath. "One, two, *three.*"

With a grimace, Mizar pulled the arrow out of the girl's side. At that moment, her eyelids sprang open, and she let loose the loudest scream he'd ever heard. It only lasted for a few seconds, though, before she slumped back to the ground and closed her eyes. Her breath slowed to a raspy gurgle, and her face was pallid.

Sen, uncovering his ears, replaced his hands on her skin, and concentrated once again on his task. Mizar imagined Arantha's will penetrating the poor girl, repairing the damage, trying to pump life back into her body before it shut down completely. As he watched, the blood oozing from her gaping wound slowed, then stopped.

Mizar watched his apprentice with pride. The lad had come a long way from the inexperienced, overwhelmed kid he was when he first stood on the Nexus of Arantha.

"Now the leg," Sen panted.

Removing the second arrow was easier than the first, but there was just as much blood. Thankfully, the girl didn't scream this time. By the time that wound sealed itself, Sen's face was ashen. His head drooped, and he almost collapsed on top of her. Mizar grasped his shoulder, keeping him upright. "Are you all right, Sen?"

He nodded, his eyes closed.

"Is she healed?" Mizar asked.

Sen opened his eyes again, still catching his breath. He put his ear to her mouth again, and an exhausted smile materialized on his face. "She's breathing better now." He straightened up again. "I think she's healed, but it's not safe to move her right now. She's lost a lot of blood, and she'll be weak for a while. We need to keep her warm."

"Agreed. I'll build a new fire right here," Mizar said.

The sun had almost set, so while Sen tended to the girl, Mizar gathered a few sticks, forming them into a pyramid-shape over a bed of dead grass. A wave of his hand later, he had a small fire going. "It's a start," he said, satisfied. "I'll get some more wood after I move the bodies a little further downstream. I'll also secure the Vandans' merychs."

"Thank you, Master." Sen was barely listening. He stared at the girl, pushing a few strands of her long, straight hair away from her face, which looked soft and peaceful in the dim fire-light. "She's beautiful," he whispered. "She can't be much older than me."

"She'll live, Sen. Thanks to you."

"How's the chava?" Sen glanced at the poor animal, a dark silhouette lying unmoving on the ground about ten yards away.

"It's dead, I'm afraid," Mizar said sadly.

"I thought chavas were wild."

"They are. They roam the Plains of Iyan."

Sen looked up at Mizar. "I've never heard of anyone riding one like a merych." He took the girl's hand in both of his. "Why would a teenage girl be in the Celosian Forest by herself?"

"I wish I knew."

"But … you said you had a vision."

"I did."

"And Arantha didn't show you what was going to happen?"

Mizar shook his head. "No. He just showed me *where* it was going to happen."

Sen drew in a sharp breath. "If you hadn't been here –"

"If *we* hadn't been here," Mizar corrected, "she would have died." He smiled. "Arantha sees everything."

The tiniest of sounds escaped the girl's mouth. She was stir-ring, murmuring something under her breath. Her eyes were still closed.

Sen leaned down closer to her. "Don't try to move."

At the sound of his voice, the girl's eyes popped open, and she stared directly at him. Her mouth was slightly agape, but no words came out.

"Hello," Sen said, "How are –"

He didn't get another word out because the girl, moving faster than someone with her wounds should have, swung her left fist around, cracking Sen square in the jaw. The impact sent him flying backwards. Because of his weakened state, he was out cold by the time he hit the ground.

Mizar's eyes widened as the girl, having apparently used all her energy in that one punch, slumped back to the ground. Her head lolled to the side, and her eyes closed again. He stood up, regarding the two unconscious teenagers at his feet, and smiled wryly to himself. "Well, almost everything."

Chapter Thirty-Seven

"**S**HE DIDN'T tell you anything?" Sarja said, loosing another arrow at the target, missing just left.

"Not a thing," Nyla said.

With all the drama surrounding Kelia's return and Susarra's dismissal, Liana canceled Nyla's Wielding lesson for the day. She returned home with her mother and Liana, where Kelia informed both of them that Liana would be taking Susarra's spot on the Council. It took a lot more convincing than Nyla would have expected, but Liana finally acquiesced. A swearing-in ritual in front of the entire tribe was scheduled for the next day. Kelia then told Nyla she could have the rest of the day to herself, so with nothing else to do, she decided to join Sarja on the archery range. She sat on the ground, her knees pulled up to her chin, watching her friend practice.

"It's such a mess, isn't it? Arantha sends my mother across the desert, and this," she made a sweeping gesture with her arms, "is what she comes home to."

"I know," Sarja said, nocking and firing another arrow, missing to the right. "But there's nothing we can do about it, is there?"

"I should have stopped her, Sar. Why didn't I stop her?"

Sarja pulled another arrow from her quiver, not meeting Nyla's gaze. "What could you have done, Ny? Used your Wielding on her? Hurt her? Knocked her out?"

"Yeah. I could've done that."

"I don't think so. She's your friend. She's *our* friend. If she thinks she's doing the right thing, who are we to question her?"

Nyla shot her a glare. "She only did it because Susarra told her to! Great Arantha, Sar ... what if she never comes back?"

Sarja aimed and fired, missing by a wide margin. "She'll be fine. I just know it."

"How?" Nyla begged. "How do you know?"

"Because it's Vaxi. If anyone can survive out there, she can."

"I hope you're right." Sarja still looked concerned, so Nyla gave her a disarming smile. "Thanks, Sar."

"You're welcome." She fired once again. This arrow fell well short.

Nyla stood up, taking a few steps forward. "What's wrong with you today?"

"What do you mean?"

Nyla pointed at the untouched target. "You've missed every shot. I haven't seen you this off since you were ten."

A glum look came over Sarja's face. "I'm just distracted, that's all."

"By what's happened?"

Sarja shook her head.

An uncomfortable sensation swept through Nyla's body. "By *me?*"

Sarja closed her eyes, then nodded. "But you don't want to talk about it."

Nyla and Sarja had been best friends their whole lives. Ever since they could walk, they'd played together, ate together, explored the world around them together. Nyla admired Sarja for her loyalty, her friendliness, her sense of humor, and for the rebellious streak she showed more and more infrequently.

If Sarja had one weakness, it was her single-mindedness. Now she'd gotten this idea about the two of them becoming companions in her head, and she wasn't going to let it go.

"You're right, I don't," Nyla said with more than a little regret, "but it's not because of you. I'm only just starting to figure out who I am, you know? Everyone expects so much of me: my mother, Liana, the tribe ... before I started Wielding, I didn't care about any of that. But all that's changed now. I don't want to be the brat anymore. I see how some people look at me, and they think it's Mother's fault that I turned out this way. But it's my fault. I've failed her."

"What are you going to do?"

"I don't know," Nyla said despondently.

"Well, whatever happens, I'm behind you."

Nyla looked at her friend's face, her gentle smile, and felt better.

"Come on, let's go get something to eat," Sarja said, taking Nyla's hand. Together they walked down the path toward the village.

* * *

A minute later, they were passing by the cave where the Stone was housed when Kelia came charging out the entrance, nearly bowling them over.

"Mother!" Nyla cried, grasping Kelia's sleeves for support.

"Duma." Kelia's eyes flicked from Nyla to Sarja. "Are you all right?"

"Yes," Nyla said. She scanned Kelia's face. She was alarmed to see Kelia's eyes red and swollen, and the remnants of tears staining her cheeks. "Mama, what's wrong?"

Kelia, as if suddenly aware of her present state, wiped her face with her hands and straightened herself up. Within moments, she was the Protectress again: stoic, austere, and emotionless. "Nothing," she said. "Everything's fine." She glanced away, down the river. No Ixtrayu were nearby.

Nyla grabbed Kelia's wrist. "Mama, please tell me what's wrong. Maybe I can help!"

Kelia looked at Nyla, conflict written all over her face. Something was wrong. Terribly wrong. "There's nothing you can do," she said.

"I don't know what's going on," Nyla said determinedly, "but I can help you. I know I've let you down before, but I can control my abilities now! Let me prove it to you!"

"Please, Protectress," Sarja piped up. "Let her try."

Kelia's eyes narrowed into slits. "What is it you're asking of me?"

Nyla squared her shoulders. "Let me touch the Stone."

"No. You're not ready."

"Mother –"

"*No!*" Kelia yelled, raising her hands. "I say you're not ready, and that's final!"

Nyla, taken aback, moved to stand by Sarja's side. Her fingers brushed the young huntress's, and she felt them interlock. Nyla did not pull away.

Rather than match her volume to Kelia's, Nyla instead spoke with a calm, even tone. "How can I prove myself to the tribe—to *you*—if you never give me the chance?"

"Your time will come, duma," Kelia said. "Now please, girls, I have things to attend to." She threw another look down the path before facing them again. Her stern visage had been replaced by a look of sadness, almost despair. "Dinner will be served shortly. Why don't you head there now?" Without waiting for a response, she strode at a fast pace along the path next to the river. Within moments, she disappeared from sight.

* * *

314

Dinner with Sarja was eerily quiet, with barely a word spoken. Minutes passed as their sister Ixtrayu came, ate their evening meal, and left, most without so much as a sideways glance in their direction. The upheaval caused by Vaxi's departure, Susarra's removal from the Council, and her mother's ultimatum to the tribe had cast a pall over the village.

After dinner, Nyla returned to her home with Sarja in tow. Kelia wasn't there, and Liana was on her way out, likely to attend some preparatory session for her induction to the Council. Nyla asked her great-aunt for permission to spend the night at Sarja's home, and Liana approved.

Runa and her companion of fifteen years, Amya, one of the tribe's foremost cloth-weavers, had gone on a total of four Sojourns between them before the Sojourns were stopped. Sarja was the only daughter born to either woman. They often expressed regret that they couldn't provide Sarja with a sister, but they all accepted it was Arantha's will, and both of them were loving mothers.

Much to the delight of Runa and Amya, Nyla demonstrated her much-improved fire-Wielding abilities, creating various symbols, geometric patterns, and swirly designs with the fire without so much as one mishap. Runa shared a loaf of honey bread she'd talked Aarna out of with the girls, and then regaled them with a story about how she singlehandedly fought off a pack of nemza cats with nothing but a skinning knife and her bare hands. Nyla had heard the story many times before, and though she was certain the tale had been embellished over time, she still loved hearing it.

It also amazed—and amused—Nyla when she saw Runa and Amya together, for they were about as different as two Ixtrayu could be. While Runa was one of the tallest women in the tribe, Amya was one of the most petite, with nearly a foot separating the two. Runa was strong and muscular with dark, tanned skin, while Amya had a lighter complexion and was slightly plump. Runa often joked that huntresses tended to wear out their clothes faster than all others, so it was in her best interest to choose the best cloth-weaver in the tribe as her companion: for one, she would always have the finest quality of clothes to wear, and also, it would cease Amya's constant complaining about the shoddy way Runa treated her best work. Amya would just laugh and reply that only the first of those two statements was true. Then they would kiss, and Sarja would turn red and cover her eyes.

Nyla also asked Runa how certain she was that Vaxi would be all right on her own, and the huntress gave Nyla her sincerest reassurance, calling Vaxi "the best student I've ever had." No mention was made about Kelia's journey or Susarra's dismissal.

When the four of them retired to their rooms and the girls changed into their sleep-robes, Sarja lit a series of candles that illuminated every corner of her room. Nyla and Sarja spoke again about companionship, and for the first time, it wasn't tension-filled or awkward. Seeing how Runa and Amya were together, still happily in love after so many years together made Nyla understand why Sarja was so determined to find someone that made her as happy as Amya made Runa.

Ever since Sarja first brought up the topic of companionship, Nyla had done her best to not think about it. It was just too bizarre. They were best friends. They couldn't be more like sisters if they'd had the same mother. The idea of *being* together was ridiculous.

But now … she was thinking about it. And the more she thought about it, the less ridiculous it seemed.

"I have an idea," Nyla said with a smile. "Let's have a Promising ceremony."

Sarja quirked an eyebrow. "A what?"

"A Promising ceremony. Right here, right now."

Sarja stared deep into Nyla's eyes for several moments, then shook her head. "I've never heard of a Promising ceremony."

Nyla feigned surprise. "You haven't? It's when two Ixtrayu promise to choose each other someday. Kind of like a pre-bonding ceremony. It's a tradition."

"Since when?"

"Since today."

Sarja laughed. "Can you just make up a tradition like that?"

"I'm the next Protectress. The embodiment of eight centuries of traditions. I think that entitles me to make up one or two of my own. So what do you say?"

A huge smile crept over Sarja's face. "Of course! What do I have to do?"

"Stand up." Both girls clambered to their feet and stood in the center of the room, facing each other. "Now, we put our hands on each other's hearts." Nyla reached over and placed her palm over Sarja's heart, and felt her friend do the same.

"Um, don't we need a witness or something?" Sarja queried.

Nyla cast a quick glance toward the ceiling. "We have Arantha as our witness."

"Okay," Sarja said, chuckling.

"Now, repeat after me: I ... "

"I."

"Nyla, daughter of Kelia."

"Nyla, daughter of ... " She caught herself. "Sorry. Sarja, daughter of Runa."

"Do pledge to one day entrust my heart."

"Do pledge to one day entrust my heart."

"To Sarja, daughter of Runa."

"To Nyla, daughter of Kelia."

"In Arantha's divine presence, do we make this vow."

"In Arantha's divine presence, do we make this vow."

Nyla took a deep breath, and Sarja followed suit. "I guess it's official now," Nyla said, beaming.

"Yeah, I guess it is." She looked expectantly at Nyla. "Are we supposed to kiss or something?"

Nyla's eyes widened, and she shuffled her feet. She definitely hadn't considered *that* as part of her brand-new ritual. "Um ... "

"Oh." Sarja glanced down at her feet. "I made it weird again, didn't I?"

"Yeah, you did." Nyla laughed. "How about just a big hug?" She enfolded Sarja in her arms, hugging her warmly, pressing her head against her friend's shoulder.

"Thanks, Ny," Sarja said, returning the hug.

They faced each other again. "Time for bed, I think," Nyla said.

"Good idea. Let's go to sleep before I say more weird stuff."

They climbed into their respective beds. Nyla waved her hand, and all the candles in the room simultaneously went out. The only light now came from the starlight leaking in through Sarja's small bedroom window.

"I love that you can do that," Sarja said from her darkened corner of the room, giggling.

"Sleep soundly, my Promised," Nyla said with a giggle of her own.

"Sleep soundly."

* * *

Nyla did not sleep soundly. In fact, she was determined not to sleep at all. There was something she had to do, and no one would stop her.

Everyone in the tribe knew that Kelia's ability to interpret Arantha's visions was inferior to Onara's. Many Ixtrayu were convinced that Arantha did, in fact, want the Sojourns to re-sume, and that Kelia had simply missed the signs. And now Susarra had forced Kelia's hand. Vaxi was gone, and the Sojourns, perhaps even her mother's position as Protectress, depended on whether or not Vaxi returned safely.

Nyla flashed back to the look on her mother's face outside the cave. Kelia had obviously seen something that disturbed her greatly, and she didn't want to share it. What could she have seen? Vaxi's death? Her being removed as leader? Or something worse?

Kelia had told Nyla that she was much more powerful than Kelia had been at thirteen. Nyla played that line over and over again in her mind. If her elemental abilities were really superior even to her mother's, could that not also mean her divinatory abilities would be superior too? Maybe Arantha would speak to Nyla in a clearer voice, provide her with the answers that had eluded Kelia since she became Protectress.

There was only one way to find out.

Silently shrugging the pelts off her body, Nyla climbed to her feet, listening for any changes in Sarja's breathing. She couldn't see her friend clearly, but it sounded as if she was fast asleep. Not even bothering to grab an extra robe or put on her shoes, she stole out of the bedroom and out of the house.

As it was two nights before when she caught Vaxi leaving, the village was quiet. There was barely any wind, and the only sound was the comforting babble of the River Ix as it flowed through the Plateau. Her feet made barely any noise upon the stone as she descended to ground level. She looked in all directions, seeing no movement, before running down the path, across the southern bridge, and into the cave.

Two torches affixed to the walls hung at eye level on both sides of the cave. Nyla lit them, dispelling the darkness and revealing the Stone to her. As it often was when dormant, the Stone was quite unimpressive on first sight, a dark lump of crystal.

She approached cautiously, each step deliberate, watching it for any reaction to her presence. She was only three steps away when it began to glow; faint at first, but ever more luminescent the nearer she got. By the time she reached the rocky altar supporting the Stone, the entire cave was bathed in a soft white hue.

She stared at it, waiting for a sign that her presence was unwelcome or unwanted. None came. She watched the slow, pulsating light, feeling it permeate her body. Then she held the palms of her hands in front of her, recalling her mother's account of her first contact with the Stone, and she shuddered.

She took a deep breath, then recited the litany. "I bask in your divine presence, O Arantha, for I am your –"

"Nyla?" said a voice behind her.

Nyla turned to see Sarja standing in the entrance, looking at her with fearful eyes. "Sar? What are you doing here?"

"I followed you. I thought you might try something like this."

"I thought you were asleep. I was sure I hadn't woken you."

Sarja smirked. "I may not be a huntress yet, but that doesn't mean I don't know a few tricks. And besides, you're not as stealthy as you think you are." She strode into the cave, stopping halfway between the entrance and the Stone. "Please, Ny, let's just go home."

Nyla met her best friend's eyes. In them, she saw what she always saw: loyalty, friendship, *love*. "I can't, Sar. I have to do this."

"Why?"

"Things are falling apart. Mother is going to need my help, and I can't do that the way things are right now." She averted her gaze. "Everyone sees me as a child. Even her."

Sarja took several more steps, pausing only a few feet away. "What if something ... bad happens? What if Arantha punishes you for this?" A choked sob escaped. "We just became Promised! I can't lose you now!"

Nyla put her arms around Sarja, holding her close. She felt her friend trembling. "You have to trust me. This is the only way."

"Are you sure?" Another sob.

"I'm sure." They faced each other again. "I have goodness in my heart now. Arantha will protect me." She hoped her words sounded convincing.

After a few tense moments, Sarja nodded, and released her. "Okay."

She gestured at the Stone, its white glow unchanged. "Maybe nothing will happen at all. But if it goes bad, you can get help. Can you do that?"

Sarja nodded again. "Be careful."

"I will."

Nyla moved to turn around, but Sarja pulled her into a sudden embrace, planting a soft, tender kiss upon her lips.

Surprised at first, Nyla just let the kiss happen, wrapping her arms around her friend. At that moment, it all became clear. All the doubts, all the awkwardness just fell away. Sarja was her closest friend, her confidant. Now, she was Nyla's Promised. And it was the right choice. There really was no one else on Elystra Nyla wanted to be keeper of her heart other than Sarja.

The all-too-brief kiss ended, and Sarja hugged her again. "I love you," Sarja whispered in her ear.

"I love you too." They released each other. "You may want to stand back a little."

Sarja did as instructed, backing up until she was near the entrance again.

Nyla faced the Stone, positioning her hands a few inches from either side of it. The glow began to intensify, becoming an almost blinding whiteness.

"Arantha protect me," Nyla said, and then her hands made contact with the Stone's glassy surface.

Intense, searing pain immediately coursed through her body. She tried to let go of the Stone, but couldn't. Her body went rigid, and her mouth opened, but she was unable to cry out.

Her mind's eye was a curtain of pure white. Gradually, the pain receded, but she was now a prisoner, locked inside a mental cage to which—she presumed—Arantha had the only key. She wondered if this pure, all-encompassing white would be her home for eternity, a soul drifting through the haze without shape or form.

After a few moments—or what felt like a few moments—blurry shapes began to emerge against the stark whiteness. As she watched, the blurs became more distinct, coalescing, focusing. An image formed. No, several images, one after another. Places she'd never been, people she'd never seen, dancing and swirling in a circular pattern through her mind.

She saw a mountain range, and within it, a dry riverbed leading to a large, serene lake. In the center of this riverbed was a woman, lying face up, her body shivering as if she was freezing to death, even though there was no snow within sight. The woman had pale skin, purple hair—*purple hair?*—and strange designs of winged creatures on her arms and chest. Kneeling at her side was another person with shoulder-length, curly red hair, who was holding the shivering woman by the shoulders, shaking her frantically. The view changed, and she saw his face.

His face. It was a young man.

Before Nyla could focus on this strange pair, the image changed again. This new image was even stranger, and much, much more disturbing.

She saw a village. But it was not her village, for the structures were wooden. And they were ablaze, every single one of them. Terrified men, women and children fled through the streets, seeking escape, but a figure emerged from the surrounding darkness. A woman, with the most horrible smile on her face. She raised her hands, and lightning shot from her fingers, striking the fleeing villagers. Nyla could not blink or turn away as the helpless victims, frozen in place by the lightning, charred and blackened before falling to the ground as lifeless husks. Right behind her, a man with a short dark beard and the same terrible smile as the woman, looked on in approval.

Nyla could only watch in horror as the slaughter continued, and then the vision faded to black. She didn't hear Sarja's scream of concern, nor her footsteps as she tore out of the cave. She didn't even feel it when her body crumpled to the floor.

Chapter Thirty-Eight

E LZOR SAT on the edge of the bed, watching his sister's sleeping form, a vast array of emotions vying for supremacy in his mind: concern, impatience, disappointment, pride.

It was a strange dichotomy, the girl Elzaria once was and the woman she'd become. She, like so many Elystran girls, were creatures to be used, abused, and discarded. He would give anything to spare her from the memories that still haunted her to this day. In fact, he hated that he couldn't compete with those memories. No matter how strong the Stone made her, no matter how much the citizens of Agrus had come to fear her, those memories would always remind her of the frail, weak child who endured the torments that monsters like Rogin and their father inflicted on her.

He found it ironic that his grand plans required so much of her, when given the choice he would keep her as far away from them as possible. He trusted his own capacity to keep her on a short leash, to prevent her from letting her abilities overwhelm her, but he couldn't help but wonder what would happen should his plans come to fruition. Bringing three Stones together would make whoever held them all-powerful, that's what the legend said. If such all-consuming power were awarded to Elzaria, would she still feel the need to obey him, to let him rule at her side? Or would she deem him unnecessary?

A frown crinkled his face. *Why does the Stone give such power to a woman who barely has the capacity to understand them, and yet I, who share the same blood, am unable to tap into that same power? Why?*

He glared at his sister. As much as he loved her, he should have been the one to be granted these abilities, not her. Still, she'd done well. Without her, his tiny army would have been slaughtered like havsu. If the armies of Darad or Imar were to show up at the city gates now, the Elzorath would be over-whelmed with Elzaria in this state. Everything depended on her.

He reached out and gently slapped her face, hoping the light sting would somehow cause her to wake from her coma. He'd been doing it ever since discovering the Vandan skeleton. He needed her to wake so they could follow the Stone's trail, wherever it led, before it was too late.

To his surprise, Elzaria began to stir. A soft groan escaped her lips, and her hands instinctively moved from her sides to cover the spot where he'd struck her. Satisfied he'd finally suc-ceeded in rousing her, he removed his gloves and used his right hand to caress his sister's cheek. At his touch, her eyes fluttered open, and she beheld his smiling face.

"Elzor?" she said, pressing her hand against his.

"I am here."

She looked left and right, taking in her surroundings. She exhaled when she seemed to recognize the bed she'd spent the past week sleeping in. "How long have I been here?"

"Two days. The guards found you lying unconscious, right outside your door. You appeared to be sleeping. Your breathing was regular and your heartbeat was strong, but nothing we did could rouse you."

She rubbed her cheek. "My face hurts."

"Yes," Elzor said without a trace of apology. "I theorized that a few sharp pains might free you from whatever was holding your mind prisoner."

Elzaria glared at him and gestured at the pitcher of water on the night table. "I'm thirsty."

"Understandable. You've not eaten since the meal we shared. I've come by on occasion to give you water, but I regret I've been rather busy." He poured a mugful of water from the pitcher and handed it to her. She grasped it with both hands, raised her head and quaffed its contents.

He watched her for a few moments. Once she'd slaked her thirst, he continued. "It might interest you to know that we finally penetrated the door. As I suspected, there was no Stone to be had."

She drained the last few drops from the mug, and then exhaled. "Morix lied. Can't say I'm surprised."

"Indeed. However, we did find the remains of an ancient raider. With no evidence to the contrary, we are assuming the Stone lies within the borders of Vanda."

"Your assumption is incorrect."

His eyebrows raised. "Oh? Where might it be, then?"

"Where is my Stone?" she asked, ignoring his question. The box inside which it normally rested sat in its usual place, on the other night table. However, the box was wide open, and there was no trace of the Stone inside other than an indentation in the crushed velvet that lined it.

Elzor began rooting through the blankets that covered her. After a brief search, his hand emerged with the Stone grasped in it. "It is here. I hoped physical contact with it might speed your recovery." He handed it to her.

"Thank you, brother," she said. "But it has done far more than that."

"What do you mean?"

A wicked smile crept over Elzaria's face. "I have quite a story to tell you."

Elzor's mouth curled into a sneer. "I don't need a story, sister, I need answers."

"Oh, you will get them." She matched his scowl with one of her own.

His eyes widened. "Did you have another vision? What did you see?"

She met his gaze, unblinking. "Everything."

Chapter Thirty-Nine

AWN HAD barely broken the morning after Mizar's fight with the raiders when he and Sen resumed their journey to Ghaldyn. The girl seemed to have slept straight through without waking, and though her external injuries looked to be far less grave than the night before, she was still quite weak. Her body accepted a few precious sips of water poured into her mouth, and swallowed them without incident. Sen still thought it best they not risk feeding her until they reached their destination.

Sen used some more of his herbs to heal the wounds beneath her skin, including a sedative that would keep her docile for the time being. He then took a couple of minutes to heal his sore jaw, after which he proclaimed her well enough to travel.

They had no choice but to leave the raiders' bodies, as well as that of the dead chava, where they were. It took a few moments to tether the girl to Mizar so they could ride his merych in tandem without both of them falling off. Once both seated, he used another rope to tie her hands around his waist. She didn't even react. She fell into a listless sleep, using Mizar's back and neck as a pillow. Then they set off at as brisk a pace as they could manage.

A patrol intercepted them just as they reached the Shardyn Crossing. Their captain instantly recognized Mizar, who informed them of the four Vandan corpses to be found along the river, as well as their merychs and the dead chava. The captain suggested they harvest the chava for its meat, but Mizar insisted that it be burned along with the thieves', out of respect for the young life it had protected with its own. The soldiers again bowed, assuring Mizar they would carry out his orders.

Six hours after bearing due east, the three of them entered Ghaldyn province, a land of sprawling farms, ranches, and orchards. The girl had still not woken when they rode up the path to a large, wooden, one-story house. They were greeted by a tall dark-haired man in his early forties with shining brown eyes and a prominent nose, who embraced Mizar in a bear-hug once he'd disentangled himself from Vaxi and alit from his merych. Mizar introduced the man as his cousin Kimur, who enveloped Sen in a similar crushing hug.

Within minutes, the entire household ran up for a greeting and an embrace, welcoming Mizar back to the place where he spent his childhood years. Sen could only stand back and watch the reunion with a heavy heart. How he wished he had a family who would welcome him so.

Sen was introduced to Mizar's family: his cousins, as well as their wives and kids, who called the farm their home. There were several little children who, after getting hugs of their own, asked—no, *demanded*—that the High Mage of Darad make them fly, and Mizar was only too happy to oblige them for a short while. Sen smiled as Mizar used his abilities to make the little ones swoop just off the ground like fledglings.

Mizar then introduced Sen to his father Deegan, a man of eighty years, who welcomed both Sen and his "beloved son" with open arms. Because of his age and the degradation of his joints, he was unable to stand for more than a few minutes, and couldn't walk without a stick.

Sen wondered upon their arrival if Deegan's house, despite its size, would have enough room to accommodate three more people. The other of Mizar's cousins, Gandrel, volunteered to give up his and his wife's bedroom for the girl, who Sen assured them would need a few more days to recover. The timing, Gandrel explained, was perfect, as he was planning on leaving that day for the provincial capital, Ghal, to attend the region's annual harvest festival, and he would be taking his wife and all the children of the household with him. Sen was grateful for this: he figured when the girl regained her full faculties, the fewer people were around, the better.

Kimur's wife, Mareta, took the job of removing the still-sleeping girl's soiled, bloody clothes, washing her, and dressing her in a clean white night-robe before settling her down in bed. Sen assumed the sedative had worn off by then, but she still hadn't woken up. Her breathing was steady, though, and it looked like she was sleeping naturally.

When Sen first learned they would be traveling to Mizar's home, he made it a point to pack several herbs that alleviated joint pain. He'd heard, ever since his apprenticeship began, about the ailments that afflicted his Master's father, and he wanted to repay Mizar's kindness by relieving as much of Deegan's suffering as he could.

With Deegan looking on while stretched out on a cushion-covered couch, Sen rubbed several fennik leaves on his own palms, before placing his hands on Deegan's knees and closing his eyes. Concentrating his abilities, he felt the power flow through his hands and into the old man, who gasped as the chronic pain left his body. He was scarcely able to believe his eyes as he flexed his knee joints, first one and then the other, with little discomfort. Then his face broke into a wide, toothy grin, and tears fell from his eyes as he hugged Sen. Mizar, too, was all smiles. Sen advised him that this remedy was only temporary, however, and that overexerting himself would only cause the pain to return sooner. Deegan nodded in understanding, and invited them to join him at the table for an early supper.

Sen could only smile at Mareta as he dug into his plate of roasted billock. These birds, useful for their egg production, were also commonly used for food. Though he ate well at the Castle Randar, Sen missed the type of home cooking one only got on a farm. He devoured his billock breast, along with a small loaf of chaska bread and some vegetables, in no time. Mareta happily gave him a second serving. And then a third.

"So who is this girl you've brought to my home?" Deegan asked, taking a sip of manza cider. He'd had Kimur open a barrel of homemade brew to celebrate his son's return.

Mizar relayed the story about the vision he had that had led them to her, about his battle with the raiders, and Sen's exemplary healing abilities.

"Vandans," Kimur scoffed, "They're like a plague of dingu bugs. Just when you think you have them under control, they rear their ugly heads again."

"Right," Deegan said. "I remember when King Armak sent the bragas packing. With my lad's help, of course." He shot a proud look at Mizar, who raised his mug of cider.

"Those were dark times," Mizar said. "And I fear there may be more ahead."

Kimur and Deegan stared at him in alarm at this ominous proclamation. Neither spoke.

"In addition to the Vandan problem, there is trouble brewing in the west," Mizar continued. "An upstart named Elzor has invaded Agrus, and slaughtered its rulers. I believe he has his sights set on larger prizes."

"Great Arantha," Kimur said. "Do you think these Vandan incursions have anything to do with this Elzor's machinations?"

"I do not know. King Aridor has gone to Imar to speak to Largo. With luck, we can broker an agreement to join forces with the Viceroy of Barju against him."

"How large an army does he command?"

"From what I've heard, six hundred."

Deegan's brows knitted. "Six hundred? How could anyone conquer Agrus with a mere six hundred men?"

Mizar's voice became hushed. "He has a Wielder under his command. A very powerful one. Her name is Elzaria. She is his twin sister."

Kimur checked Mizar's face as if wondering if he was playing a practical joke on them. "It's not in your nature to jest, cousin."

"I assure you, Kimur, I am dead serious."

Deegan was practically spluttering. "A female Wielder? How is that even possible?"

"I do not know, Father. These are strange times, to be sure."

"It is indeed," Sen spoke up. "The invasion of Agrus, Vandan raiders threatening our borders, and now this girl, riding through the Celosian Forest, alone, on a chava."

Deegan's mug froze inches from his mouth. He fixed Sen with a hard stare. "What did you just say? A chava?"

"That's right," Sen replied. "A magnificent animal. Sadly, it did not survive the raiders' arrows."

Deegan was no longer looking at them. He rose to his feet, reaching for the walking stick leaning against the near wall. All the color had drained from his face.

"Father?" Mizar asked, also rising to his feet. Sen and Kimur stood as well.

"I must ... I must get some sleep. I feel wearied by the day's excitement." He shuffled towards the door leading to his room. "It is wonderful to have you home again, my son."

"Sleep well, Father," Mizar said, and Deegan disappeared into his room, closing the door.

"Master?" Sen asked. "Did I say something wrong?"

"Worry not, lad," Kimur said. "He tends to be a bit eccentric at times. Especially after a few nips of cider."

Mizar turned to Sen. "Come, Sen, let us check on our mysterious traveler." Then, to Kimur, he said. "I want to thank you and Mareta for taking care of him. It's good that our farm is in your capable hands. There was a time I feared our land would never bear the footprints of children again."

Kimur smiled, and again Sen felt the familial bond between them. "Think nothing of it, cousin. Your name is among the most respected in all of Darad. You have brought honor to our family name, and stepping into your shoes as the caretaker to both your father and your land was the least I could do."

The two clasped hands, and Kimur bowed his head. "Sleep well, Mizzy." Sen's eyes widened, and saw Kimur leave the room with a subtle wink at him.

Sen opened his mouth, but Mizar shot him a steely-eyed glare, complete with pointed finger. "Not … one … word."

"Yes, Master." Sen tried to hide his smile, and failed.

Chapter Forty

IZAR AND Sen entered the girl's room to find Mareta sitting at her bedside.

"How is she?" Mizar asked.

Mareta was a vivacious, full-figured woman in her late thirties, with short dark hair and big blue eyes. She and Kimur had married young and now had four children. Looking at her and the happy life they shared, Mizar couldn't help but wonder what his life might have been like if he'd never made that fateful journey to Dar.

"She's still asleep, poor thing," she said. "Her dreams have been ... fitful. She's woken a few times, just long enough for me to give her a few sips of water, and she always just goes right back to sleep."

Mizar approached the bed, staring down at the girl. "What do you mean, 'fitful'?"

"She talks in her sleep. Most of the time, her voice is too low for me to hear, but I've been able to make out a few words."

"Such as?"

"She said 'Arantha' a couple of times. Maybe she was praying. She also said 'mother' once or twice. The only other word I understood was 'Protectress'."

Sen sat in a chair on the other side of the bed. " 'Protectress'? Strange word."

"Nothing else?" Mizar asked.

"No. I've also taken a close look at her clothes. It's made from strong leather, tougher even than gurn hide. It bears no country's emblem. She possesses no jewelry, no talismans. The only thing she does have are scars."

"Scars?" Sen asked, checking the girl for additional injuries.

"Yes, on her arms and back. They appear to be long healed."

Sen's eyes went to the scars on her arms. "Yes, I saw them. Whoever this girl is, she's been through a lot."

"Other than that, though," Mareta continued, "she appears to be in great physical shape. Her muscles are well-defined, and with the wounds she sustained, she must possess admirable strength to have survived them."

"Oh, she's strong all right," Sen said, absently rubbing his jaw. "Where do you suppose she's from?"

Mizar shrugged. "Her skin is too dark for her to have come from the highlands of Barju or Imar. She could be from Agrus, I suppose."

"That's a long way to travel, even by chava," Sen said.

Mareta stood up. "Well, I have chores to finish, so I'll leave her in your hands now. Please call me if you need me for anything." She walked up to Mizar, grasped his shoulders and planted a kiss on his cheek. "Welcome home, Mizar," she said, smiling. "It's wonderful to meet you, Sen."

Sen bowed, and she closed the door behind her.

Mizar searched for another chair, but couldn't find one. The room Gandrel shared with his wife Lissa was not large, containing only a few shelves for clean clothes, a hamper for dirty ones, and two small end-tables upon which several candles provided the room's only light. Taking care not to disturb the girl, Mizar sat on the edge of her bed.

They sat in silence for the next hour, watching this mysterious girl whom Arantha himself had sent them to save. Mizar

335

cast occasional glances at Sen's face, who watched her with rapt attention.

Because Sen had shouldered both his education and his duties so readily, Mizar often forgot just how young his apprentice was. He'd grown up under the same roof as a father that abused him at worst, ignored him at best. He'd spent little time around kids his own age, and apart from the occasional hellos he gave to kitchen maids he passed in the castle, he'd had no meaningful contact with females. And he'd saved this girl's life. It was no wonder he'd already formed an attachment to her, despite her rendering him unconscious.

Mizar moved to one of the night tables upon which, apart from the candles, was a pitcher of clean water. He poured some of its contents into a couple of mugs, paused briefly to lower the water's temperature to a refreshing coolness, and handed one to Sen, who took it with a quiet 'thank you'.

"Master, may I ask you something?"

"You may."

"You said your duties as High Mage prevented you from marrying and having a family." There was more than a trace of trepidation in his voice.

"That is correct."

"Is there … is there some sort of law that prevented you from doing so?"

Mizar averted his gaze to the candles flickering on the night table, choosing his words carefully. "No, no law. It just sort of happened that way."

Sen sighed heavily. "I see."

"When I first discovered my abilities, all I could think about was how miraculous a gift I'd been given. That I could repay my king and my country for the prosperity generations of my family have enjoyed. I did this freely and without hesitation."

Mizar hung his head, as if his thoughts were a great weight upon it. "I always knew that by becoming High Mage, I would have to make certain sacrifices. Instead of spending my days at my family's side, I would be advising the king. Instead of harvesting the fields and tending the flocks, I would be educated and trained for a position few men have ever had the privilege of holding. A position, as you can imagine, where isolation and seclusion are expected."

Sen nodded.

"Believe me, I would not have voluntarily chosen a life of celibacy. The people of Darad laud me as a dignitary or divine presence whenever I venture outside the castle, but I have always sensed a fair amount of fear in them as well."

Sen nodded. "They fear your abilities."

"Yes. Can you blame them? What if I were to one day decide that I no longer wanted to be subordinate to the king? What if I suddenly craved power for myself? Who would stop me? Who would save them from me?"

A pained expression crossed his apprentice's face, as if he couldn't even fathom such an event.

"Thankfully, King Aridor knows that I possess no such cravings. It took me many years to convince Armak that I had no desire whatsoever to use my power to usurp his. By the time Aridor gained the throne, trust was never an issue, as we'd had many years to become friends. But the people? They only have their king's assurances that I am not a caged, snarling beast, held in check only by my tenuous oath to serve the crown. 'Tis no small thing, wielding the power I command. Were I more faithless, or weak, or corruptible a man, I might have chosen a far more destructive path."

Mizar reached over and put a comforting hand on his apprentice's arm. "But you are a healer, Sen. My power, as you saw yesterday, can be used to take life, whereas you wield the power to restore it. The citizens of Darad, once word of your existence becomes widespread, will look upon you with far less dread than they look upon me."

"When do you think that will be?" Sen asked. "That everyone will know about me?"

"When I deem you ready," Mizar said. "You have a kind soul, Sen. You would wish to use your abilities to heal all of Elystra if you could. Am I right?"

Sen thought for a moment. "I suppose so."

"The hardest lesson you are going to have to learn is that the world, and life in general, dispenses more pain and suffering than you could hope to allay in a thousand lifetimes. You must accept this limitation, or it will drive you mad."

"I understand, Master. I was happy to ease your father's pain, though."

"I don't even have the words to properly thank you for that. Seeing my father happy again was a gift I can never repay."

Their conversation was cut short by a soft moaning sound, and both men turned to face the girl, who was turning her head from side to side, as if trying to shake the cobwebs out. As they watched, her eyes fluttered open. She blinked a few times, scanning her surroundings. After a few moments, she seemed to realize she wasn't alone. Mizar caught a flash of what looked like fear in her eyes as she focused first on his face and then Sen's.

Her eyes shot to her hand, which Sen was once again holding. She took in his features, lit only by the three candles that hadn't yet sputtered and died. Then, for the first time since she burst from the forest, she spoke.

"Sershi?" It came out as the softest of whispers, but in the quiet of the room, both men clearly heard it.

Every land on Elystra spoke basically the same language. One would notice a few idiosyncrasies if they were to travel to another land, but for the most part, one would be able to understand more than enough to get by. This word was unknown to Mizar.

Sen leaned forward expectantly. "Hello. How are you –"

Upon hearing his voice, the girl gave a sudden, shrill shriek. Yanking her hand free from Sen's grasp, she struggled to sit up quickly. As she did so, she swung her other hand around, balled it into a fist, and struck Sen square on the nose. He flew backwards, toppling his chair and sending the contents of his mug onto the wall, the floor, and his own face and clothes. Sen hit the floor with a *thud* and a cry of pain as he brought his hands to his nose.

Mizar watched his apprentice hit the ground, knocked silly for the second time in as many days.

Oh, for the love of ...

Chapter Forty-One

D AVIN HAD night watch again the night before, so Maeve let him sleep in. When he awoke at just past three in the afternoon, Maeve gave him a minimal account of the disagreement she'd had with Kelia the day before, and it was a struggle for her to internalize the anger she had for herself.

Davin, as she expected, consoled her as best he could. He pointed out that despite numerous setbacks—a severe manpower shortage, engine troubles, a lyrax attack, wonky PTs, and a woeful lack of appropriate celebratory libations—their mission was a success. They'd found the energy source they sought in less than two weeks, and Maeve had become the universe's first Earth-born proto-human. Oh, and he'd gotten to see a woman naked. That was definitely the best thing that happened. Maeve wanted to smack him.

Not much was said over lunch. There was nothing left to do but pack up and leave Elystra.

To go where?

Davin was convinced he could figure out how the quantigraphic rift drive worked. He just wasn't sure how long it would take. The good news was, they had plenty of time. Maeve would let Davin dismantle and reassemble the thing to his heart's content if it would help them get home. Failing that, they would have to scan every planet in the neighboring systems for fissionable material that they could use to power the supralight engines. Davin calculated they had enough fuel to get them to any of several systems, so at least they had options.

Yeah. What a great plan. We found the pot of gold at the end of the rainbow, and now the farking rainbow is broken. Maybe we could just form our own country here in the mountains. Davin can be the prince, and I'll be the empress. Every bird, every animal will do my bidding. It'll be fun.

She shook this ridiculous notion out of her head as she and Davin set to breaking down their equipment and moving it back into the *Talon*'s hold. After stowing the generator, they secured both the purifier and the synthesizer to the walls of the crew room so they could have easy access to them without having to return to eating rations. Next, they filled up several large containers with lake water, enough to last them for several months in space. After that came the smaller stuff: the table and chairs, the sensor rods, and the flood-lamps. That just left the excavator.

And the Stone.

While Davin treated himself to one final swim in the lake, Maeve placed the Stone in the securest case they had. It was two cubic feet in volume, triple-lined with lightweight quadranium. Hopefully it would be enough to block the Stone's super-rays, or whatever it was that made their instruments go tits-up. Then she placed the crate in a compartment built into the floor of the crew quarters, reasoning it should be as far away from as many of the ship's vital systems as she could put it.

After stowing the last sensor rod back in the hold, she walked down the ramp to the riverbed. It took a few seconds for her to locate Davin, who had dried off and stood, fully clothed, near the rocky overhang beneath which they'd buried Gaspar.

"Hey, kiddo, you all right?" she asked as she approached. His eyes were closed, his hands were crossed in front of him, and his head was bowed.

"Yeah," he said softly. "Do you think it's okay for us to just leave him here? I'd hate to think of those lyrax things digging him up and ... you know."

Maeve put a comforting arm around him. "I'm sure he'll be all right. We did bury him pretty deep. And besides, whether we bury him here or out in space, he's still gone."

"I know. I just miss him."

She leaned her head on his shoulder. "So do I, Dav. So do I."

He let out a deep exhale. "This is a good spot for him. He always did like the mountains."

"That's true."

"So what's next?"

"You take the excavator and retrieve all our lights and digging tools from inside the cave. I'm going to do a systems check, make sure everything's good to go. I'm thankful Roisin and her friends haven't put in a return appearance, but I don't want to push our luck now that I've put the Stone away."

"Where'd you put it?"

"It's safe on board. I'll show you where later. Now, though, we gotta get back to work. I'd just as soon we were on our way before sunset, which according to the ship's clock will be in just under an hour. Collect our stuff, and then we'll stow the excavator and be on our way."

"All right. See ya soon." He gave a weary smile and strolled toward the cave.

Maeve entered the cockpit and sat down in the pilot's chair. Out the viewport, the Elystran sun was beginning its descent behind the western peak.

Her mind flashed back to two days before, when she first saw Kelia, standing in her thick brown robe, that same peak in the background, with that same sun setting behind it.

My first ever "first contact" mission, and I damn near killed the poor woman. Not exactly something to be recorded in the annals of diplomacy, is it?

Thoughts of Kelia filled her head. Maeve had expected a savage, and got the exact opposite. Kelia could have killed her. And not only did she not do that, she'd saved her. Healed her. Freed her from the despair that was slowly crushing her. She'd shared something miraculous with Kelia, but Maeve had to go and get all high-and-mighty on her.

If only things could have ended dif–

Her reverie was interrupted by a flashing icon that appeared in the center of her console screen. Had it been blinking the entire time? This was odd, because Maeve hadn't even begun to power up the ship's systems. The computer should not have been on.

But it was.

The words on the screen read "MESSAGE – PLEASE PLAY," in big bold letters.

What the hell? Where is the computer drawing power from?

It didn't take long to find a tiny power module behind an access panel at the foot of the main console. It didn't seem to be connected to anything but the main computer. It was definitely Terran in origin.

Intrigued, she placed the module on the console and tapped the "PLAY" icon. Immediately, a face appeared in the center of the screen. A very familiar face. A face she never expected to see again.

Richard.

Maeve let out a short gasp, then caught herself. She recognized the room Richard was in: Sahara Base's security office. And from the time code on the playback, it looked like he'd recorded it at 3:15 a.m., the morning before the base was attacked, everyone else was killed except for her, Davin, and Gaspar, and the three of them escaped.

She took in the details of Richard's face: his intelligent eyes, aquiline nose, strong jaw and slightly-receding hairline. He looked exhausted, of course, which he usually did after he'd gone two days with barely any sleep. God, how she missed that face.

And just like that, she started to well up with tears. At that moment, however, the recording began.

"Hey, Starbird," he said with his usual crooked half-smile. "Betcha never expected to see this handsome face again. What I wouldn't give to have this be a two-way conversation. But, that's not possible."

A smile pushed its way past the sadness as she beheld his image. She stabbed at the "pause playback" icon, but nothing happened. He just kept smiling at her.

"I know you're probably thinking 'I should go get Davin right now,' darlin', but this message is for your ears alone. It can't be paused or rewound, and I've programmed the computer to delete it as soon as I'm done speaking. So just listen."

Taken aback by his words, she slumped back in her chair. Her eyes locked on the screen, afraid to even blink lest his image disappear forever.

"I'm not sure you're going to believe the story I'm about to tell you. Fark, I pray to the Saints you do. I'm still not sure *I* believe it. But it's all true, and you need to hear every word I have to say.

"I'm recording this only seven hours before we're scheduled to leave the Terran system on the *Talon*. Our little solar flare is set to disrupt the Jegg dampening field so we can escape. Unfortunately, it won't work." He threw his hands up as if frustrated by the realization.

Maeve's breath hitched in her throat.

"You know this already, but just before we make our attempt, the Jegg will attack. Don't know how they found us, but they do, and there's nothing we can do to stop them. You'll be in the cockpit doing your pre-flight checks, Davin and Gaspar will be performing the final diagnostics on the quantigraphic rift drive. The rest of us won't be there."

He knew*? He knew the Jegg were going to attack? And he did* nothing*? How could–*

"Obviously, we're going to have to activate the base's self-destruct. If the Jegg discovered our plans, if they knew where you're heading, it would screw up everything we've worked for.

"No doubt you were surprised when you opened the box of PT's and only found four instead of ten. Mahesh will remove the other six right before the attack, and he and the rest of the team will use them to evacuate to Himalaya Base. They'll be quite safe. As for me ... not so much. Someone has to stay behind."

His face became somber. "There's something I have to tell you, Starbird. You're going to hate me for it, but this is my last chance to tell you the truth. I told you my first contact with Banikar was two years ago, when we began drawing up plans for this mission. Where we would somehow fuse a Jegg QRD with a Terran supralight engine and use it to escape. The fact is, I've been speaking to Banikar for thirty years."

Maeve's mouth went slack, and she felt her head shake involuntarily. She couldn't believe what she was hearing. She wanted to scream at the image on the screen. *Make sense, damn you!*

"I was just a kid. Scared the fark out of me the first time he appeared. Right there in my bedroom, floating above my bed like a cheap holographic ghost. I couldn't even scream. But he calmed my fears and we talked. He was a blob really, no eyes, no mouth, nothing. But he talked to me, inside my mind. Maeve, he was wise beyond all measure.

"He told me that I was going to change the course of human history. That's all he said, and then he disappeared. I was sure I'd dreamt the whole thing. But when you're eight years old and someone tells you that, you actually believe it. From that day forward I poured every angstrom of energy I had into achieving greatness. By the time I turned eighteen, I had three doctorates and a Hawking Prize. And I was just getting started."

Maeve remembered a younger version of Richard than the one she saw on the screen now. He was always handsome, but he also had a whimsical charm when he was younger that the invasion robbed him of. She smiled in spite of all he wasn't telling her.

"Every night from that first day in Texas, I slept with one eye open, hoping my glowing friend would drop in on me again. It didn't happen, though, until I was twenty-one, after I joined Dr. Hochstetter's team. We had just finished building our new Aldebaran prototype ship and were all set to begin flight testing when Banikar appeared. I was shocked as hell. I mean, it'd been thirteen years, for God's sake. I'd long since written off my memory of him as a product of my overactive imagination.

"I asked him all sorts of questions, but the Eth aren't much for small talk. He told me 'all was as it should be,' which made me really happy, like I was fulfilling my great cosmic purpose. He told me to go celebrate. He even told me where to go, a dive bar near Fort Bailey. It was June 18, 2719. I'm sure you remember that day."

Maeve's lips pursed. She remembered it well. It was the day they met. Richard had looked so out of place. An engineer in a bar frequented by military personnel. He was lucky he didn't get his arse handed to him. When he asked her to dance, it was so clumsy and pathetic it was hard not to laugh. But there was something so sincere, so endearing about him that she accepted, despite the snickering of her friends.

Wait ... Banikar told *him to go there?* This was making less and less sense.

"When we crossed paths two weeks later when you were assigned to pilot our prototype, it must have seemed like co-incidence. But it wasn't. It was meant to happen." He paused, a hard edge wrinkling his face. "Everything, every single god-damn meaningful thing that has ever happened to me, to you, to everyone in our lives, was part of some grand plan. Every-thing. Me becoming an engineer. Us meeting, marrying, having a son. And oh, remember when the Diplomatic Corps asked if you wanted to lead the mission to the Denebian system? You wanted to turn it down, but I talked you into going. Because, to quote our friend, 'it was necessary'."

Maeve wanted to scream, to run away. She didn't want to hear any more. She wanted to smash the console with her fists, stand up and run out of the room. But indecision, fear, and morbid curiosity kept her glued to her seat.

"And then, five years ago, the Jegg came. Governments have had bunkers hidden all over the world for centuries. From our little hole in the ground, we watched as our world, our colonies, even our allies, fell to the Jegg.

"I felt like the biggest sucker in the universe. 'Change the course of human history', my ass. We lost everything. Half of humanity: gone. Nine billion people, spread across forty-two worlds, dead. My entire family ... " he trailed off, removing his glasses, placing his thumb and forefinger against his eyelids.

"I was so angry. I felt so useless. I wanted to give up, to lie down on a sand dune and die. I actually climbed that ten-story ladder to the surface once. I was prepared to just walk until I couldn't walk anymore. That's when old Glowface appeared to me again."

Maeve vaguely remembered a time when her husband seemed to be more distant, more upset than normal. He even-tually came around and she chalked it up to stress and the war. Eventually the old Richard surfaced and she never thought about it again.

"I hated him. All my life, he made me believe I was ... special, destined for greatness even. But he led me up the proverbial garden path. Now we sat, rotting away underground, watching the Jegg siphon away our resources, one molecule at a time. I felt used. Betrayed. So I screamed at him. I screamed and cursed for what felt like hours. If he'd had a neck, I would have wrung it. I didn't want to look at him. I didn't want to hear anything he had to say."

Richard leaned back in his chair and looked up at something off camera. "Of course, Banikar being Banikar, had all the time in the world. So he let me scream myself raw and throw punches at the air until I collapsed from exhaustion. And then he spoke to me again. I didn't want to listen, but when someone speaks to you in your mind, you have no choice but to listen.

"Believe me, Maeve, I know how this is going to sound." He sighed. "There's nothing we could have done. The Jegg are centuries ahead of us. Whether humanity had colonized ten worlds or ten thousand, or whether we'd just chosen to stay on Earth and leave the galaxy be, it wouldn't have mattered. The Jegg would have come and kicked our butts. Because it was *meant to happen*." He spat out the last three words before he stood up, walked a few paces away, and leaned his head on the far wall.

Maeve's heartbeat was frantic. But he wasn't done speaking.

"I've spent a lifetime mulling over the concept of destiny. Why Banikar chose me. All my life, it's been like I'm an actor, on a stage, waiting for the director to tell me what to do, where to go, what to say. But that's not what I am. I'm a pawn. A pawn in some giant cosmic chess game. The Eth are on one side, and on the other ... " He threw up his hands. "Who the hell knows. Banikar wouldn't say, but my guess is whoever this other player is, the Jegg are *its* pawns. As to what the winner of this game gets ... well, that's beyond even my puny mortal brain's ability to figure out."

He crossed the room and sat down in his chair again, moving his face until it filled most of the screen. "It took me a long time to deal with this revelation. It damn near destroyed me to keep it secret. I mean, who would believe such a crazy thing? I think the others only went along with me because, to put it simply, what choice did they have?

"I need you to remember this, Maeve: all that matters, all that really matters is that, pawns or not, we're playing for the good guys.

"And now, if everything worked out as Banikar foresaw it, you are sitting on the *Talon*, with the Stone. And it's done things to you that you can't begin to explain, just like the one on Denebius IV that protected you and Davin all those years ago. I may be a pawn, but you, darlin', are a queen in this chess game. But you have no idea which move comes next. Well, I'm going to tell you."

No. Don't say it. Don't you farking say it!

"Banikar showed me everything. Your destiny lies *there*, Starbird. On Elystra. You're about to go where the proverbial angels fear to tread. But you won't be doing it alone. Yours and Davin's paths are linked to that woman you just chased away. Kelia, I think is her name?"

Stop. I'm begging you. In the name of all that's holy, stop fark-ing talking!

She looked at his face. The man she thought she loved. He'd kept secrets, monstrous secrets from her, all this time. He'd never loved her. He was just following orders. He'd built their relationship like he was using a manual or a schematic. He'd used her, in every way a person can be used.

For the last two weeks, she'd grieved his loss. The sadness that gnawed at her insides, the shame she'd felt because of her dalliance with Kelia, it was all for nothing. That sadness, that shame had now morphed into white-hot hatred. She was glad he was dead. He deserved to die.

Through the sound of the blood pounding in her ears, she realized he was still talking.

"… you know why I agreed to stay behind while all the others transported to safety. I know what I did to you, and I know I'll probably go to hell for it. But I believe in my heart of hearts, it had to be done." He gave a humorless smirk. "When you're an engineer, you never want to believe that there's a problem that can't be solved. And when you're an arrogant bastard like me, you never want to believe that the universe is a better place without you in it.

"But I've made peace with my sins. I know you will never forgive me, and I don't deserve to be forgiven. That's why I'm glad it's over for me. My part in this little play is done. This pawn is taking himself off the board. All I can hope is that Banikar has a hotline to God, and lets Him know that I did what I had to do. Then maybe, just maybe, I can be reunited with the rest of my family."

He looked directly at her, his deep brown eyes boring into her soul. "You're the strongest woman I've ever known, Maeve. Whatever is about to happen, I know you're going to kick ass. Win this game. For humanity."

One last lingering look, and Richard switched off the recording. The screen went dark, and two seconds later, the words "RECORDING DELETED" appeared. Then it went dark again.

Maeve was numb. Her entire life, her entire existence had been ripped apart like so much tissue paper.

Slowly, she pushed herself up from the pilot's chair. Observing the room around her, like she'd done a thousand times before, she could not comprehend the innumerable switches and lights along the panels. Richard's words swirled around her head, supplanting every other impulse struggling for her consciousness. She descended the ramp and immediately broke into a run.

Her blood pounded in her ears as she sprinted down the wadi, toward the western peak where the sun was now hidden behind its uppermost crag. After five hundred yards, just as she was about to round the bend in the riverbed, she stopped, gasping for breath. She bent over, clutching her knees, begging to every Saint in heaven to make her forget every single word she just heard.

With her back to the camp, she balled up her fists and screamed. She screamed over and over again. She screamed once for every lie he'd ever told her. Every year of her life she'd wasted thinking he really loved her. *Loved her*. Bullshite. She was just a tool to him, to be used at his whim.

She couldn't deal with this. If even a fraction of what Richard said was true, this was a matter for philosophers and theologians and cosmologists to discuss. Geniuses, scholars, holy men. She was a soldier, not a queen. She was meant to fight battles, not end wars.

Arantha has chosen you, Kelia's words echoed.

"No!" she screamed at the mountain looming before her. "Fark you! Fark destiny! Fark the Jegg and the Eth and *FARK YOU,* Richard!"

Physically, mentally, and emotionally spent, she dragged herself to a nearby rock, sitting down upon its flat surface. She buried her face in her hands, unable to process it all. If she thought she was broken two nights before when she cracked in front of Kelia, that was nothing compared to this.

Free will. For millennia, humanity did everything it could to destroy their planet, and each other. Holy wars, crusades, inquisitions, world wars, holocausts, they'd survived it all. They pulled together as a species, grew out of their infancy and evolved. They became the beings they always knew they could be. And it all amounted to precisely zero. Free will? What a crock of shite.

Is every decision I make part of some grand design, a thread in some infinite tapestry? Do I go left or right? Do I drink water or whiskey? Do I become a pilot or a schoolteacher?

It's all meaningless. Utterly meaningless.

Do we stay here, on Elystra? Or do we leave?

We.

Davin.

My son.

It didn't matter whether he was the product of somebody's twisted game of fate. He was just a boy, who didn't know any of this. She'd given birth to him. She'd helped raise him into an amazing young man. She would die to protect him, and nothing would ever change that.

He was not meaningless. In this whole farked-up universe, he was the only thing that mattered anymore. He was her son, and she was his –

"Mom?" his voice called, echoing down the wadi.

She looked up to see him, fifty yards away, jogging toward her. Behind him was the *Talon*, the last remaining sunlight reflecting off its bird-shaped hull.

It would only be a few moments before he reached her. She had to compose herself, fast. She would put on a brave face for him, just like she always did. She couldn't tell him what she just learned. Had he heard her screams? Had he seen her run away?

She stood up, screwing the fakest fake smile she could onto her face, and walked toward him.

Off to her right, she heard the faintest of hisses. By the time her brain registered it, processed it, and made her realize it wasn't the wind or the scurrying of rodents, she felt a sharp stab of pain in her leg, causing her to cry out in alarm.

She looked down to see something attached to her leg. It was serpentine, about three feet long, and the same color as the dirt of the riverbed. It had two sharp fangs that were now embedded in her shin.

Snakes? They have snakes on Elystra? Figures. The day I'm having, I'll probably get infected. Thank the Saints I can heal now. I hope it's not poi–

A flash of white-hot pain engulfed her brain, overwhelming all her other senses. A cocoon of agony wrapped itself around her like a second skin, suffocating her, smothering her. She barely heard Davin's cry of alarm as he came charging up to her.

Then, all at once, the pain receded, replaced by a numbness that seeped into every corner of her mind. The whiteness faded, and a fog of inky blackness took its place.

Her last thought before the abyss stole her consciousness was for her son, who would now be all alone in this terrible, cruel, unforgiving, not-worth-a-shite universe. And then, nothing.

Chapter Forty-Two

THE IXTRAYAN Plateau loomed before Vaxi as she trudged up the path to the village. On both sides of her, the fields where dozens of Ixtrayu normally tilled the soil, watered the plants, or harvested the grain, were all empty. There were no signs of life to be seen.

She ascended the path, cradling her enormously pregnant belly. Very soon, she would give birth to the first daughter born to her tribe in fourteen years. Or it would be a son, which she would return to his father, a man she strangely had no memory of.

Why can't I remember him? Why can't I remember any of it?

She crossed the threshold into the Plateau. Her sisters were there, standing still as statues on the banks of the River Ix, which was bone-dry. She strode down the middle of the waterless riverbed, through the gauntlet of women staring down at her. She scanned their faces, expecting welcoming smiles. What she saw instead chilled her blood. Many of their expressions were inscrutable, while others were looking upon her with disapproval, disgust, loathing.

At the end of the gauntlet were the people who mattered to her the most: Kelia, Nyla, Sarja, and, of course, her grandmother. She smiled, hoping they would greet her, but their faces showed even more disdain.

And then, one by one, her sisters wordlessly turned their backs until only a few remained facing her.

Vaxi felt her will crumbling, and the knot in her stomach intensified as she felt the baby kick. A pitiful whimper escaped her lips.

Sarja was the first to speak. "You left us." Her voice, tinged with sadness, cut through Vaxi like a knife. "How could you do that?"

"You were our friend," Nyla said, her hazel eyes brimming with tears. "You left us behind."

"I had to –" Vaxi began.

"You abandoned us!" Sarja and Nyla shouted in unison.

"Please, let me –"

"You are not our friend," Nyla said, and then she and Sarja turned their backs on her.

"You are a disappointment," said another voice, and she turned to see Susarra glowering at her. "Why couldn't you be more like your mother?"

Vaxi could not believe what she was hearing. "I only did what you wanted! You said it was Arantha's will! And I succeeded! See?"

She looked down at her belly, and was shocked to find she was no longer pregnant. The baby that grew inside her was now cradled in her arms, looking up at her with loving eyes as naked as its body. Such a beautiful baby ...

... *boy.*

She met her grandmother's derisive gaze again. "You have failed me," Susarra spat, and then she, too, turned her back.

Kelia had moved to stand directly in front of her. "You have failed me," she echoed.

"Protectress –"

The baby began to wail, thrashing his little arms and legs.

With a terrible scowl, Kelia snatched the infant from Vaxi's arms, rapidly ascending the bank of the river and hurrying to the entrance of the cave. She gave the baby one contemptuous look, and then threw him inside. Within seconds, a great stone door descended across the entrance, slamming shut with a crash and cutting off the baby's screams.

This couldn't be happening. Never had Vaxi thought Kelia capable of such cruelty. She turned, aghast, from the stone slab separating her from her son, preparing to beg for the life of a beautiful, innocent boy. But it was not Kelia standing before her anymore. It was her mother.

Vaxi looked around wildly, only to discover that her sisters had all vanished into thin air. The Ixtrayu, the village, the Plateau, all gone. She now stood on the edge of a cliff overlooking an abyss so black it seemed to swallow all light. Ilora stood before her. She was just as Vaxi remembered her the day she died: a young woman, tall and beautiful, only a few years older than she was now. Vaxi did not know how or why Ilora had come back to her, but if there was one person who might forgive her, it would surely be her mother.

"Mama," she begged, searching for words that weren't coming. Tears burst through her eyes, falling in salty rivers down her cheeks.

"Who are you?" Ilora said, just above a whisper.

Despair such as she'd never felt clutched at Vaxi's heart. "Mother," she whimpered. "I'm your daughter. Please –"

"I have no daughter," Ilora interrupted. And then, without another word, she flung herself off the precipice, spreading her arms wide as she fell.

"Mother!" Vaxi cried, but it was too late. The darkness swallowed her mother up, leaving her completely and utterly alone.

She sank to her knees, consumed by hopelessness. She had failed. She had failed everybody she loved. She had nothing left, not even her baby. There was only one thing left for her: oblivion.

The chasm called to her. It sounded like … a voice. No, voices, several of them. She tried to make out words, but they were too faint.

And then, without warning, a blinding whiteness shattered the empty black of the abyss, rushing at her at breakneck speed. Her body disappeared, and she lost all sense of self. All that remained were the voices, getting ever louder.

One by one, the rest of her senses returned. She felt warmth surrounding her, softness underneath and on top of her. A bed. A blanket. She moved her head, felt her neck muscles working.

She was alive. The abyss hadn't claimed her.

She couldn't remember what had happened. How she'd gotten … wherever she was.

Where am I?

She opened her eyelids just a crack, then all the way. She scanned her surroundings, blinking her eyes. She tried to focus on something, anything, and came up with the unmistakable sensation of someone grasping her hand.

A slight movement caught her eyes as they continued to focus. Two figures were nearby, blurry and indistinct. They were watching her. One was standing against the back wall on her left, while the one holding her hand sat on a chair to her right. She concentrated on the near figure's face. It looked young, with a wide mouth and high cheekbones, much like someone she knew.

Sershi's here? Vaxi thought. *Maybe I didn't die after all. I'm safe. I'm home. I'm healed.*

"Sershi?" she said, barely audible to even her own ears.

Her eyes continued to focus, the blurry images resolving. She was in a room, roughly the same size as her room back in the village. However, she could tell she was nowhere near her home. The walls were made of wood and not the stone of the Plateau. The blanket that covered her was most assuredly not made from lyrax pelts. And what was she wearing? It did not feel like her sleep-robes.

The figure holding her hand cast a glance at the one standing in the background, and shrugged. Neither spoke.

After a few moments of silence, the near figure turned to face her, leaning forward and finally speaking. "Hello," it said. "How are you –"

Vaxi caught a clear glimpse of the figure's face.

It was a man.

Every memory of her encounter with the bearded brigands flooded back. The last thing she remembered was being thrown from her chava immediately before pain overwhelmed her.

But she was still alive. They'd kept her alive. For what? Humiliation, rape, torture and murder?

Not while she still had an ounce of strength to retaliate.

Vaxi let loose the loudest, most piercing scream she could muster, jerking her hand free from the man's grasp. Simultaneously, she pushed with her legs to reach some semblance of a sitting position while swinging her left fist at the man's face. The man, startled by her sudden burst of energy, did not have time to react before her fist connected with his nose.

Her punch struck hard. His chair toppled backward, spilling both him and the contents of the mug he'd been holding in his other hand all over the wall. He hit the ground with a resounding thump. She immediately turned her attention to the other figure, who hadn't moved. One more to overpower, and perhaps she could escape.

She looked around for some kind of weapon, but all she could see within arm's reach were a couple of wooden sticks holding the candles providing the room's illumination. She grabbed one, causing the candle to fall over. Thankfully, the sudden movement snuffed the candle out before it hit the ground, though the increased dimness made it even harder for her to see her captor, who appeared to be much older than the other. He, like the men who attacked her, had a tuft of hair descending from his chin, though his wasn't as thick or scraggly.

She made a motion to kick the blanket off and swing her legs off the bed, but before she could, the other man strode forward and placed one hand on her legs, holding them in place, while showing the palm of his other hand to her.

"Please, child," he said. "We mean you no harm."

She hesitated. His voice was much more soothing than she expected. Not only that, but his words came out in a practiced, even tone, a far cry from the rough, guttural dialect the thieves used. It seemed like he was being honest. But he was a man, and her grandmother had warned her that gentle words from a man always hid a more insidious nature.

Rearing back her hand, she threw the candlestick at him, and it passed harmlessly over his shoulder. Before it had even hit the wall, she made a grab for another one. Again, the lit candle toppled over, but this one did not go out. It fell upon a small pile of clothes bundled together in the corner, and within moments, it had caught fire.

The man's eyes flicked to the fire, and he released his hold on her leg. Hoping the fire would distract him long enough for her to get the upper hand, she attempted again to climb out of bed.

And then the last thing she expected to happen, happened.

Taking a step back, he made a wide, sweeping motion with his hands, and just like that, the flames flickered and died, snuffed out by a sudden, concentrated gust of air. Only a patch of blackened cloth and a tiny wisp of smoke gave evidence there'd ever been a fire.

She ceased her struggling, rendered mute by what she just saw. Somehow, he had put out the fire. With nothing but a wave of his hand. There was only one possible explanation for such a feat.

"You're a Wielder," she said in a hushed voice.

He had resumed his stance near the back wall, straight and non-threatening. If he truly meant her ill, he sure wasn't showing it. "Yes."

"But you're a man." Her mind raced. "I only know of one man with Wielding abilities, and that is –"

"Mizar, High Mage of Darad." He gave a wry smile and a slight bow. "At your service." He gestured to the young man on her right, who had regained a sitting position, leaning his back against the wall and holding his hand over his nose. "And this is my apprentice, Sen."

She looked back and forth between them for several moments. Neither made a move toward her, so she relaxed slightly, though she kept a firm grip on the candlestick. It wasn't much of a weapon, but it could still cause pain. "Where am I? What happened? Where are my clothes? Where's Tig?"

Before Mizar could answer, the door opened and a plump woman with short black hair entered, rushing immediately to Vaxi's bedside. "Oh, my dear!" she said. "You're awake! Thank Arantha! I heard the most dreadful scream! Are you all right?"

Vaxi stared up at the woman, at her kindly blue eyes, which were rife with genuine concern. Susarra had instructed her to be wary of Daradian men. Daradian women, her grandmother had led her to believe, were little more than servants. At that moment, she felt her surge of strength drain from her limbs, and the fight-or-flight instinct ebbed.

"I am … all right," Vaxi answered. Her hand drifted to her side, and more memories rushed through her mind. She remembered being wounded, the intense waves of pain that washed over her as the arrows pierced her skin. But there was no pain. The flesh beneath her sleep-robe felt tender, even sore, but it was little more than a dull throb. She threw off the bed-cover and hiked up her robe so she could inspect her thigh. Her eyes widened when she saw that it, too, was miraculously healed but for a rough nodule of skin where the arrow penetrated it. She looked incredulously at Mizar. "Did you do this? I was not aware that healing was one of your abilities."

He gave a friendly grin, gesturing across the room to the young man she'd punched, Sen, who had righted the chair and resumed his seat. "Actually, that was me," Sen said. As if in demonstration, he leaned his head forward, showing off his perfectly-healed nose. Only a few drops of dried blood gave any indication he'd ever been injured.

"You ... saved me?"

Sen nodded.

Her brow furrowed. "Why would you do that?"

He cast a puzzled glance at Mizar, then back at her. "Why wouldn't we?"

"I am a stranger. And a woman."

"My dear," said the plump woman. "I can understand your reluctance to trust men after your encounter with those horrible Vandans, but I can assure you, there are few on all of Elystra more worthy of your trust than Mizar. And though I've only just met Sen, I am willing to vouch for him as well."

"Mareta," said Mizar, "would you mind giving our young guest some water?"

"Yes, of course." Mareta filled a mug from the pitcher and held it out to Vaxi, who handed her the candlestick, took the offered mug, and downed its contents. "When was the last time you ate?"

"I don't know," Vaxi replied, pouring the last few drops into her mouth. She hadn't realized until that moment just how thirsty she really was. This revelation brought forth other sensations, most notably her growling stomach. "It was several hours before I was attacked."

"That was more than a day ago," Mizar said. "You've been drifting in and out of consciousness since we found you."

Mareta took the empty mug, refilled it and handed it back to Vaxi. "You poor thing, you must be starving! I will fix you a plate of food right away—assuming the men left anything of the evening meal, that is." She smiled warmly, and Vaxi couldn't help but return it. "I will be right back." She gave Vaxi's hand a squeeze, stood up, and left the room, closing the door behind her.

Mizar, suddenly looking weary, sat on the foot of the bed. "I must commend you, young lady. There's not many who can say they were accosted by four Vandan raiders and lived to tell the tale."

"Six," Vaxi said, taking another long gulp from her mug.

"I beg your pardon?"

"Six," she repeated. "There were six of them. I killed two with my bow."

Mizar's eyebrows went up. "Did you, now?"

She nodded. "What became of the other four?"

Sen's mouth curled into a smile. "Let's just say they'll never bother anyone ever again."

"You killed them?"

"Yes," Mizar answered.

"Good," she scoffed. "May their souls be sent to the blackest part of the Great Veil."

She studied Mizar for a few moments. She didn't know much about him, only what Susarra had told her: like Kelia, he was an Elemental Wielder who, as of the time of the last Sojourn, served the king of Darad, Aridor. He looked to be in good physical condition for a man of his age, which she guessed was several years younger than her grandmother. "Is this your home?"

"Not precisely. This farm, this land, has belonged to my family for many generations. Had I not received the call from Arantha when I was a lad, I would no doubt have taken over for my father as keeper. Thankfully, my cousins and their families have more than fulfilled that role for me." He shifted position, causing the wooden bed-frame to creak. "How came you to be in the forest by yourself?"

Before Vaxi could answer, Mareta returned with the food. The scent of the meat that assailed her nostrils, though unfamiliar, made her mouth water. She snatched what looked like a bird leg off the plate and tore into it. Then she ripped a chunk off a small loaf of bread and downed that just as quickly.

"My goodness! Slow down, dear!" Mareta cautioned.

"She's right," Sen added. "Too much food after a long fast will bring you much discomfort. Better to not take the risk."

Vaxi just nodded, and began eating at a much more leisurely pace.

"Now then," Mizar said. "You were about to explain your presence in the forest?"

Mareta shot him a withering glare. "This young lady is our guest, cousin, as are you. I'm sure at the Castle Randar you are accustomed to having all your questions answered, but I'll not have you interrogating her until she's regained her strength."

"Hardly an interrogation, Mareta," he said bemusedly. "They are simple questions –"

"That can wait until tomorrow," Mareta interrupted. "Now go, both of you."

Sen looked shocked, but Mizar just chuckled. "Very well. I look forward to resuming our conversation in the morning." He stood, as did Sen. Mizar moved toward the door, but fixed Vaxi with a piercing stare. "At the risk of being intrusive … may we at least know your name?"

She thought of the prayer she'd made while being hounded by the Vandans. She'd begged Arantha to spare her life, to forgive her sins. Arantha had responded by sending no less than the High Mage of Darad and his apprentice—a healer—to rescue her, and rescue her they did. And this woman, Mareta, had already shown more compassion, more concern for her wellbeing than her grandmother ever did.

Vaxi had no idea what would come next, but Arantha had obviously put her in their care for a reason. And if Arantha trusted them, she would too.

"Vaxi," she said. "My name is Vaxi."

Mareta smiled, and her warmth seeped into Vaxi's heart. "Welcome to our home, Vaxi. You will be well looked after here, I promise."

"Thank you." Vaxi looked at her hands, scarcely able to reconcile the tales of what she'd heard about foreigners with the hospitality these people offered so freely. "I ... I owe you my life. I do not know how I can repay you for your kindness."

Mizar smiled. "We'll get to that tomorrow. I suspect you will have an interesting story to tell us."

"Actually, there is one thing," Sen said, turning to face her.

"What is that?"

He grazed his fingers over his cheek. "If you could refrain from hitting me again, I would be grateful." Both Mizar and Mareta chuckled under their breath.

Vaxi, too, laughed. "I will do my best."

Both men said their goodnights and left the room.

Mareta waited patiently for Vaxi to finish her meal, pouring her yet another mug of water. She set aside the empty plate, rose to her feet, and instructed Vaxi to resume a lying position. As she covered Vaxi with the blanket from the chest down, she said, "If you need to relieve yourself, there's a clean pot right over there." She gestured to a medium-sized clay pot sitting conspicuously in the far corner. "Is there anything else you need?"

"No, I don't think so."

Mareta smiled, and surprised Vaxi by leaning over and kissing her forehead. Then she retrieved the empty plate and blew out the remaining candles.

Before she could exit the room, Vaxi asked, "Do you know what happened to Tig?"

"Tig?"

"My chava. Is she nearby?"

Mareta's brow crinkled. "Oh, my dear, I'm so sorry. I'm afraid she didn't make it."

Vaxi's heart turned into a lump of packed snow in her chest. She felt tears well up in her eyes, but she held them in. "Thank you, Mareta," she croaked.

Mareta gave her one more sympathetic look, nodded, and left, leaving Vaxi to sob into her pillow.

Chapter Forty-Three

ITH A sigh, Davin demagnetized the bolt holding the last of the portable lamps from the wall of the tunnel they'd spent a week creating. Hefting it in his hands, he deactivated it and flung it into the back of the excavator, along with the other nineteen he'd already removed. The upward-sloping tunnel behind him was now in darkness except for the lamps blaring from the roof of the excavator.

He couldn't believe they were just packing up and leaving, after everything that had happened. They'd found what they came to Elystra to find, and that should've been all there was to it. But it wasn't, and he knew it. And he knew his mother knew it too. The sudden manifestation of her incredible abilities, which was immediately followed by the appearance of Kelia, who possessed supernatural powers from another Stone, was something that needed to be explored. But it wasn't to be.

Though he was barely fifteen, Davin, having inherited his father's smarts, was already studying at a university level by the age of ten. Had the Jegg not reared their ugly insectoid heads, he would surely be on the fast track to follow Richard's path, the one that led straight to the Engineering Corps.

Living for five years underground had been difficult. He had many childhood friends that he knew he'd never see again.

They were likely dead or in some internment camp some-where, including Emma Donnelly, the girl he'd built his first laser with. Recalling his childhood friend, and the fun they'd had together, made him curse the Jegg.

He never let on how lonely he was, being the only kid at the Sahara Base, but given his ability to build things, no one on the team had ever treated him like he didn't belong. As bad as it was, spending one third of his life without seeing the light of day, he knew it could have been so much worse. At least he was alive, and he was with his parents, and they were working toward a solution. It beat being dead, a fate that befell untold billions.

Maeve let Davin sleep late into the day, after he'd taken sen-try duty for a third straight night. When he woke a couple of hours ago, he discovered Kelia had gone without so much as a goodbye to him, only a three-word message spelled out in rocks. Maeve was tight-lipped about the circumstances sur-rounding Kelia's departure, despite his persistent questions. All his mother had revealed was that, even though Kelia could provide Maeve with the knowledge and training she would need to use her new abilities in some way against the Jegg, their world-views were just too different to reach an accord.

Davin couldn't hide his disappointment. He'd read many stories about humans achieving supernatural powers through various extraordinary means. Some invented technologies to augment themselves, some tapped into extra-dimensional sources, and there was even one ancient story about a boy not much older than he who got bitten by a radioactive spider and soon thereafter developed the proportionate abilities of a human arachnid. *A truly ridiculous notion,* he often thought, *but entertaining.* He always thought of his mom as a hero—she was a veteran combat pilot, trained in several martial arts dis-ciplines and a variety of weapons—but when you throw the ability to talk to animals and heal herself into the mix? That redefines the word *riff*.

As he maneuvered the excavator back up the tunnel, he harbored an evil thought of leaving some innocuous artifact, like one of their hand-shovels, behind. Or maybe he should carve "DAVIN WAS HERE" in four-foot-high letters on the cave wall. Then, centuries from now, some Elystran archaeologist might find it, and it would blow his ever-loving mind.

The excavator passed through the entrance and out into the waning daylight. All the things he'd gotten used to seeing—the tables and chairs, the generator, the purifier and food synthesizer—had already been packed away. There was nothing left to put back on the ship except the metal beast he was now driving.

He killed the machine's engine several yards away from the *Talon*. Almost immediately, he heard a high–pitched, agonized scream come from down the wadi. It was followed by another, and then another. It could only have come from his mother.

Had the lyraxes returned? Even though they hadn't revealed themselves beyond the occasional distant howl since the night they breached the camp, it wasn't out of the realm of possibility that they might return. It was now late in the afternoon, same as it had been on that night.

This led to another terrible thought: now that Maeve had packed the Stone into a quadranium-lined crate so that it wouldn't interfere with the ship's sensors, did that mean that her ability to talk to the lyraxes also went away? Maybe they had come out of hiding, and were tearing his mother limb from limb.

The screams continued unabated as he sped down the wadi. When he rounded the slight curve in the riverbed, he saw his mother, sitting upon a flat stone, apparently uninjured. He heaved a sigh of relief as he slowed his pace, coming to a stop about fifty yards away. There was no sign of any lyraxes, and she seemed unharmed. So why was she screaming like a banshee?

He resumed walking, approaching her position. Her shoulders were drooped, and her face was buried in the palms of her hands. He heard several loud sniffles, and he could only conclude she'd been crying.

Only a few minutes ago, she was fine. He knew they weren't leaving under the best of circumstances, but still ... what could possibly have happened to upset her like this?

"Mom?" he called out. She raised her head and saw him. She stood up immediately, clumsily straightened her shirt, wiped her face with the backs of her hands, and faced him with the most disingenuous smile in her repertoire. He might have rolled his eyes if he wasn't so concerned.

She began walking towards him. At that same moment, a small patch of dirt several feet away stirred, as if displaced by a burrowing rodent. Before he could cry out, something long and serpentine shot forth from the ground, quickly covering the distance between its hiding place and his mother. It curled its body like a spring and launched itself at her, burying its fangs in Maeve's leg. The thin material of her pants was built to withstand the elements, but it was inadequate to shield her from an attack by an angry snake.

"Mom!" he yelled, breaking into a sprint, his eyes locked on the snake.

At first, his mother didn't appear affected, and for a moment, he held out hope that either she wasn't badly wounded or that her healing ability had somehow countered the pain caused by the bite. The horror at hearing her scream returned in full force a moment later, though. Her body jerked spasmodically, and she doubled over before collapsing to the ground.

Davin screamed as loud as he could, trying to get the snake's attention. It worked. The creature turned its beady black eyes upon him, flicking its tongue in and out as it assessed him.

Before he could make up his mind how best to attack the thing, however, it slithered away. Almost invisible against the dirt of the riverbed, it disappeared into its hole.

He reached his mother, who continued to jerk and writhe, and he pulled her into his arms. Trying in vain to quell his rising terror, he could only watch as her eyelids fluttered, her face twitched, and her legs kicked out.

"Mom!" he screamed, over and over again, trying to get through to her. No luck.

He'd heard of people's lives flashing before their eyes as they died, but he suddenly felt himself seeing his entire life. He remembered blowing out candles on his birthday cake. His school and his friends. A forgotten corner in the Sahara Base sub-basement he'd converted into his own personal fortress. Finally, the flight from Earth. In each of these memories was a woman, smiling and proud, to guide him through it all. His mother, the woman who now lay seemingly dying in his arms.

It was just a snakebite! Why wasn't she healing herself? Wasn't the Stone supposed to make her invulnerable?

The Stone. Which was now locked in a shielded box, somewhere on the *Talon*.

With a frantic sob, he swept her into his arms, running as fast as he could back to the ship. He was quite tall, just over six feet in height, and he was in above-average physical shape—he spent a lot of down-time at Sahara Base working out with Calvin, Ji-Yan, and sometimes even his mother—but Maeve was no lightweight. It took a full minute, and all of Davin's strength, to carry her to the *Talon's* exit ramp. The longest minute of his life, where he could have sworn he heard his mother's heartbeat slowing down with every step he took.

He set her down as gently as he could on the ramp and ran to the crew quarters to retrieve the med-kit, praying to God there was some kind of antiserum. He rooted through the supplies like a man possessed, his eyes lighting up when he found an ampoule of antitoxin. The label was worn, and it was likely several years old, but he couldn't stop to worry if the stuff had expired or lost its potency. He jammed the ampoule into the derma-hypo, grabbed the med-kit with his other hand, and ran back to his mother.

He let out an exhale as he heard the hiss of the serum being injected into her body. Her twitching had lessened, but her breathing was erratic, and her eyes were still closed. He grasped her hand, feeling for a pulse, a sign that the medicine was working, *something*.

For another agonizingly long minute, he listened for signs of change in her breathing, which was now reduced to low, shallow pants. Her spasms had stopped, and it felt like her pulse was becoming weaker by the moment.

His mind raced. This wasn't working. He'd bought her a few more minutes, but unless he did something else, he would lose her. And then he'd be all alone.

"Shite!" he cried, leaping to his feet. He ran back to the crew quarters, scanning every corner for the box Maeve would have used to contain the Stone. He saw nothing. He searched every place he could reach, but turned up zilch.

No. No. God, don't you DARE take her away from me! Not now!

Davin barreled down the ladder to the hold, where most of their containers lay stacked around the perimeter. A large gap filled one end of the room where the excavator was to be parked. Most of the crates were too big to be the one she would use to keep the Stone in. He tore the lid off the only one that might have been the right size, only to realize he'd just opened the box with the PT's in them. Four of them, thrown carelessly into their container.

He and Maeve had stopped using them the night of the lyrax attack. When they found the Stone, the source of the interference that rendered them nearly useless, they hadn't bothered checking to see if the PT's were even still operable. Now that the Stone was, presumably, ensconced in its shielded box somewhere on board, the rational part of his brain was surprised to learn that all four devices still held a minimal charge, their power readings ranging from seven percent to nineteen percent.

Panic now taking over, he left the hold and returned to his mother's side. Her convulsions had subsided, and she was lying still as death. Her body was going into shock. Soon, the venom that was paralyzing her one bodily system at a time would reach her heart.

With a desperate scream, he dumped the entire contents of the med-kit onto the ground, scanning each bottle, vial and ampoule in turn for something that might help. He found nothing.

Utter helplessness is what Davin had felt as a ten-year-old when, safely hidden beneath a hundred feet of desolate African desert, every major city and minor town on Earth fell to the Jegg. It was the worst experience he'd ever had. But he knew there was nothing that he could do to stop it from happening. There was nothing anyone could do. This situation, however, was much, much worse. A thousand years of medical advances, and his mother would die from a goddamn snakebite. It was ridiculous.

He grasped Maeve's hand in both of his, his voice a full octave higher than normal as he screamed at the top of his lungs. "Mom! Heal yourself! Please! You gotta do it! I can't help you! You're the only one on this planet who can –"

A sudden idea struck him. It was crazy, and it might end up getting both of them killed, but he had to take that chance. He had no other choice.

With a sudden surge of adrenaline, he sprinted back up the ramp.

Chapter Forty-Four

KELIA STARED down at Nyla's still form, anguish pulling her soul in a thousand directions.

The night before, Kelia had just drifted into sleep when a frantic Sarja barreled through her bedroom door and informed her that Nyla had gone and done exactly what she'd been expressly forbidden from doing. Kelia carried her daughter's limp body straight to the Room of Healing, rousing Lyala and Sershi from their slumber. After a brief examination, Lyala concluded that Nyla's contact with the Stone had shocked her into a dream-like state, and there was no telling when she would come out of it.

Kelia remembered the same thing happening to her when she first touched the Stone, and prayed to Arantha that Nyla's condition was the same as hers had been. The difference was, Onara had prepared Kelia for months beforehand, while Nyla had received no preparation at all. Nyla was strong, she realized; much stronger than she was at thirteen.

In her mind, Kelia replayed her conversation with Nyla from outside the cave. Nyla had begged her for a chance, and she refused, like she'd refused all of Nyla's requests.

She squeezed her daughter's hand, her breath quickening.

Why couldn't she just do what I asked? Why is she so willful and stubborn?

Because she's just like me, that's why.

Nyla wasn't a child anymore. She'd grown into a young woman, who wanted nothing more than to prove herself. And Kelia had turned her back on her.

Despair gripped Kelia's heart.

I've failed. I've failed as a daughter, as a mother, and as a leader. I've led my people, my family *straight to their doom.*

"Please, Arantha," she whimpered under her breath, bringing Nyla's hand up to her lips and kissing it. "I beg of you. Tell me what to do. Please tell me what to do."

Emotionally spent, she sank to the floor next to her daughter's body, and after many minutes of silent prayer, she reluctantly succumbed to sleep.

* * *

Smoke swirled around her as Kelia found herself at the Plateau. Flames engulfed the fields of grain and the fruit vines, the searing heat pricking at her skin. The only thing not aflame was the River Ix, which wound its way through the dead or dying croplands.

Kelia ran as fast as she could toward the village, passing many huddled forms who lay unmoving. The smoke obscured their faces, but they were dressed in the garb of the Ixtrayu. Her sisters, dead, littered the ground.

She climbed the last hill to the Plateau, scanning both sides of the river frantically for signs of life, seeing nothing. There was too much smoke. It stung her eyes, its acrid smell filling her nose. She covered her mouth, trying not to cough as she searched for survivors.

On and on she ran, when in the distance she saw movement. A body, silhouetted against the smoke, still moving. She ran up to it, and the figure's identity became clear.

"Nyla!" she screamed, her guts twisting inside her. Her daughter's beautiful face was badly burned, ugly red blisters dotting her arms and legs, her breath coming in shallow rasps. "It's okay, duma, mama's here!" She enfolded Nyla's body in her arms, trying to keep her alive by sheer force of will.

Nyla's eyes fluttered open. She stared vacantly up at her mother. "You must save me," she whispered. Then her head lolled to one side, her body went limp, and her breath ceased.

"No!" Kelia screamed, shaking her daughter's lifeless body. "Please, duma! Don't leave me!"

Another figure stirred nearby. It was Sarja, lying on her side, staring at her. She, too, was covered in burns. Her large, sad eyes bored right into Kelia's. "You must save me," she said, and then she, too, lowered her head, the life gone from her body.

Beyond Sarja, in the near distance, another body clung to life. Gently placing Nyla's head on the ground, Kelia ran to this new figure. She did not detect any burns or scorch marks on this one's skin or clothes. However, her body was jerking and twitching as it convulsed in pain. Kelia grabbed hold of her shoulders, staring into her face.

"Ilora?" Kelia cried. It couldn't be. Her companion died, many years ago.

I must be dreaming.

Just like that, Ilora's spasms eased and renewed hope filled Kelia's heart. Ilora's eyes sprang open, looking lovingly up at her. She lifted her hand to Kelia's cheek, caressing it gently. "You must save me," she spoke in a gentle, dulcet tone.

"No!" Kelia screamed. "You're dead! I couldn't save you!" Fat tears poured from her eyes. "I couldn't save you ..."

She heard a hiss, and looked down to see a hugar, it's black eyes staring back at her as its fangs pumped their deadly venom into Ilora's leg. "Get away!" She batted at the thing, but missed. Its work done, it disengaged its bite and slithered away, disappearing into the smoke.

"You must save me," Ilora repeated, her voice much weaker this time.

"No," Kelia sobbed. "Please don't leave me again. Please." She cradled Ilora's head in her hands, leaning forward to plant a tender kiss on her lips. She closed her eyes, feeling Ilora's hand cup the back of her head. Dream or not, she would get what she was denied twelve years ago: one last kiss.

She felt the hand fall away, and lifted herself up to meet Ilora's gaze one more time. But this was not Ilora. It was Maeve.

"You must save me," the Terran woman said in a choked voice.

Despair overwhelmed Kelia, her heart crushed. "I can't," she sobbed. "I can't save you. I can't save anyone."

"You must," said another voice.

Kelia looked up to see another figure. This one was standing, but it was not obscured by smoke. Rather, the sunlight framed it in a brilliant yellow aura. It stood over her, smiling down with a wise, careworn face.

"Mother?"

"You must save them," Onara said, stepping forward, the light continuing to dispel the smoke.

"How?" Kelia cried. "How can I save them? Please tell me! Tell me what to do! I'll do whatever it takes!"

"You must save them," Onara repeated, and then her form faded into nothingness.

"Come back!" Kelia reached for her mother, but it was too late. She was gone, vanished in a cloud of light. She looked down to see that Maeve's body had disappeared. So, too, had the bodies of Nyla and Sarja. There was nothing left.

Kelia pressed her face to the ground, pounding the dirt with her fists, over and over again, ignoring the pain as she wailed in misery.

* * *

She awoke to find Lyala standing over her, shaking her shoulder, her ovular face scrunched up in concern. "Protectress! Wake up!" she was saying.

Kelia sat up, getting her bearings. She was still in the Room of Healing. Nyla lay on a bed of lyrax pelts, her face serene and peaceful.

"Lyala?" she panted.

"Oh, thank Arantha," the healer said. "I've been trying to wake you for several minutes."

Kelia reached out a hand, and Lyala helped her to her feet. "I–I must have fallen asleep."

"You fell asleep hours ago. I thought it best to let you rest, but then you seemed to be having a nightmare. A really bad one, I would say. Are you all right, Protectress?"

Kelia drew herself up, trying to dispel the ghastly images from her mind and restore order to her psyche. "I am all right."

Lyala looked like she didn't believe it for a moment, but said nothing. "I'll have Sershi bring you some camirra-root tea," she said. "It will soothe your nerves."

Kelia exhaled and nodded. "Thank you, Lyala."

Lyala bowed, moving away just as Liana entered the room. She wore a white robe, a long-sleeved ceremonial garment reserved for official ceremonies. "Nima," she said, striding to Kelia's side. "How are you feeling?"

Kelia considered lying to her, but decided against it. "I don't know what to do, ama. It feels like I have no control over anything anymore."

Liana wrapped her arms around her niece, pulling Kelia onto her shoulder. "All will be well, nima. Just you wait."

Not for the first time, Kelia drew strength from Liana. She could always count on her aunt to keep her grounded. "I pray you're right."

"Nyla's a fighter, just like you," Liana said, moving several strands of hair, which had come loose from Kelia's braid, away from her face. "You came through your first consultation, and so will she."

Kelia nodded, gesturing at Liana's robe. "The ceremony?"

Liana held up her hands. "We had it an hour ago. I know custom dictates that the Protectress be present, but we didn't want to tear you away from Nyla for something so simple. In front of the tribe, I spoke the Councilor's oath and Katura and Eloni welcomed me in."

"Was the tribe supportive?"

"Very much so." Liana beamed, and then became serious. "Have you decided what's to be done with Susarra?"

Kelia had to admit she hadn't come up with a solution. Never in the Ixtrayu's history had someone been guilty of an infraction as serious as Susarra's. What could be done? The thought of some form of physical punishment or exile was repugnant to Kelia, given Susarra's age and infirmity, but neither could the former Councilor be allowed to walk free, continuing to sow dissension. "I regret that I have not."

"Fear not, nima," Liana said. "My first conclave was just adjourned, and that was the main topic of discussion. We have a proposal that I think is a fair punishment, as long as it meets with your approval."

"What is it?"

"For the foreseeable future, Susarra will be confined to her home. A wooden barricade will be constructed and placed over her door—light enough to be moved when needed, but strong enough to keep her inside. Once a day, Runa or one of her huntresses will escort her down to the cistern so she may bathe. Meals and clean robes will be passed to her through her window."

Kelia thought it over for a few moments. "That sounds acceptable. Do you think she will put up a fight?"

"I doubt it. She seems convinced that she's accomplished her goal."

"That's good. Maybe just one thing can go smoothly today." Kelia's shoulders sagged.

Liana patted her cheek. "You just take care of Nyla, and we'll see to the rest."

"Thank you, ama."

"By the way, Sarja's waiting outside. She's been out there all morning."

"Really? Send her in, please."

Liana bowed and left the room. Moments later, Sarja gingerly entered, each footstep more hesitant than the last.

"Come in, Sarja," Kelia said. The grisly image from her dream of the girl's dying plea flashed through her mind, but she brushed it aside. Sarja was still very much alive, though her moist eyes were just as sad as in her nightmare.

Sarja cast a worried glance at Nyla, wrapped in lyrax pelts, and out the tears came. She ran up to Kelia, making frantic gestures with her hands and talking a mile a minute. "I'm so sorry, Protectress! This is all my fault! I knew she was going to do this, and I tried to stop her, and she said it was the only way, and Great Arantha I'm so, so sorry! Please forgive me!"

Kelia pulled Sarja into an embrace and didn't let go until the girl had calmed. "It's all right, Sarja. Nyla will be just fine. You know how strong she is."

"I know," she panted, her eyes still mournful. "It's just ... I'm so worried about her. She's my Promised, you know."

Kelia quirked an eyebrow. "Your what?"

Sarja explained their impromptu ceremony from the night before, and a tired smile crept onto Kelia's face as she realized the true depth of the relationship Sarja had with her daughter.

"I know, it's silly, but it really meant a lot to me," Sarja said.

Kelia put both hands on Sarja's shoulders. "It's not silly at all. I think it's a great tradition you two have started. And I can't think of anyone I'd rather have my daughter pledge her heart to than you."

Sarja gave a half-chuckle, half-cry. "Thank you, Protectress. May I sit with her for a while?"

Kelia cast a glance at Nyla, then nodded. "Of course you may."

A spasm of pain twisted Kelia's stomach, and she realized she hadn't eaten a thing all day. Judging from the position of the sun, it was almost time for evening meal. "I am going to get some supper," she said. "Shall I bring something back for you?"

"Yes, please, Protectress, thank you." Sarja gave a head-bow and sat down next to Nyla's bed. Kelia watched as the young huntress took Nyla's hand, and her heart swelled. She and Ilora were several years older than Sarja when they first developed feelings for each other, but the gestures of love were the same back then as they were now. She always knew Nyla and Sarja would end up together, but seeing it happen in front of her was just another reminder that her daughter was not the child she once was.

Straightening her tunic, Kelia exited the Room of Healing, on her way to the dining area.

* * *

Kelia chewed thoughtfully on her kova steak. It tasted under-seasoned, and she wondered if Aarna was just having an off-day, as her preparations were usually delicious. It wouldn't surprise her if that was the case; nothing had been normal for a long, long time, and she'd been so wrapped up in being a good Protectress she hadn't realized how badly she was failing at it.

The rest of the tribe gave her a wide berth, not wanting to disturb her reverie. Though Nyla wasn't always well-liked within the tribe, she was still one of them. No one wanted something bad to happen to her, and her current condition brought out the mother in all of them. Kelia just hoped that they wouldn't attribute her coma as punishment meted out by Arantha for all those years of mischief.

Runa's face was stoic as she sat down opposite Kelia. She placed her plate down in front of her and immediately pushed it to the side. With a humorless grin, she said, "If you want to switch jobs now, I'm game."

Kelia returned the smile. Yet again, her best friend was there to pull her away from the cliff's edge. "Believe me, you don't want all this on your shoulders. It's enough to drive even the sanest woman mad."

"You'll come through it, Kelia." It was rare Runa called her by her actual name in public, but Runa always seemed to know the perfect times to do so. Like now, when the mantle of Protectress felt like a boulder around her neck.

Kelia reached over and squeezed Runa's hand before grabbing another morsel of bread and popping it in her mouth. "Have you talked to Sarja today?"

"She's not really in a talking mood. She's been beside herself ever since Nyla's … accident."

Kelia nodded. "I just spoke with her. In the Room of Healing. She wants to stay by Nyla's side." She smirked. "I think she's in love."

Runa's eyes widened. "With Nyla?"

"Yes."

She blew out a breath. "I'm not surprised." She grimaced. "Remember that talk our mothers gave us when we were that age? Looks like it's our turn to give it now."

"Great," Kelia said, looking down at her plate with a mock-frown. "We've officially become our mothers. Now my day is completely ruined." Then she laughed.

She glanced up to see that Runa was not looking at her any more. She was looking past her, over her shoulder, at the far corner of the dining area. She also noticed that the room, which held about fifteen Ixtrayu, had gone deathly silent. Several women were staring in goggle-eyed, dumbfounded surprise at something behind her.

Kelia rose from her chair and spun around, and her jaw dropped in astonishment.

Standing there, in an empty space between several tables, was Davin. His face bore a horrified expression, and he was carrying Maeve in his arms. Her sister Wielder's eyes were closed, and her arm hung limply downward. She wasn't moving. Or breathing.

Several Ixtrayu, after getting over the shock of a man materializing out of thin air, grabbed for whatever they could find to defend themselves. Three huntresses snatched up their bows from next to the door. Others picked up their empty plates, perhaps to use them as clubs. The rest just backed away from the pair, not taking their eyes off them.

Kelia stepped forward, her arms spread wide, hoping her sisters would correctly interpret her silent instructions to keep still and not do anything rash. "Davin?"

Davin's eyes flicked wildly from side to side, scanning the stunned faces of the women around him before finally locking onto her. His bottom lip was trembling, and his already-pale face had gone ghostly white. She could see the remnants of tears staining his face. "Kelia?" His voice was a taut whisper.

Runa was the first Ixtrayu to speak. "You *know* him?"

At that moment, Kelia realized she still hadn't told any but the Council about Maeve and Davin, and their mission to Elystra. And now, there they were, thanks, Kelia guessed, to four connected metal tubes ringing Davin's waist like a belt. These were the devices Maeve had used before, the PT's.

Kelia shot a glance back at Runa before sweeping her eyes over the rest of the crowd. "It's all right," she said, hoping no one would panic and start screaming, or worse, shooting. "He's a friend." She could see the stupefied reactions this statement elicited.

She focused on Maeve's body, which still hadn't moved. Her eyes were drawn to Maeve's left leg, and the two bite marks that tainted her skin in an all-too-familiar pattern.

She'd been bitten by a hugar. Just like Ilora.

Her dream, and Onara's words echoed through her mind.

You must—

"Save her!" Davin begged, tears trickling down his face. His knees were starting to wobble, and he looked like he was going to pass out. "Please save her! She's dying!"

Kelia rushed forward, helping brace Davin's fall as he sank to his knees, his mother's weight too much to bear. She placed her hands underneath Maeve's body, lowering it gently to the ground.

You must save me.

She took Maeve's hand in hers and closed her eyes. She reached out with her mind, searching for any trace of the mental bond they'd built through the Sharing. There was nothing. No life. No energy. Only darkness.

You must save me.

Desperation grew within Kelia as she searched, in vain, for any spark of life within her sister Wielder. She saw, felt the hugar's poison, coursing through Maeve's veins, gripping her heart with icy fingers. Smothering it. Extinguishing its ...

There.

A single spark, a faint ember of life, hidden deep within Maeve's mind, fighting to stay lit as darkness closed around it.

Kelia tightened her grip on Maeve's hand, pushing her concentration to its limit. She called forth the energy Arantha had gifted her with, surrounding the spark and keeping the inky blackness out. She built a wall around it, tempering it with every ounce of will she could muster.

She hadn't been there to save Ilora. Despite her protestations to Susarra to the contrary, a part of her blamed herself for her lover's death. It couldn't happen again. It wouldn't. She wouldn't let it.

That's when it hit her. *This is why Arantha sent me to Maeve. To bond with her. To Share with her.*

To save her.

The wall complete, she opened her eyes, meeting Davin's gaze. His teeth were clenched together so tightly she thought they might snap, and tears continued to leak from his eyes.

"Is she ..."

"She's alive," Kelia said. "Just barely. Why does she not heal herself?"

Relief erupted on his face. "Sh-she put the Stone on the ship somewhere. In a shielded box. She didn't tell me where. I–I didn't have time to look for it."

Kelia's thoughts raced. As long as the two of them were connected, she could keep Maeve alive. Eventually, though, her strength would wane. She needed–

That's it!

She turned around to see that the crowd of Ixtrayu had grown in size over the last few minutes, silently staring at them from a respectful distance.

"Eleri!" she called to a young girl with short brown hair and hazel eyes standing by the entrance.

The girl took a nervous step forward, separating herself from the crowd. "Yes, Protectress?"

"Get the healers! Have them meet us in the cave! Go now!"

She nodded, turned on her heels and ran out the door without a word.

Kelia faced Davin again. "Pick her up. Come with me. We don't have much time."

Davin attempted to rise to his feet with Maeve in his arms, but he looked completely drained.

"Runa!" Kelia called, and her friend ran forward to hoist Maeve's limp body up, lifting her as if she weighed nothing.

"Now what?" Davin said.

"Follow me. Quickly."

News of the aliens' arrival must have spread through the entire village, judging by the throng of women gathered to catch a glimpse. Kelia and Davin, with Runa carrying Maeve right behind her, hurried down the path, across the bridge and into the cave.

She lit all the torches with a quick wave of her hand, striding to the Stone. As she laid eyes on it, its glow appeared, growing in luminosity until it bathed the cave in its light.

"Bring her here." She motioned to Runa, who gently laid her on the ground right next to the altar. Davin sat down next to her, clutching her hand.

The light's intensity grew even more.

Kelia took her other hand, reaching out with her mind again. The spark was still there, but the protective wall surrounding it had weakened. She quickly rebuilt it, but her strength was flagging. She wasn't a healer. Even in the presence of the Stone, there was only so much she could do.

Maeve confessed to Kelia that she'd healed decades of scars unconsciously. To fight the hugar's venom, however, required knowledge and training she didn't possess. The poison had overwhelmed her mind and body so quickly that she hadn't had time to react. On top of that, she'd foolishly placed a barrier between herself and her Stone. If Kelia and the healers couldn't rid her body of the poison, Maeve would die.

You must save me.

A commotion from outside the cave drew Kelia's attention. She turned to see a crowd of Ixtrayu, craning their necks to see inside. "Runa, keep everyone out of here! Let only the healers in!"

Runa nodded. "They're here."

Lyala and Sershi pushed through the crowd and entered the cave. Runa took up a position at the entrance, filling the doorway with her large frame.

The two healers gaped in astonishment at the sight of the two strangers on the floor. Kelia understood their shock. Maeve and Davin's clothes, not to mention their pale skin, Maeve's hair and skin drawings, and Davin's maleness was the very definition of *unique* in their village. "Protectress?" Lyala asked, her eyes widening.

"Thank Arantha," Kelia said. "She's been bitten by a hugar. The venom has almost shut her heart down. You must heal her."

Lyala exchanged a harrowed look with her daughter. "We've never done that before," she stammered, her lip trembling. "Hugar bites are lethal. No one's ever survived long enough for me to –"

"She's alive, Lyala!" Kelia shouted, her sudden anger boiling over. "Do *something!* I command you!"

With an obedient nod, both healers rushed forward, kneeling next to Maeve's body. Davin grudgingly released her hand and stood back, his eyes never leaving his mother.

Sershi moved around behind Maeve's head, placing her fingertips on the sides of the unconscious woman's skull. Lyala folded the palm of her left hand over her right, and placed both of them over Maeve's heart. The two healers shared a glance and a nod, took a deep breath, and closed their eyes.

Kelia, too, closed her eyes, returning to the spot in Maeve's mind where the last spark of life remained. Once again, the poison was breaking through her defenses. She tried once again to rebuild it, but without success. The link between them was breaking.

"Hurry," Kelia whispered, a sob choking her voice.

The wall of darkness closed in. The ember's light flickered. *Arantha,* she prayed. *I beg of you, do not let this woman die!*

A blinding light swept through the darkness, flowing over the ember, coating it like a blanket. A light so blinding, it hurt her to look into it.

She opened her eyes with a gasp, letting go of Maeve's hand. Lyala and Sershi still had their hands pressed to her heart and head, and Kelia could see—no, *feel*—Arantha's energy pour out of them and into Maeve's weakened body. She stared at her friend's face, looking desperately for a sign of life.

The glow emitted by the Stone diminished until it was faint again, giving way to the torchlight. Kelia's heart soared at what she saw.

Maeve opened her mouth, sucking in a huge lungful of air. Once, twice, three times. Her eyelids fluttered, but didn't open.

Kelia scanned the faces of Lyala and Sershi, who, as one, removed their hands from Maeve's body. They looked haggard, especially Lyala. She'd never seen Lyala looking this spent. The elder healer inched backwards and almost fell, but Sershi was there to catch her.

Davin, who had been standing against the cave wall watching silently, knelt once again at Maeve's side. He lifted her shoulders, placing her head in his lap. "Mom?" He sniffed. His tears still hadn't stopped. "Mom?"

Her eyes opened and quickly closed again, her brow creasing. A silent moan escaped her lips. "Dav?"

A weak smile broke out on his face. He lifted her gently into a sitting position, wrapped his arms around her, and hugged her hard. "I'm here, Mom. I'm here," he sobbed, kissing her cheek.

"I'm alright, kiddo." Her eyes still closed, she let out a soft groan. "What a farked-up week I'm having."

Davin grinned and hugged her again. "Love you, Mom."

"Love you too, Little Bug." She smiled as well.

Kelia smiled, too, as a tear rolled down her own cheek.

Still out of breath, Davin stared with gracious eyes at Kelia and the two healers. "Thank you," he said softly.

Kelia faced the healers as well. "Take your mother home, Sershi, and then prepare a bed in the Room of Healing. We will be there shortly."

Sershi stood, helping her mother to her feet. Lyala clutched at her daughter's arms for support.

"Lyala?" Kelia said.

Lyala's face was ashen, but she could still speak. "Protectress?"

"I am beyond grateful. To both of you." The words were woefully inadequate for the gratitude she felt, but they would have to do for now.

The two ladies bowed their heads and, still supporting each other, walked past Runa and out of the cave.

Kelia turned back to Maeve, whose eyes were now fully open. And staring right at her.

The last bit of Kelia's resolve crumbled, and her own tears flowed unabated. She thought of her time with Maeve: the Sharing, their flight, their kiss. She thought of Ilora, and of her failure to save her companion's life; a failure she'd atoned for today.

She unconsciously moved her hand to the lumpy metallic pendant around her neck. For the first time in years, she felt fulfilled. Arantha had set forth a path, and she'd followed it correctly. It was her will that this strange, incredible turn of events transpire. Where the path would lead from here, she had no idea. There was only one thing of which she could be certain: after eight hundred years of uniformity, things had changed. And they would never be the same again.

"Kelia?" Maeve said, staring up at her. "You came back?"

Kelia briefly met Davin's gaze, then looked at Maeve again, brushing a strand of her amazing purple hair away from her face. "Not exactly," she said with a wry smile.

Maeve's expression was blank, but then it scrunched up in anguish. "I'm sorry," she said, her voice scratchy and raw. "I'm so sorry. For everything I said to you."

"As am I, my friend. Rest now."

Maeve's eyes darted around the cave as if searching for something familiar. "Dav? Where are we?"

"We're in Kelia's village," he said sheepishly.

"How –"

"The PTs had enough juice for one final jump," he said. "It was the only thing I could think of."

"Nice work, Dav." She looked down at her body. "Why can't I move?" Before Kelia could answer, Maeve added, "The snake."

"You were bitten, Maeve," Kelia said, "by a hugar. Its venom kills quickly. I believe you are the first person to ever survive a bite from one."

"Yay me," Maeve said with a light chuckle.

"Your mobility will return in time. Now that you're awake, your healing ability should take effect."

A faraway look appeared on Maeve's face. "It felt like I was … in a room. With no light, and no exits. I felt the darkness closing in around me. It was cold, so cold. But then I felt something else. A sort of warmth, keeping me alive. Was that you?"

"It was," Kelia said. "It would seem our Sharing has benefited us both once again."

A shuffle of footsteps came from the entrance. Without turning, Kelia said, "Runa, I told you not to let anyone else in."

"Don't blame Runa," Liana said. "I'm afraid we insisted."

Kelia turned to see all three members of the Council standing just inside the entrance. Runa, standing behind them, gave her an apologetic shrug.

"Councilors," Kelia said.

"Protectress," Katura's normally placid expression bore a mixture of surprise and disappointment. "It would seem you left a few details out of the story you told us yesterday. I trust, in the near future, you will see fit to tell us what *really* happened."

Kelia, caught in her own half-truth, nodded. "I promise I will do so, Councilors. In the meantime ..." She looked at her guests. "Maeve, Davin, meet the Council: Katura, Eloni, and Liana."

Maeve cracked a weak smile. "Hi," she and Davin said in unison.

"Hello," Liana said. Although apprehensive, the three bowed respectfully.

"Councilors," Kelia continued, "may I present to you: Major Maeve Cromack, daughter of Helen, retired Space Corps pilot, commander of the 308th Antares Squadron ..."

The three elderly women stared blankly at her. Maeve chuckled under her breath.

"... and her son, Davin," Kelia finished.

"Nice to meet you all," Davin said, flashing a wide, innocent smile. "Sorry to drop in on you like this."

A smile creased Katura's kind face. "Given the events of the past week, I believe I speak for my fellow Councilors when I say that it is clearly Arantha's will that you have found your way to us. You are welcome here."

"Thank you," Maeve said. Davin pulled her close to him again.

Kelia turned her attention back to Maeve. "I have things to discuss with you, and the Council, when you've recovered."

Then, Maeve's face became serious. "That's nothing compared to my news," she said. "If you thought what I told you in the mountains was unbelievable, trust me, you ain't heard nothing yet."

Chapter Forty-Five

Elzor drummed his fingers on the table impatiently as Elzaria finished her meal. Sitting silently in the surrounding chairs were Langon and several other high-ranking Elzorath, who looked like they'd rather be doing anything else. None said a word, though. They'd been summoned back to Castle Tynal's dining hall by Elzor; not for a meal, but to hear news of monumental importance.

Elzaria popped the last morsel of bread into her mouth, chewed, swallowed, and leaned back in her chair with a contented sigh, dabbing her face with a small cloth.

"If you still have room, I can have a servant bring you some dessert as well," Elzor said with surprising sincerity.

"Yes, that would be wonderful," she said. She knew perfectly well the men assembled were waiting to hear what she had to say, but she was famished. She'd never eaten like a royal before, and wanted to relish it while it lasted.

Elzor waved a hand at a servant, a frumpy woman standing in the corner, and she scurried through the back door to relay his order to the kitchen staff. "Now that you're no longer in danger of starving to death, sister, I would prefer we get down to business."

She looked at him with a catty smile, thumped her chest lightly, and let out a belch. Then she balled up her napkin and dropped it on the table. "Very well. Thank you for indulging me, my liege." She straightened herself in her chair. "Did someone get the maps I asked for?"

He waved to a soldier standing at the far end of the hall, gesturing him to come forward with his burden, a stack of scrolls he'd retrieved from the castle's archive at Elzor's order. He set the stack in front of Elzor, bowed, and resumed his post.

Elzaria grabbed the scroll on top and unrolled it. It was the most comprehensive map of the main continent on Elystra ever drafted. It included the borders of all six countries, as well as forests, mountain ranges, and other points of interest that were known to exist. Nothing had been drawn of the southern half of the continent, as the wetlands were impossible to navigate and were uncharted as of yet.

"Before I begin, let me say that although my vision showed me some things that I understood, there was much that I could not comprehend. If the descriptions of my visions seem fantastical, it is because that is how I perceived them."

"Understood," Elzor said. "Begin."

"Merdeen's prophecy was correct," she said, smiling. "There *are* three Stones. I saw them come to our world. I do not know where they originated, but they are definitely from the Above."

Several Elzorath gasped. Elzor's eyes widened.

"I saw Elystra from far above. All the Stones arrived at the same time, as if thrown by some giant hand. They struck thousands, perhaps millions of years ago; I cannot say. They buried themselves deep in the rock of our world, and it is only now that all three have been unearthed."

She looked her brother in the eyes. "The Stone we found at Mogran ... that we found it the way we did, at the time we did, is nothing short of a miracle. Was it by design or an incredible coincidence? I don't know. But I believe we were meant to find it."

"That is good to know," Elzor said. "And thanks to your vision, I can assume we were equally meant to find the other two as well."

"Not necessarily. The other two Stones, as I've said, have already been found. They are held by two other Wielders who would most certainly oppose us and our plans. I don't know if they're aware of the prophecy, but it seems unlikely. So it is in our best interests to acquire the other two Stones while those that hold them are still isolated."

Elzor huffed. "As you can see, Elzaria, my general and my commanders are here. We are ready to begin formulating battle strategies for just that purpose. Can you please cut to the chase and tell us where these other Stones are?"

Elzaria jabbed a finger at the map, indicating the long, curving representation of the Kaberian Mountains. "The second Stone was just unearthed somewhere in this area," she said. "I cannot give you an exact location because one stretch of mountains looks like all the others, and there are no landmarks to pinpoint their location. All I can tell you is that the beings from the Above who found the Stone are somewhere near a large mountain lake. With luck, future visions will help us narrow down the search area."

"Beings from the Above?" Langon said in alarm. "Are you serious?"

"I am deadly serious, General," Elzaria said. "However, there appear to be only two of them, a woman and a boy. The craft they came in is ... impressive, to say the least. It is far beyond anything we could build."

Elzor recalled the mysterious light in the sky on their first night in Talcris. A light he'd dismissed as unimportant. "The day we invaded Agrus, I saw a light in the night sky. It was distant and faint, but it could have been this giant metal bird you envisioned." He met her gaze again. "You said they found a Stone. How can you be certain they won't try to acquire the other two?"

"I can't."

Elzor's face radiated tension and anger. "Well, then, what's to stop them from taking the Stone back where they came from? If that happens, all our plans are for naught!"

"They're not going anywhere," Elzaria said. "I saw, as clearly as I see you now, the woman get bitten by a hugar. She appeared to be dying, and the boy was trying to save her. Then the two of them vanished into thin air."

His eyes widened. "Where did they go?"

"This is the best part of the story." She grinned. "You see, at the time this castle was built, the Agrusian Stone had already been found centuries before. On several occasions, women exposed to the Stone developed Wielding abilities, but they were put to death as demons or sorceresses before they learned to develop them. The rulers of Agrus decided to hide the Stone in the sub-dungeon of this castle, behind a machinite door that no one could penetrate."

"We know all that!" Elzor interrupted. "So where is it now?"

Elzaria let out a frustrated breath. "I'm *getting* to that. One of the King's advisors made a bargain with the leader of a band of Vandan slavers: in return for assassinating the king, thus making him ruler of Agrus, he would give them the Agrusian Stone. However, the plan went awry. On the day the Stone was to be entombed behind that door, the King discovered his advisor's treachery. They set a trap for the Vandans, and there was a great battle inside the newly built castle. The King and his family survived, and the King had the advisor beheaded. However, when they searched for the Stone, they discovered it had vanished, as had many of the slavers. The King sent search parties after it, but the Vandans had disappeared into the Praskian Desert.

"Eight slavers survived the attack, and they rejoined their clan-brothers in their trek across the desert. It was their intention to take the Stone, and the slaves they'd acquired during numerous raids, back to Vanda. However, they never made it there."

Elzaria made a show of pointing to another spot on the map. Elzor, Langon and two commanders leaned forward to see where she'd indicated.

"Right here," she said, "is a plateau, through which the River Ix runs. It then proceeds through this forest before it breaks off into its numerous tributaries. The slavers reached this plateau, an oasis that abuts the Plains of Iyan. One night, the Vandan leader got drunk and –" she gritted her teeth, remembering her most unpleasant memories, "had his way with one of the slaves, a woman who was not as broken as she appeared to be. The fool, thinking the woman sufficiently chained, fell asleep, leaving the Stone within her reach."

"Let me guess," Elzor said. "She developed Wielding abilities?"

"Correct. The transformation nearly killed her. By the time the Vandans realized what had happened, it was far too late for them to do anything about it. She freed herself and the other slaves, and used her elemental abilities to slay the raiders." She gave a slight smile. "Several more women developed various abilities soon after: one had the power to heal, one to make the ground fertile. One learned to communicate with the beasts of the wilderness. Not all of them became Wielders, but they discovered that they had no desire to return to their homelands.

"And there, their descendants remain to this day. Right here." She used her index finger to indicate a spot on the map.

"Fascinating," Elzor said, his earlier sarcasm long abandoned. "A tribe of women, hidden on the outskirts of civilization for centuries." He surveyed the faces of his commanders, who wore equally stupefied expressions.

One commander, a tall man named Brynak, said, "How could a bunch of women possibly survive out there for centuries without men?"

Elzaria bristled at his words. Fighting down her bile, she said, "The most likely explanation is that they seek mates in other lands."

Elzor's eyes widened. "Could—could our mother have been one of these women?"

Elzaria met his gaze. "I believe that is the case, yes."

Her brother stood up, looking over the faces of his men. "So we have one Stone in the hands of beings from the Above, and one in the hands of this tribe of women. How do we go about wresting their prized possessions from their grasp? I don't imagine they're going to give them up without a fight. Can ... can you defeat these Wielders, sister?"

She bowed her head. "I will do my best, my liege."

"Langon, what are our numbers at this time?"

The burly man drew himself up. "We have eleven hundred warriors ready to march at your command, my liege."

"Very good. See to it that the merychs are properly shod and packed with provisions. We have a long journey ahead of us."

"It will be done," Brynak said, saluting.

"Do you have a plan, my liege?" Langon asked.

An evil grin spread over Elzor's face. "I most certainly do."

Chapter Forty-Six

E IZAR AWOKE just after sunrise, which was not unusual for him. He stretched his leg and back muscles as he climbed out of bed, smiling at how good it felt to be home again, sleeping under the same roof he had as a lad. After dressing in a clean set of clothes and downing a bracing mug of cold water, he decided to go for a morning walk around his family's land. Sen was still sacked out in the guest room, and a peek through Vaxi's door confirmed she was still asleep as well.

Ever since retiring the night before, he'd replayed the rather strange conversation between himself and this mysterious girl repeatedly in his mind. Something she'd said gnawed at him.

"You're a Wielder," she'd said. *"But you're a man."*

What a curious thing to say. Most denizens of the neighboring countries knew of Mizar's existence. He, like all the previous High Mages, was known far and wide as a Wielder. What Vaxi said, and the way she said it, made him believe she'd been exposed to Wielding before.

His mind immediately harkened back to his vision about the two unidentified female Wielders preparing to do battle with Elzaria. Arantha had shown him that image, and he had clearly meant for Mizar and Sen to be in the right place at the right time to save Vaxi. Mizar did not believe in coincidences, and this was just one more question he planned to ask her this morning.

His stroll took him past the fields where a small herd of gurns were grazing, and wondered how Gandrel would react when he returned to discover his milking apron now had a large hole burned through it. He wandered past the billock coops, turning a corner to see Kimur using a large axe to chop logs in front of an enormous pile of wood.

Kimur smiled as Mizar approached. "Morning, Mizzy!" he said cheerfully, splitting another section of log in two.

Mizar rolled his eyes, giving him a mock-annoyed scowl. "'Tis unwise to anger the High Mage, cousin, have you not heard?" To demonstrate, he held his palm out, creating a miniature air-spout, which ruffled the hair on Kimur's brow.

Kimur instinctively took a step back. "Okay, okay, calm down already," he said, burying the axe-head in the large stump he was using to split logs upon. "You're up early. I would have thought, living in the castle for all these years, you'd have taken to sleeping late."

"Pfft," Mizar scoffed. "My scholarly duties do indeed require a clear mind, cousin, but Arantha provides me with more than enough energy to sustain myself." A grin spread over his face. "My apprentice, on the other hand ... wild merychs couldn't rouse him."

"Say no more." Kimur's expression became serious. "I meant to ask you last night—why have you come back? Not that we're not delighted to have you, of course, but your arrival was rather unexpected."

Mizar sat down on top of the nearby log-pile, which was sturdy enough to hold his weight. "I told you of the ominous visions I've been having. I was concerned that, should the crisis escalate, I might not have the chance to see Father again." He hadn't shown it, but Mizar was alarmed at the sight of Deegan, how frail he'd become. When Mizar was a child, Deegan was robust and healthy. Now he could barely move without help.

Kimur placed another log on the stump, reared the axe back and chopped it in half. "I've had the best physicians in Ghal examine him, but sadly, there's not much we can do except keep him comfortable." He smiled. "Last night was the first time Deegan's been free of pain in years. I wish we could have Sen stay indefinitely, if only to make your father's passing more dignified and bearable."

Mizar nodded. "When Father's health began to decline, I asked the King if I could move him to Dar where I could look after him. His Majesty agreed, but Father, of course, wouldn't have it. His attachment to this land is unbreakable, and not all that difficult to comprehend."

"Indeed." Kimur split another log in two.

"Where is Father? I checked his bed, but he wasn't in it."

Kimur pointed at a large, solitary reesa tree in the distance. "He decided to visit Areca's grave this morning."

Mizar squinted in that direction and, sure enough, he could just make out a lone figure standing in the shadow of the tree. Deegan had his back to them, and he appeared to be looking at the ground.

"Did he say anything to you?" Mizar asked. "He had a rather odd look on his face when he excused himself last night."

Kimur shook his head. "He had that same look when he left the house this morning. I don't know what's gotten into him."

"I will go talk to him." Mizar stood up, gave a nod to Kimur, and strode away.

"Breakfast will be ready in about an hour," Kimur called after him.

Deegan didn't move a muscle during the several minutes it took for Mizar to cross the field. His father was still staring at the ground, at a small, square, marked stone that simply read

"ARECA." Deegan's shoulders were slumped, and it was obvious he'd been crying.

Out of respect, Mizar bowed his head and stood shoulder-to-shoulder with his father, staring down at the gravestone. He noticed Deegan's hands clenching and unclenching, and his entire body was vibrating.

Mizar put a hand on his shoulder. "Father, are you all right?"

Deegan raised his head, staring straight ahead rather than at Mizar. "It is Arantha's will that you have chosen this time to return home, my son. That is clear to me. It is equally clear that I must avail myself of this brief time we have left. I may not get another chance."

"What do you –"

"I do not have much longer to live." Deegan's eyes were moist with tears. "My heart has become weak, and it's only a matter of time before I journey to the Great Veil."

When Mizar had cited his father's ill health when asking for permission from King Aridor to return home, it was only half-true, as he hadn't wanted, at the time, to reveal the details of the vision that led him to Vaxi. Hearing now that his prediction had been correct made his heart feel as if someone was prying it from his body with a dull knife.

Composing himself, he replied, "Even the most stout-hearted man may quake when facing his own mortality. It is a journey we will all make."

Deegan shook his head. "I do not fear death, Mizar. I've had years to prepare for it. I've made my share of mistakes, as all men do, but there is still one monstrous sin that I must atone for."

Mizar's eyes widened. "What are you talking about? What sin?"

Deegan shook himself free, returning his gaze to the gravestone. "If you were to dig deep into the soil beneath this marker, you would expect to find the remains of your mother. However, you would find nothing."

Mizar felt his entire body stiffen. "Where is she, then?" he asked, trying to keep the tremor from his voice.

"I do not know, son. She left me before you were born." He hung his head in shame.

Mizar took Deegan by the hand and led him to an old wooden stool that had been placed next to the tree, sitting him down upon it.

"I didn't know her that long," Deegan continued. "Only a couple of months. But in that short time, I came to love her. I would have given anything to keep her with me."

Mizar knelt down on the ground at his side. "Perhaps you'd better tell me the story."

Deegan nodded. "My father, like his father before him, taught me everything I needed to know to run our farm. By the time I was twenty-four, I had taken over the more rigorous tasks of our day-to-day business, including making monthly trips to Ghal. But there was one trip, just weeks past my twenty-fifth birthday, that changed my life.

"Your grandfather tried several times to pair me off with daughters of other landowners, but I refused. I wanted to marry for love." He smiled. "He took quite a bit of convincing, but eventually he came around.

"I made this particular trip to purchase several head of gurn and ten bags of feed. Imagine my surprise when, on the road to Ghal, I came across the most beautiful woman I'd ever seen. Tall, elegant, beautiful sun-kissed skin, deep brown eyes ... my heart was instantly lost.

"She said her name was Areca, and that she belonged to a tribe of nomads who roamed the land from the Plains of Iyan to the southern wetlands. She told me that in her tribe, it was customary for women to seek adventures in other lands, to broaden their knowledge of the world."

"A worthy custom," Mizar said.

"Well, I couldn't let such a vision of loveliness simply pass into the night. She, too, was on her way to Ghal. I offered to get her a room at one of the more respectable inns if she would agree to share a meal with me. She accepted. We talked well into the night, and by the time I retired for the evening, I knew there was no other woman on Elystra for me.

"Over the next few days, everywhere I went, she came with me. We toured Ghal, and when I concluded my business, much to my delight, she accompanied me back home. Mother and Father were rather curious about her, of course, but they instantly warmed to her. We offered her a room and a bed, and she agreed to stay so I could continue my courtship of her.

"A month later, I was asking her almost daily to be my wife, but she seemed uncertain. Her answer was always the same: her people, her own family awaited her return, and she could not stay indefinitely. I tried everything I could to persuade her to stay. I had even convinced myself that my love for her was returned. When we began, um ... " he coughed nervously, "being intimate, I took that as a sign she was going to stay. But then, a few weeks later, she was gone. Just like that. No notes, not even a goodbye. She just got on her chava and left."

Mizar's heart skipped a beat. "Chava?"

"Yes, son. She, like all her people it would seem, rode a chava. Just like this girl you've brought to our home."

"You believe they are from the same tribe?"

"I do. They have the same complexion, the same beauty. They even wear similar clothes. Though Areca was not a fighter like this girl is, I have no doubt they are from the same place." He cast a mournful look at Mizar. "None was more surprised than I when you turned up on our doorstep. I wanted to do the best for you that I could, but I thought that ... if we told you your mother died, you wouldn't grow up thinking she abandoned you. My family agreed. The truth is, the lie was as much for me as it was for you. I didn't want you to see your father as a gullible fool who proclaimed his undying love for a woman who obviously didn't return it."

"Father," Mizar said softly. "You're not the first man to be blinded by love, and you won't be the last."

A glimmer of hope flashed through Deegan's eyes.

"But," Mizar continued, "I wish you'd told me this a long time ago."

"I should have. I am so sorry, my son."

Mizar stood up and walked over to the gravestone, staring down at it and rubbing his bearded chin thoughtfully. He shook his head as he tried to put all the pieces together.

"Son, what is it?" Deegan asked.

He met his father's concerned gaze with a stern one of his own. "Have you ever wondered why I, of all people, was given these abilities?"

Deegan tilted his head, puzzled by the question. "You were chosen by Arantha, of course."

"Arantha does speak to me, yes. But he could have chosen anybody. Without these abilities, I'm just another Daradian farmer. I come from a good family, but I am not of noble blood."

Deegan rose to his feet. "You're a good man, son. Arantha sees that. Just look at what you've done for our country."

" 'A good man.' " Mizar gave a coarse laugh. "No. There is another explanation." Before Deegan could reply, Mizar took him by the arm. "Come with me, Father. It's time we all got answers."

* * *

Mizar entered the dining room to see Kimur, Mareta, and Sen waiting for them. Six places had been set for breakfast. They were all smiles as Mizar and Deegan sat down to a plate of boiled eggs, roasted gurn meat, and a loaf of chaska bread with manza preserves. Before they ate, however, Mareta insisted Vaxi join them, so they waited as she helped their young visitor dress in a clean, loose-fitting beige tunic, socks, and boots belonging to their fourteen-year-old son, Lymus, who was of the same height and build as Vaxi.

When Vaxi appeared on Mareta's arm, she looked infinitely better than when she'd arrived. The color had returned to her face, she walked with barely a limp, and she seemed to have reached a level of trust with her hosts significant enough to share a meal with them without punches being thrown. Deegan smiled warmly at her. Vaxi, for her part, pleasantly greeted Deegan, and even thanked him for opening his home to her.

The six of them made small talk over the course of the meal. Mizar kept his overwhelming curiosity at bay with difficulty, but the breakfast table wasn't the place for such questions. A good night's sleep and Mareta's maternal ministrations had done wonders for her spirit.

Once breakfast was finished and Mareta had cleared everyone's dishes, she and Kimur excused themselves to go visit a neighboring farm in the hopes of working out a trade for supplies. The mood darkened considerably when Mizar began speaking.

"Vaxi, before we begin our discussion, I give you my word that you may trust everyone at this table, and in this house," Mizar said. "But I believe, given what I now know, that you have information vital to the future of Darad, and all of Elystra."

Vaxi seemed overwhelmed by the notion. "I don't see how that's possible. There's nothing special about me."

"I disagree, young lady. Don't forget, it was Arantha that led us to you. He wouldn't have done that if he deemed you unworthy."

Vaxi cast her eyes to the table, staring at its wooden surface for many moments as she considered this. "It is clear to me that

Arantha has brought me here for a reason. But I am at a loss as to how to proceed. Anything I say, should it become known, could mean disaster for my people. I cannot betray them any more than I already have."

Mizar folded his hands on the table. "I give you my vow as High Mage that I will protect your secrets to the best of my ability. My father here," he indicated Deegan, "never leaves the farm, and Sen," he gestured at his apprentice, "is sworn to obey any command I give him. However, there are things that I am sure you do not know, and it is my hope that when we pool our information, we will all have a better idea where our paths lead from here."

Vaxi nodded. "That is fair. Ask what you will."

"Are you a Wielder?"

Vaxi's calm expression morphed into one of astonishment. She obviously hadn't expected this question. She stared at him with wide eyes for several moments before answering, "No. I'm not."

"But there are female Wielders in your tribe. Am I right?"

Her breath caught in her throat. "How—how can you know that?"

"I will explain shortly. But first, please tell us what brought you to Darad."

Vaxi spoke slowly, as if measuring every word. "When girls in my tribe reach childbearing age, they are sent on Sojourn: we travel to distant lands and find a man to mate with."

Sen looked completely shocked by this confession. "That's why you came to Darad? To get *pregnant*?"

"It wasn't by choice," she replied drily. "My grandmother, who is on the Council, sent me here even though it was against the Protectress' wishes."

" 'Protectress'?" Mizar said. "You mentioned that word in your sleep. What does it mean?"

"The Protectress is our leader. She interprets Arantha's wishes. Thirteen years ago, right before she died, Protectress Onara decreed a halt to the Sojourns. Ever since then, my grandmother has campaigned for their reinstatement, but Onara's daughter Kelia refused, because she believes Arantha does not want them resumed yet.

"Grandmother has never been able to accept that, so several days ago, when Kelia was away, she forced me to go on Sojourn without the Protectress' approval." She sighed. "And look what happened."

"I don't understand," Sen said. "Why would you need to travel to another land to find a mate? Why not simply mate with one of the men in your tribe?"

Vaxi fixed him with a hard stare. "There are no men in my tribe."

Eyes widened, and jaws dropped.

"No men?" Mizar whispered.

"Now you see why we hide ourselves. If word of our existence got out, armies would come to enslave us or destroy us. Not just because of who we are, but because of what we are."

"So you are not nomads."

"No. That is what we tell strangers so they will not try to find us. Finding one wandering tribe among the vast Plains of Iyan would be akin to looking for a single blade of grass in a verdant field. That is why our village has been untouched, unspoiled by men, in the eight centuries since our liberation."

Vaxi went on to describe the legend of Soraya, and how she had used a Stone of Arantha to free a multitude of Vandan slaves. Now, eight hundred years later, their descendants had built a flourishing community.

"You are the first men to ever know the truth," Vaxi said, a tremor entering her voice. "I pray that you will not use such knowledge against us."

"Thank you for entrusting us with such an enormous secret, Vaxi," Mizar said. "I feel I must repay you in kind."

With Vaxi listening intently, Mizar spoke of his visions of the three female Wielders, as well as the wanton destruction wreaked by the lightning-Wielder known as Elzaria. When he mentioned the decimation of the Agrusian army, the blood drained from Vaxi's face. "No. It cannot be."

"What is it?" Sen asked.

"Lightning-Wielders are very rare. Only one family in our tribe has ever possessed that ability. The last of that family was a woman named Proda. She hoped to produce a daughter when she Sojourned to Barju more than thirty years ago. But she never returned. No Ixtrayu has Sojourned to Barju since."

Sen's eyes glossed over. "What did you just say? 'Ixtrayu'?"

"That is what my tribe is called. Why are you looking at me like that?" Vaxi said, alarmed.

"Merdeen the Sage," Mizar said, his voice hushed. "He was High Mage nearly a century ago. He spoke of a tree, its roots spreading all over Elystra. He called the tree 'Ixtrayu', which means 'Mother Tree' in ancient Elystran." He stood up from his chair, placing his palms on top of his head. "Great Arantha. This is what he meant. The Ixtrayu is not a tree. It is a tribe of women. A tribe of Wielders."

"We're not all Wielders," Vaxi corrected. "Most of us are not. But those that have been given one of Arantha's gifts have the same standing as those who haven't. The one exception is the Protectress. She is the most powerful of us; not only can she control the elements, but Arantha speaks to her through visions."

Sen snapped his head toward Mizar. "Master?"

Deegan leaned forward, a pleading look on his face. "Please, girl! Do you know Areca? Tell me!"

Vaxi stared back at him for a few moments before nodding. "How do you know that name?"

Mizar had finally recovered his voice. "She was my mother." He stumbled forward and resumed his chair, cradling his head in his hands. "I was right. I was not accorded these abilities by Arantha. I inherited them from my mother. So did Merdeen, Jerril, and every Daradian who has ever become a Wielder."

There was a loud gasp. All heads turned to Sen, who had stood up and was backing away from the table, shaking his head vigorously. Never had Mizar seen the boy looking so anguished. A tear snaked its way down his face.

"Sen?" Mizar said.

But Sen wasn't listening. With a gut-wrenching sob, he ran from the room. Seconds later, the front door slammed shut.

"Vaxi, I beg you," Deegan seemed not to have noticed Sen's tearful departure. "Areca ... does she live?"

So many revelations at once had stolen Vaxi's voice. Meeting Deegan's gaze, she slowly shook her head.

"When did she die?" Deegan said with a muffled sob.

"It was many years ago, before I was born. Her granddaughter, Kelia, is Protectress now. And Kelia's daughter Nyla is ..." She caught herself. "*Was* one of my best friends."

Deegan turned to Mizar. "Do you know what this means, son? This woman, Kelia, and her daughter ... are your blood. You have the same abilities. They're your family. Our *family*."

Mizar struggled mightily to recover his wits. Vaxi hadn't moved, and was still staring at him. "Vaxi," he said, "this third Wielder from my vision ... do you have any idea who it might be?"

She shook her head. "I'm sorry, I don't." Her breath became rapid. "What are you going to do now?"

Mizar stood up, gripping the table to steady himself. "Do you understand the enormity of this? Your tribe, without even realizing it, has shifted the entire balance of power on this world. A war is coming, my dear, and no matter which side wins, the Ixtrayu are indirectly responsible."

Vaxi was rendered speechless, finally grasping his meaning.

Mizar continued, "Should these revelations become common knowledge, it will rock Elystra to its foundations. Arantha help us all."

END OF PART ONE

Author's Note

If you enjoyed *Wielders of Arantha – Book One: Pawns*, you would be doing me a tremendous service by leaving a review on the book's pages on Amazon and/or Goodreads. Reviews are critical to independent authors like me, as it helps to elevate our books above the millions of others that make up the literary landscape. A review need not be long, just a few paragraphs or even a couple of sentences.

I hope to have Part Two of the series, entitled *Queens*, available to you sometime in summer 2017. Part 3, which is tentatively titled *Endgame*, will hopefully be out in winter 2017.

In the meantime, if you love my writing so much that you just can't get enough, feel free to download my Young Adult Contemporary trilogy, *The James Madison Series*. The three books, which include the multi-award winning *Joshua's Island*, as well as *Ethan's Secret* and *Sophie's Different*, are wonderful reads for preteens, teens and adults.

Keep reading for a preview of Book Two of the Wielders of Arantha series, Queens, due out in late summer 2017!

Chapter One

EGHTEEN DAYS AGO

A man whose posture, rumpled clothes, and scruffy beard gave him the appearance of one much older than his thirty-eight years sat at the main computer console. His ginger hair bore streaks of grey, and the eyeglasses that usually clung to his face now perched precariously on the tip of his nose.

Though he kept a watchful eye on the vast bank of monitors that scanned the sands of the Sahara Desert five hundred miles in every direction, his attention remained primarily fixed on the screen in front of him. His own image filled the screen, staring back at him as he spoke into a tiny microphone. "You're the strongest woman I've ever known, Maeve. Whatever is about to happen, I know you're going to kick ass. Win this game. For humanity." Then he shut off the recording.

Feeling the sting of fatigue behind his eyes, he removed his glasses and set them on the console. "One down, one to go," he muttered to himself.

He heard a shuffle of footsteps and turned around to see a young, olive-skinned man in a blue jumpsuit standing in the security office's doorway. A short yet thick beard and mustache covered the bottom half of his face, and his piercing brown eyes were far more alert than they should have been, given the late hour. "Hey, Richard. Mind if I join you?"

Sahara Base had been built decades earlier as an R&D lab for the purpose of exploring propulsion methods that exceeded even supralight capabilities, one of the Terran Confederation's best-kept secrets. Though designed to house several hundred personnel, only ten people lived there now.

Richard waved the man in. "C'mon in, Mahesh. I just made some coffee; help yourself."

Mahesh sat in the chair opposite Richard. "No thanks, I'll stick to tea. Besides, we packed the synthesizer yesterday, which can only mean you brewed the coffee yourself. And no offense, Richard, but your coffee could strip the paint off a starship."

"Screw you," Richard said with a sardonic smile. "Besides, I got just the thing to make it taste better."

Mahesh gave him a bemused smile. "Drain cleaner?"

Richard opened a nearby drawer and pulled out a small flask, waggling it in front of his friend. "Eighteen-year-old Scotch. 2719 was a very good year."

"Pass. If I come back to the room with that on my breath, Suri will read me the riot act."

"Suit yourself." Richard unscrewed the top of the flask and took a swig, throwing it back with a satisfied exhale. "Is everything prepared?"

"Yes." Mahesh scooted his chair forward until it rested only a few feet away from Richard's. "Is there any way I can talk you into coming with us?"

Five years before, Earth had been invaded by the Jegg, an insectoid race whose vastly superior technology made short work of the Confederation's defenses. Nine billion people—more than half of humanity—were wiped out. Richard, his wife and son, and the rest of his engineering team escaped subjugation by sealing themselves inside Sahara Base. They'd reasoned that even if the Jegg knew of the base's existence, their small team posed no semblance of a threat, and therefore left them alone.

They were wrong.

Richard's breath hitched at his friend's concern. "Someone has to be here to make sure the *Talon* gets away safely, to say nothing of activating the base's self-destruct."

"It doesn't have to be you."

"Yes, it does."

"Is that what Banikar said?"

"In so many words."

Mahesh folded his arms across his chest. "I'm not buying it."

Richard drew himself up. "Excuse me?"

"This mission has been two years in the making. Have you ever wondered why the rest of us—who have never so much as laid eyes on this mysterious trans-dimensional being who has been influencing your decisions since childhood—follow your instructions without question?"

Richard shrugged. "Because the Jegg have had us farked twelve ways from Sunday since the day they dropped from the sky?"

"Well, there is that, of course. But there's more to it."

"What are you talking about?"

Mahesh stared at the ground. "People have believed in a higher power for thousands of years, Richard. Whether they call that higher power Jehovah, or Vishnu, or Allah, or Banikar, it doesn't matter. When things are at their most hopeless, sometimes all a person has is his faith." He raised his head again. "For the last two years, I've watched you feed this team information you couldn't have gotten from any human source."

Catching sight of Richard's raised eyebrows, Mahesh held his hands out, palms up. "Believe me, things would've gone so much smoother if Banikar had decided to include the entire group in his briefings instead of insisting on appearing to you exclusively. God works in mysterious ways, and for whatever reason, he chose you as his messenger. As a man of faith, it's not my place to question that."

Richard took another gulp. "But you're a scientist. You're supposed to question everything."

"Whether I question it or not doesn't matter." Mahesh smirked. "I'm going to heaven regardless."

"Sure, rub it in." Richard rolled his eyes. "Make sure you look for me when you get there. If you don't find me, well ... you know where I'll be."

Mahesh's deep brown eyes bore into his. "I know you're the captain of this metaphorical ship, but that doesn't mean you have to go down with it."

"I know." Richard's eyes flicked toward the security monitor to his right, taking in the wide-angle view of the hangar, inside which sat the rebuilt, refurbished, soon-to-depart hulk of the *Talon*. "But I'm tired, Mahesh. I'm so tired. I lost my whole family to the Jegg: my parents, my brothers, my little sister ... all gone." His hands curled into fists. "After tomorrow, I will never see my wife or son again. And it's probably for the best. When Maeve plays that recording, I don't know what's gonna piss her off more: hearing the truth or that she won't get to kill me herself."

"You don't know that."

Richard sneered. "This is Maeve we're talking about, Mahesh. She's Irish *and* a combat veteran. If there's one thing she's better at than piloting spacecraft, it's holding a grudge."

Mahesh's face was, as always, infuriatingly calm. "Richard, come with us. The Resistance still needs people like you."

"The Resistance?" Richard turned his flask over and over in his hand. "It sounds so noble, doesn't it? Like we're a shining example to humanity, who dares to hope that we may gain victory, cast off our vile oppressors, and regain our freedom." He chuckled. "What horseshit. Humanity doesn't even know we exist. And as for victory? This is it right here." He gestured again at the *Talon* on the monitor. "This is mankind's last, *very last* chance. Either this works, or the next millennium will be exactly like the last five years: watching the Jegg carve up every planet in the Confederation, and unable to do jack about it."

Mahesh arched an eyebrow. "Well, that doesn't mean you have to be an asshole."

"I'm not an asshole. I'm from Texas."

"Not sure those two things are mutually exclusive."

"Well, that's certainly true." He downed another gulp from his flask. "You've told the other five what's going to happen?"

Mahesh leaned back in his chair with a heavy sigh. "Yes, everything Banikar told you. In four hours, I'll load the crate with the personal transporters onto the *Talon,* having removed six of the ten for ourselves. In seven hours, Gaspar will activate both our borrowed Jegg quantigraphic rift drive and the ship's supralight engines for final testing, and Maeve will begin the pre-flight checks. Twenty-one minutes later, the base will come under attack, by which time, the rest of us will have already transported away to Himalaya Base. You'll make sure Davin is on board?"

"Don't worry about that. He goes wherever Gaspar goes."

Mahesh idly cast his eyes at the monitors, and he lowered his voice to a whisper. "Does Gaspar know what's going to happen to him?"

Richard shook his head. "That would only distract him. We need his entire brain on this, or they'll never make it."

"Have you recorded the messages?"

Richard turned back to face the console in front of him. "I just did Maeve's. I'm going to do Davin's in a minute." He sighed. "For years, I've known this moment was coming, and now that it has ... I don't know what the fark I'm gonna say."

"Tell him what he needs to hear," Mahesh said, standing up. He reached over and put a hand on Richard's shoulder. "Nothing else matters."

"Is that another one of your pearls of Hindu wisdom?"

"Nope. Metallica."

"You and that old heavy metal of yours." Richard stood up and extended his hand. "Thank you. For everything."

Mahesh took the offered hand, shaking it firmly. "It's been an honor serving with you."

"Well, it's right you should feel that way," Richard said with a grim smile.

Mahesh rolled his eyes as he moved toward the door. "*Definitely* not mutually exclusive." He gave a brief wave, and then was gone.

Richard listened to his friend's footsteps fade away. He closed the door to the Security Office and resumed his seat in front of the console. He downed one more swig as he gathered his thoughts, and his courage, then pressed the Record button on the screen. One more deep breath, and he began to speak.

Chapter Two

ELIA CHOKED back a sob as she removed her hands from the Stone.

Her heart raced, thumping wildly in her chest. This was not unusual when she consulted Arantha, but it was made worse by the unfathomable horror of her latest vision, the same vision she'd been subjected to repeatedly since returning from the Kaberian Mountains.

Perspiration beading on her brow and acid roiling in her stomach, she lurched across the dusty stone floor and out through the narrow entrance, stumbling as she crossed the threshold. She squinted in the light of the morning sun as her eyes adjusted from the dimness of the cave.

She turned to the right, taking in the view of the Ixtrayu village that had been her people's home for eight centuries. Built directly into the walls of the plateau on either side of the River Ix, it was a sight she'd seen countless times since she was a little girl walking at the side of her mother, Onara. Back then, the sight was welcome, familiar, but with every unhelpful vision she'd had since donning the mantle of Protectress, it felt less and less so. On this day, the comforting babble of the river did nothing to calm her turbulent thoughts.

Rather than cross the nearest bridge to the other side of the river, where her home lay invitingly close at the top of a large stone staircase, she moved down the narrow footpath along the eastern bank toward the Room of Healing. Upon entering, she scanned the spacious room for either of the tribe's two healers. She spotted Sershi near the back wall, watching as the young, willowy woman removed a kettle from over a small fire and filled three mugs with its contents. The spicy fragrance of jingal-root tea filled the air, and Kelia instantly felt her mind quiet.

"Protectress," Sershi said, her mouth morphing into a tired smile that wasn't reflected in her eyes.

Kelia strode forward, picked up a mug of tea from the table and held it under her nose, closing her eyes as it filled her senses. She took another deep breath before blowing on the tea and taking a cautious sip. She felt the hot liquid slide down her throat, savoring its piquant taste.

"Oh, I needed that." Kelia took another quenching sip and set the mug back down. "How is your mother doing?"

"Still weak," Sershi said. "It may be another day before she's up and around. Extracting the hugar's venom from our ... guest's body took more out of her than either of us realized."

"I understand," Kelia said, casting a glance at several huddled forms sleeping on beds of lyrax pelts on the other side of the room. Davin lay curled up next to his mother, snoring peacefully, his curly red hair spilling over his face. "How are they doing?"

"The woman has improved," Sershi said, following Kelia's gaze. "She seems to have regained some movement in her extremities. I believe we eradicated all of the poison, but now it's up to her body to rejuvenate itself."

"There's nothing more you can do?" Kelia glanced at her half-empty mug, wishing its restorative powers would have a similar effect on her friend.

Sershi shook her head. "As you know, we've never had to heal something like this before. We're monitoring her, and I assure you, we'll chronicle every detail in our records in case it ever happens again."

Kelia nodded. "And Nyla?"

The healer took two steps forward, shifting her gaze to Kelia's thirteen-year-old daughter, lying on a different pallet of furs. "Her heartbeat is strong, and the burns on her palms have healed. Beyond that, she's in Arantha's hands. I'm sorry I don't have more to tell you than that, Protectress."

Kelia just nodded again.

Sershi's voice became even more tentative. "What are we going to do about the boy?"

Kelia remained silent. It was a good question, and one she didn't have an answer for. Davin was the first male to set foot in the village. Ever. And as such, he couldn't be allowed to roam around unattended. Having spent two days getting to know Davin, she knew him to be an intelligent, personable young man, playful and mischievous at times but a devoted son. Until she could convince her sisters of his good nature, however, he would be considered dangerous, and thus in danger himself. For eight hundred years, her people had looked upon men with suspicion and contempt, only interacting with them when seeking mates on Sojourn.

Additionally, he was from the Above, as was his mother. She only hoped she could get her sisters to understand that their new friends, just like the Ixtrayu, were following a path set forth by Arantha, and it was at that moment in time that those paths were converging. Kelia desperately needed the Council's help in that regard.

"He will stay by his mother's side. Should he wake, tell him I will have their food brought to them. But they are not to leave this room until I say otherwise. Can you keep the more curious of our sisters out, or shall I have Runa assign one of the huntresses to stand guard?"

"That might be wise, Protectress," Sershi said. "At least until my mother has recovered."

"I will arrange it right away. No one is to enter but me, Lyala, or the Council. Oh, and Sarja." Kelia allowed herself a brief smile, remembering Runa's daughter's recent declaration of affection for Nyla. The two had created their very own tradition before Nyla laid her hands on the Stone for the first time, pledging their hearts to each other. But Nyla's first consultation had been too much for her, overwhelming her just as it did to Kelia when she was that age. She silently prayed that her willful daughter would wake soon.

With final glances at Nyla, Maeve, and Davin, she strode from the room.

* * *

From her large chair at the head of the Council Chamber, Kelia sat, spine rigid, as she looked at the three older women facing her.

"We'll try not to keep you long, Protectress," said Katura, concern etched into her aged but kindly face. "Rumors abound about our mysterious visitors, and our people look to the four of us for explanations."

"Agreed," said Eloni, her short, dark hair as elegant as ever. "While I'm thankful the woman's life was saved, hers and the boy's arrival couldn't have been more ill-timed. Thanks to Susarra, emotions have been running high since Vaxi's departure. We need to speak as one voice if we are to subdue the unrest she created."

Kelia felt a knot form in her stomach at the mention of Vaxi. Despite her best efforts to free the young huntress from the clutches of her domineering grandmother Susarra, she'd failed to do so. Only four days earlier, the vision that sent Kelia to the Kaberian Mountains gave Susarra the perfect opportunity to send Vaxi on Sojourn without Kelia's permission. Now the girl was beyond their reach, and Kelia could only pray she would come to no harm.

"Councilors," Kelia addressed the triumvirate, "I apologize for keeping secrets from you. I did not tell you about my bond with Maeve because I couldn't discern Arantha's purpose for creating that bond. When I left Maeve, I didn't think I would ever see her again. Believe me, last night's turn of events was as much a surprise to me as it was to you."

"Let's put that aside for a moment," said Liana. Though Kelia's aunt had only been on the Council for two days—a replacement that became necessary after Susarra's disobedience came to light—she'd slipped into the role as easily as the white robe she now wore. "Let us instead focus on the circumstances that led you to Share with a woman from the Above."

"It happened in a moment of weakness," Kelia confessed, her fingers idly grasping the familiar lump of metal that dangled from the necklace she wore. Featureless and spherical, it had been given to her by her mother right before her death, so Kelia had turned it into a pendant as part of the necklace that Nyla had crafted many years before. "I was fatigued from my journey across the desert. My first meeting with Maeve precipitated a show of force on my part, and using my abilities drained the last drops of my strength. I was at her mercy. She could have killed me if she so desired, but instead she rushed to my aid. Though we did not speak the same language, I knew at that moment that she wasn't my enemy. Her eyes bore no malevolence, only sorrow."

Kelia took a deep breath, staring at the floor as she relived the memory. "There is something about her, Councilors, something I'm not even sure I can explain. Before I even made my trek to the mountains, Arantha provided me with visions of her. I felt ... drawn to her, somehow. Like our meeting was destined, preordained by Arantha, and it was the divine goddess guiding me."

Katura raised her bony fingers, briefly covering her mouth. "In the cave, she spoke in our language. Was this also a result of the Sharing?"

"It was." Kelia nodded. "From what I gather, though she and her son are speaking in their native language—she called it 'English'—we are able to *hear* her in Elystran. And likewise, they can understand us equally well."

"Remarkable," said Eloni. "Thank Arantha for providing us with such a gift."

"There is another factor at play here, which I must now inform you of. At the time of our Sharing, I came to discover she'd already developed Wielding abilities."

The eyes of the entire Council widened. Eloni let out a gasp.

"Great Arantha," whispered Liana.

Kelia continued, "Her healing ability manifested itself before they even found the Stone. When I first envisioned Maeve, her back bore many large, deep scars. But because of the Stone, the scars are no longer there. With my guidance, she discovered she could also heal others." She pulled up the sleeve of her tunic, showing off the upper arm where Maeve's gunshot had grazed her. Only a tiny patch of rough skin remained where the bullet wound had been.

"Soon afterward, we discovered she could communicate with animals. She was able to command my chava with nothing but a word and a gesture." She recalled the moment when her wide-bodied mount, with whom she'd spent years building a rapport, completely ignored her and ran straight to Maeve. "She also told me she'd used this ability to pacify a pack of lyraxes several nights before."

She paused, scanning the faces of the Council. "But the biggest surprise came after we found the Stone. I attempted to use my air-Wielding to levitate myself, and just as I felt my strength begin to slip, Maeve … empowered me. Somehow, she added her strength to my own. We floated above the ground like hovering birds." Kelia smiled at the memory. "It was the most exhilarating moment of my life."

Of course, this was followed by a brief but passionate kiss between her and Maeve, but she saw no need to inform the Council of this.

"Simply unbelievable," said Liana, "that Arantha would bestow such power upon a woman not of our world."

"Agreed," said Kelia. A sorrowful look crossed her face. "However, we must not fall into the trap of believing we always know the divine goddess's wishes. And as you heard, Maeve has matters of extreme importance to discuss with us when she's recovered. In her brief moments of clarity before sleep claimed her, she told me there was more at stake than just the future of Elystra. I do not know what it could possibly mean, or what our future holds for us."

This was a lie. Kelia knew exactly what was coming. She'd seen it in her last three consultations. The same terrible, horrible images being shoved into her mind.

The nearby forest, ablaze.

The Ixtrayu croplands, aflame.

The charred, smoking bodies of her sisters, scattered on the ground.

If this is the future, Kelia thought, *why does Arantha torment me so? Is it so we may find a way to escape such a fate? Or are we doomed no matter which way we turn?*

Chapter Three

A TORRENT OF water roused Rahne from his slumber. The shade of the so-called "Tree of Justice" protected him from the heat of the sun, but exhaustion had taken over several hours before, and he'd lapsed into a fitful sleep.

Whipping his head back and forth to clear several strands of dark hair from his eyes, he squinted up to see Sekker leering at him with no small amount of disgust.

Sekker was by far the fattest man Rahne had ever seen. He was callous, officious, and puffed up on his own sense of self-importance. His favorite boast was that he was a distant cousin to King Morix—a *very* distant cousin, Rahne reasoned, to be given the title of High Magistrate of an insignificant little coastal town like Larth, where the air perpetually smelled of fish and nothing of consequence ever happened.

"Rise and shine, thief." An ugly smile formed between his jowls.

Every one of Rahne's muscles ached in protest as he attempted to sit up straight against the tree he'd been manacled to for the last twenty-four hours. Everyone in Larth knew this tree, the tallest in the area. Located in the middle of a large, open meadow a half-mile east of town, it was a common punishment site, where victims of the magistrate's whims were chained, sometimes for days, without food, only yards away from the nearest of several wells nearly full to the brim with fresh water.

With great effort, Rahne dug his boots into the soft grass and pushed himself upright. Now fully awake, he stared up at the magistrate. "Like I told you yesterday during that farce you called a trial, I'm not a thief. That boat belongs to me."

"Not anymore, it doesn't," Sekker retorted, throwing the empty bucket on the ground next to the nearby well. "Your boat, or should I say your father's boat, became the property of the crown upon his death."

Rahne flexed, but his arms had very little range of movement, spread wide as they were against the bark of the tree. "That's a lie! My grandfather built that ship with his own two hands! He passed it down to my father, and as his only living relative, it goes to me! That's what the law says!"

Sekker chortled, his ample belly quivering. "We went over this yesterday. Of course, you were only half-conscious during most of your trial, so I guess that explains your lapse in memory."

Rahne remembered being struck on the head by one of the local constables on the way into Sekker's office, his punishment for a particularly choice insult about the man's questionable lineage. "What are you talking about?"

Sekker leaned forward, speaking to him as if to a naughty child. "The law states that property can only be transferred to a relative if said relative has reached his nineteenth year. By your own admission, you are only eighteen."

"I'll be nineteen in ten days."

"Doesn't matter. You're eighteen now."

"Fine," Rahne said through clenched teeth. "Let me go, and in ten days I'll take ownership of my boat."

"Doesn't work that way, boy," Sekker said, using the toe of his boot to kick Rahne's heels; not enough to hurt, just enough to annoy. "Your father died with unpaid debts, as you may or

may not know. Those debts have come due now that he's journeyed to the Great Veil."

"What debts?" Rahne asked. "He paid the taxes on the fish
he caught for years. It was too much, but he paid it anyway.
We barely had enough to get by."

"Ah, but your father docked his boat at a public pier. I just
recently enacted a law regarding a harbor tax that all boatmen
must pay, and it seems he neglected to pay the harbor master
this additional duty since the law's enactment."

An increasing sense of helplessness flashed through Rahne.
"How much did he owe? At least let me try to pay it back!"

"It's too late for that, I'm afraid. Your father's boat was by
far the most valuable thing he owned, and that's already been
sold. It only covered about half his debts."

Rahne felt his stomach clench. "You slimy braga."

Sekker flashed an evil grin. "You're more than welcome to
travel to Talcris and complain to the King. Oh, wait, you can't."
He laughed again.

Fourteen days before, a Barjan captain named Elzor and his
army, the six-hundred-strong Elzorath, had laid siege to the
capital city of Agrus. It took several days for news to filter
down the coast to Larth, the southernmost city in the region.
Stories had been told at the local taverns ever since about how
Elzor's twin sister Elzaria singlehandedly decimated the Agrusian army. She was a Wielder, the first female in the history of
Elystra to wield the power of Arantha.

Rahne could hardly believe his ears when he heard the story
about how lightning shot forth from Elzaria's hands, killing or
wounding more than two-thirds of Agrus's soldiers, and Elzor's men had scored an easy victory after that. King Morix, the
entire royal family, and most of the nobles were dead within
days. Everyone expected Elzor to send someone to Larth de-
manding some token of fealty or tribute, but there had been
none.

"Larth's small size puts it beneath the notice of that pernicious whelp who now dares call himself Lord of Agrus. And as the only citizen of Larth with royal blood, that means I can adjust the law how I see fit. Which puts you … well, right where you are now." He chuckled. "Tomorrow, you will be released into the custody of a local fishmonger, in whose employ you will remain until the rest of your family's debts have been paid."

"You mean Joor?"

"Ah, you know him?"

"We've met," Rahne said with a scowl.

"Good. I wouldn't count on getting much downtime during your stint at his shop. Or food. And I'd sleep with one eye open if I were you." Sekker's bushy eyebrows raised, and his enormous girth seemed to expand even further with his perceived victory.

A faint sound from down the road leading north and slightly inland caught Rahne's attention. Sekker hadn't yet heard it, as he was in the middle of another fit of cackling.

Several men on merychs appeared through a dense copse of trees. As he watched, an entire procession appeared, dozens becoming hundreds, headed right for where he was chained. He realized with a start that the one leading this army could only be Elzor.

After a few moments, Sekker heard the clamor as well and turned to see the heavily-armed mass approaching. A look of horror appeared on his face, and he started to waddle away toward the road to his merych-drawn cart.

Two soldiers in high-quality armor broke away from the rest, spurring their merychs into a full gallop and easily closing the distance between the procession and Sekker. The magistrate had just managed to clamber into the driver's seat of his cart when he found himself facing two large men with swords pointed right at him.

"Stand down," one of them growled. "Now."

Though he was twenty yards away, Rahne could see Sekker's face had gone deep crimson. The setting sun glinted off the sweat pouring from the man's plump face. Raising his hands in surrender, he gingerly climbed off the cart.

For almost a minute, no one moved a muscle, like figures in a tableau. Finally, the rest of the procession caught up, and Rahne caught his first good look of the man who had invaded his homeland as he alit from his merych, a powerful-looking black steed with an equally impressive mane. The man was tall, dark-haired and dark-bearded. His eyes were as cold as morning frost, and an air of ruthless authority emanated from him.

Right next to him was a raven-haired beauty clad in a black dress cinched at the waist by a leather belt. This had to be Elzaria, and if he thought Elzor's eyes were icy, they were blazing suns compared to Elzaria's. He'd seen fish with warmer eyes.

Rahne wondered if he'd seen his last sunrise.